Conrad's
TIME MACHINE

BAEN BOOKS by LEO FRANKOWSKI

A Boy and His Tank
Fata Morgana
Conrad's Time Machine

Conrad's TIME MACHINE

A Prequel to the Adventures of Conrad Stargard

LEO FRANKOWSKI

CONRAD'S TIME MACHINE

A Baen Books Original

Baen Publishing Enterprises
P.O. Box 1403
Riverdale, NY 10471
www.baen.com

ISBN: 0-7434-3557-5

Cover art by David Mattingly

First printing, September 2002

Library of Congress Cataloging-in-Publication Data

Frankowski, Leo, 1943–
    Conrad's time machine / by Leo Frankowski.
      p. cm.
    ISBN 9-7434-3557-5
    1. Time travel—Fiction. 2. Male friendship—Fiction. 3. Motorcyle gangs—Fiction. I. Title.

PS3556.R347 C66 2002
813'.54—dc21   2002071203

Distributed by Simon & Schuster
1230 Avenue of the Americas
New York, NY 10020

Production by Windhaven Press, Auburn, NH
Printed in the United States of America

10   9   8   7   6   5   4   3   2   1

DEDICATION

This book is dedicated to my new wife, Marina.
She is beautiful, intelligent, warm, loving, and
more than any man could possibly deserve.

ACKNOWLEDGEMENTS

This story had been rattling around for so long that virtually
every person that I have ever known has read parts of it
and made useful suggestions. I've gotten feedback from
hundreds and hundreds of people, and I can't
possibly give them all the credit that they deserve.
Dave Grossman gave me the idea for the ending,
but the rest must remain unnamed.

FOREWORD

Many of my books were a long time getting finished, but unless I live to be a hundred, this one is the record setter.

I was in high school in the fifties when I asked myself the classic science fiction question, "What if?" In this case, it was what if time travel were really possible? I wasn't concerned with the paradoxes that other writers had explored to more than completion. I was wondering what else you could do with it.

My first attempts at writing were pretty amateurish. I didn't know much about writing, but having cut my teeth on Robert Heinlein juveniles, I knew good writing from bad. Wisely, I kept my smudged pages to myself. Anyway, I was too busy flunking out of Senior English to have much time for anything else. Back then, I had some truly wretched English teachers, who forced the poetry and Shakespeare that I had loved down my throat so hard that I soon hated it and him— and them. I eventually regained my love for it and him, but never for them. It never occurred to me that I would end up as a professional writer.

Not when I had some really great science teachers, who knew their subjects and taught them well. A career in science, technology, and/or maybe business seemed to be my obvious life path.

Still, the thoughts kept on welling up, like bubbles in a cesspool. If you could move something, maybe even yourself, from one position in the space-time continuum to any other position, then you would immediately have effectively infinite wealth and power. You could always win the lotteries, always buy the best stock on the market, always bet on the winning horse.

So, with that going for you, what would you do with your life, aside from getting filthy rich? Well? No quick answer? I didn't have one either. It took me forty-three years to work it out, and even then it took the help of my good friend, Lieutenant Colonel David Grossman, to finally give me a good ending for the story.

I hope you enjoy it.

—Leo Frankowski
Tver, Russia
2002

CHAPTER ONE
Sad Leavings

The war in Vietnam was heating up, half the people in the country were smoking dope, and the Flower Children were sprouting peace and free love all over the place.

I was only vaguely aware of it.

It was 1968, and I was leaving.

The Air Force never said goodbye, but I didn't love them either. I'd made a few good friends in the service, but Chris was in the guardhouse again, SelfCheck had been discharged the week before, Crazy Mormon was on leave, and Johnny Sleewa was on duty at the time. No one was there to see me off. I finished up my paperwork, gathered my few belongings, and walked past the dead trees in front of the squadron area.

They were my one lasting accomplishment in the United States Air Force.

It happened like this. Last fall, I'd gotten a whole weekend off, and I figured to make it with this girl I knew in Toronto, which was a little outside of the hundred mile limit they had us on. I'd put a fictitious address on the official checkout sheet, but left the chick's phone number with Johnny, so if something really important happened, he could get in touch with me.

1

Around one-thirty on a Saturday morning, I'd just gotten to her place when a sergeant phoned. He asked for me, and said that I was scheduled for "special duty" at eight that morning. He didn't know what it was all about, but I'd better be there.

Well, I thought it must have been important or Johnny wouldn't have handed out the number. See, I was one of only three techs who were trained to fix the Alert Transmit Console, and it was about the only piece of equipment at The Notch that wasn't duplicated.

The machine had a keyboard on it that was used to send messages like "fire all of your missiles," but it wasn't a QWERTY. The keys were arranged in alphabetical order.

None of the officers could type, since among our masters, such abilities were considered unmanly.

The ATC had two Chevrolet ignition keys, mounted ten feet apart, so that it took two men to operate it, at least from the front. They used it for calling practice alerts, scrambling the bombers, and starting wars.

The controls inside the back of the ATC were a different matter. Once, Chris got to playing with the buttons back there and managed to scramble the 99th Bomb Wing. Those guys were over Hudson Bay, fueled up and with bombs ready, awaiting orders from the President, before anybody else knew they were gone.

Nobody got on Chris's case for it, though, since none of the brass would believe that an airman had enough brains to pull a stunt like that. Me, I knew that Chris had an IQ in the 160s, but it would never occur to them to ask me about it. To them, I was just another dumb trooper, too.

What got Chris thrown into the guardhouse this time was sweeping dirt under the floor. Not under the carpet, you understand, but actually under the floor. Chris was very strong, and he had a penchant for doing things the hard way.

Well, what with Chris in the guardhouse and me gone for the weekend, that only left Johnny Quest qualified to work on the machine. If something happened to Johnny and the ATC went west, SAC's third alternate Combat Operations Center would be out of business, and you never could tell when they might want to start a war.

And while I hated the Air Force, I still loved my country, so on the girl's phone, I admitted to the sergeant that I was me.

I had to turn around and leave. I tried to kiss the chick goodbye, but she wasn't the understanding sort. She screamed a lot about my wasting her whole weekend and told me not to come back.

That night, I drove all the way back to Massachusetts without sleeping and got on base with seven spare minutes to change into fatigues, report, and find out what was happening.

What it was, was that the colonel had decided that the squadron area needed some beautification.

Having a full bird colonel in command of a squadron was strange, but then a nine-hundred-man squadron was pretty weird, too. The guy had been a hot fighter jockey during World War II. He'd made all his rank during his first three years in the service, and hadn't been promoted since. This made him an unhappy man, and he didn't lead a happy squadron.

Boots were new troops who had finished tech school and were now idle for three months, awaiting their security clearances before they were allowed to work on the equipment that they had just spent a year learning how to fix. Why these clearances weren't obtained while they were still in school, saving fifteen percent of their useful careers, was one of those little unexplained military mysteries.

Our colonel's beautification plan was that I should drive ten of the boots out into the nearby woods, have them dig up nine likely looking trees, and drive the trees and boots back. We would then plant the trees about the squadron area at the points specified on the enclosed sketch by that evening. Why we couldn't do this during the week, when all of those guys were idle, or doing useless make-work, was also not explained. Neither was why this qualified as an emergency sufficient to pull me in from a weekend pass, but then the Air Force never bothered to explain things to an airman.

So I did it, making the boots do all the work.

Then I showered up, and, too tired to sleep, I went to

a blind pig hidden below its neon sign in the basement of a Baptist church just outside the gate. Sensibly, I got stinking drunk while mulling over the injustices of the world. I was still unhappy when I returned to the barracks at three in the morning. The colonel wasn't available to hear my suggestions, so I ripped the newly planted trees out by the roots and threw them halfway to the parking lot.

Feeling much better, I found my room and went to sleep.

I'm bigger than most people.

When I got up late on Sunday afternoon, the sun was setting, somebody had replanted the trees, and the girl in Toronto wouldn't talk to me on the phone. It was thus reasonable to get drunk again, and wandering back, I came across the replanted trees.

I ripped them all out again, and this time, using a hammer-throw technique, sailed one of them all the way to the parking lot, narrowly missing somebody's fifty-seven Chevy.

The same thing happened Monday night, too, since by then somebody had once more replanted the trees. Actually, it happened almost every night for about a month, and after a while it got so that I didn't even have to get drunk first. I had found a certain relief from tension and a deep-seated satisfaction in ripping up those trees and giving them a good toss.

The strange thing is that nobody ever saw me do it, or if they did, they didn't talk about it, but then most people don't realize that I'm really a very gentle person, if you give me half a chance.

In a month or so, I was pretty sure that the trees were dead, what with the way the bark was falling off, and after that I left them alone.

That had been six months ago and they were still out there, because the colonel hadn't given any orders about them. Likely, he hadn't noticed.

My mark on the Air Force. Nine dead trees.

I carried my belongings to the garage outside of the gate and settled up with the owner of the place.

Motorcycles weren't allowed on base. They had the wrong image by Air Force standards, although they were allowed up at The Notch, since civilians weren't allowed within sight of the place. They'd give you a sticker for one to let you past the Elite Guard, through the gate, and to the small parking lot. From there it was a short walk past more guards, past the thick steel blast doors, and into the generator-packed tunnel that led deep into the hollowed-out mountain.

I packed up, kick started her with one hand and rode off. I never put a foot on the kick starter, my theory being that if hand cranking wouldn't do it, she needed a tune-up. Electric starters, of course, are for wimps.

I stopped a hundred yards outside the Westover Field gate and peeled the SAC sticker from the Wixom Ranger faring on my BMW R-60. I no longer felt any hate. I just didn't want it there, defacing my bike, now that I was free.

I had joined the Air Force for many reasons. Without the money to finish my degree, I needed a trade, and they'd promised to teach me electronics, the one promise they'd actually kept. Mostly, though, I'd wanted have some adventures while I was still young, to spread my wings a little, and see a bit of the world.

Instead, they'd stuffed me under a mountain for the duration.

More than anything else, I'd wanted to do something . . . significant. To do something important for my country, and maybe even for the world.

But there's nothing glorious about fixing machinery, especially when the stuff almost never broke down. Ninety percent of my actual work time had been spent cleaning floors, dusting equipment, and trying to look busy. Most of the rest of it was spent filling out paperwork, an occupation that took six times longer that the actual repair work did.

Mostly, I just sat there at a grey metal desk. The lighting was cool, efficient fluorescent. The temperature was kept at a constant 70.4 degrees Fahrenheit. The relative humidity was at 48.6 percent. The floors and ceilings were white. The walls were beige. The equipment was a uniform dove grey, with small, unblinking colored lights.

The silence was deafening.

You sat there for eight hours every day, forbidden to read anything but technical manuals, staring at the walls and waiting for someone up in the cab to tell the heavy bombers and all the land-based missiles to go and blow up the world.

Off duty, you drank a lot, but it didn't help all that much.

My outfit had a suicide rate that was higher than the casualty rate of most combat outfits in time of war. And it wasn't just the young kids who "took the pipe." Old, balding sergeants would somehow get sort of listless, and then you'd hear, unofficially, that they'd put a bullet behind their ear. You never heard a word officially, of course, not even a notification of the funeral service. It didn't fit the public image the Air Force wanted everybody to believe in.

Soon, you learned to hate the bastards.

The hate I'd felt for years for the organization that had kept me in useless bondage had become a bigger part of my life than I had imagined, and now that those bonds were finally parted, I was left with a vast hollowness inside of me.

I'd sold off almost everything I owned except my camping gear. Even my uniforms were gone, which wasn't precisely legal since I was still supposed to be a member of the inactive reserves. But I didn't have any family or anyplace to send that junk for storage, so if I couldn't fit it into my saddlebags, I couldn't see keeping it.

I really didn't know *what* I wanted, but I had a strong handle on some negatives. Like I never wanted to see another officer again in my life. Mostly, I needed to get way far away from petty rules and silly regulations and people who outranked me, which in the Air Force was just about everybody.

I wasn't the kind who got promoted.

My BMW sort of automatically took me to the Mass Pike and just as naturally pointed west, which was fine. There isn't much east of Massachusetts that you can get to on a bike.

Well. My motorcycle was paid for. My savings and accumulated leave added up to just under $2,000.00. It was springtime and I figured I could live for six months without the need to reconnect myself to society. Then, maybe I'd go back and finish my degree. Or maybe not.

The Mass Pike dumped me onto the New York Thruway and a green-and-white sign read "Rochester—231 Miles."

That got me thinking about Jim Hasenpfeffer, since he was working on his Ph.D. at the University of Rochester and this naturally got me thinking about Ian McTavish as well.

CHAPTER TWO
An Old Friend

Actually, we never did have much in common.

Take religion.

Now, I was a defrocked altar boy whose convictions varied between my normal atheism to militant Agnosticism when I'm argued into a corner. Militant agnostics say that they don't know anything about God, *and you don't either, dammit*!

Ian was sort of conventional about religion. He always went to church on Sunday, but he never much talked about it. I think he was about the only Christian I'd ever met who was capable of being polite about religion. Or at least he was always annoyingly polite with me.

And nobody ever had the slightest idea of what—if anything—Hasenpfeffer believed in. He had this talent for side-stepping whatever he felt wouldn't be personally rewarding.

Or take women.

I always tried like hell, but never got anywhere with them. Or even when I did score, they usually didn't want to see me again the next day.

I'm pretty sure that Ian knew that women were necessary for the continuation of the species, but he acted as though they were something that a rational man shouldn't waste his time on.

Like, once I brought these two girls home because I didn't know what else to do with them. They'd been hitchhiking in Detroit, a profoundly unsafe procedure. They were very young, very pretty, and very stoned on God knew what. Ian was sitting in an easy chair, reading my *Scientific American*, when one of them latched onto his leg. She was kneeling at his feet, babbling something about running barefoot through the forest together, and sliding down rainbows.

Ian looked down from his article, said "Rainbows lack structural integrity," and went back to reading. He wasn't queer. Just sort of indifferent.

Hasenpfeffer always seemed to have a woman within arm's reach. Even baching it with us, I don't think he ever slept alone. They seemed to follow him like flies going after shit.

Or, take politics.

Back then, I was an awfully liberal Libertarian and Ian was a conservative Republican. I'm not sure, but I think Hasenpfeffer was pretty left-wing.

Or take partying. I like to drink and sing a lot. Ian was an absolute teetotaler about all drugs beyond coffee. And Hasenpfeffer did moderate amounts of *everything*.

Or take sports. Or hobbies. Or damn nearly anything.

Hell, I'm six foot six and Ian was five one with his elevator shoes on.

Yet when we met in the freshman registration line at U of M, we hit it off pretty quick. Hasenpfeffer had found this huge three-bedroom apartment and was looking for two people to share expenses.

We moved in that day. Oh, it was a fourth-floor walkup and the six-foot ceilings were—for me—an absolute pain, but it was cheap and that was the deciding factor. None of us had a family to fall back on for money.

I guess we did have something in common. We were all orphans.

Ian pulled a straight four point and had no difficulty in keeping his church scholarship. Hasenpfeffer had this talent for pulling dollars out of all sorts of organizations. But

I was only an average student and I wasn't much good at filling out forms and begging.

I'd used up a small inheritance by the end of my junior year, and joining the Air Farce seemed like a better shot than getting drafted into the Army. They put me through a year of electronics school and then had me spend three years pretending to fix computers under this mountain in Massachusetts. They'd never even let me ride on a military airplane. . . .

Towards sunset, looking up old friends seemed like a good idea, and my bike made a right turn into Rochester, a strange little town.

The locals claim that the engineer who laid out the street plan was drunk for eight weeks before he drew the first line, but I knew better. It takes large groups of people working earnestly together to do something that stupid.

The arithmetic average of the number of streets coming into an intersection is probably somewhere around four, but the modal number is three, with the next most likely number being five and after that seven. The whole town is like a quilt made by crazy old ladies out of random polygons. There's even one frightening crossroads called "Twelve Points." No shit.

Right downtown, doubtless by accident, there are these two streets that cross at almost right angles, although one of them changes its name in the process. This oddity so astounded the locals that they built this big office structure there and called it "The Four Corners Building."

I passed it seven times trying to find Hasenpfeffer's address, and it was pretty late when I finally got there.

I recognized it right off when I saw it. It was exactly the sort of place he had to live in. It was an ancient clapboard mansion that had long ago been converted into housing for the perpetually poor class, students. It was painted barn red and had a yellow external staircase with fully eleven odd-angle turns in it that led up to the sixth-floor attic. I didn't have to read the mailboxes to know that Hasenpfeffer had to live on top. He was home, and—A Wonderment!—was actually alone, bereft of all female accompaniment.

"Well, Tom. The parallelism of truly linked souls."

Hasenpfeffer hadn't changed much. The same blue eyes, blond hair, and straight features. Only now he had a full beard, his hair brushed his shoulders, and he no longer belonged on a poster advertising the Hitler Youth Movement. Instead, he was ready to compete in a Jesus Christ Look-Alike contest.

He was wearing this yellow scholar's robe with a garish collar.

"Huh?" My first comment to him in four years, barring a few letters.

"Your motorcycle. I saw you pull up. I have one just like it, but without the Ranger faring." He stood up and twirled to show off the gaudy cadmium yellow circus tent he was wearing. It had two broad strips of bright blue velvet running up the front, over the shoulders, and then meeting at the back of this oversized hood. Not that he could have put up the hood, since he wore this black tam-o'-shanter with a gold tassel.

"What do you think?"

"They make you wear that all the time, or just when you're on duty?"

"None of the above. I'm getting my doctorate in Behavioral Psychology tomorrow. That *is* why you came, isn't it?"

"Well, no. Just passing through. But I'll stick around if you want."

"You are out of the Air Force?"

"Yeah."

"Any plans?"

"Uh, none, really." I didn't think that he'd understand about officers.

"Excellent! Then we can leave in two days."

"Leave? Where are we going?"

"No place in particular. I have a Department of Defense grant to study social interactions within motorcycle gangs. That's how I bought the BMW. Forming our own gang will be much pleasanter and safer than trying to join the Hell's Angels."

Great. Me they stuff under a mountain. For him, they buy a motorcycle.

"Hell, why not?"

"Excellent! Ian will be with us, at least at first."

"Ian McTavish? What's he doing with himself?"

"He got his bachelor's in Mechanical Engineering two years after you left, and a second one in World History at the same time. He has been working for General Motors ever since. He has three weeks vacation due him, and we're to pick him up in Michigan this coming Friday."

"Great. Who else?"

"No one. Just the three of us."

"So three people constitute a motorcycle gang? I mean, if you've got this paper to write . . ."

"I can pad it out a bit. No one reads these DOD things anyway."

Hasenpfeffer lent me a tie and made me wear it to the graduation ceremony. I thought it looked funny with a T-shirt and a leather jacket, but it was his show. It was about six hours of boring people proving how boring they could be, and after all that, they didn't even give him his diploma, just a blank roll of paper. The real one was to be sent later. Much later, as it turned out.

The party afterwards was worse than the ceremony itself, with all the grads and their families standing around while the professors came in, "made an appearance," and left as soon as possible.

I'm patient enough to put up with things like that for old friends. Once in a while. At least I didn't have to stand in formation.

In the course of the day, about a dozen slender young women came up to say goodbye to Hasenpfeffer. They each got a smile, a hug, and some vague promises about see-ing each other again. He politely introduced each of them to me, but it seemed that I wasn't somebody that they wanted to meet. They each left as soon as possible.

That night and the next morning, we got all his stuff packed and a moving company hauled most of it away for storage. A half dozen more girls came by for their goodbye kisses, and one of them spent the night with him. He actually invited the last two of them to spend the night, but with me, since he was already occupied, but they developed pressing engagements elsewhere. They both left at a dead run, although one of them stopped to see if I was following, and to pick up a rock.

The two of us were on the road Friday morning at ten with a clear blue sky above us.

We took the shortcut through Canada, and 401 is a good place for road bikes. I was glad that Hasenpfeffer had bought a BMW because people who own them don't much like rolling with those who ride all the lesser breeds.

It's not that we're uppity, so much, though pride has a certain amount to do with it. It's just that a BMW is about the only machine that can go on forever without breaking down. I had to stop running with a buddy in the service because his Honda had an average of three mechanical problems a day, and that sure ruins a trip.

But with good machinery between our legs, we knew that there wouldn't be any holdups, so we could afford the time to make about four beer stops and load up on that fine Canadian brew. I never could figure out how one people could make such great beer and such lousy cigarettes.

CHAPTER THREE
The Other Friend

We got to Ian's condo that evening. It was quite a place, with carefully tended gardens and an impressive entranceway. It looked as though GM was doing well by our boy. The living room was spacious and nicely furnished with Danish Modern stuff. Indeed, it looked a lot bigger than it actually was. I found out the reason when I sat down. The furniture was tiny! It turned out that he had furnished his "pad" with the three-quarter-sized stuff they make to put in model homes, so they can fool people into thinking they're buying more than they're actually going to get.

It all fit Ian just fine, though, and it was his place after all. It got me to wondering if anybody made furniture to fit proper-sized people like me. Not that I could afford any furniture, much less a place to put it in.

But what wasn't undersized was Ian's motorcycle.

"Hey, you bought a Harley?" I said.

"What's wrong with buying American, Tom?" Ian said.

Ian was using my name, and Hasenpfeffer's as well, a whole lot more than he used to. Obviously, while I was gone, he'd taken a Dale Carnegie course. "How to Win Friends, Influence People, and Be A Complete Phony in Ten Easy Lessons."

14

"Well, nothing, when you're buying cigarettes or cars," I said. "But the engineering in that thing is forty years out of date."

"It's tried-and-true engineering, Tom."

"Tell you what, little buddy. I'll lend you a hand the first two times a day it breaks down. After that, you can find me at the next bar up the road."

"Have you ever considered the advantages of auto-copulation, Tom?"

Back in college, I'd ragged Ian a lot about swearing as much as he did while at the same time being such a regular churchgoer. This last statement obviously represented his attempt to cut down. It didn't last.

The next morning, we were on I-75 heading north. The plan was to go to Washington State by way of Minnesota, head south through California, and then get Ian home in three weeks by way of Louisiana.

By noon, we were off the expressways. We didn't plan to use the Interstate system all that much. The best way to travel while on vacation is get a map, figure out where you are, and where you want to be that night. Then you draw a straight line on the map between those two points. After that, you try to stay as close to that line as possible while staying on paved roads. This gets you into the country, where things can get interesting. The expressways are efficient, but they're also boring.

Ian's Duo-Glide held up better than I had feared, with only a half hour lost for repairs that day. We went over Big Mac (the bridge, not the junk food) that afternoon, but an hour later it started sprinkling, so we pulled up to the only building in Pine Stump, Michigan.

It was a combination gas station (one pump), general store (one small shelf of canned goods), and tavern (four stools at a linoleum-topped bar and two chairs at a small table).

The town's mayor and sole inhabitant was the little old lady who ran the place, tended the bar, and lived in the building's other room, in back. She looked to be eighty years old. She was skinny, and about as frail as a crowbar.

The surrounding area really did have pine stumps. Thousands of them! They were huge for white pine, probably world record setters when they'd been cut maybe eighty years before, when the area had been logged over. Nothing growing there now was even close.

The three of us packed the place, since there were a couple of locals at the table and an Indian at the bar. He was dressed in blue jeans and was wearing a bow-hunter's cap, but he wasted no time explaining that he was a full-blooded Ojibwa. Then he stood up, shouted "Jesus Christ!" at the top of his lungs, slammed his can of Blatz down on the linoleum bar, and sat down.

I asked him what seemed to be the problem, and he launched into a tirade about the hunting and fishing rights he had as a result of a treaty between his people and the government. I had a hard time understanding exactly what he was talking about, not because of any accent—he spoke perfect, standard English—but because every so often he would stop in the middle of a sentence, stand up, shout "Jesus Christ!", slam down his increasingly flat can of beer, and then sit down again as though nothing had happened. After this happened about six times, Hasenpfeffer whispered to me that the fellow was on a fifty-three-second cycle. He'd been timing the guy.

After maybe a half hour of this, I figured out that the treaty said that the Indians could hunt and fish whenever they wanted to, without needing a license, and it didn't say anything about the manner in which they should accomplish this.

Now the government game warden had written him up for dynamiting fish, a thing he felt he had a perfect right to do.

Well, that was interesting, and shot down all the nonsense you hear about Indians being natural ecologists, but the constant standing up and screaming was starting to get to me. It was getting to Ian worse, nursing his Coke while everyone else was into their second six pack, him being a Christian and all, and he was on the side that was being sprayed with beer every fifty-three seconds. I think Ian was just trying to quiet the Indian down in a friendly, humorous way.

"My friend, you swear too fucking much," Ian said, a

perfectly normal statement to make in a Detroit auto plant, but not, as it turned out, in the UP. (That's pronounced You Pee, with an equal accent on each syllable.)

Things quieted down in a hurry. There was dead silence for a few seconds, then one of the locals got up from his chair and knocked Ian off his bar stool.

"What—what's wrong?" Ian said from the floor. He was more shocked than hurt.

"You was using *vulgarity*, and in front of a *lady!*" the man explained. The barkeeper nodded in agreement, happy to have her honor defended.

"Vulgarity? After all the swearing that has been going on in here? You're out of your fucking mind!"

"That was taking the Name in vain, and it ain't the same thing!"

"Shouldn't simple vulgarity be the lesser offense?" Ian said, still flat on his back.

The local didn't know how to answer that, so he hauled off to kick Ian when he was down, and, naturally, I couldn't sit quiet for that. I picked up the would-be kicker from behind with my right hand on his belt and said, "Gentlemen, please fight politely."

At this point the other local and the Indian piled onto me, ignoring Ian entirely. I thought it best to take them outside, since the furnishings of the little place didn't look too sturdy. There wasn't much to it since I was already carrying the one, and the other two were crawling all over me trying to wrestle me to the ground. I even had a free hand with which to open the door.

I walked over to a twenty-foot gully near the road, threw them rolling down it and went back into the bar, locking the flimsy screen door behind me.

"I think I've deduced the problem," Hasenpfeffer said, writing hurriedly in a new notebook. "It seems that in this subculture they differentiate between two types of swearing. . . ."

"Yeah, I got that much," I said. "You all right, Ian?"

"I think so, Tom. Geeze, I thought I was making a joke!"

"It was a nasty joke!" the old bartender said. "Nasty!"

"Yeah. Well guys, the rain's stopped. Let's drink up before they think about knocking over our bikes."

"These are good, solid interactions," Hasenpfeffer said as we left.

Later, the three of us were camped way off the road in someplace called Ontonagon County. It was Sunday morning, and Ian was trying to talk us into going to church with him, since he had stopped at all those bars with us. I allowed as how that seemed fair, but did he know of a church that served beer? After all, he'd been able to get a Coke at each of our bars.

"Maybe we can find one that serves wine with communion," Hasenpfeffer suggested.

Ian looked disgruntled, and a change of topic seemed in order. I was doing the cooking, and thus by ancient custom I had certain conversational rights.

I said, "Back to what you were saying last night, Ian, I still maintain that stupidity, *true stupidity* mind you, is not an individual function. Oh, anybody can do something dumb, and usually does, but to create truly monumentally ridiculous edifices, it takes large groups of people working diligently together. A case in point can be taken from my recent Air Force experience.

"This organization, if I may use such a term on a group of more than ten people, which are inherently disorganized, is obviously—"

"Share out some coffee, and your ramblatory obfuscation will be sharply reduced by the caffeine," Jim said.

"Yeah, and you won't talk so funny either, Tom," Ian added.

"Right," I said, pouring. "So like I was saying, somebody at the Chief of Staff level became convinced that the best way to insure that the United States Air Force had officers of the finest quality was to require that all such new people were college graduates. Just who this person was, I'm not sure, but you can be certain that *he* was a college graduate.

"As an aside, I point out that General Chuck Yeager (the first man to crack the sound barrier, an ace pilot in WWII and the commander of the most efficient flying unit in Viet Nam), was only a *temporary* general. His permanent rank was *sergeant,* since he talked funny and didn't have any Ivy League accent at all. They figured that he didn't measure up since all he knew about was flying, fighting and getting things organized. How could anybody with a redneck accent be officer material?

"Anyway, in some very different nook or cranny of that same service, some committee looked out and observed that enlisted men who had been trained in fields like electronics, and who could thus earn three times their Air Force pay working on the outside, rarely reenlisted. Since there was nothing that this committee could do about pay rates (those being the prerogative of some other committee somewhere else), but needing sergeants trained in electronics to boss the peons they were perforce training in vast droves, and yet heaven forbid that they should make a sergeant out of anyone without first giving him grey hair, passed the following ruling: As an incentive to reenlistment, any troop choosing to reenlist could pick the career field (like electronics) of his choice, and receive up to two years worth of training in that new field.

"Unbeknownst to any of the above committees, the Air Training Command decided that all that an instructor had to know was what was in the training guide, and that practical experience was unimportant in such a fast-moving field as electronics, where things were obsolete before they were installed anyway. Furthermore, they didn't have any sergeants trained in electronics in the first place, what with none of the airmen reenlisting, so they might as well use airmen right out of school to teach the next class. This set up a situation where airmen were training sergeants who were taking advantage of the reenlistment training bonus, sergeants they could very well be subordinate to on their next tour of duty. Oddly enough, those sergeants all got very good grades, whether they proved capable of learning Ohm's Law or not.

"The committee that had set up the retraining program compiled all these grades on neat charts that proved that the experienced troop was always the best student.

"Then the Air Force bought the 465L Command Control System, which at that time was the most complicated computerized control system known to man. And the committee in charge of manning this monster decided that it would take some pretty bright boys to keep it working, so they scheduled troops to be trained for repairing it on the basis of IQ. I was one of them they selected.

"So they paid me to go to school for a year, drink a lot, and do pushups in the sandburrs. Once I got to my duty station, I found that my boss was a sergeant with an IQ of about ninety. While he wasn't a bad guy, he had been too dumb to make it as a sheet-metal repairman, so he had been retrained by the Air Force in the exciting new career field of electronics.

"He was running a major computer repair section and he was afraid of electricity. The fact that all of our equipment ran on five volts, and was as safe as a flashlight, didn't faze him. He knew that the stuff could electrocute you, so he wouldn't touch it. He made sure that we kept the floors clean, though, so no one of any importance suggested replacing him.

"My Officer In Charge was a college graduate, as per regulations. Only there weren't any Degreed Electrical Engineers around who wanted to take on a low-rent job like Second Lieutenant, and the Air Force, with no sensible candidates available, had to take what it could get. The only officers we got were those who had taken degrees in fields where there were no civilian jobs available. My OIC, who was in charge of a quarter acre of computers supposedly defending North America, had his degree in Marine Biology and didn't know for shit about computers. *His* boss had a degree in Forestry and *his* had a master's in Music Appreciation.

"Then, at the bottom of this strange pyramid, surrounded by a half billion dollars worth of inoperative equipment, were us four hundred misfits. None of us had the social graces to get a college degree of our own and every one of us had a sad story as to how he ended up in uniform. Yet *all of us had IQs of over one-forty*! All of us were subordinate to sergeants with IQs of under ninety. All of whom were commanded by officers who hadn't the slightest idea of what was going on.

"The result was obvious chaos, and there are stories to be told about it, but not just now, breakfast being over and it being Jim's turn to do something about the mess. But on some future date I shall relate the tale of the atomic clock that failed."

"Tom, you fry a good pancake, but they weren't worth having to listen to your bullshit."

"Every word of it is true, I swear it! Do you think that I could have invented a story like that?"

"Hmm. You have a point there. You're not that smart. In fact, I don't think that anybody could invent a story like that one. Yet could such a situation actually be?" Jim said.

"There could and there is, for I was just there and it's not likely to change. But my point is that each step of the above was sensible, or at least not thoroughly insane when looked at in its own small context. But when an organization gets so large that nobody can possibly know everything that is happening elsewhere, many small sensible steps generally congeal into a major conglomeration of mass stupidity."

CHAPTER FOUR
An Explosion in Time

We were packing up after breakfast when we heard the explosion.

Sort of a deep, heavy, ground-shaking *FUMP!*

"Is there some sort of mining operation going on around here?" Hasenpfeffer said.

"Not in the last forty years, Jim, and certainly not on a Sunday," Ian said. "I doubt if there's a farm or factory within ten miles of here."

"Hey, we're not that far from Kincheloe Field," I said. "Could be some Weekend Warrior broke his bird. We'd better check it out. I think it came from that way."

A BMW isn't ideal for cross-country work, but Ian's Harley was worse. Anyhow, I got there first.

It wasn't like any explosion that I'd ever heard of. There was a hole there—maybe ten yards across and five deep—clean and hemispherical. It hadn't been there long, because there wasn't any erosion to speak of. Just a little rubble at the bottom.

But there wasn't any blast damage around it. If you blow a hole in the ground, the dirt has to go *somewhere*. I was standing on what looked like a lawn, and the grass wasn't even dirty.

22

Hasenpfeffer came up.

"Strange. Look at that. The rocks are polished," he said.

There was some stonework at the end of the hole, made of rounded field stones, the sort that I had seen used locally for chimneys. It was as though somebody had sliced and polished the stones in the same plane as the edge of the hole. No, let me take that back. It wasn't a plane. It was as though the hemisphere of the hole just sort of continued up through the fireplace and chimney. Spooky.

Ian came in from the other direction, skirting a newly planted garden. He killed the ignition on his overheated Harley and it knocked a dozen times before it died.

"Either you've got the wrong hole, or this is some kind of a joke." Ian was on the far side of the pit.

"How so?"

"There wasn't any explosion, Jim. Explosions blow things outwards. This was an *im*plosion. Look at his garden here. The sticks with the seed envelopes on them are all lying *towards* the hole."

We had to go the long way around the pit because there was an old station wagon in the way. Half of the front bumper was missing. In fact, the bumper ended exactly at the same invisible sphere that the hole and the fireplace did.

We heard a "pop" and a thin oval of shiny wire fell from the bumper into the hole. It slid to the bottom and was half buried by some sand and thin slices of stone.

"Hey, it's getting bigger!" I said.

"Bullshit. It's getting smaller, Tom. The stuff fell into the hole, not out of it."

Nothing happened for the next few minutes. There wasn't much to see, so I said, "Look, anybody got a rope or something? I'm going to go see what's down there."

"Are you out of your fucking mind?" Ian suggested.

"Uh, what do you mean?"

"I mean whatever is down there can slice steel like cheese, and now you want to put your whole body into it."

"Huh. You've got a point there."

There was another pop and more rubble fell into the hole.

"Maybe we should get the police," Ian said.

"Has a crime been committed?" Hasenpfeffer asked.

"I don't know."

"Neither do I. And until we have positive evidence of criminal activity, I suggest that we leave the authorities out of this." Hasenpfeffer dug out his notebook.

"But, just sit here, Jim?"

"And observe. This could be the basis of an excellent paper, even though it probably does not concern my own field. One's progress in Academia is largely dependent on what one has written." Hasenpfeffer dug out the tape recorder and camera that he'd planned to use recording our "interactions."

"They had to spend a lot of time getting the hole this smooth." Ian crumbled the edge of the pit in with the heel of his engineer's boot.

There was another "pop" and Ian's scream must have been heard in Sault Sainte Marie.

"The 'pops' seem to be happening at eight-minute, forty-second intervals," Hasenpfeffer noted.

Ian would have fallen into the hole, except that I happened to be right there and a lot bigger than most people. I managed to get a hand on his belt and carried him over to the lawn. Across the arch of his boot there was a quarter-inch-wide stripe where the leather and rubber were puffed out and dirty. Ian had stopped screaming and started swearing, so I figured that it wasn't too serious.

When I got his boot and sock off, I saw that his right foot had the same quarter-inch stripe, only now it was black and purple, as well as puffed out and dirty. Nothing seemed to be broken or cut, but I got out my canteen and first-aid kit. I washed and bandaged the guy's foot, just for form's sake.

Ian still wasn't all that coherent. The only anesthetic I had was a forty-ounce bottle of Jim Beam that I'd bought along with a carton of Pall Malls at the tax-free shop at the Canadian border, and he was a teetotaler. I got the bottle out of my saddlebags anyway.

"Come on, amigo. It's a good painkiller."

"You know I never touch the stuff, Tom."

"Hey, this is purely medicinal." I took a drink to demonstrate its virtues.

"I'll pass, Tom."

"But Ian, my boy, this is the true ancient panacea, historically proven to cure cancer, ease childbirth and improve virility in your old age."

"Crawl off and die a lonely death, Tom."

"Why, this elixir is so beneficial that were you cleaved from head to knave, I would only have to fit the two halves precisely together, and then by placing only the smallest of drops on your sadly mutilated tongue . . ."

"God Dammit!" He grabbed the bottle. "If it'll shut you and Don Quixote up . . ."

My purposes accomplished, I wandered back to Hasenpfeffer.

"I think Ian'll be all right," I said. "How's the hole?"

"Filling in. The time between 'pops' is decreasing, logarithmically I think. It is down to eight minutes, twelve seconds. Do you think that you could retrieve some samples of the debris without injuring yourself?"

"Well, I can try," I said.

"The next pop is due in about a minute."

I got an old, dry stick from the garden and held it next to the edge of the polished stonework, keeping my hand well away from it. The pop came on schedule and this time it was accompanied by a minor explosion coming from the bottom of the hole. Startled, I jumped back, but kept hold of the stick. Looking at it, I had a wafer of polished stone—the kind you see in lapidary shops—stuck through the end of my stick. I mean, the stick just went in one side and out the other, without the stone having a hole in it.

"I should have warned you about the explosion," Hasenpfeffer said. "What have you got there?"

"Well, it looks like we've got a good stone-cutting technique," I said.

"We might have a great deal more than that. Tell me, how far was it from the stone to where this wafer appeared?"

"Oh, about an inch and a quarter."

"About three centimeters. Excellent. That confirms my theory," Hasenpfeffer said.

"Enlighten me."

"This wafer is just under a half centimeter thick. We have

observed six pops since we arrived, and the debris at the bottom of the hole indicated that a pop occurred before we got here."

"So?"

"So seven times less than a half equals about three."

Maybe in psychology they use a different kind of arithmetic than we use in electronics, but I don't think that I'd want Hasenpfeffer to design a circuit for me.

"Yeah?"

"Isn't it obvious?" Hasenpfeffer said. "The material that once occupied a spherical volume of space went someplace else and now it's returning to its original position in small pieces."

"Uh huh," I said. "Where did it go when it wasn't here?"

"How should I know? I would imagine that it went into some alternate spatial or temporal continuum."

"Alternate . . . ?"

"Don't you read any science fiction? Come, there's work to do. And get Ian," Hasenpfeffer said.

Well, Ian was still there, and the bottle was still there, but the contents of the latter had been transferred to the former.

"Ian's going to be out of it for a while."

"Oh. I see. Well, we will simply have to do it ourselves."

"Do what?"

"Rig some sort of net to recover as much as of the debris as possible."

"What on earth for?"

Hasenpfeffer looked at me sadly. Then he started speaking slowly and with small words. "Something made a big ball of earth and air go away. Now it is coming back. Big balls of earth don't usually go away, so something unusual must have made it go away. Maybe that something is in the middle of the big ball that went away. If we can get it, maybe we can find out how to make other big balls of dirt go away."

"Go drag your knuckles in your shit."

Obnoxious son of a bitch. I went and cut down two thin saplings for poles. The twit needed me because he was too clumsy to cut down a tree without chopping off both of his thumbs in the process. I heard another "pop" while I rigged up a butterfly net of sorts out of the poles, my sleeping bag, and some bungee cords. Dumb bastard, anyway.

"You'll notice that there was some sort of structure here," Hasenpfeffer said. "The last few pops have contained bits of wood and shingles, located precisely where you would expect them to be if a thin spherical shell were to materialize in our space. While none of the debris so far has been very heavy, some of it looks quite sharp, so do be careful. Oh, yes. The explosions are becoming less violent. I think that the additional material at the bottom has a muffling action."

My "butterfly net" weighed about fifty pounds.

"Hey, I should be careful? Damn it, Jim, give me a hand with this thing!"

"Well, if you really feel that you require physical assistance . . ." But he didn't come any closer to me.

Pop.

"What is that?" he said.

"That" was a bunch of hundred-dollar bills that materialized right in front of me. I had them scooped out of the air before they fell into the hole.

I said, "Hey, good idea about the net!"

"Thank you. They're coming in at six-minute intervals now, so be ready. I'll watch for anything else that might be useful."

So I was left holding the stick, but it didn't trouble me any more. In the next eight pops, with Hasenpfeffer warning me of each impending pop, I raked in an even two hundred and fifty thousand dollars, which was a lot of money back then. Some of the bills were cut up, but I got all the pieces. We could Scotch tape them back together later on.

Then there was nothing much except wood and plumbing fixtures for a few hours, so I took a lunch break. I was halfway through my fourth salami sandwich when Hasenpfeffer started yelling.

"His papers! There are papers coming in!"

"What? Whose papers?"

No answer. The pops were coming two minutes apart now,

so I inhaled the sandwich and went back to work. Actually, my net was a little big for Hasenpfeffer to handle alone.

Paper came in, but it was more like confetti than anything else. You see, the money had been laid parallel to the surface of the sphere, whereas this stuff was perpendicular to it. It came as thin, curved walls of confetti that gently exploded on arrival. The first bits were followed by a deluge of paper.

"Jim, this is ridiculous. A whole library has been run through the grandmother of all paper schredders here. No way in hell will we ever get it together," I said.

"But we must try! It's critical!"

"Maybe, but it's also impossible. I'm going back to lunch. Call me if anything useful turns up."

Ian hadn't moved, but he still had a pulse.

Towards four o'clock the gore started. I had been scooping up bits of electronic parts, circuit boards and workbench when I got a bit of meat on my sleeping bag. At first I thought that I was going through another refrigerator. At this point the sphere was about two yards in diameter. I was standing knee deep in sharp splinters of wood veneer, thankful for my leather pants and shit-kicker boots. The pops were coming every ten seconds and it was about five scoops before I realized what was happening. I was pitching people!

"Omigod," I said.

"You noticed," Hasenpfeffer said. "Don't let it throw you. We're almost to the end."

"But . . ."

"Hang on just a little longer, Tom. We can't save him, but maybe we can save his work."

The last hundred or so shells came in a long *BBRRIIIP!*
And then it was over.

I was dead tired and went over to the lawn, by Ian, who had rolled over on his side, and had his pants unzipped. I lay down upwind of him, because he was doing the vomit and urine routine. Forty ounces of sour mash is quite a bit for a little fellow who'd never been drunk before.

I guess I sacked out.

CHAPTER FIVE
The Venture

It was dusk when Hasenpfeffer shook me awake.

"Hey, Tom. Are you all right?"

"Huh? Yeah. I guess so."

"I just wanted to tell you that actually, we were able to salvage very little. Only the money, some wrecked circuits— that you may or may not be able to do something with— and this. It was the only piece of legible paper that I was able to save. Do you have any idea of what it is?"

I was feeling sort of woozy.

"Uh, sure. It's a circuit schematic."

"I deduced that. But does it mean anything to you?"

"Well, it's strange. He's got digital, analog and R-F components in the same circuit. Maybe I can figure it out. Later. Look, I don't feel so good."

"You don't look so good, either. I have already sent Ian for an ambulance. He said to tell you that alcohol is not a painkiller. It's a pain delayer and relocator."

"Uh, if Ian was all hung over, why didn't you go yourself?"

"Because I don't feel so good either."

Then for a while there my memory gets sort of spotty. It was a lot like when you're on a good drunk only without any of the fun involved.

Medical types were always waking me up to do something to me. Hauling me into an ambulance, out of an ambulance, into bed, out of bed. Asking weird questions I couldn't quite follow. Waking me up to get some more shots. Waking me up again to take my sleeping pills. I tell you that medics have less respect for your personal individuality than the average Air Force sergeant.

Eventually, the fog cleared some and Hasenpfeffer was leaning over me.

"Radiation sickness and some sort of chemical poisoning," Hasenpfeffer said. "You are going to be all right, but you came about as close to being dead as you could get."

"So, why didn't you get it, too?" I said.

"I did. But you spent much more time in the rubble than I. Ian was the least affected, due to his distance from the event and all that Jim Beam you poured into him. It seems that alcohol reduces the effects of radiation on the system."

"He poured it into himself. Look, where is Ian?"

"In his room. He still has difficulty getting around."

"Hey, I thought that you said he was okay."

"From the radiation," Hasenpfeffer said. "But that sand in his foot blocked off the blood supply to his toes. Gangrene. He lost half his right foot."

"Christ. We should have gotten him to the hospital sooner."

"Perhaps. But the doctors said that it wouldn't have helped any. There is no technique for pulling sand out of someone's foot when it didn't make a hole getting in there in the first place. No prior medical art."

"Shit. Uh, what about the money?"

"When it became obvious that we were having medical difficulties, I locked the money and the rest of our salvage into those detachable saddlebags of mine and hid them a few kilometers from the site. This was fortunate, because by morning the medical types had reported the radiation sickness and the place was crawling with government types."

"And the money?" I asked.

"Safe and sound. I picked it up this morning."

"Hey, great! What about the guy who got sliced up?"

"Woman. Her name was Barbara Elaine Kruger. Nobody seems to know anything about her, except that she was maybe sixty, and her neighbors didn't like her. She had no relatives that anybody knows about," Hasenpfeffer said.

"Weird. Just her up there puttering all alone?"

"That's what it looks like. But now you are in for a grilling by the AEC, the FBI and Air Force Intelligence."

"Uh, that last is a contradiction in terms."

"Hush. Your story is that we heard an explosion and went to investigate. When we got there, we all fell asleep. You woke up once or twice and saw a number of flying saucers cruising in formation. Then you went to sleep again and woke up in the hospital."

"Hey, why not just . . ."

"Tell the truth? If we did that, we would lose a quarter of a million dollars, and possibly a good deal more," Hasenpfeffer said.

"Uh, okay. Why the flying saucers?"

"Because mentioning them is the best way to get things hushed up."

So for the next three weeks, until I got out of the hospital, I was grilled about twice a day by different people wearing white shirts and narrow ties. I just played dumb. Four years as a SAC Trained Killer made me a past master at the game of pretending that you're stupider than your boss, even though you've got seventy IQ points on him. Since most of the government bozos grilling me were even dumber than your average sergeant, none of them caught me at it.

Ian had more problems, since his training in college and at GM was all about how to look smart even when you don't have the slightest idea of what's going on. I wish I could have given him some pointers, but the rooms were generally bugged.

The hubbub about the radioactive explosion site died out surprisingly fast, without a single word of it getting into the papers.

Hasenpfeffer was released from the hospital in a few days, but another month went by before Ian and I were mobile.

Ian's company-paid Blue Cross-Blue Shield covered all his bills, and Hasenpfeffer somehow talked the Air Force into picking up my hospital tab. At least I had to sign a paper saying that it wasn't the fault of the U.S. Air Force, but they were treating me for radiation poisoning purely out of the goodness of their hearts and I wasn't allowed to sue the shit out of them for it later.

Hasenpfeffer didn't have to pay for his own bills, either, though I'm not quite sure how he worked that. Maybe he got one of the girls in billing to pad his bill into mine or Ian's. He was good at that sort of thing.

Because of the repeated interrogations we'd been through, with a strange assortment of unmannerly government types asking us nonsensical questions that varied from the stupid to the rude, we had been afraid to talk freely with each other in the hospital. Once I actually found a tape recorder in my room, and Ian was acting downright paranoid.

Finally, the ordeal over, we celebrated in a private dining room at the best restaurant Hasenpfeffer could find. He picked the place while we were in the taxicab on the way there, so we figured that they couldn't possibly have the place bugged.

"Gentlemen, I feel that a serious discussion is in order," Hasenpfeffer said as we sat back, stuffed with high-calorie, greasy, salty, and glorious *food* after weeks of that disgustingly healthy hospital pap.

"Well, I don't feel like anything should be in order, except maybe another glass of this Grand Mariner stuff." I puffed on a two-dollar cigar. "Then, let's play vegetable for three hours, followed by having *another* pretty waitress bring us four more bottles of wine, another round of caviar, three more steaks, some more Cherry Jubilees, and then some more cigars and . . ."

"Tom, you sound like a first-century Roman glutton," Ian said. "I'm due back at the plant in a few days. If I go back."

"Then again, I don't feel much like arguing, either."

"Excellent. To sum up, we find ourselves in a unique position. We are suddenly the proprietors of both some radical technology and the capital with which to develop it."

"*If* it's ours, Jim," Ian said. "They both really belong to that Kruger woman."

"Who is irretrievably dead, with no apparent heirs or relatives. I'm sure that she would have wanted someone to carry on her work. Now, the question is, what do we do with our windfall?"

"Hey, *you* might call it a windfall, but for Ian and me it was pretty damned expensive. He lost half his foot, and my radiation poisoning cost me every hair on my body. I'll be on chemotherapy for a year, and—"

"Gentlemen, in our ignorance we have sustained accidents and injuries, but nothing devastating. When you consider that Ian couldn't dance *before* his accident, and the fact that you weren't beautiful *with* your hair, you must conclude that your collective losses aren't that severe."

"Yeah, but I still think you ought to pitch in your part. Like maybe your left testicle. What say, Ian?"

"I think it's time that you cut your Polish blarney. Nobody made me stick my foot into that hole, and none of us knew about the radiation. If it hadn't been for Jim's quick thinking, we probably wouldn't have either the money or those bits of circuits. The only fair way to handle this is as an even three-way partnership."

"An excellent suggestion. I second it." Hasenpfeffer smiled.

"Oh, what the hell. I'll third it."

"We are agreed, then. The next obvious question is, 'Besides the money, what exactly do we have?' Tom, you've had time to look over that circuit. Could you duplicate it?"

"Sure. No sweat. It's all standard parts, so I could probably get it together in a week or so. But I couldn't tell you *why* it did whatever it did. And I'd want to be about four miles away when we turned it on."

"You feel that we could produce something useful in a relatively short time?"

"Well, that depends on what you mean by useful. Lookit, a few ounces of electronics stuff did about as much damage as a two-thousand-pound bomb. The Air Farce would call that *damn* useful."

"You are suggesting that we develop the military aspects of this?"

"Hell, no! If uncle found out about this thing, we'd be under tight security for the rest of our lives. Look, do you know what it's like working in a government top-secret area? Showing your badge to armed guards six times a day? Filling out forms in triplicate to get a resistor? Having a TV camera in the john watching you crap?" I shivered.

"More important," Ian said. "If we develop the military side of this before we have the civilian uses on the market, we might never be allowed to develop the industrial products at all."

"Then you see commercial uses in this?"

"Dozens of them, so many that I feel like a phlogiston chemist who just got a good look at the Periodic Table of Elements. Think about mining. Put one of those circuits against the side of a cliff. Turn it on, and before the chips come back, get a conveyor belt in there to haul them out. Then put another circuit against the far wall and repeat the process. I tell you that we could tunnel at a cost of a few dollars a foot, where the competition would have to charge thousands!"

"I see. And the difference between those two figures is called profit?"

"Sure. You think I'm a 1930s-style socialist? But more important, think about what we could do with cheap tunnels. A lot of mountain ranges—the Rockies and the Andes—are too wet on one side and too dry on the other. Think about big tunnels to carry irrigation water to the deserts. Or, think about an underground highway system. No snow on the roads to cause accidents. No rain to wash out bridges. No bridges at all, for that matter. No fog or other problems with visibility. No dogs or other animals to hit. No children to worry about. Without all the obstructions, it would be easy to automate, so bad drivers wouldn't be a problem, either! I tell you it would save billions of dollars and fifty thousand lives a year!"

"So you are suggesting that we become involved with the construction industry?"

"Sure. But it's even more than that. Do you realize that half of the lumber that's harvested is turned into sawdust and scrap? You saw what the circuit did to the wood in that house. Smooth polished surfaces on both sides of the cut, with absolutely no waste. That translates out to less-expensive wood and fewer trees cut."

"Hey, aren't some of those sawmills powered by burning sawdust?" I asked.

"Let 'em buy coal. We can tunnel it out cheap. Or better still—well, maybe I don't believe this one myself, but think of a piston engine with one of these gadgets where the spark plug used to be. If we could somehow work it so that the circuit didn't destroy itself, and could make the air in the cylinder go away without hurting the engine, atmospheric pressure would naturally force the piston into the cylinder, and if we can make the air come back at the right time, we push the piston back out. It sounds like nearly free power. I mean, the circuit was powered by a transistor-radio battery, and when you do the math about how much stuff was removed . . ."

"Uh, huh. What about the Second Law of Thermodynamics?" I said.

"That's what bugs me about the idea. . . . Anyway, back to cutting techniques. Do we have to make chips that are spheric segments, or can we shape this field, or whatever it is, into other contours? Do you know what we have to do to make an automotive quarter panel? You take an ingot of steel and run it through ten million dollars worth of rolling mills to turn it into sheet metal. Then you take the sheet metal and run it through typically six dies worth a half million each. Dies you have to throw away to make next year's model. Maybe with a properly shaped field, we could cut parts directly off the original ingot. Then all we'd have to do is weld 'em together."

"Hey, maybe not even that," I said. "You saw that stick I put through the stone?"

"Hey, yeah! Look, we clamp our support brackets right where the fender is going to reemerge. Then—"

CHAPTER SIX
The Partnership

"Gentlemen, I gather that you are both enthusiastic about the technical and financial prospects of our venture. But the question before us is 'Do we have a venture?' Is Ian going to leave tomorrow and return to Pontiac Motors? I have an offer to start teaching in the fall. Am I going to be there? Is Tom going to go and do whatever he had in mind before all this came up? Or are we going to take our newfound capital and work together to develop this new technology?"

"Well, uh, of course!" I said. "I mean, this is a clean shot at a fifteen-point buck! We'd be dumbshits to pass it by! A man would be a fool—"

"I quite agree. We have stumbled upon our chance at success. Wealth. Fame, if we want it. Power to change the world into a better place. Most definitely I second your motion."

"But it's . . . it's so *wild*!" Then Ian said softly, "I've got a place, now. I've got security. I'm moving up in a good company. . . ."

"Ian, there is nothing as secure as money in the bank," Hasenpfeffer said. "You now have seven years' pay in your third of our account. Why not spend those years testing your mettle? General Motors knows that you are competent. They will be happy to take you back, if we fail. Come with us! Screw your courage to the hitching post!"

Ian stared at the table. "I've bought this condo, and I've got mortgage payments. I've got car payments. And payments on the Harley. I owe on my credit cards. . . ."

"Hmm . . . Tom, what would you say if the company were to take over all of Ian's debts and assets—whatever they are—and bring him to exactly the same financial status that you and I presently enjoy?"

"Hey, sure. No question. Bankers are all leeches, bastards, the lot of them. All for one!"

"And one for all!" Ian suddenly shouted. "I'm with you! We'll do it!"

As things fell out, and with Hasenpfeffer selling the condo, our little company cleared $2,954.26, and kept Ian's Corvette as group property. And Ian got his Harley paid off, since Hasenpfeffer and I owned our BMWs clear. But I get ahead of myself.

"Well then, we are agreed," Hasenpfeffer said. "The next question is 'Where are we going to do it?' I would like to suggest Ann Arbor. It is a town that we all know—we went to school there. It has a major university, with all that that implies. It is near a major airport. It has hundreds of high-tech companies, and it is within easy driving distance of the Detroit area, with its thousands of diverse manufacturing facilities."

"Uh, sure. Why not?"

"Fine, Jim. It'd be nice to walk in Ann Arbor with some money in my pocket."

"Walk? There is, of course, the parking problem, but what I have in mind is some ten miles outside the city limits. While you two were hospitalized, I took the liberty of investigating the real estate market in that area. I located an interesting property. It has forty acres of wooded land, so if we need to make big balls of earth go away, we shall have plenty of dirt to do it with. It has a large, modern three-bedroom house with four baths, and it has an eight-thousand-square-foot metalworking shop, complete with milling machines, surface grinders and that sort of thing."

"You say that this is all new?" Ian asked.

"The buildings are three years old. I have the machinery specifications here somewhere. . . ." Hasenpfeffer fumbled through his inner jacket pockets. "Ah. Here, eight thousand square feet . . . ten-ton overhead bridge crane . . . five thousand CFM air compressor with piping . . . truck wells . . . six-hundred-AMP, 480-volt service . . . three Bridgeports, one with readouts and one with CNC . . . two lathes . . . but here, Ian. You know more about this sort of thing than I do."

Ian went down the list, mumbling. "Yes. Yes. With this stuff, I could build anything. But with only a quarter of a million, we can't afford to buy all this."

"However, I did buy it. It was an estate sale. The heirs were faced with selling it at auction for twenty cents on the dollar (and then paying a ten-percent auctioneer's fee) or selling to me at twenty-two cents on the dollar, cash. They accepted my offer, and I paid them."

"What did this cost . . . us?"

"$226,000.00."

"Hey, that's most of what we have!" I yelled.

"True. Which is precisely why I sold it."

"You sold the place!" Ian shouted.

"Yes, for $358,000.00, retaining the chattels—furniture, machinery and so on. Then, of course, since we needed it, I bought it back for $480,000.00, on a lease with option to purchase, with the first five years rent paid in advance. And a balloon payment, due after that period, of $470,000.00—should we decide to exercise our option to purchase. Actually, we probably won't want to buy it then. If our venture is not successful, we won't need the property. If it is, we will probably need something bigger. But it looks nice on the lease."

"Uh . . ." I said. "You bought it for $226K. You sold it for $358K. Then you bought it back for $480K. . . . Why?"

"Surely it is obvious. When the smoke clears, we get the facilities we need for five years at no cost to us, except that we have to pay the taxes and insurance, which will be assessed at the $226,000.00 price."

"You mean that you conned somebody into giving us the place almost free?" Ian's eyes were tall.

"Conned? Swindled? Nonsense, Ian. My principal here will

be quite handsomely rewarded. See here. We are working with Dr. Bernstein, who has a medical practice in Ann Arbor. He bought the property from us—well, from me, actually, since you two weren't available. Anyway, he bought the property for $358,000.00, putting $132,000.00 down and easily obtained a $226,000.00 mortgage for the balance. After all, he is a solid citizen, he put thirty-seven percent down, and he had a long-term lease—with us—on the property. We rent it at $2,200.00 a month. His payments are $1,361.00 to the bank. It is the sort of arrangement that financial institutions love."

"So we owe rent on it," Ian said.

"No. The rent has already been paid, five years in advance. I gave Bernstein a check for $132,000.00, which he used for his down payment."

"He got it for free, but he's making our mortgage payment? Why?"

"Because Bernstein saves money by paying it. Of that $1,361.00 payment, $1,155.00 is interest, which is tax deductible. At twenty-year straight-line depreciation, he can deduct an additional $1,491.00 per month for a total of $2,646.00 in tax deductions. His tax bracket is well over fifty percent, so he comes out ahead, cash-wise, in addition to building valuable equity."

"Jim, I thought that that kind of wheeling and dealing went out with Diamond Jim Brady. What happens to his taxes on the $132,000.00?"

"Oh, that never really existed. The checks were never cashed."

"But . . ."

Which was the start of a two-hour discussion that I would just as soon not remember and in fact have forgotten. Long experience had taught me that Hasenpfeffer can do magic and that Ian can keep him honest.

I went through two more cigars and four more Grand Marniers, and had the waitress to the point where she didn't mind my arm around her waist. She was stroking my bald head.

Then I got the bill. It was over a week's pay at my Air Force job, and more than I had on me. Being unable to attract Hasenpfeffer's attention, I picked his pocket. It was my money, or ours, anyway. I returned it discreetly, after giving the waitress a twenty-percent tip and a squeeze, one of which made her squeal with joy. I told her that we'd be needing further services.

She went off shift and I never saw her again.

Her replacement was even better looking, having all of her teeth, and I was starting to repeat the process when my partners came to some sort of an understanding.

"So, Ian. It's all honest?" I asked.

"Well, yes, of course. At least I think so, I mean . . ."

"Hey, are we going to go to jail for it?"

"No. Or at least not until the deceased first owner gets jailed first."

"Well, good enough for a veteran. So we are decided?"

"One last thing." Hasenpfeffer shooed the waitress out. "Security. I know that that's a bad word with some of us, but a certain degree of it is necessary. I am not proposing armed guards and television cameras. At this stage they could do nothing more than attract attention. I am merely suggesting that we keep silent and tell no one, absolutely no one, about our plans, objectives, or intentions. Are you with me?"

"Of course."

"Yeah, sure," I said. "What about the waitresses?"

"How could they know what we're talking about when we don't know ourselves?" Ian asked.

"Good points, gentlemen. The fact is that I have already ascertained that they are both local people with no outside affiliations. In the future we must be more cautious. One last thought: we must agree that everything we learn or accomplish must be kept within the group. Absolutely nothing may be released to outsiders without our unanimous agreement. Are we together on this?"

"Certainly, Jim."

"Well, yeah, okay. Remember that *I'm* the only one here with a top-secret clearance. But I've got a question or two of my own. Jim, you've been pulling your little strings on us all evening long, but you haven't told us what you're thinking."

"I have led the discussion in examining certain obvious questions, but I have not concealed anything."

"The hell you say. You bought and sold a major piece of property with our money without even asking us about it first, or telling us about it later, second. Now, I've said how this thing could be a weapon and Ian's talked about using it as a tool. What do *you* think we have here?"

"I am not sure that my opinions are relevant. You two are the technical ones."

"Not a chance. Spill it," I said. Ian nodded his agreement.

"This is premature, but very well. *If* you technical gentlemen can perfect it, I expect that we shall eventually have a time machine."

CHAPTER SEVEN
Girlfriends and Grandfathers

The place outside of Ann Arbor was everything that Hasenpfeffer said it would be. Everything was well built, clean
and new. The house was a big brick ranch-style thing, and
while I would have picked some other color than pink for
the bricks, even that sort of grew on you.

There was a big living room that we dubbed a "parlor" and filled with Ian's old three-quarter-sized furniture,
agreeing among ourselves that we wouldn't use it except
for entertaining people we didn't like. I mean, it had a
white carpet and white walls. Ian was a painfully neat
person, but the best thing you could say about Hasenpfeffer
and me was that he was a filthy slob, and that I was a
filthier one. Obviously, the room wouldn't stay white if
we were allowed to use it. Anyway, you've got to have
someplace to use if the girl's folks want to come over,
right?

There was a big family room with a fireplace and enough
bookshelves to hold all of Hasenpfeffer's books and Ian's
as well. Ian put his little leather easy chair in there, and
Hasenpfeffer found out that there *were* companies that made
stuff big enough to fit me, for a price. I got this glorious
real leather recliner that actually fit my back while

Hasenpfeffer chose a leather-and-chrome Eames swivel chair and hassock for himself.

Of course, Danish Modern, chrome-and-leather, and Lazy Boy don't match, but then we didn't match, either.

The kitchen was full of gadgets that I wasn't used to, like a microwave oven, a garbage disposal and a dishwasher, but modern man is pretty adaptable, and it's remarkable how quickly these fabulous luxuries became absolute necessities.

I got a new set of bedroom furniture, and that was wonderful. For the first time since I started to grow hair below my waist, I had a bed long enough to fit me! I got the master bedroom, too, since I needed it to get my new bed and an oversized desk into it. It had its own bathroom, but then so did the other two bedrooms.

The door into my room was of only normal size, so I could still bump my head on it. I was half tempted to cut the doorframe out on top so I could walk through standing straight up, but I decided against it. The guys had been pretty reasonable about everything else, and I thought it wise not to push them too far.

The place had a three-car garage, and that was filled up pretty quickly. We kept Ian's Corvette as group property, since he owed more on it than it was worth, and I think Hasenpfeffer liked it even more than Ian did.

Only, while the 'vette was a pretty little plastic toy, the damn thing was too small for me to get into. I threw a temper tantrum about it, so we bought a secondhand Chrysler as group property so I had something to drive in the winter, too. The bikes took up the third stall, and we soon had to buy an old pickup truck to run errands for the factory. The truck was never granted garage privileges.

There was a full basement with a ten-foot ceiling, and I took that over for my electronics lab. It was air-conditioned and the factory wasn't. Electronic equipment works better at a constant temperature, and so do I. I'm one of those people who think that sixty-five is a wonderful temperature, provided that I can sit naked in front of a fan.

All told, the move was a big step up for all of us, and for me more than the others.

We settled into our new quarters in a few weeks, although

a month went by before all of my oversized furniture arrived. I had to camp in my bedroom until then.

While the shop already had most of what Ian thought he would need, I had to put together an electronics lab from scratch. It took two months before I got all the big stuff in. I was another five weeks building the first breadboard circuit, mostly awaiting parts. Having *almost* everything doesn't make it. Not in electronics.

Cheop's Law: Everything costs more and takes longer.

But the very first time we tried the thing out—from a quarter mile away—it worked perfectly, dutifully putting a thirty-yard hole in our back forty.

This meant that we could have gotten into the mining and tunneling business almost immediately, but after a nine-hour-long meeting, we decided to hold off on that until we could develop the whole concept a bit further. We still didn't know the basic principles that the gadget worked on, and without knowing those, we'd be hard pressed to get an all-inclusive patent.

If we started using or selling the circuit, well, I'd copied the thing easily enough, and so could any other competent tech. Given a hint on what we were doing, hundreds of outfits would soon be out there competing with us.

Competition might be a good thing for the economy as a whole, but it is a bad thing for an underfinanced little company like ours was.

For the rest of that first year, we made solid, steady progress. The field did not have to be generated from a point source. We found out how to set up steady-state fields, where a given volume was irradiated evenly and could be transported through time without being sliced into sushi.

We found out how to shield the field, so we could send what we wanted to send without cratering the landscape.

We learned how to operate it with the circuitry inside the field, so it acted sort of like a car, taking its motive power with it. We also figured out how to work it with the circuitry outside the field. We got to calling this the "cannon" technique.

All this time, we were only putting things into the future. From a practical point of view, we could have accomplished much the same thing by locking whatever it was in a box, and taking it out of the box later. The real prize would be to be able to send things into the past.

From everything we had been able to learn, it looked as though if you simply reversed the phase in one section of the circuit, it should reverse the circuit's total temporal effect.

A circuit thusly configured should have been able to send things back in time, but when I tried it, the circuit overloaded, every time, and burned to a blackened pile of ashes and melted metal. We had no idea what the problem was. Coupled with it was the impossibility of just how a tiny, nine-volt transistor battery could possibly put out enough power to so thoroughly fry a good-sized epoxy-glass circuit board. Ian calculated that over its entire lifetime, such a battery couldn't put out a thousandth of the power we saw repeatedly generated.

"So, gentlemen, it appears that in addition to everything else, you have discovered a new source of industrial power!" Hasenpfeffer said one morning at breakfast.

"A fucking expensive source of power, if you ask me," Ian said. "When you spend thirty dollars worth of circuitry to generate thirty cents worth of power, you aren't making a profit."

Nobody had a good way of answering that, and in the momentary silence, Hasenpfeffer's lady of the night walked in, wearing one of his old housecoats. She was a gorgeous, slender young thing, with long, straight blond hair, like most of the others. Ian offered to make her breakfast, and since Hasenpfeffer was here, she nodded acceptance. After that, it was as though Ian and I didn't exist, as far as she was concerned. After a bit, we picked up our coffee cups and drifted off, leaving the two lovers, or at least sex partners, alone.

We were used to it. The same sort of thing had been happening for seven years, since we all were freshmen in college. But being used to something doesn't mean that it no longer hurts. I couldn't help but look on Hasenpfeffer's success with the ladies with mixed emotions, the most prominent of which was envy.

We settled into the family room, out of earshot of Hasenpfeffer's latest.

"Over the years, he's got to have had two hundred of them over," Ian said.

"Counting college, yeah, it has to have been at least that."

"Well, you'd think that at least one of them would want to have something to do with at least one of us."

"It seems statistically likely, only it just hasn't happened. The books all say that women want permanence in a relationship, yet all of Hasenpfeffer's chicks have to know that he'll drop them in a week or three, just like he dropped all of the others. If either of us latched onto a girl as fine as any of his, we'd want to keep her forever. They've got to know that, too. But will one of them even talk to us for ten minutes? No!"

"Tom, I don't think that we'll ever understand women. It's like they're a strange, alien species."

"You could be right. You know, the biologists, or maybe the biochemists, figure the separation of two species by computing the time since the two groups had a common ancestor. If the chimpanzee's branch separated from the human branch five million years ago, then that's the measure of separation between the two species. Now then, biologically, sex was discovered back in the days when single-celled critters were the most advanced things around. Even bacteria occasionally get together and exchange genetic information. So male was separated from female at least a billion years ago. By the rules the biologists use, you and I are two hundred times more closely related to the chimps that we are to women. That makes them a very alien species, indeed."

"That argument is so ridiculous that it's probably true. Shall we accuse Hasenpfeffer of sodomy? What I want to know is why I can't get laid."

I said, "Look, don't ask me about it. All I know is that whatever the typical woman wants, it ain't me. Try asking Hasenpfeffer, or better still, one of his many chicks."

"Dammit, I've done that very thing. Jim can't explain a thing, except to say it might have something to do with pheromones. The girls always say that there's a good woman out there for me somewhere, and then they take off at a dead run. I'm totally lost."

"I was never found in the first place."

After a silence, the conversation dropped back to an old, unresolved issue. The paradoxes of time travel.

"So what are you going to do when I kill your grandfather?" I asked.

"Well, I can't kill one of yours in retaliation, since nobody knows who they were. Anyway, why would you want to kill one of my grandfathers? By all accounts, they were both fine, decent gentlemen."

"You know what I mean. If we can really get it together, and get our time machine built, and go into the past, what happens if we change something? It wouldn't have to be a big change, you know. The tiniest change in the wrong place could make everything different. How many alternate-history science fiction stories have we read between the three of us? Dozens?"

"I'd guess it to be more like hundreds, Tom, and fully a third of them seemed pretty plausible. If you really want to know what I think, it's that we shouldn't fuck with it."

"You mean that we should build the thing and then not use it? That's crazy! If we aren't going to use it, why bother to build it in the first place?"

"No, that's not what I mean, stupid. I just mean that we should at least try not to change anything. Even an atheist like you should know that none of us is God. We shouldn't try to act as if we are Him!"

"I'll second that one," Hasenpfeffer said as he came in from the kitchen. "Be it moved that we should not play God."

"Third, and be it so moved," I said. "At least at first, we've got to be super cautious, until we get a better handle on this thing, anyway."

Before long we'd agreed that it would take a unanimous vote to change the rule. Nothing new, there, of course. All of our agreements were unanimous, the thought being that if one of us couldn't go along with the others, we just hadn't talked it over long enough, and anyway, none of us had any way of forcing anybody to do anything.

Future planning is something that every company ought to do now and then, even though we were still a long way from having our time machine.

CHAPTER EIGHT
Cosmology

We still really didn't understand what we were doing, but then we humans never understand anything absolutely. I mean, I've been working competently with electronics all my adult life, but I've never seen an electron. Thinking about it, I'm not at all sure that I've been dealing with some sort of tiny particle. I'm even less sure that I've been playing with a zillion tiny negative indentations in the space-time continua. But I know how to build a circuit, how to make it do what I originally had in mind, and how to fix it when it breaks.

And that is all that I need to know.

So we were starting to get a feel for how to use this stuff, and of what could be done with it. That is to say, we had a bit of practical experience, but we didn't have a codified theory yet. We didn't have an algebraic formula that worked every time.

Ian was fond of pointing out that the builders of the medieval cathedrals didn't know anything formal about the strength of materials, let alone stress analysis, but they built some vast, beautiful buildings, and most of them didn't fall down.

He loved to point out that the first steam engines were

built by men who had never heard of the laws of thermodynamics. Nonetheless, their steam ships made it across the
Atlantic on schedule, and their railroad trains ran on time.

And I had to agree that DeForest and Armstrong really
didn't know what they were doing, but they got the job done.
The world now enjoys radio, television, and the rest.

It was the same thing with our explorations of this new
technology. Some of the time, things worked out pretty much
as we'd planned, and when it didn't, we often were able
to figure out why. Jim and I decided that this was fairly
good. We worked well together, and made a good team.

Only, we had this problem with Hasenpfeffer.

You see, Ian is a first-rate mechanical engineer and a good
machinist, besides. I can usually handle anything electrical
or electronic. Further, we each knew enough about the other's
field to lend the other a hand when circumstances made
that a good idea.

But Hasenpfeffer got his doctorate in Behavioral Psychology, and I guess that's what caused most of the pain.

The man was an absolute genius when it came to working
out a complicated business deal, or talking a beautiful
woman into his bed, or solving any other sort of person-
to-person problem. This wasn't something he learned in
college. It was some sort of a talent, or an innate gift.

He could do it on day one of his freshman year, when
I saw him take a future homecoming queen to bed, cold
sober, on the first day he met her. I swear that they hadn't
talked for more than four minutes before they were grinning ear to ear at each other and walking hand in hand
to his bedroom.

Yet he was an absolute idiot when it came to anything
technical. This, too, had to be innate. Nobody could possibly *learn* to be that incompetent.

To make it worse, he was always so pitifully eager to help.
He wanted to be "in" on things, and he'd follow you around
like a puppy dog, wagging his tail and trying to understand
it all. And like a puppy, he'd always make a mess of things.

It wasn't that Hasenpfeffer was stupid, or that he was
malicious, or even careless. It was just that he had the innate
ability and compulsion to stick his finger into whatever was

most likely to break. And he was god-awful clumsy besides.

Like the time I asked him to clean off some printed circuit boards with MEK—I'd given up trying to use him as an assembler.

Hasenpfeffer eagerly took the boards out of my lab and into a small enclosed bathroom. When he was about two-thirds done, I guess he felt a little light-headed, because he sat down on the toilet seat and tried to light a cigarette.

The Fire Marshall wasn't the least bit reasonable, the boards were a complete loss, and the doctor bills were absurd.

So Hasenpfeffer mostly wandered around feeling useless. He was *trying* to help. He kept the place clean and did the dishes. He even did the laundry so Ian and I could keep at it fifteen hours a day. And he took care of the books. Not that there was much to that. No income. All out-go.

Yet there was nothing grim about us or what we were doing. Looking back, yeah, we had a good time. There was a constant round of bull sessions, arguments and practical jokes. Mostly, we disagreed on practically everything, often for no other reason than the rollicking fun of a good argument.

I remember one night when Hasenpfeffer was carrying on about the latest cosmological theory that some academician—Hawker, I think he said his name was—had been writing about. Something about how the universe started as something the size of a dime, sixteen billion years ago, had expanded up to the size of the solar system in a few seconds, and had been expanding ever since.

I used our customary method of stating that I wished to engage in a debate on the current subject at hand. I stood, raised my fist, and shouted at the top of my voice, "Bullshit!"

Following protocol, he stared at me, pretending to be aghast, as if he was shocked at my disagreement.

"It's all bullshit. First off, the solar system is many light-hours across. You have the leading edge of your universe traveling way faster than the speed of light. Explain that one away!"

"You know, Tom, I met a noted physicist from the university at a party, and I asked him that very question. He told me that it wasn't a matter of going faster than light so much as it was that space was being created behind the leading edge." He noted my dubious look, and continued, "I confess that I didn't fully understand his statement myself, but the man's reputation is that he is one of the finest theoretical . . ."

But I was already rolling up my pant cuffs, signifying that I wished them to remain unsoiled, even though the bullshit being spread around had already ruined my shoes and socks.

"Right," I said. "Then there's this whole 'expanding universe' nonsense. Now, the only proof we have that the whole universe is expanding is the shift in the spectrums of certain apparently small, and therefore supposedly far away, galaxies, into somewhat lower frequencies."

"Of course. The famous Red Shift."

" 'Famous' just means that all the fools have had time to hear about it. Let's look at this red shift. Photons lower their frequency when their energy level is lowered. A blue photon is stronger than a red photon. An X-ray photon is vastly more powerful than a microwave photon. It is true that if an object is traveling away from you, the photons it emits will be relatively less energetic than a photon emitted by a stationary object. In exactly the same way, a rock thrown at you by someone in a departing car will hurt less than one thrown from a stationary one. But is that the *only* way a photon can lose energy? You don't know? Well, I don't know either! Nobody knows. Nobody knows because nobody has ever observed a photon for anything but a very short time, the longest of which is the time it takes a radar beam to leave the reflector, hit the target, and return. A few milliseconds at the most."

"A few *minutes*," Ian interjected. "They've bounced radar beams off the moon and some of the planets."

"Call it hours for all I care! What are hours compared to sixteen billion years? What I'm trying to say is that we don't have any idea what happens to a photon over long periods of time. Yet these half-baked 'cosmologists' blithely assume that photons are absolutely unaffected even though they have been winging it through space for billions of years. Personally, I can't imagine *anything* remaining unaffected after traveling at light speed for ten billion years! Yet all that would have to happen would be for the tiny photons to get just a little bit tired, lose a little bit of energy, and your expanding universe theory is right out the window!"

"But all the theories prove—" Hasenpfeffer started to say.

"Theories don't prove anything! Theories are things we invent to make the world more comprehensible to our inadequate little brains. Facts prove—or disprove—theories, not the other way around. If we don't have the facts, then theories are nothing more than wild ass guesses! We aren't any closer to the truth than if we just said, 'God did it, so He must want it that way.' "

I could see Ian tightening up when I brought God into the argument, which I did fairly often, for an atheist. My theory was that if He didn't want me to do something, He had the wherewithal to stop me. And if He didn't care, or He wasn't around to care, then who was Ian to object?

Ian, of course, had heard all that years before, and decided that just now he didn't feel like plowing up old turds. So he said, "What troubles me about all this cosmology stuff is the way the cosmologists have of speaking so definitively about what happened ten or twenty billion years ago. I mean, shit, there's no way that you can get a bunch of historians to agree on what exactly happened during the Civil War! And that was an event that had millions of observers, and thousands of people recording their observations. I tell you that cosmology is just a silly game that physicists like to play, probably because they don't have anything else to do."

"That seems like an extreme statement," Hasenpfeffer said.

"Extreme, Hell. Those guys with their super-expensive toys haven't come up with anything useful and new since they came up with atomic power, long before the beginning of World War II."

"But surely, all of the dozens and hundreds of subatomic particles must count for something, even to one of your sadly restricted intellect."

"For the last part of that, *up your ass, Hasenpfeffer*! For the first, I said 'useful.' Nobody has ever found a use for a Mu-Meson, an Electron-Neutrino, or a Left-Handed Boson."

"I met a left-handed bos'n's mate, once," I said, but was ignored.

"Furthermore," Ian continued, "I doubt the very existence of the things. Subatomic particles are things that their inventors have painted with the colors of their own minds, and then glued together with their own shit. Data? They don't have no stinking data! Those overpaid academicians sit around and try to 'interpret' tiny, meaningless squiggles on photographic plates the way ancient Roman soothsayers tried to predict the future by interpreting the bumps on the liver of a sacrificed owl. And in both cases, the stupid politicians lap up every irrational word of it, and reward the rip-off artists with gold from the public coffers! If we had spent on biology what we've wasted on all those cyclotrons and accelerators and what not, the world would be a lot better off!"

Hasenpfeffer whispered aside to me, "Oh, my. I do believe the poor boy is going to start in on Taxes again. Try and head him off, won't you?"

I turned to Jim and said quietly, "You feel that way because you have never had to pay any, or found a way around it if you did. *You* fork out a major chunk of *your* income every week and see what you think about taxes, and what the bozos spend it all on."

Ian had indeed started in on his often-told Speech On Taxes before noticing that he had lost his audience. Eventually, his sermon wound itself down.

"Be that as it may," Hasenpfeffer said in a normal voice, "I wonder if the reason that Ian is such a regular churchgoer is that his is one of those sects where they let lay people get up and speak. I mean, with a less critical audience, he could go on ranting for hours about anything that comes into his curious little mind."

Ian glowered at him, but didn't say anything, so I suppose that much of what Hasenpfeffer said about Ian's church was true. I was curious, but not quite curious enough to take Ian up on one of his frequent offers to take me to church.

CHAPTER NINE
Autum Leaves and Temporal Swords

About the only non-time-travel thing the three of us did agree on was that the smell of burning autumn leaves was the finest of perfumes, gaseous ambrosia and vastly superior to all commercial olfactory products. Also, that any governmental official who called it pollution was obviously a Fascist Left-Wing Atheist. (As named by Jim, me, and Ian, respectively.)

One day, just as Hasenpfeffer completed raking all the leaves from our huge front lawn into a humongous pile on the gravel drive in front of the shop, Ian came screeching up in the Corvette. He had this bright idea burning a hole in his mind, and was so eager to try it out that he simply didn't notice the six-foot-high pile of leaves on the driveway. He just plowed through them, jumped out of the car and hobbled as fast as his damaged foot would take him into the shop.

Hasenpfeffer, less than amused, proceeded to pack the little car solid with leaves, raise the rag top, and then bury the car with the rest of the pile. This procedure left him with a feeling of contentment, accomplishment, and proper vindication.

An hour later, Ian realized that he needed a few parts

from the industrial supply store down the road. He rushed to what he still thought of as "his" car, jumped in and actually fired it up before he realized that he couldn't see out the windshield, or breathe either, for that matter.

The next day, Hasenpfeffer's bedroom was stuffed nearly solid with leaves, leaving Ian looking smug while Jim, with a new lady friend on his arm, screamed.

And the day after that it was Ian's bed and closet that got the full treatment.

I watched this leafy dialogue go on all winter, the same pile of leaves being handed back and forth, and growing smaller and increasingly tattered in the process.

Wisely, I stayed neutral.

Towards spring, they were down to one leaf. You might pull on a roll of toilet paper and out would float this battered tree leaf.

If I happened to find it, I always returned it to its place. After all, they weren't talking to me. I didn't want to get involved, it wasn't my fight, and furthermore, in the service I had seen this sort of thing get dangerously out of hand.

Still, they played it safe enough, this time. Usually, an exchange of practical jokes tends to escalate, each side trying to outdo the other, every round, but in this case they were saved by the self-destructibility of autumn leaves.

The leaf appeared in magazines and books, under the place mats and in the breakfast cereal. Finally, it had been abraded down to a stem and six fragile veins before it was retired by mutual consent.

Meanwhile, the work went on. We learned to calibrate our circuits to amazing accuracies—things sent for weeks reemerged within microseconds of the predicted time.

We learned how to focus the field and project it as tight as a laser beam, which made an incredible knife or sword. This was nothing like a *Star Wars* light saber. It was a lot better. Switched on, it projected a thin needle of nothingness that looked like a tightly stretched black thread. Everything that entered that line was sent forward, an atom at a time, I think, for hundreds and thousands of years, reemerging imperceptibly except as an immeasurably tiny addition to the background radiation.

It was a neat toy, and I spent a few weeks "polishing" it into a tidy, handheld package. For safety reasons, I put in four trigger switches, complete with anti-tiedowns. To turn it on, you had to have a finger on each trigger, and lifting any one of them turned the beam off. Then, you had to release all the buttons before it could be turned back on. This was so that Hasenpfeffer wouldn't try to tape down three of the buttons, and hurt himself, or me either.

The blade length was adjustable from an eighth of an inch out to twelve feet, by means of a sliding potentiometer built into the side, easily reachable with your right thumb. For power, it had solar cells charging Ni-Cad batteries, and everything that had to penetrate the housing—switches and so forth—was guaranteed to be dust tight and water tight, down to thirty meters.

Ian machined up three stainless-steel housings for them, complete with belt clips, and these were hermetically sealed as well.

We christened them "Temporal Swords."

Switched on, it made a crackly hissing sound that was caused by air molecules leaving rapidly for elsewhen. The sword was a glorious thing, the ultimate cutting tool and the deadliest possible short-range weapon.

As a cutting tool, it could cut absolutely anything as quickly and as smoothly as you could feed the stock to the tool. There were no vibrations, and with the right beam width, no chips to clear away. Over the coming months, Ian adapted all of his cutting tools from conventional cutting bits to temporal swords. The lathes didn't look much different, but the Bridgeports looked like they were decapitated with their motors and gearboxes gone. And the saws were reduced down to being little more than holding fixtures! Eventually, Ian replaced all five of his saws with simple clamps to hold the swords accurately, and had Hasenpfeffer sell the surplus machine tools.

At the other end of the spectrum, as a weapon, it was something to make a combat veteran perk up, drool, and pant with lust. With a flick of your wrist, you could cut through *anything* with this puppy! I mean that if a Sherman tank offended you, you could turn it into a pile of small metal chunks in seconds. And the only sounds anybody would hear would be a quiet hiss and the much louder sound of bits of dead tank hitting the ground.

But you couldn't fence with one because you couldn't parry. Two beams interpenetrated without difficulty. I figured that it was just as well, since I think that Hasenpfeffer has a Zorro streak in him, and a temporal sword wasn't a play toy.   ·

I put a lightbulb in the butt, letting it serve as a flashlight as well as a cutting tool. This use was not encouraged because it quickly ran down the batteries.

Ian and I talked about high-output, long-range pulsed models—rifles and pistols—but, probably because none of us hunted, it was a long while before we got around to making any.

Anyway, when the first "production" model was done, I took it outside to run a real-world test, or, in the popular vernacular, to play with it.

It was a beautiful day and Hasenpfeffer was trimming the hedge with a pair of huge, two-handed scissors. He was still doing most of the drudge work around the place because he wasn't of much use elsewhere.

I went to the shaggy end of the hedge, adjusted the blade to about three feet, and held the beam horizontally at shoulder level, where the hedge should be topped. Then I walked steadily towards Hasenpfeffer, neatly trimming the shrubs to height. He saw me, stared at me, and registered pleasant shock.

"Give me that thing!"

"Hey, sure Jim." I laughed. "Only it's as dangerous as sin and not quite as much fun. Look, you hold all four of these triggers down to make it work. Then this slide controls blade length and . . ."

"Got it!" He took it out of my hand, ignorant of the fact that it is *very* bad form to take a tool out of any workingman's hands. It's a fighting offense in the Society of the Competent.

He slashed at the hedge, gouging a hole that would take

years to grow back in. He laughed and ran to some blue Spruce lawn trees that were in need of clipping. He began vigorously trimming them, slicing thin cuts into the lawn that made hash out of the automatic sprinkler system.

I once read the report of an early Spanish explorer who had given a jungle native a sharp steel machete. This Indian had spent much of his life pushing thick greenery aside so that he could walk upright, forcing his way around it when he had to, and bowing under it when nothing else would suffice.

The Indian tried a few swings with the machete and suddenly realized that he now had the power to slash his lifelong tormentor asunder! He ran off laughing, screaming and yelling war cries while butchering the vines and shrubs of the Amazon. A little technology sometimes goes a long way. . . .

Eventually, hours later, the Indian came back to camp with his new blade hanging from his exhausted right arm. He was slick with sweat, and the explorer described his facial expression as of "one who had just enjoyed sexual release."

Hasenpfeffer acted just like that Indian. He trimmed a few more small fir trees, laughing and shouting, working his way to the "back forty." He slashed a big, ornamental boulder in half, screaming like a cowboy, or maybe a Rebel cavalryman. Then he fixed his attention on a big sugar maple which grew at the edge of the lawn.

Ian heard the shouting and came out in time to see the ancient tree fall to a single cut! With great, uncharacteristic agility, Hasenpfeffer leaped at his foe, gleefully chopping it into firewood in seconds.

"Hasenpfeffer, what happened to your ecology thing?" Ian shouted.

It was one of our many continuing arguments. I figured that it was our world and we shouldn't make it dirty, but Ian had this semi-religious idea that we were morally obligated to *use* everything that God had given to us here on earth.

Hasenpfeffer was a flaming, left-wing ecology freak. He loudly defended the "right to life" of leeches, snail darters, puff adders and every other living creature except for mosquitoes, of course, and the cow he was currently eating.

And here he was, butchering this innocent tree.

"We've already got a five-year supply of firewood!" Ian added.

"My God. You're right." Shocked at his own actions, Hasenpfeffer dropped to his knees. Forgetting that all he had to do to turn off the blade was to let go of any one of the four triggers, he stupidly reached for the blade length adjustment with his left hand. His mania over, his clumsiness returned, and that's when Hasenpfeffer pitched in his part.

The thin, black thread of nothingness crossed his palm, and four still-connected fingers hit the dirt before he felt the pain.

I got a tourniquet around his wrist and we drove him to the U of M Hospital, where things were considerably more sophisticated than they are in the Upper Peninsula. Ian had had the brains to pick up the severed fingers, put them on ice, and bring them along. The doctors were able to sew them back on, blood vessels, tendons, and all.

In a few months they worked again, after a fashion, but the nerves never regenerated. Most of his left hand was numb.

The medical bills made a major dent in our cash reserves.

Despite Jim's accident, Ian and I got to wearing our swords all the time, just like we both always carried our calculators clipped to our belts.

Hasenpfeffer wouldn't touch a sword after his accident. He claimed that our carrying them was an atavistic fetish, a response to our primitive blood lusts, and a stupid macho stunt.

Well, he rarely touched a calculator, either.

Admittedly, a sword was rarely useful as a tool. After the first week, I used my Swiss Army jackknife ten times for every time I used my sword. It was just too powerful for most ordinary things—it was too easy to cut the circuit board you were working on in half when you only meant to trim a lead.

Out in the shop, cutting steel and ceramics, Ian used variations of the sword all the time. By then, he had replaced them as the cutting tools on all of his lathes and mills and saws. But I rarely remember seeing him using the one that was clipped to his waist.

A feeling of power? Maybe. I suppose that I could have cut a truck in half if I ever needed to. But that same line of reasoning said that my calculator, my wallet and my keys each gave me, in their own ways, a similar feeling of power. I felt naked with any one of them missing.

All I know is that it *felt good* to have my sword there.

CHAPTER TEN
Lateral Displacement and Practical Jokes

Work continued, but we started hitting technical snags, the worst of which was the lateral displacement problem.

At first, we'd been running most of our tests for short time periods, a few seconds or so, for the sake of convenience, so the problem wasn't immediately noticeable, but when something was transported, it didn't reemerge in exactly the same place as it left. It never moved up or down much, but it shifted sideways in a random direction that averaged six inches per hour, assuming "drunkard's walk" statistics.

We sometimes had a hard time finding a test object when it emerged in the air, and because of this, we got to sending small, Citizens Band radios as test objects. A receiver was wired up to a commercial time clock, so if the walkie-talkie emerged when we weren't there to observe it, we at least knew when it happened.

From there it was a simple matter, if nothing was broken, of using a radio direction finder to locate our vagrant test object. Later, we got to putting them in steel canisters, to protect the radios from the shock of hitting the ground.

What made this lateral displacement problem so serious was that on reemergence our test object suddenly coexisted in the same space as whatever else was there. Emerging in air killed anything alive and degraded electronic circuits something fierce. Emerging within a solid or liquid usually caused an explosion.

If we could tell exactly *where* something would emerge, it would be easy, or at least possible, to arrange to have a hard vacuum waiting there. But when a thing could drift a mile in a year . . .

Well, things started getting grim. We spent more than a year trying to get a handle on the problem, making hundreds of tests and wrecking a circuit and a radio on most of them. We had test objects reemerging in the damndest places, blasting twenty trees, destroying a drill press in the shop, and blowing out Hasenpfeffer's bedroom wall, just when he was getting into his latest chick.

But eventually something useful emerged. After tediously charting the exact times and places of every departure and arrival, Ian discovered that, while the actual displacement seemed to be random, nonetheless it *tracked* according to the sidereal day. If you sent something at noon for (say) exactly fifteen hours into the future, leaving point A and reemerging at point B, then you could do the same thing tomorrow at 11:56 and it would go from the same point A to the same point B.

This gave us a handle on the lateral-displacement problem.

The three of us celebrated by going out to a good restaurant, a seafood place since it was my turn to pick, and I had developed a taste for critters with hard skins during my years in Massachusetts. Hasenpfeffer ordered us a dozen raw oysters for an appetizer, and he and I dug into them.

Ian held back. He had been raised in a conservative, WASP household which apparently subsisted on boiled chicken, boiled potatoes, and boiled beef on Sundays. No seafoods, no foreign foods, and no spices at all.

"Come on, Ian. At least *try* one! They're delicious!" Hasenpfeffer said.

Ian picked one up and looked at it dubiously.

"It looks like a glob of grey snot," he said.

"Yeah, it looks funny, but it tastes strange, too," I said. "Sort of salty and slippery, since you swallow them whole.

But they really are delicious, even though I can't say exactly why."

Hasenpfeffer, as always, was more persuasive than I was. Eventually Ian closed his eyes and slurped the little bivalve down. He had a strange expression on his face, as though he knew that, somehow, another joke was being played on him.

That expression must have been where Hasenpfeffer got his clue for the stunt he pulled.

"But, but, you DIDN'T KILL IT!" he yelled. "You were supposed to kill it with your fork first, just before you ate it! It's still alive, man! My God, it'll eat your guts out! You've got to kill the damned thing before it perforates your intestines and kills you! Here, quick, drink this!"

And with that, Hasenpfeffer handed our terrified friend a large bottle of Cajun Hot Sauce, something that Ian had never seen before, let alone tasted. And before I could stop him, the little fellow upended the bottle and drank it all down at one gulp.

Ian had never even eaten a taco, so I'll let you imagine the results of Hasenpfeffer's sadistic stunt. It wrecked the evening, and Ian couldn't talk properly for days. I gave Hasenpfeffer a military-style chewing out, once we got home, and he was pretty contrite about the whole thing. Ian just shook his head and walked out.

I saw Ian the next day, heading out to the woods behind our place. He had a four-foot-long one-by-six board under his arm, and was further equipped with a roll of toilet paper, one of those cardboard tubes you get when the toilet paper is used up, a plastic garbage bag, and a pair of heavy rubber gloves.

"Not meaning to invade your privacy, you understand, but just what in the *hell* are you up to?" I asked.

He looked at me and smiled. He gestured to his throat, as if to say he couldn't speak, and continued on his way, leaving me standing there.

A week later, he was sitting at the kitchen table with the same rubber gloves on. Ian had always been an incredibly neat person, and the table was now covered with neatly aligned newspapers. He was carefully unrolling an oversized roll of toilet paper, taking out hundreds of now-dried poison ivy leaves, and dropping them carefully into a lined trash container. He then rerolled the paper on another cardboard tube, and was doing so neat a job of it that it looked like a brand-new roll, even though it had soaked up a deadly oil from the green and red leaves.

I shuddered to think about what this meant, but again I had brains enough not to get involved.

The next day, Hasenpfeffer developed a terrible rash on his ass, and his current lady friend went home carrying her underpants in her hand, never to be seen again. She was angry, and muttering something about V.D.

Venereal diseases were nearly nonexistent in the early seventies, having been almost wiped out accidentally by doctors who were handing out antibiotics for everything from head colds to sprained ankles. Of course, at the time, nobody knew that, and government ads still harped about how deadly V.D. was.

I found Jim lying naked on his stomach in bed, with his legs spread. I told him that it didn't look like any sort of V.D. that I'd ever seen, and suggested that a trip to a dermatologist might be appropriate.

The doctor insisted that it was poison ivy, even though Hasenpfeffer insisted that such a thing was impossible. One shot cleared the problem up, though, and you can't argue with success.

Except, of course, that the next day, having perforce used his toilet and toilet paper again, he had a relapse. I drove him back to the same doctor, who gave him another shot, and warned him to launder *everything* he owned, and especially anything his butt might have touched.

For eight days, each morning I drove Hasenpfeffer to the doctor, who was becoming increasingly agitated. I can't begin to describe Hasenpfeffer's mood, except to say that it involved a lot of raw hate, with a suicidal backdrop.

It was time to talk to Ian.

"And you are positive that he has now suffered more than I did?" Ian said.

"Absolutely. That poor boy now knows suffering like the way he knows how to talk a chick into bed."

"Well, perhaps I could remove the toilet paper from his john in a day or two."

"Do it now. Please."

"But . . ."

"Now, or I'll tell Hasenpfeffer the cause of his troubles."

"So now it's threats, is it?"

"Not really, but look. I've let you have fair vengeance for what he did to you. But enough is enough! End this thing, before he figures out that all of his pain, and his last girlfriend's pain, has been deliberately caused by you!"

"I did not *deliberately* hurt her. That was an accident."

"It was rank carelessness on your part, and as an engineer, you should have planned more carefully. Anyway, when Hasenpfeffer finds out that you pulled this on him, he will retaliate, and whatever his response is, it is sure to be much worse that an ass full of poison ivy. And you know full well that after he does that, you'll do something even worse to him. In time, this thing is likely to escalate until one of you is dead."

"You think it would actually go that far?"

"Yeah. I do."

"Well, okay. You talked me into it. I'll do it now while he's still gone. The roll's nearly empty, anyway."

So, thanks to me, they didn't kill each other, the three-way partnership didn't self-destruct, and time travel would still have a chance to be invented.

I'd spent a lot of time mulling over the problem of going backward in time. Since I couldn't handle more than three dimensions in my head, I started by imagining two of the ordinary ones out of existence. This left me with a one-dimensional string, or sometimes it was a line on a piece of paper. Then, I could imagine the fourth dimension, time, as being like an infinite number of strings, lying one beside another. Well, I can't really think in infinities, either, but call it a large number of strings.

Each second that goes by, a zillion or so new strings are laid down. Now, the strings that will go onward into the future don't exist yet, so it isn't hard to take the NOW string and push part of it in that direction. It lands ahead of everything else, and waits there (can I really say that?) until the rest of the world catches up with it.

At that time, the *now* and the transported thing may or may not interact, depending on whether or not there was any matter at that time and place in the *now*.

On the other hand, all of the strings that lie behind the *now* string still exist. You can't go straight backward because the space behind you is all filled up. Maybe that could explain all the extra energy we kicked up when I threw the circuit into reverse. It was like we had an infinite line of railroad cars rolling free behind us, and I was jamming on the brake. Of course things heated up!

It took me two hours to explain my admittedly fuzzy thoughts to Ian, who was less than violently enthusiastic about the concept.

"It's an interesting analogy, Tom, but that's all it is. An analogy. Analogies are slippery things, and not to be confused with reality. And even if it is a good analogy, which we have no way of knowing, where does it get us? If you are right, then we never will be able to go to the past, and I, for one, will be profoundly disappointed. I don't know if I've ever mentioned this, but the big reason why I want access to the past isn't in order to know which stock to buy, or what horse to bet on. I want to know exactly what happened, all through human history. And you're telling me that I can't do it!"

"Not quite, my friend! You can't go back there only if A) my analogy is correct, and B) we live in a four-dimensional universe. That is to say, the two that I threw away, the one represented by the length of the line, and the one we like to call time."

"So? Isn't that obviously the case?"

"I don't know. Is it? All I'm thinking is that if all we've got are four dimensions, then we can't have backward time travel. But imagine if there was one more dimension. Put it at right angles to the time dimension, and hope it doesn't have any matter in it. If both those things turned out to be true, we should be able to pick something in the *now* lineup off the paper, move it backward however far we want, and then come back onto the paper in the past."

"Interesting. So we have to start by imagining the world was made the way it would have to be for our project to succeed, and then seeing if we do succeed to know whether it's built that way or not."

"Close, although if we don't succeed, it proves nothing. After all, our failure just could be because we're stupid. But yes, we either have to assume that success is possible in this universe, or give up."

"Put that way, it's not so farfetched, Tom. So what precisely do you think we should do next? Just how do we handle this possibly imaginary but absolutely necessary fifth dimension?"

"I think that maybe the place to start is with varying the phase angles in that part of the circuit that seemed to be trying to take us back. I mean, if a 180-degree shift took us backward, what would all the other possibilities do?"

A month later, we had an instrument canister leave and never come back anywhere or anywhen that we were aware of. Since it was only powered to be gone for a few minutes at most, we guessed that this meant that it went off sideways, and got lost there. It seemed only fair to call that a victory.

Next, we would have to arrange for a canister to swing out sideways in the fifth dimension, stop swinging, go back in time, and then swing in sideways exactly as far as we had swung out. It seemed simple enough at the time, but remember that this was happening in the early seventies, before large-scale integration was more than a gleam in an engineer's eye. Before we were done, we needed two hundred pounds of computer to do the navigating, and each test had a twenty percent chance of destroying everything electronic on reemergence.

Things started getting very expensive.

CHAPTER ELEVEN
Robbing a Bank

We were making progress, but we were also going broke, and every time we plotted both curves on graph paper, it always showed going broke winning the race.

A quarter of a million dollars had seemed like a fabulous sum when we started, but research is expensive. While we were living as frugally as possible, there were bills that just had to be paid. The power bill, for example, and food.

Oh, we already had a number of useful and probably highly profitable products, but we knew that time travel was the biggie. If we sold the bomb or the sword, even if we manufactured them ourselves, somebody else would inevitably figure out what we were doing. We toyed with the idea of setting ourselves up as a subcontracting job shop, specializing in working with hard-to-cut materials, but the same problem was there. Subcontracting from other engineering companies, we'd get a lot of bright people curious about how we were doing what we were doing, and there would go security. Then where would we be? The thought of two or more teams out killing each other's grandfathers was scary.

I figured the safest thing to do was to rob a bank.

"I don't know what Hasenpfeffer will think about robbing

a bank," Ian said over a cup of tea in my lab. "His morality wouldn't have pleased Martin Luther, but he does seem to have a certain sort of ethics."

"Hell, he'll probably enjoy it. At least it'll give him something to do."

"Tom, it's so damned frustrating!" Ian said. "We've had working time travel for almost a year and it's totally useless."

"Hey, not completely useless. It's erratic, and we can't send animate objects yet, but we can rob a bank with it," I said.

"I just wish we knew more about the theory. There has got to be some way of easing back into the continuum, instead of this bang-bang thing we've been doing."

"Well, you've got your choice. I can give you a uniform field, and you can emerge all at once in the same volume of space that the air insists on occupying, at which point you can die painfully of the bends. Or, I can give you a non-uniform field, and you can come back a little bit at a time, and die painlessly as each little bit falls on the floor. Assuming that you don't come back *in* the floor, that is. I think that as far as the fifth dimension is concerned, our three normal ones don't seem to have any thickness at all. You can't ease a hole into something that is infinitely thin. You either punch the hole in it, or you don't."

"Maybe if we could somehow tilt the canister in either the fourth or fifth dimensions. Then we could come in at a sort of an angle, and gently push the existing matter out of the way."

"We can do roll, pitch, and yaw things in the normal three. We've seen no indication that they're possible in the other ones. Anyway, doing all three supposes at least six dimensions out there, and that gets to be more than my little brain can handle. Now, about robbing a bank . . ."

"It's definite now that the radiation is caused by random nuclear fusions on reemergence. When two objects are suddenly in the same place at the same time, a small percentage of the atomic nuclei are close enough to fuse, generating some strange isotopes. And we know the field correlates somehow with the local gravitational gradient. But why the random lateral displacement on reemergence? We know that it tracks on the sidereal day and year, but we still haven't the foggiest notion of *why* it does it!" Ian wasn't biting.

"Hell, continental drift, for all I know. Or magma flows. Or solar flares. Or phases of the moon. Look, I'm to the point where I'm starting to understand why something is *when* it is. I've got no idea why it's *where* it is. They buried what was left of the only person who could give us some straight answers. Dammit, we're running out of money! In three months we'll be out of credit. We've got to rob a bank!"

"We could have a breakthrough at any time, Tom. You're talking about grand larceny!"

"Hey, we've been looking for that breakthrough for eleven months. And we can rig the robbery to take place a year after we get the money. We can even deposit it in the same bank we're going to rob. We'd never get caught."

"But theft, Tom?"

"So, banks are insured. Nobody will get hurt."

"Nobody? Look at all the damage we've caused around the property here. Nobody's been hurt, because we're out in the country. You're talking about doing it in downtown Ann Arbor! We'd kill someone for sure."

"We can have the whole thing happen at three in the morning, when no one's around," I said. "Look. We rent the garage across from the bank. We build a time cabinet large enough to hold a big truck. We send the truck back maybe three hundred years, before this town was built, before there was any significant number of people around. The truck drives forward exactly eighty feet. Inside the truck we have another time cabinet. It goes forward three hundred and one years—right to the sidereal second—and emerges in the same space as the bank vault, so the money is inside the time field. It comes back with the contents of the vault to the truck. The truck backs up to where the garage will be and the whole thing comes back to now. We have a year to loot the vault before the robbery takes place! I can have the controls ready in a week, and it shouldn't take you much longer to make the cabinets."

"You've been thinking about this for some time, haven't you?"

"Yeah."

"Well, you've been thinking stupid, the whole while! First off, aside from the moral questions, you're talking about cabinets a hundred times larger than anything we've ever built. Scaling up isn't always as easy as it sounds. We don't know what problems we'll run into. Two. If your truck gets hung up driving that eighty feet across who knows what, we've got a first-class anachronism on our hands. And three, worst of all, you're expecting the inner time cabinet to emerge four times in air, or something worse. It'll be as radioactive as sin and shot through with rust. There's not a chance in hell of it being operational for that trip back."

"You weren't listening. Any one time circuit only has to operate twice. The money itself will only be transferred twice," I said, "so it won't be too bad. Paper outgasses easily. And to heck with the time cabinet. We can build another one."

"And the truck?"

"We rent it."

"Well, maybe," Ian said, "but it's going to be more work and money than you're counting on. And we've got to get Hasenpfeffer in on it."

Hasenpfeffer walked into the lab on cue, wearing the gaudy, bell-bottom trousers that were currently fashionable, but looking glumly at the floor.

I turned off my power supplies, hid the breadboard I'd been working on, and put the dust cover over my Textronics scope. It was just conditioned reflexes on my part. He hadn't actually gotten close enough to break anything, which was probably conditioned reflexes on his part.

As I finished, Hasenpfeffer said, "There is something that I have to talk over with you gentlemen."

"Shoot." I'd never seen him this far down.

"I have been trying," he said. "For well over two years I have been trying to make a meaningful contribution to our endeavor. I have done whatever I could, even the most menial of tasks. But this just is not sensible. The only rational thing is for me to get a job elsewhere, and to hire someone to do the trivia around here. After all, washing your underwear is not the best use I can make of my doctorate."

"Cheer up, Jim. We're all doing a lot of dirty work. The twelve hours I have just spent at a well-named boring mill didn't have much to do with thermodynamics," Ian said.

"True, but we can't afford a machinist, and we *could* afford a housekeeper. I can make a better contribution with a paycheck."

"Look, there's something we're going to be doing over the next few weeks where we'll need your help. After that we can talk this over."

"What do you have in mind, Tom?" Hasenpfeffer perked up.

"Well, we're going to rob this bank."

"What!"

"Look, we're running out of money," I said. "See, we get this truck, and we build a big time cabinet in the garage across from the bank and . . ."

"Shit!" Hasenpfeffer looked at me disgustedly. "We aren't *that* hard up." He went over to a small test canister sitting on my workbench. "But if we really need large amounts of capital, there are more rational ways of obtaining it."

He opened the canister and took out a copy of next week's *Wall Street Journal*.

CHAPTER TWELVE
Rich Again

We didn't see Hasenpfeffer for three months. He rented an office in town and as best as we could tell, he was sleeping in it. At any rate, he sent over a middle-aged and overweight housekeeper who moved into his old room.

She complained a lot about dirty socks in the family room and cigarette butts in the coffee cups, but she stayed clear of the lab and the shop. She was annoying, but Ian and I found ourselves working longer hours than ever.

Truth was, we missed Hasenpfeffer. He phoned us maybe once a week and told us to just send all the bills of any kind over to him, to spend whatever we had to, but to get the job done. A courier, always an attractive young woman, but always a different one, arrived every Monday afternoon to pick up the bills. From the first, she dropped off a paycheck for the housekeeper and two more for Ian and me. Whatever Hasenpfeffer was doing, it must have been profitable, because Ian and I were now each drawing more than Ian had made working for General Motors.

We started eating better and dressing better as well. Clothes for somebody my size almost always have to be hand tailored, which is clothing store talk for expensive. Ian had trouble buying clothes, too, unless he wanted to go to the children's department.

Men's clothing styles went through a major evolution in the early seventies, and now the two of us could look a little more "with it." Ian was especially happy that a man could now wear high heels and platform boots in public without being considered a queer, and he still wore his heel lifters inside them. I stuck with low heels, of course, but with boots, nobody much noticed.

Women's clothing was changing, too. Skirts had been creeping happily upward for a decade, and had now gotten about as short as they could get without becoming a wide belt. See-through blouses were getting popular, and were often worn without a bra, although they usually had two strategically located pockets in front. The scenery was thus better than ever, even if the two of us never got any of it to take home.

Strange to say, we also missed the parade of Hasenpfeffer's ladies. For years, Ian and I had placed bets about the hair color and probable measurements of his next one, and just when this slender young thing would come along, but with Jim gone, his ladies were gone, too.

So we technical types had little left to do but work and spend money. And spend we did, I don't know how much. We farmed out a lot of the work but we always did the final assembly and programing ourselves.

And the work progressed. Money has a lot to do with the creative process. When you're broke, you spend all of your energy trying to come up with inexpensive solutions to your problems. Since we were flush again, Ian and I fell into an attitude of "Hell, it's only twenty thousand! Let's try it!"

One of the expensive things that worked was our discovery that you could make a circuit reemerge below ground by starting off below ground. And if you triggered the circuit again within three nanoseconds after reemergence, before it had time to explode, it would usually still work.

This meant that, working from a pressure chamber in the basement, we could transmit back a second, smaller sacrificial pressure chamber, which contained its own temporal circuitry. Immediately on reemergence, it sent itself and its contents way out sideways, scattering it harmlessly out over the fifth dimension. At least we hoped it was harmless. At any rate, we never saw anything of any of them again.

Ten nanoseconds later, a second very sturdy pressure chamber arrived, which stopped the walls of the hole from collapsing. Also, the pressure chamber had a second time circuit. This was used in "cannon" mode, to send any air that managed to leak into the chamber out to oblivion just before the next, third, canister was due to arrive, insuring that it emerged into an absolutely hard vacuum.

The net result was a precisely located hard vacuum, the position of which tracked with the chamber in the basement. Exactly where it was physically was a moot point, but a sidereal day later we could transmit to that time or receive from it. Our first stopover station in the past went to exactly four years before.

Four years was an inconveniently long time from an experimental point of view, but any shorter and there was the statical danger of having the canister reemerge too close to the experimenter, namely your humble narrator, snuffing him mightily.

What we had dreamed about for years was a time machine much like an automobile, where you could get in and go to whenever you wanted. What we had succeeded in building had more in common with a railroad, with discrete stations at least four years apart along its "track."

To get any closer to a given point in time, you either had to go back to the nearest time before your target date, and then wait around until the time you wanted happened, or you had to build other lines with spacings of longer than four years, and then change lines several times to get closer to when you wanted to be.

This was less than ideal, but you had to admit that traveling by railroad was superior to having absolutely no transportation at all.

We got to the point where we sent a mouse back to 1967, let it stay there a day, and then brought it back healthy and a day or so older. I say "or so" because instruments indicated 5.4 seconds of "travel time," which was very puzzling.

It took time to travel through time.

Why did whatever we sent "think" that it was traveling through the fourth dimension, the way we normally do, when in fact it was flipping back and forth through the fifth dimension and *backward* in the fourth?

We argued for months over that one, and slowly a lot of things started to make sense.

CHAPTER THIRTEEN
Hasenpfeffer's Place

Until the housekeeper arrived, lunch happened at some random time between eleven and three, whenever someone got hungry enough to cook enough for the three of us. With Mrs. Kelly around, well, lunch was served at noon, whether we were ready to eat or not. I think that she considered anything else to be sinful. Breakfast at seven and dinner at six were also prime tenets of her religion.

Her only saving grace was that she would always put the food on the table and leave, which let the two of us talk shop over the dining room table without breaching security.

At one point, discussing something having to do with causality, Ian said, "It's undefinable. It's like asking which came first, the chicken or the egg?"

"That's a perfectly stupid question. Obviously, the egg came first."

"You seem remarkably positive about that. Would you care to illuminate me with the glow of this newfound wisdom?"

"Certainly, my conventional little friend. Consider that what we call a chicken is in fact a domesticated Ceylonese jungle fowl. That domestication could not possibly have taken place more than ten thousand years ago."

"I'll accept that for the sake of argument. What has it to do with the subject at hand?"

"Why, everything. Eggs have been around for hundreds of millions of years. Billions, maybe. Dinosaurs laid eggs, you know, and fishes were laying eggs long, long before that. The time difference between ten thousand years and a billion years is so great as to make the question of priority blatantly obvious. Now, had you asked about the chicken and the *chicken egg*, the problem might have been less easily resolvable, but fortunately that's not what you said."

Ian's rejoinder was lost for all time because I had to get up to answer the telephone.

"Tom, can you and Ian get over here at one this afternoon? It's important." Hasenpfeffer sounded tired over the phone.

"Sure. Where are you?" I said.

"I have the top two floors of the Madison Building."

"The big new one on Third?"

"Yes. And put a suit on, will you? Appearances, you know."

It was already half past noon, so we changed quickly without bothering to wash up. We left on the run, not realizing that we'd never see our home again. Ten minutes after we were gone, a small fleet of moving vans arrived and cleaned the place out in two hours flat. And I do mean cleaned out. They even took all the trash in the garbage cans.

When we got to the Madison Building, we found that the top floor button on the elevator had been replaced with a key lock, so we got off on the sixteenth. The elevator door opened on a large room half-filled with impressively dressed and manicured people. Silk ties. Leather attaché cases. Three-piece grey wool suits.

Presiding over it all was an incredibly beautiful and efficient-looking woman. She sat behind this nine-foot desk that was just encrusted with gadgets.

"Quite a layout," Ian said, looking past his dirty fingernails to his unshined shoes.

"Yeah. Look, let's go somewheres and buy a tie or something."

The woman at the desk spotted us and came over quickly, smiling. "You must be Mr. McTavish and Mr. Kolczyskrenski."

An angel. She even pronounced my name right. She ushered us past the briefcase crowd and through a much larger room. There were scores of desks with intent people sitting at them, talking quickly on an equal number of telephones. Word processors were being operated. A big computer on the far wall was in operation, with dozens of big tape decks whirling and stopping and whirling once more with simpleminded diligence. All told, maybe a hundred people doing important-looking things.

At the top of an escalator, where they couldn't be seen from the floor below, stood two uniformed guards, festooned with radios, side arms and submachine guns. These were not your usual rent-a-cops. They were deadly types.

"This way, sir." The angel put her hand on a wall mirror and a heavy door opened electrically.

"The screen is keyed to my palm print," she said. "This is as far as I am allowed to go. The next door is keyed to both of your prints."

"Hey, this is getting a little ridiculous," I said.

"Dr. Hasenpfeffer's orders."

"Look, Hasenpfeffer isn't God."

"Indeed?"

I didn't know how to answer that one, so I went in and Ian limped after me. Inside were more guards with that sleepy look and more guns with thirty-round clips. Ian opened the next door and we finally saw Hasenpfeffer, sitting behind a huge desk in a big, dirty, and profoundly cluttered office. There were old newspapers and computer printouts all over the place.

"I see that you gentlemen made it."

"Quite a setup you have here, Jim."

"Thank you. It's quite necessary, I assure you."

"Look, what's with the guards and bank-vault doors?" I asked.

"My friends, you must understand that when you convert twelve thousand dollars into something in excess of twenty-six million within six months, people are bound to ask questions. For obvious reasons, it is preferable that they do not receive accurate answers."

"Twenty-six million!" I gasped.

"At present. Six times that amount by this time tomorrow, if all goes well," Hasenpfeffer said.

"How in the hell did you do it?" Ian rasped.

"The stock market. The race tracks. And real estate. I asked you both here to sign several warranty deeds. We have four closings scheduled this afternoon, but I have arranged them at forty-five minute intervals so as to interrupt your schedules as little as possible."

"Like, what schedules? We work and we sleep."

"Jim," Ian said. "With the staff you have here, what do you need with our help?"

"In most things I can act in your names with relatively little difficulty, but when a major corporation pays thirty-one million dollars for a parcel of oil-producing land, they naturally expect a clear title."

"Hey, back up," I said. "*Our* signatures? You mean I own a piece of this?"

"One third, of course. This *is* a group venture."

The year before, Hasenpfeffer had taken my four-channel, two-gigahertz, delayed-sweep Textronics storage scope and dropped it down the basement steps. It was at this moment that I finally forgave him.

"But we must hurry," he continued. "It is imperative that we finish by 4:15. Soybean futures will be hitting a three-year low this afternoon, Great Stag will be paying thirty-seven to one this evening, and Mitsubishi will be announcing a three-to-one split at 11:30 local time. Come, now."

Hasenpfeffer led us quickly to the corridor.

"Is that all?" Ian was having trouble keeping up with Hasenpfeffer's rapid, jerky stride.

"Of course not. There's the heavyweight championship, National Robotics is going public in the morning, and Exxon will announce an inexpensive shale-oil recovery process. It won't prove to be practical, but there will still be plenty of money to be made in trading its stocks for a few months." Hasenpfeffer broke into a trot. "We'll be receiving fifty-five million dollars in certified checks, which must be in the bank before it closes."

"Hey, calm down," I said. "The universe will still be here."

"If we upset today's schedule, we'll slow our growth by four months. So many highly profitable things are happening today! We are at a cusp, and there is a sea tide in these things. We must not miss it!"

The office was empty except for the angel.

"Where are they, Haskins?"

"Standard Oil called from Chicago. They'll be at least an hour late, Dr. Hasenpfeffer," the angel said.

"Reschedule this afternoon's appointments."

"I've been trying to, sir. I haven't been able to contact the Texaco group or Bradford Development. Mobil will get here on time, but not before. And they are the last of the four."

"Most annoying. Keep trying, Haskins."

When she left, Hasenpfeffer said, "Shit!" and flopped down on a couch. "Oh, yes. There is the matter of your new laboratory. I have taken the liberty of having a moving company clean out your present quarters. I think the new facility in Arizona will be very much to your liking."

"New facility!" Ian cried. "What on earth for? We've got pretty much what we need right where we're at."

"Primarily for security. Your coming here has announced your presence. We can not have our project known to the public."

"Security! Damn it, if you think that I'm going to let a gang of armed thugs into my lab . . ." I said.

"Tom, security forces are the lesser of the possible evils. Your staff can isolate you from any unpleasantries."

"Staff?" Ian said. "Jim, one of our primary goals with the time field was to keep it to ourselves. With a staff, there's bound to be a leak."

"They will be quite reliable people, selected from my own personnel here. Many of them are very competent, technically, and Haskins will set up the organization along the lines of the Manhattan Project."

"Haskins? The angel?" I said.

"Yes, she'll be going with us as General Manager. You'll find that she's quite efficient."

I pondered maybe twenty milliseconds.

"Ian," I announced, "if you're against it, you're outvoted." Arizona suddenly sounded good.

"Don't worry, gentlemen," Hasenpfeffer said. "Soon, I'm sure you will be successful and we will soon be able to travel in the fourth dimension."

"Fourth? Jim, we are working with at least nine."

"Yeah, and I figure there's got to be at least two more that we can't use, just for the sake of symmetry," I added.

"Having *eleven dimensions* is symmetrical?"

"Sure, when you think about it properly," I said. "Look, you can't go straight back in time. If you tried to, you'd run into yourself before you left. You got to go sideways through dimension five first, then work yourself back through four, six and seven to your destination, then back through five to our own continuum."

"Indeed? I didn't realize that. But you said eleven dimensions. What about the rest of them?"

"There are only nine that we are really sure about, Jim," Ian said. "The other two exist only in Tom's current half-baked theory. He'll change his mind about them tomorrow."

"The hell you say. Tomorrow's Wednesday."

"Right. Jim, we've decided that until further data is in, there are eleven dimensions on Monday, Tuesday and Wednesday, and nine of them on Thursday, Friday and Saturday. It shortens the arguments that way."

"On Sunday, God Himself doesn't know," I added.

"Hush! On Sunday, it's indeterminate."

"I am still confused, gentlemen. Whether it is nine or eleven, you have still only mentioned using the first seven."

"Oh, you wouldn't like those other two," Ian said. "You wouldn't like them at all."

"What?"

"Uh, he means that when we tried to use them, things go away and don't come back," I said. "Ever."

"I wish I understood all that," Hasenpfeffer said. "Perhaps if I had studied some more technical field."

"Well, don't let it trouble you. We don't know what we're doing, either."

"I suppose that your last statement should cause me some relief, but somehow it doesn't."

The angel popped in and announced that Standard Oil had arrived. The problem was that the V.P. brought along four corporate lawyers, each of whom tried to justify his existence by delaying the proceedings. Those bozos are paid by the hour and like to sandbag it. It was 3:45 before the deal closed.

Haskins popped in again. "Texaco is waiting in Office Nine, Mobil is in Eighteen, and Bradford is in Twelve."

"Lord!" Hasenpfeffer said as we ran to Office Nine. Texaco's lawyers delayed us an additional twenty-five minutes and Hasenpfeffer looked like he was getting ready to chew a hole in the conference table. We had five minutes left to close two deals and get the money to the bank.

"Just maybe!" Hasenpfeffer shouted as he rounded the corner to Office Eighteen. He ran crunch into a man who was running in the opposite direction. They both went sprawling on the floor.

"Excuse me! But I've got to run!" Hasenpfeffer jumped up. His nose was bleeding.

"Relax. Everything is all right." The stranger felt his own bandaged nose. "Shit! Twice!"

"He's you!" Ian's mouth was open.

"Obviously," the two of them said in unison.

"But you can't do that, Jim! We don't have it working for short time periods yet!"

"Of course not," they said in unison again. Then the bandaged Hasenpfeffer, who had been there before, stopped talking. "But you will."

CHAPTER FOURTEEN

Arizona by the Sea

Ian and I quickly signed the remaining two deeds and the bank's courier ran out with the checks. Then we drove the bleeding Hasenpfeffer to the hospital and got his broken nose fixed up. He promptly ducked out of the side door of the hospital lobby.

"I'll see you gentlemen shortly," Hasenpfeffer said through his bandages.

"Hey! Hold on!" Ian yelled. "I want to see this gadget I'm going to invent!"

"I would advise against that. Seeing it might hamper your creative processes," he said from the doorway. And then he left.

And came in the front door six seconds later with his suit more crumpled and wearing a bigger bandage.

"Am I gone yet? Excellent! Come! Onwards! On to the airport, and a glorious future!"

"Is he drunk?"

"Hell, he's more likely stoned," I said, but it turned out to be just high spirits. We were hustled into a chauffeured stretched Cadillac that raced us to the airport, abandoning our old Chrysler in the process. I have no idea what became of it.

On the way to Detroit Metro, I pretty much convinced myself that having a couple of guys around who understood soldering irons and printed-circuit layouts might speed things up a bit.

In front of the first terminal, a gorgeous airline stewardess flagged us down, hopped in the car, slithered in tight beside me, and directed us to a smaller terminal for private aircraft.

What none of us realized was that about the time we were boarding the plane, a fair-sized horde of police and government types was descending on our facility outside of Ann Arbor. All they found was a couple of very empty buildings. Even the overhead cranes were gone from the shop.

We took off in our own plane, a big wide-bodied jet no less, with a KMH corporate logo on the tail. It had things like showers and a sauna and six of the most magnificent stewardesses I'd ever seen this side of an Alfred Hitchcock movie. Like, any one of these women could have made it big in Hollywood.

Ian was embarrassed at first when one of them joined us in the sauna. I guess she was some sort of dancer, because after a bit she went through a most amazing series of stretching exercises.

"It's almost like she's *displaying* for us, the way a bird does during a courtship ritual," I whispered to Ian.

"I think that that's exactly what she's doing," Ian whispered back. "I've never seen anything quite like it. Have you?"

"No, I haven't, my son. But I have looked on it, and found it to be good."

Hasenpfeffer just took it all in and acted smug.

I was still trying to get up my nerve to ask the dancer out to dinner some night when the plane landed at our own airport.

Ian and I had found a bunch of suits and things—all of which fit!—in the closets of our bedrooms on the plane, so we didn't feel grubby entering the terminal building.

"Gentlemen," this big fellow said as we stepped into the airport lobby. "It is certainly a great personal pleasure to meet you all personally at last. I am Bradford Jenkins, and

I have the personal honor of being the mayor of your city of Morrow."

My mind had been blown totally away by the plane we flew in on, and Ian was standing there silent with his eyes unfocused, so it was kind of fun to see Hasenpfeffer get flustered.

"Mayor?"

"Yes, sir. In the first few years there were some minor problems with lost tourists and fishermen. Some representative of civil authority was needed to greet them and shoo them away. So, while it wasn't in your original instructions, I was elected."

First few years? Hold on now.

"Uh, how long did this take to build?" I asked.

"Six years, of course, sir. And we were able to stay exactly on schedule the entire time."

All I could think of to say was, "Sure. That's uh, very good. You did a nice job."

"Why, thank you, sir!" Jenkins' smile was too big to be anything but genuine. He acted like a suburban teenager being given his first car.

Ian came out of his daze long enough to say, "And how much did it cost?"

"Less than thirty billion, sir. I can get you the exact figure from accounting, but I can personally assure you that we are well within budget."

"Of course." Hasenpfeffer was looking at a long line of people in the lobby, all of whom were looking at us. "We would not have put you gentlemen in charge if we did not have absolute confidence in your abilities. Naturally, we will want a complete tour of the facilities, but for right now, we should not keep these people waiting."

You had to admit that Hasenpfeffer was pretty quick when it came to people situations.

"Yes sir. I've taken the liberty of arranging your itinerary for the next few days, but for now I would like the personal honor of introducing some of my colleagues."

That was my first—and last, damn it!—experience with a reception line. I was introduced to well over a hundred men and women, all of whom looked as though they had spent *hours* grooming themselves for the glorious occasion of meeting yours truly. All I could think of to do was to imitate Hasenpfeffer, who was smiling, shaking hands and saying things like "How are you?" and "It is so good to meet you at last!"

Most of them were in suits and dresses, but there were a dozen towards the middle in bright green military outfits. I'd spent four years as a second class airman—or worse—and it was kind of strange having a bird colonel clicking his heels and saying "Thank you, sir!"

It wasn't until I got near the end of the line that I noticed that there was a certain sameness to all of them. All of the men were big and athletic looking. That's to say, big as ordinary people go. Not my size, of course. The women were all healthy and remarkably pretty.

Why pretty? I mean, these ladies weren't decorations or somebody's second wife. They were all officials of one sort or another. Hasenpfeffer had always loved the ladies, but he wasn't the sort of guy who would promote a woman on the basis of her sex appeal.

Anyhow, everybody seemed to know who *we* were, as if they'd seen photographs or something. It was only when we were being ushered into a waiting private subway car that I realized that I hadn't remembered one single name.

Five minutes later, Jenkins led the three of us up an escalator into a tastefully lighted park. In the distance, I could see the moon glinting off the ocean; I could hear the surf and smell the salt air. The park was flanked on three sides by palaces. "Mansions" would have been a derogatory term applied to these places.

"We've arranged these quarters for you," Jenkins said. "I hope that they will prove adequate. You are doubtless tired from your journey, so, with your permission, I will leave you now. Would it be convenient if I personally picked you up at nine tomorrow morning?"

"That would be excellent." Hasenpfeffer turned and started walking towards a huge free-form concrete-and-glass structure that he had apparently claimed for his own.

Ian and I just stood there.

I had spent the morning in my lab in the basement in

Michigan, burning my fingers on a soldering iron. Now, it was quiet for the first time in twelve hours. Silence, with just the hiss of the surf and the smell of salt air in a manicured park in front of my palace in my city by the sea in Arizona . . .

"HASENPFEFFER!" I yelled when he was two hundred yards away. "GET YOUR ASS BACK HERE!"

He trudged back to us. "Gentlemen, it has been a long day. It has been four hours longer for me than it has for you. My nose hurts. We apparently have a busy day ahead of us tomorrow. Please, let's get some sleep."

"Dammit, not 'til you do some explaining!"

"Yeah," Ian said. "The office I could believe, and *maybe* the airplane, Jim. But this . . . this *city* is flat shit impossible!"

"It should be obvious that your technical endeavors will be quite successful, and that sometime in the future—our subjective futures, that is—we are going to fund a group to build this facility for us. Yes. It should be perfectly obvious."

"Look, what about the goddamn *ocean* in *Arizona*?" I said.

"I assume that we will decide to build this in some place other than in Arizona."

"Other place? . . . *You mean you've never been here before either?*" I tried to point at him but my hand was shaking.

"I decided this morning that we needed something better in the way of a physical plant, since we could now afford it, and that if I was sending newspapers back to myself, why not letters and money so as to get us a facility when we needed it? Then, when it became obvious that you would solve the problem of transporting people, I realized that it would be more convenient to go back and do it personally, rather than bothering with clumsy correspondence."

"So you just went to the plane and assumed that the pilot would know where to go?" Ian was staring wide-eyed.

"True. Although I didn't expect such an elaborate aircraft."

"*You didn't even know about the fucking airplane!*" For a Christian, Ian sure swears a lot.

"I assumed that I would arrange something. It is really quite amusing. You see, the Ann Arbor facility is called

Hasenpfeffer Investments. I have been buying and selling
KMH Corporation stock for months without realizing that
KMH must stand for Kolczyskrenski, McTavish and Hasen-
pfeffer."

"How come Tom's name comes first?"

"We will probably flip a coin about it. I am perfectly
content with my name being last. Please, gentlemen, let us
get some sleep." Hasenpfeffer headed back to the concrete-
and-glass thing.

"Well, take your pick." I pointed to the other two palaces.

"It's already been decided, I think. I like the Taj Mahal,
so you must want Camelot."

"Yeah. I guess so. See you in the morning."

"Wait. Tom, do you have a quarter?"

"Huh? Yeah," I said.

"Flip it. Let it fall on the ground. Heads your name comes
first, tails mine."

"Hell, that's ridiculous. After a day like today you're
worried about the company logo?"

"No. It's important."

"Christ." I dug out the quarter I had in my right pocket.
I'd been carrying the two of them around for over a year,
waiting for the right opportunity. I flipped it and of course
it came up heads.

"So much for predestination and free will." Ian limped
over to his palace.

Making a two-headed coin is fairly simple once you have
access to a Browne and Sharp surface grinder and a soldering gun. You just grind the tails off two quarters and
solder them neatly together. I ask you, would it really be
sensible to repaint the airplane, change all the signs on all
the buildings, and print up new letterheads and stock cer-
tificates? And just because Ian has this religious hangup?

Anyway, KMH sounds better than MKH, and one must
never underestimate the importance of esthetics.

CHAPTER FIFTEEN
My Princess in My Palace

My palace wasn't so much an English castle as it was Germanic with heavy Slavic overtones. It had lots of gold leaf and curlicues, and I liked it. I found myself grinning as I walked towards the place. A huge ornamental draw-bridge was lowering on massive iron chains, while a heavy portcullis was rising. So, if there is a God, and he wants to smile at you, wouldn't it be sacrilegious not to smile back?

God wasn't standing in the entranceway, but a goddess was. An amazing woman who was wearing a sideless, backless outfit that I maybe saw once on *Star Trek*, where the girls are all sexy. She walked over and came close, much closer than women normally come to me. I caught a slight whiff of burning autumn leaves.

She looked up at me with these huge violet eyes.

"Good evening, sir. I'm Barbara Prescott, your majordomo."

By this time, of course, I didn't have much mind left to be blown away, so I said, "Hi."

"Hello, sir." Barb had this intense, eager look.

"Uh, Barb, where are we?"

"At your home, sir."

"No. I mean this place."

"We're on the outskirts of Morrow, in San Sebastian, sir."

"Better. Now what and where is San Sebastian?"

"San Sebastian is an independent island nation in the Leeward Islands of the Lesser Antilles."

"Yeah. Where are the Lesser Antilles?" I wasn't doing much to impress her, but heck, I'd never make it with a woman this good-looking anyway.

"North of Venezuela and east of Cuba, sir."

"Okay, got it. This is some sort of banana republic?"

"No, sir. Bananas don't grow here and this is—or was—a kingdom. Actually, the governmental system is somewhat undefined, just now."

"Lord. A revolution going on?"

"No, sir."

"Well, we bought off the local government, or what?"

"I think that 'bought out' would be a better term, sir. The former 'king' was a Greek shipping magnate. He'd only visited San Sebastian once."

"Oh. We bought an entire country?"

"It really isn't much of a country, sir. It's only about twenty kilometers long and eleven wide, depending on the tides. We only paid six million dollars for it. San Sebastian had no economic value, but it had the political advantage of being a sovereign nation."

"Wow. I didn't know such things still existed."

"Oh, yes, sir. Actually, we had our choice of four of them."

"Yeah? What happened to the people?"

"There were only eighteen inhabitants, sir. They were paid a few thousand dollars each to move to another—non-sovereign—island that we bought for them."

"And that was six years ago?"

"Yes, sir. Then we built Morrow with KMH Corporation funds and re-inhabited it with our own people."

So when I was joining the Air Farce because I couldn't afford college tuition, I was also a king or something, with billions of dollars. Weird.

"Yeah. How many of you are there?" I asked.

"Our present population here is about sixty-five thousand, sir."

"Sixty-five . . . Where did they all come from?"

"I'm not allowed to tell you that, sir."

"Not allowed? I thought that I was one of the bosses around here?"

"You are, sir."

"Then answer my question."

"No, sir." Barb wasn't angry, but I could see that she wasn't going to budge. I remembered what Hasenpfeffer said about how we would probably have good reasons for doing what ever it was that we did, so I let it drop for the time being. Mostly, I was still too fuzzy-headed to want to argue.

"Okay. It was just that I was under the impression that this was going to be built in Arizona."

"Yes, sir. Would you like to meet your staff now?"

"Staff?"

"Yes, sir."

I figured that if I met my soldering-iron crew at this point, they'd likely think that I was a mumbling idiot, and they'd be right.

"Uh, no. Barb, I'm pretty far into stimulus saturation."

"As you wish, sir. Perhaps you would like dinner."

She kept looking at me straight in the eyes, sort of eager and switching her gaze from one eye to another. It kind of scared me. I mean, look, I'd been in the Fat Boy's Club at Westover Field, and I'd put on fifty pounds since leaving the service. I was sort of pudgy. Make that fat. I was completely hairless and my skin was still pretty blotchy. And while I've never been quite sure what the typical American woman wanted, a long series of hard knocks had taught me that whatever it is, it ain't me. Girls just don't look at me like that. And certainly not the most beautiful woman I'd ever seen.

"Yeah. Sure. I could use a bite to eat." I tried grinning back at her and Barb looked ecstatic.

"Very good, sir. The banquet hall is this way."

"Banquet? No. No. Please, Barb, just, just something small and informal."

"As you wish, sir. Anything in particular? Polish? Syrian? Chinese?"

"Chinese, I guess."

"Yes, sir. The Confucian Room is this way."

Barb led me through an entrance hall that would have put a Hyatt hotel to shame, and then down a long corridor.

It was obvious that the building had been built with me in mind. All of the doorways were at least eight feet high, and all of the furniture was properly oversized.

She led me into a candle-lit room. It was decorated with a lot of jade, Ming dynasty, maybe, and what looked like Shang bronze work. It was all imitation, of course, because it all looked new. The window overlooked an enclosed garden that was more Japanese than Chinese, but the total effect was stunning.

Also stunning was the tiny Oriental girl who was kneeling at my feet undoing my shoelaces. After that she started taking off the rest of my clothes. For a while there I wasn't sure when she was going to stop undressing me, but I was soon led—barefoot, and without my tie or jacket—to a low table.

Barb was still standing at the door, like she was waiting for something.

"Would you, uh, care to join me?" I said.

And Barb was grinning ecstatically again.

Our ninety-pound waitress (maid?) (servant?) was named Ming Po. I let Barb order the meal, since I'd been getting along mostly on Big Macs and Gallo Paisano, which didn't seem to be quite appropriate. I missed the name of the wine Barb picked, but Mr. Gallo has some catching up to do.

Ming Po had this habit of kneeling behind a pierced screen, watching to see if we wanted anything. When she went to get the food, I said to Barb, "You know, she's as pretty as that ballerina on the plane."

"Yes, sir." She was dead cold again. "You must mean Gloria McCluskey."

"I didn't catch her name."

"She's an awful social climber."

That sort of killed conversation until halfway through the meal. I was all out of things to say, and I finally figured out that Barb didn't feel free to speak until spoken to.

"Look, you mentioned a staff. Could you tell me about it?" I said.

"Yes, sir. There are nine personal secretaries. . . ."

"Nine? You mean I have a whole steno pool?"

"No, sir. The steno pool comes under the administrative section of your laboratory. That's not under my jurisdiction. You have nine secretaries."

"Uh, why so many?"

"To maintain continuity, sir. We were told that you preferred to work rather long and irregular hours. With nine, we can offer you three shifts a day, with each woman working four days on and two days off. This allows for two secretaries on duty at all times."

"Like, I need a typist sitting outside my bedroom door?"

"If you wish, sir. Or we can change the schedule if you prefer."

"Uh, no. Let it ride." There *have* been times when I was hot on the track of something and worked thirty hours straight, and I guess that that's a bit much to ask somebody else to do. Anyway, I'd hate to make some girl lose her job.

"So, who else do I have?"

"In the household staff, there are forty-five each in food services and housekeeping."

"Twenty people on duty all the time? That means that I've got—what—ninety-nine people here?"

"There are a hundred on the inside staff, including myself, sir."

"Wow. And you're the only one who is not available at all hours?"

"But I am, sir. I don't sleep. It's the main reason that I was able to get this position."

I'd heard of people like that, but I'd never met one before. Another thought hit me halfway through the Peking duck.

"Say, you mean to tell me that an hour ago, there were a hundred people spruced up and lined up to shake my hand?"

"One hundred twenty-nine, sir. There are thirty more on the gardening staff. Would you like me to call them back?"

"Uh, no. No. I'll meet them all eventually. I'm just not used to this kind of attention. I can't understand why it was decided to blow so much money on these palaces."

"I suppose it's relative, sir. The cost of constructing, furnishing and maintaining these three 'palaces' was less than one percent of our total budget for your facility."

I didn't know what to say to that, so I kept quiet.

Towards midnight, Barb showed me the way to the Master's bedroom. Catch that? Not the master bedroom. Apostrophe Ess. There were two more women in the bedroom. One was my adolescent dream. The other was better looking.

"Sir, these are Michelle and Carolyn," Barb said.

More embarrassing bows, handshakes and inane words.

"I think that that will be all for tonight, girls," Barb said.

As they went out, Michelle gave Barb a look that would have flattened a boar hog.

I was sitting on the frame of the massive waterbed, taking my shirt off, when I noticed Barb standing in the doorway, like she was waiting for something.

I figured that she couldn't leave without permission. We might as well get it over with. Best to let the girl leave and get some rest. I was used to being rejected.

"Would you, uh, care to join me?" I said.

And Barb was all ecstatic-looking again.

CHAPTER SIXTEEN
A Surfeit of Ladies

That night was indescribable, and I'm going to leave it that way except to say that I'd been celibate for a year and I darned nearly made up for it in one night.

I woke up the next morning with Barb sleeping on my arm. On an ordinary bed, that would have meant a numb arm, but waterbeds have their good points.

There was a glorious smile on Barb's face. It was as if she was in the middle of a beautiful dream, so I didn't want to wake her. Hell, I was the one who had to be dreaming. Then I remembered that Barb said that she didn't sleep.

"Uh, Barb."

Eyes open. "Yes, Tom."

Last night I'd told her to knock off that "sir" stuff and to spread the word about it.

"Uh, I guess I should have asked you last night. Are you safe?"

"I suppose so, Tom." Somehow, she made my name sound like "sir." "Why? Are we under attack?"

"Uh, no. I mean with contraceptives."

"Oh. No. I just went off the pill and I'm at the peak of my cycle." She stretched her arms and looked unbelievably happy. "I was so glad that you wanted me last

97

night. There's a sixty-percent chance that I've conceived your child."

Shit.

I'm rich *one day* and already I've got a gold digger on my hands. Christ, I'm dumb. Like, why else would a chick who was this beautiful, this intelligent, and this classy want a bald, oversized jelly belly like me?

"Dammit, don't you think that you should have told me?"

"But, you didn't ask!" She looked surprised, then her face started to crumble.

"Dammit! That's one hell of a low-rent stunt!"

She lay on the bed, quietly crying. I rolled out of the waterbed, got up, and tried to find my clothes. Damn. Somebody had snuck in while I was sleeping and swiped my clothes. They'd swiped my wallet and keys and sword and everything. My driver's license and calculator and everything.

Somebody had hid my stuff on top of the dresser. Sneaky bastards, anyway. I rummaged through an oversized chest of drawers hunting up the socks and undershorts I was sure they would have put there.

I turned to the closet and nearly tripped over my major-domo. She was kneeling, still naked, at my feet. And still sobbing.

I guess I'm a born sucker, because I softened up quite a bit.

"Hey, take it easy, kid." I touched her shoulder and she looked up.

"I'm sorry, sir. I should have known that *you* wouldn't have wanted a child by *me*."

I lifted her to her feet. She looked so tiny.

"Easy, Barb, easy. It'll be okay." Hell. Probably time I got married, anyway.

"I'll kill him if you want me to."

"Huh? Kill who?"

"Our son. I'll have him aborted," Barb said.

"Oh, no need for anything like that."

Shit. I probably wouldn't ever find a woman brighter or more attractive. There likely wasn't one, anywhere.

"I can keep him?" I never saw a woman change so quick.

She was smiling before the last tear hit the ground. And I swear it wasn't phony.

"Sure, Barb, sure. You just sort of took me by surprise. We'll work something out."

She was pure joy again.

"Look, we'll talk about it at breakfast," I said. "For now, just point me towards the bathroom."

There were two new women in the bathroom. Tammy and somebody else. One to suds me down and the other to dry me off. I think Tammy was planning to brush my teeth before I took the toothbrush away from her. They were both nude and both used any excuse to touch me or brush their bodies up against me.

Actually, it was kind of annoying. I mean, here I was, trying to think seriously about the possibility of marriage, and there they were, trying to get me involved in adultery before I'd proposed matrimony in the first place!

Just where did Hasenpfeffer *find* these chicks? They were all knockouts! Playmate quality and above! And what did he do? Brainwash them? Even the very, *very* rich couldn't live like *this* without people finding out.

Anyway, it got my mind off Barb. Just as well, because when I was led to the breakfast room—passing more scantily clad women in the halls—was the whole staff female?—Ian was already there working on a stack of pancakes.

"Ian, about all these women . . ."

"You too?" He sounded downright hostile.

Hasenpfeffer walked in. He looked haggard.

"Uh, me three, from the looks of it," I said.

"Gentlemen, I think that a conference is in order." Hasenpfeffer made hand signals to a waitress wearing the shortest skirt and the lowest top I'd ever seen this side of a go-go bar. She understood that she was to bring us more of everything that Ian was eating.

"Yeah. And you broads clear out of here," Ian grumbled.

"Right after bringing us our breakfast and coffee." Hasenpfeffer smiled.

Service was quick and the women evaporated.

"Now, you are probably curious why we have, collectively,

some four hundred attractive and eager women running around us."

"Talk about an understatement," I said.

"Yeah. I'm no prude, Jim, but this time you've gone way too damn far."

"Gentlemen, in the first place, I refuse to take full credit"— looking at me—"or blame"—looking at Ian—"for our present situation. This city, indeed this country, is the result of something that we all will do. No. That's not right, it's already here. 'Have done?' Absurd. 'Will did?' I think that might be correct, but it certainly sounds strange. You know, we will have to modify the English tense structure to accommodate both the subjective and the objective aspects of time travel. Perhaps if we adopted the convention of—"

"Cut the damned English lesson!" Ian shouted. "I was raped last night!"

"Ian, it is physiologically impossible for a woman to rape a male *Homo Sapiens*. You must have been at least subconsciously eager for the liaison in order—"

"Cut it!"

"Well, whatever else these women are, they are at least extremely obedient. I believe that if you gave direct orders as to how you want your household to behave, you would be obeyed."

"Bet?"

"Stop being childish. You do not look physically damaged, and I'm sure your libido had a marvelous time. Now then. As to how we will have managed all this, the answer is that I do not know, but I do have a hypothesis. Consider that none of our household staffs have had any experience as domestic servants. They are all very bright and well educated, but not as servants. Consider my people at Hasenpfeffer Investments. Because of distractions, I did not realize it until last night, but every one of my employees there— and there are over two hundred of them—is intelligent, hardworking, physically fit, competent, honest, and attractive. I never had to terminate a single one of them. And yet I hired all of them by placing a few newspaper ads."

"Back up a bit," I said. "What distractions?"

"In the first place, I did not have any experience in

running a large organization, so I had nothing to compare the staff's level of competence with. As to attractiveness, well, my first employee was Angela Haskins. She was simply the first person to answer my advertisement and I hired her. We were soon involved in an affair of such intensity that I really did not notice any other women."

"So, go on with your hypothesis."

"Have you noticed that all of the people here at Morrow and at Hasenpfeffer Investments speak perfect Midwest Standard English, the language of Walter Cronkite? That alone should have tipped me off months ago. Consider that they adamantly refuse to say anything about their origins. And consider that their value systems are not American."

"You mean the Russians, or . . ." Ian said.

"No. They would not and could not be behind it. One Mata Hari, perhaps. But four hundred of them? I doubt if there are four hundred women in the world who could approach our staffs on attractiveness alone, not to mention intelligence."

"You mean . . ." Ian was gesturing upwards with his thumb.

"Extraterrestrials? Possible, but improbable. What would be their motivation? From what you gentlemen tell me, time travel is relatively simple from a mechanical and electronic standpoint. Any race that had star travel would certainly have time travel. Why would they want to steal the idea from us?" Hasenpfeffer said.

"But, if they already had it, and wanted to stop us . . ." I said.

"Had they wished us ill, they could have quite easily stopped us with three small-caliber bullets. After all, they *found* us with no difficulty. No. The conclusion is inescapable. These people are superior human beings, obviously the result of a culture that places considerable emphasis on eugenics. The men are eager to help us and the women are anxious to conserve our genes. I suggest that they are the results of a culture that we ourselves will create."

We were all quiet for a while. Then some of it seeped in.

"So, the women are out for breeding?" I said.

"Certainly. You are one of their founding fathers, one of their great patriarchs. If their culture places a high value on finding the best possible father for one's children, you would be a perfect catch."

So much for marital bliss.

"So you didn't let your affair with the angel upset your stud work last night," Ian said.

"Not once I had deduced their cultural parameters. Actually, I indulged in one of my teenage fantasies and took four of them to bed at once. Not that I recommend the practice, or intend to repeat it myself. It was a classic example of one-trial extinction. What I *do* recommend is that you spread yourselves as evenly as possible among your household staffs. Tell your majordomos to set up an optimal breeding program, and I'm sure they'll oblige. Mine did."

"But, what about love and affection and . . ." I said.

"I am sure that they will be as affectionate as you want them to be. But as for lovers and life partners— Did you take a good look at the *men* in that reception line? They made the three of us look like diseased Neanderthals. No. I expect that everyone on our staffs has a lover or husband or boyfriend or whatever they do here. They merely want our genes, and I think that we should oblige them."

"Fuck 'em," Ian said.

"That is precisely what I am encouraging you to do."

CHAPTER SEVENTEEN
Rebellion

A woman in an abbreviated French maid's outfit (a frilly see-through apron, a black microskirt, high heels, mesh stockings and very long legs) announced that Mayor Jenkins had arrived to escort us on our tour of the city.

My watch said 9:00:01. "Well, tell him to wait. I'm having breakfast."

The maid nodded, started to leave and stopped abruptly when Ian added, "Better still, tell him to wait at his office. We'll call him if we need him. Later."

"Yeah, much later," I said.

"As in perhaps next month."

She started to leave again when Hasenpfeffer yelled, "Stop! Just what is the matter with you two? There are probably thousands of people awaiting us!"

"So let them wait," Ian said.

"Yeah, or tell 'em to get back to work."

"Or give them the day off."

"Good idea," I seconded. "I hereby declare a national holiday until further notice."

"You are both being preposterous!"

"So, how do you figure?" I asked. "If I'm the boss, I can

give my people a day off if I feel like it, or a month off for that matter."

"At full pay," Ian added.

"Uh, time and a half. I made it a holiday."

"That makes it double time."

"Well, be it so moved." I resumed work on my blueberry pancakes.

"You guys can't be serious!"

"Can't we?" Ian poured more hot Vermont maple syrup on his last Famo Buckwheat pancake.

"But . . . But why?"

"Jim, I can't speak for Tom, but personally I'm getting a little ticked off about being pushed around."

"Hell, you *can* speak for me. People have been pushing me around for the past twenty years, first at that damned orphanage and then at the damned university and then at the double-damned Air Farce. But this is the first goddamn time that people have told me that I'm in charge, but they want to push me around anyway."

"But . . ."

"Jim, have you thought it out?" Ian asked. "Does it make any difference *what* we do? We're going to be successful. Whether we do it today, or tomorrow, or next year, we are predestined to get this city—and doubtless a lot more—accomplished. This place is an accomplished fact, and it is futile to try to change facts."

"But . . ."

"Futile," Ian repeated.

"Look," I said. "If you feel some kind of social obligation, why don't you go and satisfy it. If you want, you can give us a complete report."

"What do *you* plan to do?"

"Well, I don't know about Ian, but I'm going to find myself a book and a bottle and a small room with a big chair."

"Make that two chairs, Tom, and add a pot of tea."

We left with Hasenpfeffer looking at us with his mouth open. I stopped a beautiful, underdressed woman in the hall and asked, "So where do I find a book?"

"The library is this way, Tom." She said my name like it was a title.

"Yeah, a whole library. I should have known. Lead us there."

My library would have done justice to a small university, maybe a half million volumes. The librarian was, of course, yet another gorgeous female. She wore a trim, grey wool suit over a figure like a Barbie doll's. Her hair was pulled tightly into a bun, and she wore large, round, horn-rimmed glasses that I was sure were made with flat, plain glass.

"Fiction," Ian said curtly.

We followed her down another hall.

In the fiction room, I found myself in the "H's" and pulled down a copy of *Stranger in a Strange Land*. It was a first edition, unread, and signed by the master himself. It felt Holy.

I ran to Ian with it, but he'd already found Verne's autograph on *20,000 Leagues Under the Sea*. He turned to the librarian.

"Are all the books here like this? First editions and autographed?"

"Uh . . . Effectively, sir."

"Effectively?" I smelled a rat. "Exactly what percentage of the books here are autographed?"

"About two point six percent, Tom."

"Then, how is two point six percent 'effectively' all?"

"All of the books that you will touch are first-edition autographs, Tom. The rest were regarded as unimportant so we economized."

Ian groaned, grabbed an armful of Mark Twain and hobbled out. I stopped to pick up a few books for myself, and caught up to him. He pointed to a heavy oak door.

"I'll have a reading room right there, with two comfortable leather chairs and a fireplace. And I'll have a pot of tea, Twining's Earl Grey."

"And a bottle of Jim Beam," I added.

Ian opened the door and the room was as described, with a cheerful fire, one oversized and one undersized leather chair, with a marble-topped table between them. There was a bottle of Kentucky sour mash next to the big chair, with a glass and a full ice chest. A cup and a pot of hot tea stood next to the small one.

"Ian . . . How . . . ?"

"Sheer brilliance and accurate deduction, my son. Only I've changed my mind about the Earl Grey. I've heard that there are some Chinese teas that cost more than their weight in gold. I'd like to try some."

A "French" maid came quietly in and removed the silver English teapot, and Ming Po came in with a tray of tea-making stuff, bowing a lot.

She was the first of my servants that I'd ever seen twice, and she went through this little ceremony of whipping a tiny amount of green powder into a bowl of hot water.

"The water . . . ?" Ian asked.

"Dew from rose blossoms, sir. I gather this morning." She bowed some more and left the room.

Ian tasted his tea. "Interesting . . . You know, if they were all like that last one, having servants wouldn't be so bad."

"Dammit, if you'll tell me what you're doing, I'll give her to you."

"*Give* a human being? Shame on you for the thought."

"I mean, I'll have her transferred to your staff. *That* can't be immoral. Now what gives?"

"You're slow, and here I'd had such hopes for you. Perhaps if we arranged a suitable course of study, starting with John Calvin and . . ."

"Dammit . . ."

"Okay, Tom. Make a wish."

"All right. I'm rich now, so I'll have Beam's Choice instead of his regular sour mash, and make it a ten-gallon bottle."

Within moments, a new bunch of nearly naked women removed the old bottle and rolled in a cart with a huge, pivoted bottle of booze. It was a gorgeous cart, with all sorts of intricate hand carving and fancy inlay work. The women left us alone again.

"Uh . . . They couldn't have had that ready and waiting. I don't think that Jim Beam makes a ten-gallon bottle."

"They probably had a glassblower do it up special. They had plenty of time, since that cart must have been a year in the making."

"Huh . . . ?"

"If you must be spoonfed, consider the situation of pre-destination along with the knowledge of future events. They probably have a microphone hidden in this room, and are placing orders far enough in the past so that we get things on request."

"Uh, is that how you knew this room was here?"

"I *didn't* know that this room was here! I ordered it here and they incorporated it into the architectural plans when they built the place."

"Good God! But why are they doing all this?"

"A good question! A magnificent question! Another good one is 'How far are they willing to go?' "

I was starting to catch on.

"Look, did you know that just beyond that wall is a scene that would entice the most decadent caliph of the ancient Saracen world? That this very wall, fireplace and all, can be slowly slid downwards, starting now, to expose a vast pleasure garden with a thousand naked odalisques undulating in their passion for our tender bodies to the slithering music of a hundred blind musicians. . . ."

The wall was moving downwards. Arabic music was coming in.

"No!" Ian yelled. "Damn it, Tom, they might do it! Would you have a man blinded?"

"Jesus Christ, you're right! Cancel the blind musicians! Make that a full symphony orchestra, black tie and tails, and they can stare at the girls all they want."

The wall vanished into the floor and there it was, as ordered. Pleasure garden. Orchestra. A thousand naked dancing girls. At least I think that there were a thousand.

Hell, I didn't count.

But having ordered it, we felt obligated to watch it, which we did for at least fifteen minutes.

"Bored yet, Tom?"

"Yeah. And embarrassed. For the last ten minutes."

"Then up with the wall. Let's have the fireplace back."

We shortly had the fireplace back, although I never did figure out how that chimney worked. I tried to get interested in my sour mash and a bound manuscript copy of H. Beam Piper's *Only the Arquebus*. Good book. Good booze.

But I couldn't get into either one of them. Still, I tried, hoping perhaps that my subconscious could solve the problems that fuddled my rational self. But the words on the paper didn't seem to mean much and mostly I just listened to the hum of the overworked air conditioner, fighting the heat from the fire in a decadent waste of power. After what seemed like a few hours, Ian broke the tension.

"God damn it!" Ian slammed a copy of *Life on the Mississippi* to the table, upsetting his tea cup. "These people have robbed us of all that is worthwhile in life!"

"Robbed us? They've smothered us under tons of everything we always thought we wanted."

"That's just it, Tom! By giving us everything, these bastards have taken from us every reason for *doing* anything. I'm a builder, a designer, an engineer. My role in God's world is to make things to better myself and to better humanity, *and you're not much different*! What's to become of us now? Are we to lose ourselves in mindless carnal pleasure like the first-century Roman patricians? Or spend our only lives in stupid mind games like the decadent Russian aristocracy? We'd be better off in prison!"

"Well, it's a very nice prison."

"Too damned nice! Tom, what I can't figure out is *why* they are doing what they are doing. What do they want of us?"

"Well, whatever it is, they're willing to pay one hell of a price for it."

"If they want something, why are they paying without bargaining first?" His face was red and tight.

"So maybe they're as ignorant of us as we are of them."

"They have pre-knowledge and Hasenpfeffer says they have high intelligence."

"Well, intelligence and knowledge don't necessarily make you smart. Look at your typical college professor. All I know is that whatever is happening, *we're* not in the driver's seat, but it's a pleasant enough trip. Let's ride with it for a while. Maybe it's just a colossal joke we're playing on ourselves. We're smart. In time, we'll figure it out. Until then, I say we should take the Chinaman's advice, relax and enjoy it."

"Tom, that's a disgusting attitude!"

"So what's so disgusting about a vacation on a tropical island? We've been busting balls for two years without a break, let alone a proper vacation. Let's lay back for a few weeks. We can always leave if things get sticky."

"Are you sure that we *can* leave?"

"Hell, they've done everything we've asked so far."

"Except answer certain basic questions."

"So if push comes to shove, we're still American citizens. We can call in the Coast Guard, if we need them, or the Marines, for that matter. They owe us something for all the taxes we've paid."

"And just how do you plan to contact them?"

"Well, I think I'd start by making a phone call."

"Good luck. I tried that last night. There are no outside lines."

"So, if we need to, we'll think of something else. I could build us a radio transmitter out of a broken stereo, if I had to. Look, all that's happened so far is that we've got a whole lot of people who say they'll do anything we want. Fine. Let's see what develops. I haven't noticed anything like violence, but if it gets rough, I have this gut-level feeling that we're a whole lot rougher than they are."

"Tom, it isn't violence I'm afraid of . . . it's ennui!"

"Well, that can't hit us for at least three weeks. Look, there's got to be a good beach here, with palm trees and a grass hut. We could take a picnic lunch."

"With McDonald's hamburgers and Colonel Sanders' chicken?"

"You're on. Some Gallo Paisano for me and we'll have Ming Po make some tea for you. We'll take Barb along in case we need anything else."

"What the hell, Tom. It beats just sitting here. One thing, though. I'm not going to do one damn thing for these people until such time as I have figured out what's going on!"

"Seconded and be it so moved!"

CHAPTER EIGHTEEN
The Uses of Time

We got to the beach in a converted VW dune buggy, with Ian driving and Ming Po respectfully apologizing while giving directions. Ian's right foot being what it wasn't, accelerator control was pretty haphazard. I wasn't troubled. If Ian flipped us, these people would likely arrange it so that we fell safely into a few tons of marshmallows.

The sky was a clear blue, the palm trees grew in profusion, and the beach was glistening white and clean. I even saw a few rake marks; nature's little unpleasantries had been removed. The grass hut was right where I expected it to be. Everything looked suitably primitive except for a line of buoys a half mile out. Barb told me that they supported shark screens.

The girls seemed to have never heard of a nudity taboo, and Ian and I had often taken saunas together, so we soon dispensed with bathing suits.

It was an idyllic afternoon, complete with friends, sun, wine, food, and sex. At one point, Barb and I went swimming, leaving the others on the beach. Afterward, we walked arm and waist back to the hut. Suddenly Barb stopped.

"Perhaps we shouldn't intrude," she said.

Through the doorless doorway, I caught flashes of rhythmically moving flesh.

"Well, I'll be damned. That just might be his first time, assuming that he wasn't really raped last night. Ming Po's persona must really appeal to him."

"Persona?"

"You know, the character she's portraying. Hey, I know that this is all an act, some kind of game you people are playing."

"An act?"

"Look, I'm just saying that if you want Ian on your side, have all his girls be like Ming Po."

"We don't have that many Orientals."

"Well, I don't think it's the race that matters. Just tell them not to get pushy. Give him some space, and he'll probably start chasing them."

"I'll do that, Tom. Do you really think that we're just playing a game?"

"You're all as phony as a pile of forty-cent pieces."

"We're not phony, you know. We're really very deadly serious."

"Fine. So tell me what you're so deadly serious about."

Barb didn't answer, and I knew enough about her to know that she wasn't going to answer until she was ready to. But circumstances were pleasant and I can be patient.

Hell, I can outstubborn a cat.

We wandered up the beach and then through a grove of palm trees. Just when the drying salt water was starting to make me itch, I saw it.

Coming out of the side of a curving royal palm tree was a golden shower nozzle, with a pair of gold faucets within easy reach.

I didn't say anything. I just used it and Barb joined me. It was not only fresh water, but heated fresh water. Disregarding the technical problems of a water spigot in a tree—I mean the bark wasn't damaged, and that tree trunk started out being horizontal and then bent a full ninety degrees to become vertical.

How did they drill a fifteen-foot-long curving hole to put the water pipe through?

But disregarding that, how did they know that I wanted a shower at just that time? If it was that they could read my mind, why were they going through this hugely expensive charade of trying to please me? Or was I going to say something about it in the future, my future, so that they would know what to do in the past?

By damn, I would *not* say anything about it! I never did, ever, to anyone. I had, in fact, entirely forgotten the incident until I came to be writing this narrative, years later, and . . . No! Damn it, they got me again!

When we were through showering, Barb opened a concealed door in the side of a boulder and took out a few towels. I stared at her in surprise.

"Did you think that we were the first people ever to use this beach, Tom?"

But I was resolved on the strong, silent technique. I went over to the gold faucets and gave them a yank. They came loose in my hand. They weren't connected to any water pipes. There were potentiometers on the back of the faucets and they were wired to this tape recorder still inside the tree trunk. Barb looked amused as I shimmied up the tree and tore out the shower spigot. There was nothing behind it. Absolutely nothing but a short hole drilled in the wood. And the end of the pipe was capped. There was no way for the water to get into the shower nozzle that I had just used!

"Barb, how the hell . . . ?"

"I'm not allowed to answer technical questions, Tom."

"Grunt," I said.

I went back down with the nozzle and turned the water on. I'd half expected the water to come out of the nozzle in my hand, but no, it came out of the hole in the tree. Still holding the nozzle, I went back up the tree. Looking in the hole, I could see the water appearing just inside, about at the level of the bark on the tree. It just appeared out of nowhere. I stared at this for a while, then tried to put the nozzle back into the tree. Barb started to shout something, but I ignored her. That was my big mistake.

It exploded in my hand, blowing a fair chunk of the tree away and sending me flying to the ground.

Barb had a first-aid kit ready and was soon using it competently.

"It blew just when I tried to push the metal cap through the interface where the water was coming out. That was a temporal explosion if I ever saw one," I said. "So you guys have it so down pat that you can send something to the time and place that you want it, and it's cheaper to do it that way than to run a water pipe all the way out here. But tell me, do they send a truck of hot water around every few months, or do they just work it all from some central location, somehow?"

"I'm not allowed to say, Tom," she said as she finished with my hand and started on the wood splinters scattered about my body.

"You know, a few simple answers would have saved me a lot of grief," I said. "I could have been killed there, and then where would your little game be?"

"You're not going to die, Tom." I didn't know just how she meant that, but she was pretty positive about it.

It was dusk when we returned to the palaces. Ian was in a quiet, smiling mood on the way back. He let me drive, probably so he could hold Ming Po's hand in the backseat.

"Dinner at my place, Tom?"

Ian's Taj Mahal was as spectacular, in its own way, as my place, but the thing that grabbed you was his womenfolk.

They were the same racial mix as my crowd—mostly northern European, with a sprinkling of everything else—but every one of them was trying her honest and phony best to act Oriental. It was like they'd all taken a six-week crash course in bowing and groveling.

Barb could not have told them to do this since she had not left my side since I had suggested that Ian's crew adopt Ming Po's manners, so—datum: it wasn't necessary to do something in order to get something done. It was sufficient to merely *intend* to do something. Only, what would happen if you meant to do something and then didn't do it?

I hadn't figured that one out yet.

One odd point about the place was that while much of the furniture was specifically intended for little Ian's use, the building itself seemed to be designed for someone my size or bigger. Whereas the doorways on my palace were all eight feet high, those in the Taj Mahal looked to be closer to eight and a half. Maybe these people just liked to build palaces with big doorways.

The meal was excellent—about thirty Chinese dishes, half of them on fire when they were brought out, and some Siamese food that wasn't actually burning, but tasted like it should have been. That last was for my benefit only. Ian, of course, wouldn't touch it. He was spending all of his time touching Ming Po.

He was soon hinting that Barb and I might want to leave.

I slept with Barb again that night, but the next morning I made full use of the bath girls. When in Rome, eat all the pasta you can get.

Ian invited himself and five of his women over to breakfast, a bit of a crowd for the small breakfast room. I had the meal set up on a big porch that overlooked the ocean. Or that is to say, I moved the party out to the porch and breakfast was waiting for us.

It was another beautiful day. Actually, the weather on San Sebastian was usually great, barring the odd hurricane, and those were fun, too. I knew I couldn't be hurt. Who would invent all this stuff if I wasn't here to do it?

"Tom, the girls tell me there are some nine-meter racing yachts in the harbor. My crew and I challenge you and yours to twice around the island. What do you say?"

"Well, sure. Barb'll line up our four best sailors and we'll take you on. Care to make a wager on it?"

"A bet, Tom? How? When you have everything possible in a material sense, what significance can there possibly be in winning or losing money?"

"Huh. You got a point there. Okay. My complete Poul Anderson collection up against your Harley. Assuming they're still in Michigan."

"Hardly a fair bet, Tom, but then it's not going to be a fair race. You've forgotten that I'm a whiz at fluid dynamics, whereas you've never even had a course in it. And what is sailing but simply applied fluid dynamics? I'm going to beat your socks off."

The twelve of us were walking across the drawbridge in yachting garb when Hasenpfeffer ran up. His bandage was gone and his nose looked as straight as ever.

"What are you gentlemen up to? There's work to be done!"

"Well then, you better get cracking, son, because you get to handle it all by your lonesome! We're going to go ride on some sailboats!"

Actually, I'd never been sailing before.

"But don't you realize our obligations to these people? And what they can do for us?"

"Look, I don't remember signing any contracts and I like what they're doing just fine." I had my arms around Barb and Tammy, and gave them both a squeeze.

"Oh, that, certainly. But look, look here." Hasenpfeffer was vigorously sticking a pencil into the fingers of his left hand. "That hurts, I tell you. It hurts painfully."

"Then stop doing it, stupid!"

"No, Tom! He's telling us that the nerves in his hand have regenerated, that their medical technology is better than ours."

"So?"

"So then they might be able to get me back my foot and you your hair."

"Good idea. Somebody make us some doctor appointments for right after the boat ride. And thinking about it, I want to ride horses down to the harbor."

Two cowgirls promptly rode up with a dozen empty horses. We saddled up and left a frustrated Hasenpfeffer standing in the plaza.

"Tom, maybe we should have invited him along."

"So send one of the girls back with an invite. But he won't come. He's too busy pontificating with the local bureaucrats."

The palaces were at the north end of the island, and we were a good hour riding to the city. The land between was flat and fertile, with well-tended fields and orchards. We passed one big dairy farm, but mostly it was all in fruit and vegetables.

The few farmers we saw were smiling, well-built fellows, and the one woman I saw driving a Ford tractor was as beautiful as any of the dozen girls in our party.

The city did not have the usual suburban sprawl of single-family homes. The fields stopped where a half mile of parks started, and where the parks ended, high-rise buildings began.

No, that's not quite true. The parks never actually stopped, but continued right through most of the city. It was a city without streets. Sidewalks, yes, but no provisions were made for motor vehicles unless you drove on the lawns. There weren't any cars at all.

"Subways," Ian said. "These buildings all have to be connected with subways. Somebody really spent with a lavish hand. . . ."

"Well, maybe not. Remember what you were saying once about cheap tunneling and underground highways?"

"Hey, yeah." Ian obviously regretted being on the surface. "We'll have to explore the things on the way back."

We were attracting a fair amount of attention. People were leaning out of windows, waving. The park around us was starting to fill up.

"Barb, if we get involved in a ticker-tape parade, I'm turning back. Somehow, tell everybody to just go about their usual business."

"Yes, Tom," she said, and glanced at her watch. Without any one individual doing anything unusual, the crowds quickly thinned out.

Most of the city was high-rise, but there was a certain eclecticism about it. No two buildings were alike, and there was a cluster of amusement sections, "Old Town," "China Town" and "Greek Town," which had a feeling of brand-new quaintness, sort of like a world's fair.

Yet, despite the phoniness of it all, the city of Morrow was truly beautiful, with sweeping modern structures and meticulous copies of every great piece of architecture in the world.

And it had such healthy, happy population! Thinking about it, I saw no one who looked over forty nor any under fifteen.

I turned to Ian. "Hey. They don't have any old people."

"Perhaps their medical technology is such that people don't have to look old."

"Maybe. They don't have any kids, either."

"Good God, you're right! Ming Po! Where are the children?"

She stared at the pommel of her saddle and was silent.

"Barb?" She just looked away. All twelve of our companions had been chattering a moment before, but suddenly they were silent.

"Well. Another little mystery."

"But . . . But it's so unnatural, Tom!"

"Yeah, it's that and more."

We wound our way towards the harbor through an industrial section. Here suddenly the parks ended, and what wasn't built of concrete was made of steel. Huge blocks of grey buildings surrounded us, identified only by large, painted numbers. Thinking about it, except in old town, where garish signs were part of the decor, there had been very few signs, and those few were small and discreet.

These were factories with very little noise, and no smoke or dirt at all. There were trucks here, and Hysters scurrying between buildings. Our nautical garb and horses were more out of place than ever.

The harbor was more of the same. A fair-sized tanker was being pumped out, a huge container ship was being unloaded and a second was steaming into the bay. There were a hundred small pleasure craft coming and going, and three sleek racing yachts were tied to a dock. But what caught my eye were two very deadly looking gunboats. They were small, as naval vessels go, maybe a hundred fifty feet long and thirty wide. They had big flat areas that told of phase-array radar antennas, and each sported a dozen gun turrets. There was some sort of covered torpedo tube high on the bow, above the waterline.

"Tom, that unloading platform . . . It looks like the hoists are somehow sticking to the ceiling of the bodacious thing. . . . Would you mind if we delayed the race for an hour or so? I mean, they're so damn fast and efficient. . . ."

"Yeah, sure. Only I want to check out the gunboats."

My crowd automatically split off to join me for my naval tour. Both of the cowgirls (alias French maid and bath girl. *I recognized them.*) stayed on the dock to take the horses back to wherever they came from, while the rest of us took an "impromptu" tour of the gunboat *Hotspur.*

CHAPTER NINETEEN
Gunboats and Yachts

There were about fifty people working on deck, and we eventually found another fifty doing maintenance below.

The boat's skipper, *Leftenant* Fitzsimmons, spoke with a crisp British accent that he probably got out of a World War II English propaganda film. His mannerisms followed suit, with much flashing of eyes and a tendency to strike heroic poses. He was a decent enough looking fellow, yet somehow he lacked the beefy smoothness of most of the other men I'd seen on the island.

"Right, sir. Shall we start at the bottom and work up?"

I don't know much about boats, but I know when to be impressed by good machinery. That little ship carried at least four inches of armor on all of her external surfaces, and twice that in some places. Her hull was a single, huge alloy casting, and her streamlined deck and upper works was a second single piece. There were no portholes, no windows except on the bridge, and two massive powered doors provided the only entrances.

"Hey, wouldn't that make it hard if you had to get out in a hurry?"

"Not a very likely circumstance, sir. Oh, I suppose that if more than three of her watertights were badly holed, she'd sink. But even then I think I'd rather go down with her than put to sea in a rubber raft."

Seeing me stare, he continued, "Oh, no heroics, sir. It's just that she's as strong as any submarine and just as watertight. If she sank, likely someone would be along directly to pull the old girl up."

So they did the "get it when you want it" routine with themselves as well as with us. It figured.

Much of the interior space was taken up by four huge Rolls-Royce gas turbine engines.

"She'll cruise at fifty knots, and hit sixty in a pinch. Planing hull, don't you know. She draws eighteen feet in harbor, but at cruise she'll raise up to six."

"Yeah, but those engines look hungry."

"Quite right, sir, and I suppose you'd say that's her weak point. She can only cruise for twelve hours without refueling. Yet in a left-handed way, it increases our security. We could defend San Sebastian fairly adequately, I expect, but we simply don't have the range to attack anyone. It makes us a safe neighbor, don't you think?"

Fire control was just forward of the engines and below the bridge. Judging by the heavily padded chairs and the seat belts, the *Hotspur* had a pretty rough ride.

"Twelve turret-control stations here, sir. One for each of the deck turrets. We have eight machine-gun turrets and four missile launchers. This station is for the fire-control chief and that forward is for the Exocet operator."

"Exocet?"

"It's a French surface-to-surface missile, sir, with enough of a punch to take out just about any modern warship. Not an old battlewagon like the *Missouri*, of course. At least not with one shot, but we carry four aboard. Our Monday punch, as it were. Launched from the bow tube you doubtless noticed."

"Oh, I thought that was for torpedoes."

"No, no torpedoes, I'm afraid. We carry a dozen homing depth charges though, which are fairly similar. They pop out the back."

Leftenant Fitzsimmons's accent sort of came and went depending on whether he was thinking about it.

The auxiliary bridge was forward of gun control. Most of the electronic equipment was down here, with repeaters going up to the "main" bridge. One odd fitting turned out to be a periscope.

"It eliminates the need of having lookouts up in a crow's nest, sir. It has a pair of gyro-stabilized lends' a hundred feet or so above the deck, and doesn't retract like the periscopes used on subs. Also, it doubles as a range finder, in case our radar goes west."

The story below was taken up with fuel and ammunition storage.

"That's about it down here, sir. Shall we go up to the main bridge?"

"That's it? Don't you have any crew's quarters or a galley?"

"No, sir. With only twelve hours of fuel, our usual patrol is eight hours. There's a coffee pot on the bridge, and we brown-bag it for lunch."

Barb and the others followed us up a ladder to the bridge. They'd been quiet, probably bored, having seen it all before.

The machine-gun turrets were hemispherical, reminiscent of a belly gun on an old bomber. Four of them hung over the side of the deck so as to be able to defend against boarders. They could actually shoot straight downward. The other four were mounted more conventionally. Repairmen had the covering of one of them removed, exposing a Vulcan 20mm Gatling gun with a smaller thirty-caliber "mini" beside it. Above the two sat a telescope with a TV camera attached. There was a third, empty mounting on the servo platform between the two guns.

"Hey, what normally goes here?"

"Well, nothing, sir. Presently that is, but you never can tell what the designers will come up with." I noticed that he was trying not to stare enviously at the "sword" clipped to my belt.

"Right. I don't see how you operate these guns. Where does the man sit?"

"Below, sir, in gun control. I showed you."

"What, nobody up here at all?"

"At full speed, this deck is a dangerous place in peacetime and in daylight. Fighting from it would be absurd. Between the radar and a TV camera on each turret, the operator can see everything he needs to. Loading is automatic, of course."

"Well then, what do you need with all these people? There must be a hundred aboard."

"This isn't my crew, sir. Maintenance comes under the Harbor Master. The *Hotspur*'s complement is twenty-four. They'll be along directly. We're due to go out in a half hour to relieve the *Nonesuch*."

"So, there are more ships than just these two?"

"Six, sir. The other four are on patrol."

"Oh. Is that usual? Two in and four out?"

"It's typical, sir, although we try not to be too regular in our movements."

I did some quick calculations. "I see. I gather then that you have multiple crews, like some of the U.S. Navy submarines."

"Oh no, sir. I wouldn't want to share the *Hotspur* with another skipper."

Out of the corner of my eye, I could see Barb turning red, shading to purple.

"Hey, but you've told me that this ship averages two eight-hour patrols a day, every day, with no facilities for sleeping or eating. If you're the only captain, that's an absolutely killing schedule."

"Hardly that, sir. In fact, we're just coming off a two-week holiday."

Barb looked like she was ready to explode.

"So, who was driving the boat when you were away?"

"Why, *we* were! One doubles back and that sort of thing. Surely you understand that the *Hotspur* represents a considerable capital investment, and it would be foolish to let her sit idle."

Oh yeah. These people were pulling the same stunt that Hasenpfeffer pulled in his office. Only they did it on an everyday basis!

"Yeah. Yeah. I see. Leftenant, you have a fine ship. A lot of the equipment has familiar manufacturers' name tags, but I've never seen anything like her. Where was she built?"

"Right here, sir, in that dry dock."

"All six of them?"

"Well, not exactly, sir. I mean we only had to build her once, of course, and then refit her each time she came back."

Oh. Whoopee. Shit.

"Yeah, thanks for the tour, Leftenant. I'd probably think of some more questions only my head's hurting. Barb! Gather up the girls! Let's go sailboating!"

We met Ian's party by the yachts, and he was babbling on about a building big enough to drive a container ship into, and these hoists that ran on variable tracks on the ceiling that unloaded and reloaded the thing in a half hour. I wasn't interested.

"Hey, you girls! Get busy casting off the scuppers and shivering the bowlines and doing all that other nautical stuff to make this thing go!" I went down into a spartan cabin to rub my temples and let this latest set of data get digested.

Soon, one of the women came in and started rubbing my neck and shoulders, which felt delicious. Before long, she was rubbing me all over. I found out that her name was Kathy. She was my librarian with her hair fixed differently and without her phony horn-rimmed glasses. We enjoyed each other.

I was back on deck in time to wave at the *Hotspur* as she went by.

There was a complicated-looking radio aboard. "I want to talk to Leftenant Fitzsimmons. Any of you girls know how to work this thing?"

Tammy did, and Fitzsimmons was on the air within seconds. At the same time the *Hotspur* made a fast "U" turn.

"Yes, sir. Can we be of assistance?"

"No problems, Leftenant. I just thought of another question."

The gunboat made another about-face. "Of course, sir."

"The five times your ship "came back," was it damaged? Shot up, I mean."

"I really couldn't tell you, sir. I wasn't there at the time, and it's not the sort of thing that they'd tell a bloke about. Rather like telling him when he's going to die, what? Simply not done. Anything else I can help you with?"

"Yes. Just what is it that you do out there for sixteen hours a day?"

"It's mostly a matter of dashing about and staring at empty

ocean, sir. About every fifth day we come on a fisherman inside the ten-mile limit. At least they say they're just fishermen. Just a matter of escorting them back out, usually. Once we assisted the Brazilian Navy in a rescue job. It's been pretty boring since the submarines stopped coming."

"Submarines, you say?"

"Yes, sir. Used to be scads of them. American, Russian, French, British—even a Chinaman, once. Lots of chaps were curious about what we were doing out here."

"Right. Just what *are* we doing out here?"

"*I'm* out here patrolling the ten-mile limit, sir. Couldn't rightly say about the rest."

"Huh. Okay. What did you do about the subs?"

"At first, we couldn't do much at all but stay on top of them and drop the odd hand grenade now and then to let them know we still cared, sir. Then one of the technical boffins came up with a variation on our homing depth charges. It has a magnetic grapple that clamps onto the beggar's hull. Then it has an underwater speaker and a tape recorder that says—I think I can recite it—'I am a five-hundred-pound bomb. You are violating the territorial sovereignty of the State of San Sebastian. If you depart immediately, I will detach at the ten-mile limit. If you continue in your violation, I will detonate in sixty seconds. I repeat . . . ' It worked wonders, sir, even if the equipment took up all the available room, and there was none left for a bomb. None of the blighters saw fit to call our bluff, so it was jolly well effective!"

Years later, I found out that the real reason that the various world powers stopped sending subs around was that satellites and U-2 style aircraft could do a better job of keeping an eye on us, and do it cheaper. Ian and I were pretty much unaware of the fact that a lot of very powerful people were very interested in what we were doing.

"Lovely," I said. "But is it a good idea to go around transmitting stuff like that unencrypted on the radio?"

"We're not exactly transmitting, sir. We have our ways. Any other questions, sir?"

"Uh, no. Thank you."

I looked suspiciously at the radio. It had a big, complicated face, but it was only about two inches thick. Not much room for batteries, and the yacht was strictly sail powered. There wasn't even a small auxiliary engine. Checking further, I found no antenna leads and no power wires leading into the thing. It was completely self-contained. I might not know much about boats, but I know quite a bit about communications equipment. I got out my Swiss Army knife and dismantled the "radio."

The silly thing had no transmitter section at all! Instead, it had a pair of small tape decks! Bloody be damned tape decks! I had been talking to a God damn tape deck! I stared at this for maybe ten minutes before I recognized two simple timers. Daylight slowly dawned in the swamp. If Fitzsimmons had a pair of tape decks on his boat, and he talked to it the same way I did, and then if somebody sent both "transmit" tapes back in time to before we both left port and then *switched tapes*, so my old "transmit" tape was his new "receive" tape, and vice versa, then we'd both hear what the other had to say, just as if we'd been connected by radio! Damn.

I put the set back together and called up the gunboat.

"Fitzsimmons, I've just inspected the 'radio.' Question: What happens if the *Hotspur* is going to sink?"

"Well, in my case, sir, I have a set of normal if less secure communications gear as a backup. We mostly use it to talk to foreign ships. In your case, if you have problems of any kind, just have one of your girls press her red button and help will be on the way. Ah, I've just received the most atrocious communication from your lovely majordomo, and I think I would be wise to sign off. Cheerio!"

Another set of data to muddle out!

CHAPTER TWENTY
Two New Bodies

I looked back to check out the competition. Ian had insisted on commanding his own yacht, so he still wasn't out of the harbor. We had to "hove to" for an hour until he caught up. It was noon, so Mary broke out lunch—salami sandwiches and Budweiser beer. Right after that, and completely without encouragement, the girls stripped to the buff to sun themselves. None of them had bathing suit marks on their suntans, so it apparently wasn't entirely for my benefit. I motioned Barb to come with me into the cabin, and I caught a few glances of envy directed at her from the crew.

After only a day and a half here, I was beginning to take this as part of the ordinary course of events. It's remarkable how adaptable the human organism is.

But just then, I didn't want her for sex.

"Okay, Barb. Are you ready to 'fess up?"

"About what?"

"For starters, about why I need nine secretaries when you people go zipping to last Thursday as often as an American housewife goes to the grocery store."

"I am going to gouge Leftenant Fitzsimmons's eyes out."

"Well, from what I hear, your doctors could put them back."

"Then I'll take a try at his gonads!"

"Spilled a few beans, did he? Answer my question."

"Tom, you must understand that there was a lot of social pressure—from the women, I mean. A lot of them wanted the chance to . . . to meet you. Your culture uses secretaries and servants, doesn't it? It . . . it seemed the natural thing to do."

"Hah! So you admit that you're from a different culture!"

"You knew that already."

"Yes, but I still don't know which one. Spill."

"I'm not allowed to answer that."

"Then who is?"

"I can't answer that either."

"So, what do I have to do to get the truth out of you? Slap you around?"

"You can if you want to. No one will stop you, Tom."

Shit. She'd called my bluff. I couldn't hit a woman, even if she did deserve it, and Barb hadn't gone nearly that far, yet.

"Well, okay. Now what's this about your culture not having any children?"

"We have children. Beautiful children."

"So where are they?"

"Tom, you can't expect us to have them here!"

"Well, what's wrong with here? This is a lovely tropical island, and you people have built a fine little city on it."

"Because it's *dangerous* here!"

With that she ran out of the cabin.

When I got on deck, Ian's yacht, *The Scot's Revenge*, was within shouting distance. It sported a remarkable set of dark scrape marks on its white hull. My girls, still nude, were getting our sails back up, and Ian's women, seeing mine, promptly adopted the same uniform. Ian was fully clothed while I was wearing a hat because of the sun, and shorts so I'd have some pockets and something to clip my calculator and "sword" to.

I leaned over the side and read the name on my own boat. Written upside down, so I could read it easily looking down from the top, it said *The Polish Prince*.

Getting on this particular yacht had been simply the natural thing to do. All three were identical, and I just stepped aboard the middle one without noticing any names. They had me again, and somehow I just couldn't get into relaxing while being raped.

The race wasn't much of a contest. We did two laps before Ian completed one.

I'd read about the twelve-hour days, no matter what the season, and the rapid sunsets that the tropics boast of, but this was the first time I'd been outside at the right time to see one. It was dusk when we got the boats tied up next to the third yacht, *The Teutonic Humorist.*

"Hey, some names, huh? I mean, the Scots never got their revenge, Poland doesn't have a prince and Germans aren't very funny!"

"Screw it! Tom, just where in the hell did you learn to sail a boat?"

"Well, no place. I never did. I just had the girls sail it."

"But what about our bet?"

"So what about it? I won."

"The hell you did! Your girls won!"

"So? It was me and my crew against you and yours. If you don't have brains enough to delegate a task to the people most competent to do it, well, it's not *my* problem."

"You cheated!"

"Hey! I did not! And I'll thank you for an IOU on your Harley."

"Damn it. Okay, Tom. You'll find a Duo-glide in your goddamn bedroom."

"Look, not *a* Duo-glide. *Your* Duo-glide. Bets have to be meaningful, remember?"

"Yeah, okay. But let's make it an IOU, then, like you suggested. I wouldn't want her left here when we leave."

"Well, you mean *if* we leave. Calling the Coast Guard is out. You didn't see that gunboat. Maybe the U.S. Navy could make it through, but there'd be a bigger butcher's bill than I'd want to be responsible for."

"I saw lots of gunboats today, Tom, along with jet fighters and helicopters. But should we talk about such things, in front of . . . you know?"

"Hell, does it matter? They've got us monitored twelve ways from Friday, anyway."

"Like you said, it's a very nice prison. Let's go check out that subway system."

"Fine. But we've got those doctors' appointments first."

"Oh, yeah, Tom. That."

The doctor was a nervous, skinny fellow who looked like he'd rather be chain smoking. He fluttered around, asked twenty minutes worth of questions, and was rude about it. Finally he had me strip naked and stand in front of this machine.

"Disgusting," he said from behind a control console. "The things you've done to your liver with your debauched drinking are absolutely disgusting! If you really *must* drink yourself into a stupor four times a day, you really should have had the brains to take vitamin supplements, B and C especially. And your lungs! Good God, the ugly things those cigars have done to your lungs! And the radiation damage! . . . Well, that's at least a decent challenge and not a matter of patching up the holes you've shot in your own feet.

"So what else do you want? Your hair back, I suppose. And something done about your blotchy complexion. And that flab! You are carrying ninety pounds of surplus fat. Do you want to get rid of it?"

"Huh? Well, sure, I suppose so, but every time I go on a diet I feel sort of *weak*."

"Okay. We'll beef up your musculature. Anything else? Any chance you'd want to be the size of a normal human being? And that ugly face—you want to join the human race?"

"Look. You leave my face alone, except I want my hair back and the scars gone. As to my height, well, why the hell should I want to be a skinny little runt like you?"

"Glad to see we're understanding one another, but I'm not a shrink. Now lie down on that bench over there."

I did so and he started closing this lid over me.

"Hey! You mean you're going to start right now?"

"Yeah. And you'll be out of here in five minutes. Now shaddup!"

The lid came down and I went to sleep. Then it went up and I awoke.

"Well, get out of there! You ought to know that what was no time at all for you was four months hard work for me! It would have been a damn sight easier to go back and fuck your mother and start again from scratch. Probably a good deal more ethical, too. Well, get up, asshole! Look at yourself in the mirror!"

I did so, and the guy looking back at me was a Greek statue in living color. I flexed my muscles and they rippled. I had this massive, wedge-shaped body with narrow hips and a flat stomach, without an ounce of fat. My hair was blond and shoulder length and I had a luxurious blond beard, and eyebrows and eyelashes!

"You need a haircut, but keep the beard. It covers some of your face."

When I finally recovered speech, I said, "Uh, thank you, Doctor. It's . . . wonderful. You . . . mentioned something about vitamins?"

"Yeah, but I knew you wouldn't have brains enough to take them so I built in a vitamin generator while I was at it. Consider it another ductless gland. That body will stay like it is. But if you keep on smoking, you'll be back here in ten years, and next time I won't be so polite. Now get out of here and send in that gimpy runt of a friend of yours."

"Look, Doc. I owe you a lot. But I've got to say that you're the most disagreeable person I've ever met."

"True. But I'm also the most competent person you've ever met, so I can get away with it. Now get out and send in the runt."

There was no point in trying on my old clothes, so I just walked out into the anteroom naked. Nobody around there seemed to care much about clothes, anyway.

Ian looked at me and said, "Jeesch! They can do things like that?"

"Some body, huh?"

"Yeah, but *nothing* like what they're going to do for me!"

Two minutes later, Ian came out on two good feet. That, and he was about six foot twelve and maybe four inches wider than me at the shoulders.

"Well. You went in to get one foot and you came out with three."

"What, Tom? Oh. I get it. One foot at the end of my leg and two feet in height. If you're counting that sort of thing, you'd better make it four, noting the improvement in my privy member."

"Good God, you're right! Shit! You could kill somebody with that thing!"

"I did always want to be a lady killer, but not in quite that way, of course. I suppose I'll have to learn caution."

"Hey, with both heads! You proceeded foolishly and without the sound advice of your experienced, learned, and wise best friend. They built this world with the little creatures in mind, rather than us people of proper size. Doorways and such are all made to deadly heights! I resolutely urge you to wear a crash helmet until further notice."

"I'll learn to duck."

"Well, they say pain is the best teacher."

Our old clothes were completely useless, so we were still naked when we joined the girls in the waiting room, looking like a pair of bit players in an Italian gladiator movie. Their reactions ran the full gamut, from Tammy's ear-to-ear grin through Barb's pleased smile through Kathy's blank-faced shock to tiny Ming Po's unconcealed open-mouthed apprehension. Naturally, they had clothes for us that fit perfectly.

Ian bashed his head fully six times getting to the subway. He had never laughed at me for doing that, so I worked hard so as not to snigger.

There wasn't much to see in the subway system, just a large room in the basement with two kinds of elevator doors in it. The ones in the middle had two buttons, and were used for going up and down.

Along the outer walls, there were three push buttons next to each of what looked like more elevator doors. You requested either a four-, eight- or sixteen-passenger car.

The door opened immediately, and inside there was a map in front of the first seat with all the possible destinations on it—about four hundred of them. You pressed where you wanted to go and it took you anywhere on the island nonstop in under five minutes.

The private car that had been waiting for us when we first got to San Sebastian had not been a special privilege. Everybody used them.

CHAPTER TWENTY-ONE
Another Race and a Party

Getting into the car, Ian bumped his head four more times that I noticed and doubtless more besides that I didn't. He hit his head again as we left the car under my place.

"Hey, maybe if you bash your head enough times, all the lumps will grow together into sort of an organic crash helmet, and . . ."

"Laugh all you want," he said. "It's a magnificent body!" He put his hands under the butts of two of his girls—Merry and Jodi—and lifted them at arm's length up to shoulder level. "Look at this, will you?"

"Hell, I can top that!" I duplicated his feat with Barb and Mary, then crouched down on my haunches and went into a high-kicking Cossack dance—with suitable verbal accompaniment—that I had learned when I was sixteen and on a diet.

Ian tried it and dropped himself and friends backwards on the thickly padded carpet.

I roared with laughter.

"Damn you, Tom, I never said I was a dancer, but I can outrun you anytime!"

"Ah hah! Do I hear another wager in the offing?" I was still holding the girls out in the air.

"You're damn straight! Once around all three of the palaces and each of us carrying two women."

"Two women? I presume they don't have to be held at arm's length."

I let my two ladies slide to the floor.

"At a dead run, it'd be a bit much, not to say dangerous." Ian remembered my supposed "cheating" at the boat race and lapsed into a "legalistic" tone of voice. "We shall each carry two ladies in any manner whatsoever, except that should any part of their bodies touch the ground, the defaulter shall forfeit the wager. The course shall be outlined by floodlights that someone shall set up around the aforesaid three palaces, and said course shall be free from any dangerous obstacles. The ladies in question shall be chosen among our own here present. . . . Oh. And we each shall move on foot entirely under our own power and without any external assistance. I think that defines it."

"Sure. What about the bet?"

"I want my Harley back."

"Okay. What are you putting up against it?"

"My Corvette."

"Hey, that's not *your* Corvette, that's group property."

"Then my share of the Corvette and my entire library back in Michigan."

"Done!" And we shook on it. I started stripping down to nothing. The soles of the feet on my new body were heavily calloused and all else was useless encumbrance.

"Okay. The lightest two of you girls front and center. Go to the bathroom and then strip."

"Tom! What are you doing?"

"Well, the bet is that I have to carry two girls over a maybe two-mile course. Nothing says that I have to carry clothes or urine." Naturally, I had a secret scheme for victory.

Ian told his ladies to follow suit, and we went outside to find a starting line set up. Word had apparently gotten around, because the entire population of all three palaces— sans Hasenpfeffer—was waiting for us, cheering. We had apparently made nudity the uniform of the day, because they were all as naked as we were. When a full-sized, ornate and highly polished brass cannon signaled the start, every one of them joined in the race. I set off with Barb over my right shoulder and Tammy over my left. As I ran, we tried other positions.

It was an absurd, hilarious, and riotous affair! We were all laughing hysterically and running as fast as our legs could push us. A few score of the girls quickly took the lead, the bulk of them paced Ian and me with our double loads, and eventually an increasing number of them fell behind.

It was wonderfully glorious, fantastically exhilarating! It was a magnificent joy, pushing a perfect body to its absolute limits! For the first time in my life, I was an athlete! Ian was stronger than I was and his legs were fully six inches longer than mine, but I was better coordinated—he hadn't learned how to use his oversized body yet. We raced evenly over the soft beach sand until we rounded the Taj Mahal. Then he started to pull ahead. I was a hundred yards behind when we rounded Hasenpfeffer's glass-and-concrete thing and got onto the better footing of a well-tended lawn.

Only a half dozen girls were in the lead now, and I saw my grand strategy starting to work. Ian's huge wong, slapping back and forth between his legs, began to tell on him, doubtless assisted by the lovely naked ladies running and bouncing around him and clinging to his neck. I caught up with him halfway back to Camelot. His erection was huge, and must have consumed a pint of blood that could have been used in oxygenating his muscles. Also, I don't think that his mind was entirely on running a race.

When I passed Ian, there was only one woman ahead of him—one of Hasenpfeffer's—and she never dropped out. I passed her a hundred yards from the finish line.

Throughout the race, I'd been shifting Barb and Tammy around, trying to find a comfortable position. There wasn't one. As we approached the finish line, Barb was on my back, with her arms around my neck and her legs wrapped tightly around my waist, and Tammy was on *her* back, with her legs under my armpits, her feet in my hands. I was bent over nearly horizontal, and pumping my legs like the devil himself was after me with two pitchforks, and we won!

We crossed the finish line to four hundred cheers and a

second booming of the brass cannon. I promptly stumbled and spilled Barb and Tammy sweating on the sand.

We were up in time to cheer Jennifer into second place and Ian into third. They had a six-quart solid gold loving cup, already engraved with my name, that said *"First Place"* and *"San Sebastian National Invitational Mini-Marathon."*

Jennifer got a similar *"Second Place"* prize, a two-quart solid silver cup. Ian got a tiny, chrome-plated plastic thing that read *"Last Place—Male Division."*

"I'll get you, Red Baron!" he shouted, because whereas our cups were filled with champagne, his held cold Lipton tea.

After taking a long pull, I passed the cup to Barb. It went from her to Tammy and then into the crowd. Three dozen dozen champagne bottles were popped besides, and musical instruments were starting to appear.

"Inadequate!" Ian shouted above the crowd. "I may be a loser, but I'm a rotten loser! Let's break up the party!"

The girls all booed.

"So we can have a bigger one!" he shouted.

They all cheered.

"You're all going to have to get dressed!"

"Boo!"

"In grass skirts and flowers!"

"HURRAH!"

"Me and Tom can't handle all of you!"

"BOO!"

"So you'll have to invite in the guys!"

"HURRAH!"

"Hey, they can only invite three hundred!" I shouted.

"BOO!"

"Well, we gotta have enough left for ourselves!"

"HURRAH!"

"McAndrews from the docks has to be here!" Ian yelled.

"HURRAH!"

"Yeah, and Fitzsimmons of the Navy!"

"HURRAH!"

It was like party time back in college, with one big exception. Ian was getting involved and taking the lead like he never had before. I was starting to get pretty worried

about it. Had they worked over his head as much as they
had enlarged his body? But I had had the same treatment,
and I wasn't acting any different, except for maybe being
more physical, and that could be explained by the way it
felt so good to move this new body. Then again, would I
know it if I was thinking differently? I'd have to get Ian
alone and talk to him about it, next time I got a chance.

Which wasn't now.

Grass skirts and flowered leis were being passed out.
Bonfires and torches were already being lit down on the
beach where we'd raced not ten minutes before. On a raised
area, a platform with seats was set up for the island's
"royalty," namely us.

Female royalty seemed to consist of only those girls we'd
actually laid—four of mine plus Ming Po on Ian's side.

A tourist-style luau was in full swing by the time we got
there. Booze was flowing freely, served in coconut shells,
hollowed-out pineapples and, in a few cases, the entire rinds
of watermelons.

A fair-sized "native" band was going and a few dozen
girls were doing a hula.

The hula was followed by some sort of all-male Polynesian
dance which featured a wide range of grunts and a lot of
body slapping—almost drumming. It was the first time I'd
taken much notice of the men on the island, female distractions being what they were. The men were the same
racial mix as the women. More than half of them were
blond, with a sprinkling of everything else from bushman
to Eskimo. They averaged around six feet tall. They were
well muscled, well coordinated and quick to laugh—usually
a sign of intelligence. Yet somehow there was something
lacking in them. Character? No, not quite. I had the feeling that these men were all decent and just.

Over-polished? Perhaps the word I was looking for was
over-civilized. . . .

The male dancers were followed by even more violent
drumming and twelve ladies came into the open area before
us doing what Barb said was a Tahitian dance, which
involved unbelievably fast hip motions.

On the other side of the platform, Ian was drinking from

a small watermelon. This was another new thing for him. I'd never seen him drinking before beyond a single glass of wine with dinner. He was pointing at the women dancing.

"Tom, I'll have that one, and that one, and . . ."

I hoped that whatever he was drinking wasn't too alcoholic. Stamina and perseverance in drinking requires diligence and long training, benefits that Ian was perforce bereft of. Still, there was only one way of obtaining such graces. One learns by doing. It was good to see the boy loosening up, if only it was really the old Ian doing the loosening.

As the "Tahitians" left, huge leaves from some kind of tropical tree were laid out at the periphery of the cleared area, and dinner was served.

Seven whole roast pigs—each slung on a pole between two men—were carried out over the leaves. With a single jerk of the pole, all of the steaming-hot flesh fell to the leaves, leaving the skeleton still hanging from the pole. The trick worked all seven times, and the cooks got more applause than the dancers.

A few hundred other dishes were brought out—there was no apparent distinction made between servers and guests. Everyone except the "royalty" seemed to have a well-choreographed part to play. Or maybe it was that these people were just naturally God-awful cooperative.

Whatever the cause, seven hundred people were served in ten minutes flat.

Ian and I didn't get a wicker platter like everyone else. Anytime we opened our mouths, some attractive lady wearing flowers, a grass skirt, and a smile rammed food down our throats. A strange custom; I came close to biting off more than one dainty finger by mistake.

As the meal progressed, another group of male dancers entered the arena. I recognized Leftenant Fitzsimmons among them, wearing a flowery cloth around his hips and a lei around his neck, but still wearing his bashed-up skipper's hat. He had two dozen men with him. I guessed them to be his crew from the *Hotspur*, which ship, with them aboard, was presently still circling the island. They did a sort of juggling dance, throwing around four dozen razor-sharp machetes in a manner that looked likely to kill somebody, but didn't.

Seeing that crew together and largely undressed, it was obvious that they were of a different breed of cat than the other men on the island. They were more varied in size and build, often wiry rather than beefy. They had a much wider range of facial features, and a few of them were down-right ugly. More than a few were shifty-eyed, and nothing about them was polished or over civilized.

Survivors, that's what they were, and my kind of people.

When the dance finished with not a drop of blood spilled, I started breathing again.

"Hey!" I shouted, then gagged and spit out the peeled grape that Tammy had stuffed into my mouth.

"Hey!" I tried again. "Leftenant Fitzsimmons! Come on up and join the royalty!"

"Right, sir!" He waved goodbye to his men, jumped up to the stage and sat down on a chair that someone had placed next to me.

"Quite a show, Leftenant. But I couldn't help noticing that your men are a bit different from the rest of the people on this island."

"I suppose the people hereabouts have their limitations, sir, but they certainly know how to throw a party!"

He gestured towards some grass-skirted ladies who must have been selected because of their overly large breasts. Their dance might have been authentic somewhere, but for me it seemed it mostly involved a lot of jumping and stomp-ing, the sole purpose of which was to get those huge breasts bouncing. It looked painful.

"Yeah, but why are you different? Where are you from?"

"Oh, elsewhere, sir. I say, look at that one on the end giving me the eye! That likely means that I'll be well entertained tonight!"

"Huh. I take it you're a bachelor."

"Oh, no sir. I'm married. Several times, in fact."

"I see. The traditional seaman's girl in every port?"

"Hardly that, sir. I'm really quite the family man. Four wives and thirteen children to date. If I had my pants and wallet, I'd show you their photos."

"Well, I'd like to meet them during my stay here."

"Oh, they're not here, sir. Wouldn't work, don't you know. For one thing, these local people are monogamous. No, I have found it wise to restrict my home life to my vacations."

"Say, that must be rough on your family."

"Most of the time, they don't realize I've been gone, sir. Children need a continuous male adult around if they're going to grow up properly, so I always arrange my departures and arrivals to happen on the same day."

"Huh. How often do you get a vacation?"

"Why, whenever I feel like it, sir. Whenever I get bored with work, I go home or elsewhere until I get bored with that. After all, as long as the *Hotspur* makes her two patrols a day, my contract's satisfied. What I do with the rest of my life is my own business. The same, of course, applies to my family." He flirted again with the dancer.

"Well then, you seem to have a perfect life, with fringe benefits." I gestured to his dancer.

"These aren't bad, sir. I've jolly well had worse. But really, they're a bit butch and thin-flanked for my taste. Back home the girls are *sexy!*"

Since I couldn't imagine any possibility of any women from any place or any time being better-looking than the ones around us, I let the matter drop.

"Uh, yeah. Where did you say your home was?"

"I didn't. Really, sir, you must understand that I have certain contractual obligations, and that that majordomo of yours, well, she might be all sweetness and joy to you, but she is also a hellion who is quite capable of making my life difficult."

The boob-bouncing dancers finished their set and were replaced by another male group. One of the large-breasted women came up, sat by Leftenant Fitzsimmons's feet, and laid her head on his knee. When he stroked her cheek, she smiled. There was no question but that the good leftenant would indeed be well taken care of.

Five others arranged themselves around Ian, crowding in among seven "Tahitians" and a half dozen "hula" girls. Ian had finished his first watermelon filled with some sort of punch, and was calling for another.

Poor kid. He was about to learn the hard way that strong drink increases the desire while it lessens the ability. Still, education is a wondrous thing, even if it is occasionally painful.

"Oh, sir, since I was a guest of honor, so to speak, I took the liberty of inviting a friend, Captain Stepanski. He heads up the fighter wing on base. That's him below with his pilots."

There were sixteen short men of the "Survivor" type doing something that involved throwing lighted torches at each other, catching them and throwing them back.

"Well, more guys from your hometown, I see. How many of your sort are here? . . . Come on, I can find out the hard way if I have to."

"Very well, sir. There are just under a hundred fifty in the Navy, about three hundred in the ground forces and perhaps thirty-five in the Air Force."

"Hey, that's a pretty tiny air force."

"Not really, sir. They're all pilots and gunners. The Smoothies handle all the maintenance and so on."

"The "Smoothies." What do they call you?"

"They call us the 'Killers.' "

The air force was the last formal act of the evening, and after they quenched their torches, the party slowly broke up into about forty smaller parties up and down the beach. The "royal" party took a walking tour among them, with Ian and me hugging all of the girls and shaking hands with all the men. Our ladies, of course, had opposite tastes.

About halfway through, Ian discarded another empty watermelon rind and led his collected girls—there must have been forty of them—back to the Taj Mahal.

It was after midnight when I finally got home. Barb said that she'd join me later, so I went to my bedroom alone. Michelle and Carolyn were there, just as they had been when I'd arrived, two days before.

Only this time I didn't disappoint them. Actually, I darned near wore them out. They soon got to calling in reinforcements, and I found myself at the center of a one-man orgy.

This new body of mine had just amazing stamina, and

before I called it quits and Barb came back, shooing the others out, I figured that I must have done proper justice to eighteen of them, and some of them several times.

CHAPTER TWENTY-TWO
The Third Wager

I woke up at dawn feeling just great. Maybe it was my new automatic vitamin generator, but if so, they must have given Ian one, too, since I found him in my breakfast room when I got there.

"Good morning, Tom. You slept well?"

"Well, they laid me soundly down. Yourself?"

"Remarkably so."

The breakfast waitress, who had not been with me last night, had taken to wearing nothing but high-heeled shoes and a small apron. I never did meet a man who could get a woman to wear what he wanted, so I didn't mention it to her. Anyway, there was a part of me that liked it.

She asked me what I wanted.

I said, "Surprise me," and sat back, wondering what she'd do.

What she did was bring me a spinach-and-cheese omelet with some kind of white sauce. It wasn't bad.

When I complimented the food, and the waitress on her choice, she told me that all of the vegetables consumed in the palaces were grown in the gardens surrounding them, and were picked within minutes of being set on the table. Hereabouts, they took the idea of freshness about as far as it could go.

Ian was working on his usual stack of pancakes. That at least hadn't changed. I was trying to figure out how to broach the subject of how his mind might have been fiddled with, but he sort of signaled that he didn't want to talk, so I let it be.

After breakfast, he suggested that we take a swim, just the two of us, so we headed for the beach in front of my place.

"What would you say to another wager?" he asked.

"You are a glutton for punishment, my young friend. In Sunday School, didn't they teach you about the virtues of moderation?"

"Yes, Tom, and long ago I vowed to strive towards those virtues as the noblest of ideals. Yet perforce, I must do my striving in extreme moderation, in order to keep the whole business within the logical bounds of internal consistency. Thus, alas, one moderate deed per week is the best I dare attain. Mainly, at the present, I want my Harley, my Corvette, and my books back." We reached the beach and started stripping down. Ian seemed to be wearing an extra doodad around his neck along with his usual religious medal, but I didn't say anything about it.

"Well, certes I would agree with your wager in principle, but do you own anything to put up against your previous foolish losses?" I said as we waded naked into the warm salt water.

"In truth, Tom, not much, but I am minded to bet it all on one figurative toss of the dice."

"A noble action, my young friend, though again a silly one. Yet faced with such knightly panache, how could I say thee nay?" We were both stroking out into deep water. "Did you have any particular method in mind with which to attain your final impoverishment?"

"I do. I propose that whichever one of us sexually penetrated and ejaculated into the largest number of attractive young ladies last night shall be the owner of all my previous property."

"Done, my sad young friend, and our present salty wetness is most appropriate, as the ocean waves shall disguise your own salt tears, for you lose. In the early hours before

I slept, I may have set a world record with over eighteen of our loveliest maidens being fully pleasured, and that is not counting the two eager bath girls I enjoyed this very morning. I wouldn't feel too badly about it, though. I mean, sew a black patch on the back of each of your hands if you really must, but I wouldn't even consider suicide."

"Only eighteen? Did you know that there was an ancient Roman general who forcibly took twenty-five virgin captives on the eve of battle, just to get his fighting spirits up for the coming conflict?"

"Did he win the battle?"

"He would have, except that he fell asleep during a counterattack."

"I feel my leg being pulled," I said.

"It's probably just a shark. This isn't a protected beach. Anyway, we are probably far enough out. One of the things that I have observed about the technology of our hosts . . ."

"And hostesses."

"Well, as the lawyers say, the male embraces the female. But as I was saying before your despicably rude interruption, their technology is exactly the same as ours, except for time travel and its various offshoots. No microphone in the modern world could possibly pick up our voices out here, what with the distance and the background noise, so I think it's safe to talk."

"It's as safe as anywhere imaginable, but I wouldn't call it one hundred percent secure. Their medical technology is way ahead of anything we've got, and these new bodies of ours could very well be bugged."

"It's not *their* medical technology. That doctor wasn't one of the Smoothies. He was one of the Killers, like the military types around here. The Killers aren't running the show. They are strictly hirelings, mercenaries, if you will."

"Makes sense, except that if they're hiring medical and military help, why not espionage agents as well?"

"Okay, you're right, Tom, but I think it's still our best shot."

"Agreed. I gather that you want to compare notes," I said as we swam slowly farther out to sea.

"True. Tell me what you've learned."

"First let me tell you what I'm worried about. It's you. Ever since you got the Zongor-the-Hunk body, you have been acting very strangely. No way would the old Ian have taken the lead at a party, for example."

"That's because the old Ian was too afraid of getting accidentally stepped on. You can't imagine how intimidating it is to be half the size of the rest of the world. I tell you that it is very difficult to assert your individuality when you only come up to other people's armpits. You spend all of your time worrying about getting a stray elbow in your eye."

"You were about as tall as Julius Caesar, Napoleon Bonaparte and Genghis Khan. They all made out okay."

"Maybe so. But can you call any one of those guys socially adjusted?"

"Point taken. However, there was also the fact that all of a sudden, you were drinking. Totally out of character. I figure they messed with your brain."

"Not to the extent that I've noticed anything. But about the drinking, that *was* their doing. I've never objected to drinking, you know. In fact, I like the taste of many drinks. What I objected to was getting drunk. I don't want chemicals in control of my mind or body, and I especially don't want to look like you do when you've drunk yourself into a stupor and lie snoring in the corner of the kitchen. Anyway, I asked the doctor if he could do something to my metabolism so that I wouldn't be affected by the stuff and he said it was no sweat. I was just testing a new ability last night, that's all."

"That's some relief, even if I don't snore. Okay. Back to the strange people we find around us."

I filled him in on what I'd learned, mostly about the many odd ways these people used time travel to replace everything from plumbing to radios. That there were two separate groups of people here from quite separate cultures, and that the Smoothies, at least, considered this a very dangerous place to be.

"Interesting. I'd picked up most of that myself, but it's good that you confirm my findings. Did you know that all the Smoothies here are college graduates, mostly from

American universities? That they all went to our high schools, too, but not to our grade schools? That about half of them have advanced degrees? That they all have two to ten years experience in industry, business, government, or some such?"

"No, I guess I missed all that." I rolled over and swam a while on my back.

"It's nothing to be embarrassed about, Tom. It's just that you're properly ashamed of your lack of a decent, formal education, so you would feel awkward asking about that sort of thing. Another point. Have you noticed that it isn't actually necessary to do anything to cause a change to be made in the past? That it is sufficient to merely *intend* to do something?"

"I have, and it bothers me. What if you meant to do something, so what you meant to happen actually does, and then you never get around to doing it? What happens to causality?"

"I don't know, and what's more, I'm convinced that *they* don't know either! These people absolutely *never* violate causality. I swear that they would murder their own grandmothers before they even thought about doing it."

"The mind boggles. What if you *can't* do what you meant to do? What if you got killed?"

"Beats me, Tom. Maybe these Smoothies don't get killed. I suspect that they live lives that are so organized and preordained that accidents simply don't happen. Compared to what they are used to, our world would seem dangerous indeed to them."

A wave ducked me and I went from swimming on my back to a side stroke. I didn't like what I saw over Ian's shoulder.

"Speaking of which, can you tell a shark's fin from a porpoise's? Like that one over there, for instance?"

"No, but I think that a quick trip to shore is in order!" He started stroking for the distant shore at full speed.

"Be it so moved!" I yelled, but I don't think he heard me.

"Ah! Something just rubbed me and took off a bit of skin!"

"That sounds like a shark! Porpoises have smooth skins. Move, boy!"

"No, wait."

Ian pulled a pencil-sized brass cylinder from the chain around his neck. In the process, he broke the chain and lost his scapular medal.

"A flare," he said needlessly, as a bright red star flashed upwards.

I ducked under water to see what was happening. At first, all I could see were some dark shapes, fuzzy as things always are when you're under water without goggles. Then, suddenly, everything came into focus. My eyes had abilities they never had before, but what I saw left me no time to be thrilled about it. There were *dozens* of sharks down there!

"Ian, we're in big trouble! There's . . ."

"Don't worry! The cavalry, in the nick of time! ARRG!"

Ian was jerked under water, only to surface again thirty feet away. The water around him darkened with his blood.

Three choppers were converging on us.

I stroked hard towards Ian, but I never got to him.

An F-105 jet streaked by the choppers and strafed the water not twenty-five feet from us. The sound of those 20mm slugs was unbelievably loud. Half of a huge blue shark was blown out of the water right in front of me, while the impact of the shells hitting the water knocked the wind out of my lungs.

I was half stunned by the blast, the smoke, and the noise, but when a rope bumped my head, I grabbed for it.

I got my hand in a loop of rope and was yanked swiftly upwards. I saw Ian dangling from another rope above me, with blood pouring off of him. Half of his right foot was gone. Again.

The chopper's crewmen got us aboard promptly and attended to Ian. They had a tourniquet and a needle of painkiller all ready, of course.

Ian looked at his foot and shook his head. "Damn. Twice! You know, Tom, I don't think I want to go swimming back there any more."

Behind us, four jets were shooting up the sharks in the water that we'd just left. Vengeance, pest control, or maybe just target practice.

"Be it so moved. As to your foot, well, they fixed it before, so they can do it again, but it sure looks like somebody is trying to tell you something."

"Maybe, but I can't imagine what He's trying to say. Maybe it's just that I shouldn't have left my sword on the beach. Can you beat that, Tom? We wore those damn swords for two years without ever really needing them, then the one time when we really do, we both left them behind! Talk about terminal stupidity!"

"No, fortunately, it was only *near* terminal. Good idea about the flare, though. What ever prompted you to bring it along?"

"Ming Po gave it to me, and insisted that I wear it. She said I might need it."

"Figures. By the way, who won our bet?"

"I did, Tom. Thirty-eight. Do you want verification?"

"No, I trust you. Do you want another bet?"

"No, thanks. I've learned my lesson."

"This is good, my son. Wisdom becomes you."

The chopper set us down on top of the hospital, where a crew was waiting to whisk Ian downstairs. I stopped to thank the men in the chopper for saving our lives and to shake their hands.

"Just doing our jobs, sir."

"Doing them damn well, Captain LeFarge!" I said, reading the name tag on his uniform. "Is there anything that I can do for you guys?"

"Can't imagine what, sir, except, well, that sure is a fine sailboat you have in the harbor," the chopper pilot said.

"It's yours any time you want it. In fact, all three of them are there for you and all of your guests, and that goes double for whoever was flying that F-105."

"That was Captain Stepanski."

I would have talked with them longer but I spotted Barb coming across the helicopter pad towards us. She had my clothes with her. Would you believe that I had been standing there naked and hadn't even noticed the fact? I suddenly realized that everybody else around me had clothes on, and immediately I felt very strange. I even stepped back into the chopper to dress.

They were the same clothes I'd left on the beach, sword,

calculator and all, except for the belt buckle. It was like the old one, only it had a red button in the middle of it, on the inside.

"It's something that I should have given you when you first arrived, Tom, but I didn't know how you'd react to it. There's a transmitter in the buckle. We all carry one, in one form or another. If you press the red button, a distress signal is sent and help arrives immediately. Today's problem wouldn't have happened if you had had one on you."

She looked like she was feeling guilty about it all.

"Not your fault, little one. Anyway, I probably would have left it on the beach along with my sword. I just wasn't thinking."

"Then you must learn to think, Tom."

"Yes, mother. Let's go find Ian."

Ian was well, dressed, and waiting for us.

"Tom, I'm having some special gold medals struck in honor of our rescuers, and forming up a special order for them, the *Order of the Two Right Feet*. But for now, let's go scuba diving, only this time let's take our swords with us."

"Climbing right back on the horse that threw you, eh? Good! Let's do it!"

CHAPTER TWENTY-THREE
Playboys in the Sun

The next three weeks went by like that, only without further bloodshed. Hasenpfeffer kept on conferring with bureaucrats, and Ian and I kept on pretending that we were wealthy tourists. We went skydiving and hang gliding, steeplechasing and auto racing, surfing and skin diving. We took flying lessons, at first on ultralights, but in a week we talked the Air Force into letting us fly a pair of their jet fighters, although they wouldn't let us do it solo. I even got to be fairly good at piloting a helicopter.

Our evenings were full, too. There was no end of good entertainment available at Morrow. They had a full symphony orchestra and a world-class ballet company. There were Olympic-grade ice skaters, and gymnasts who were the best I'd ever seen anywhere. The word gymnasium means something like "the naked place," and that's the way they did it down there. I thought it was an improvement, on the girls anyway, being prejudiced.

There were bluegrass bands and rock groups, folk singers of a dozen descriptions, and every type of ethnic music imaginable. There was even a Grand Opera Company, although we let that one pass. It was all first-quality stuff, and we were surprised to discover that there were no professional entertainers on the island.

All sports, theater, and music of of any description was done by amateurs. It seems that every Smoothie could play a musical instrument, paint a beautiful picture, and dance like Nureyev. Incredible.

Barb turned out to be a classical ballet dancer. We went to see her perform, one night, and she was great, absolutely perfect. She was pleased with her performance, herself. She told me so, sitting there beside me, watching it.

"I did this a year ago, subjectively. If that bothers you, just think of it as a movie. I could watch a movie of myself, couldn't I?"

But what Ian noticed first was that while they were all outstanding at the performing arts, not one of them could do anything creative! There wasn't a composer or a novelist or a choreographer in the whole bunch. Apparently, when you started out knowing everything that you were going to do in your whole life, it just wasn't possible to think up anything new.

The Killers weren't nearly as talented. A few played musical instruments, but most didn't. Most of them could fix almost anything that was broken, but few were real engineers. If they used a paintbrush, it was likely to be four inches wide.

In fact, most of the Killers had distinctly low-brow tastes. There were a few waterfront dives set aside for them, traditional smoke-filled dens that the Smoothies ran, but weren't too happy about. There was even a go-go bar where the dancing girls were always new. This happened because the Smoothie women drew lots to see who had to do it next, and they figured that one night of it was enough for any girl. Apparently, it was part of their contract with the Killers.

The Bucket of Blood was my favorite low-life dive, since it took something about as far as it could go, and I've always been an extremist, on just about any subject. Ian wouldn't go there a second time, but I got to be a regular.

The place was part bar and part shooting gallery. They didn't throw darts, they threw *knives*. There was a pistol range in the hallway to the john, and it was unwise to walk out of the bathroom too quickly. There was a pit where you could take on another sportsman with bare knuckles, with quarterstaves, or with sword and shield in full medieval armor, if that was your pleasure. Or you could use anything else in the way of instruments of mayhem that might be mutually agreed on. The stock of strange weapons and armor filled a basement that was bigger than the drinking areas were above. They even practiced with javelins, out in back, and sometimes played a game involving teams that each consisted of a spear chucker and a *spear catcher!*

And yes, people did get hurt there, but they had a direct subway to the hospital so hardly anybody ever died. The only things phony about the place were the Smoothie waitresses, who were trying hard to act sleazy when their hearts really weren't in it.

The first night I was there, some of the guys talked me into giving them a demonstration of my temporal sword, and they all acted very impressed. But since they all used other aspects of time travel on a regular basis, I had a feeling that their interest was faked. I think.

Or maybe it was necessary for them to learn about the swords from me, even though they already knew about them, just so causality wasn't violated. It's as confusing as Hell.

Anyway, a few of the Killers were genuinely creative artists. Leftenant Fitzsimmons wrote some remarkably good poetry, and Captain Stepanski did something that might have been called carpentry, or wood carving, or sculpting, or cabinetry, or maybe none of the above, but he filled whole rooms with oddly shaped, joined, and polished pieces of wood that I found to be strangely disturbing at first. Yet somehow, after a few hours, it sort of grew on me, and I got to liking it. Whatever he was doing, it was certainly original.

The Smoothies were bothered by his stuff, too, but I found one of them carving, cutting, and sanding away, making an accurate copy of one of his pieces.

The Red Gate Inn was Ian's favorite home away from home. It was run by some sort of social club, "The Guardians of the Red Gate," and most of the members were Killers.

Yet fully half of the clientele were Smoothies. A big place, it had some two dozen fair-sized rooms, and each of them featured a different sort of entertainment, from chess through movies past bagpipers and on to a full dance band.

I liked the place second best.

The island had a large, beautiful Gothic cathedral, in the French style, that was pretty much unused. The islanders didn't seem to have much, if any, religion, and I personally never noticed any of the Killers being of that persuasion, either.

Ian occasionally went there on Sunday mornings, and he said that a Killer lay preacher spoke to perhaps two dozen people, most of them other Killers, in the huge building. He said that the few Smoothies who came had the look of sociologists. They took notes, photos, and recordings of the proceedings, but they didn't look very prayerful.

Even more odd was the fact that the island boasted a full-sized university, with housing and facilities for ten thousand students. Completely equipped, it stood there empty, totally devoid of both faculty and students. The only people around were a small maintenance crew, who had no idea why the place had been built. Central Maintenance had assigned the area to them to keep in shape, and that's all they knew. Its existence was a mystery, and either nobody knew why it was there, or everybody was somehow forbidden to talk about it.

My best guess was that it had been built by mistake, that the City Planning Committee had changed its mind about the desirability of a university, and had so informed the Committee for Personnel Allocation, but neither organization had gotten around to telling the Architectural Council or the Builders' Guild about the change in plans.

Ian wouldn't buy my explanation. His thoughts were that with complete foreknowledge, where those in the future could always tell those in the past about what went wrong, such mistakes were impossible.

My idea was that you couldn't know about a mistake until it had already been made, at which time you were presented with a *fait accompli*. At that point, you could tear the place down, but you couldn't make it "didn't happen." Once one of my three-dimensional strings was laid down on that sheet of four-dimensional paper, that was it. You shouldn't be able to modify it.

"Or maybe," I said, "the Committee for Telling the Past Where It Screwed Up forgot to tell the Committee for Listening to the Future about the screwup. Or maybe the Committee of the Second Part just forgot to listen in the first place."

Ian didn't like that one, either. He remained convinced that there was a purpose for everything.

For three weeks, Ian and I played in the sunshine. We were well entertained in the evenings, and our nights, well, our nights were generally spent simply wallowing in the ladies of our households, like a pair of contented pigs in their sties.

But wallow though I certainly did, still I found myself sleeping most comfortably when Barb was at my side. The best of the lot was at the beginning, and I began to think that my thoughts of that first morning were right after all. I really was going to have to marry that girl. But later, I told myself, once all the rest of these women ceased fighting their way into my bed.

More and more often, Ian and I found ourselves finding that it was more fun to tour through the factories and farms of the island, than to play with all of our expensive adult toys that were laid out for our pleasure.

Not that we were about to let Hasenpfeffer know that, since taking a formal tour of the place was the first thing he wanted us to do.

He was still coming by every morning, singing the same old song about how the two of us really ought to quit goofing off, and knuckle down to business, as he claimed he was doing.

Ian and I had already said everything we wanted to say about the matter, the first morning we'd been here, but Hasenpfeffer kept on harping on the same old strings.

I quit discussing the matter with him, by simply never paying the slightest attention to him when he was ranting and raving. The easiest way to do this was to pay more attention to the breakfast waitress. When he wouldn't stop, I wouldn't either. Flirting would give way to a kiss or two and some light-hearted petting, which would eventually escalate up to concentrated foreplay. On one occasion when we were breakfasting at Ian's, it went as far as actual copulation right there at the breakfast table before Hasenpfeffer gave up and left, muttering to himself.

That day, I'd just finished up, and sent the smiling, if a bit tousled, girl out for more coffee, when Ian said, "That was quite a show."

"Thank you, sir. Not to mention that it finally got rid of Hasenpfeffer."

"Not to mention that you did it with one of my girls."

"Oooh! Territoriality raises its ugly little head! What's it to be next, Ian? Putting your private brand on each chick in your household? Tell me, do you plan on burning a big 'I-bar-M' unto all their trim little left buttocks? Or do you figure on getting creative about it? Like maybe hitting a belly button here and a right tit there?"

"Knock it off! You know damn well that I'd never do any such thing! But we never agreed to go communal with our lady friends, and to just take one without permission is damned arrogant behavior."

"I had the girl's permission, or at least her tacit consent, since she was as enthusiastic about the whole thing as I was. What? Are you her father? Her brother? Her husband? Her owner, maybe? Whatever you are, you just sat there while the two of us got carried away a little. If you had a complaint, you should have aired it before the act took place!"

"Maybe so, but I still think that you owe me one."

"No, you owe me one. I transferred Ming Po over to you, and you never returned the favor."

"Would you take that maid in trade? She hasn't come up on my schedule yet, and now I don't think that I'd feel right about taking her."

"Fine. She's a good woman. But you're sure getting uppity in your old age. Remember those forty women you took home after the party? A third of them were from my staff, and an equal number came from Hasenpfeffer's. Did either of us complain about that? A few hundred of the girls went home with other guys after that party, and certainly no one objected to that! In fact, I have yet to meet a woman on this island who was either underaged, half-witted, or a virgin. These are all mature, experienced women who are in full command of their own lives. For some strange, yet-to-be explained reason, they all seem to want to enjoy our succulent bodies, in just exactly the same way that all the women back home didn't. It always has been the women who do the choosing, not us men. You're enough of a historian to know that! We couldn't do any getting when they weren't doing any giving, and now that they are, I say that we should take all we can get. Personally, I intend to continue doing just what I have been doing all along, and if that bothers you, tough!"

"Oh, just forget it."

"The hell I will." The waitress came back precisely on cue, the way everything happened around the island. "Mona, my fine girl, I think that you are not sufficiently appreciated around here, so if you're willing, how about coming to work for me? You could report to Barb as soon as you got through here. Does that sound good to you?"

"Why, yes, Tom! That's wonderful!"

"Good." Turning back to Ian, I said, "*Now* we can forget it."

I slapped Mona on the butt as she left, and said to Ian, "So. Do you want to talk about what's really bugging you?"

"No, Tom. Not just yet."

CHAPTER TWENTY-FOUR
Amoebas and Our Factory

I said, "Did you ever think about an amoeba?"

"Rarely. In fact, I've been known to go whole weeks at a time without doing such a thing, even after breakfast."

"Then consider that when times are good, an amoeba duplicates itself, reproduces by fission, about once every half an hour."

"And two little amoebas wiggle off. So?"

"Well, would you consider that act of fission to be the death of the animal?"

"Certainly not," Ian said.

"Then one can reasonably say that every amoeba now on earth has been around since the very first single-celled animal came into existence, perhaps a billion or more years ago. They are immortal."

"I suppose that that would follow, yes. Interesting."

"Now consider the fact that the total number of amoebas on earth doesn't change much. That there were about as many of them a half an hour ago as there are now. Therefore, on the average, one amoeba must die for each one that is created by fission. Think about what it must be like to be such an animal. There you are, billions of years old, knowing for the entire time that there is a fifty-fifty chance that you will be dead in the next half an hour," I said.

"Well, fortunately, as far as we know, they don't know, think, or remember anything, which together makes worrying pretty much impossible."

"True. But if they could, each and every one of the zillions of amoebas in the world would be perfectly justified in thinking of himself as being a fantastically *lucky* individual, having won that fifty-fifty bet with death almost every single half hour for billions of years."

"I see what you mean, Tom. Each one has seen—what?— maybe ten to the fifteenth of its clones die, while it has kept on living! Every one of them is so improbable that it couldn't possibly happen, yet there they all are in uncountable numbers, immortals waiting to die at any instant. Remarkable. Does this little parable of yours have any point?"

"No, but it sure makes you think, doesn't it? So what do you want to do today?"

"I don't know, except let's not try to be amoebas," Ian said. "I think that we have just about exhausted all of the possibilities before us. Nothing comes to mind. Can you think of anything interesting?"

"Well, okay, look. Neither one of us has ever tried anything really kinky. Now, I'll bet that if we looked for it, this palace of yours will turn out to have a dungeon, complete with cages full of nearly naked slave girls in leather, eager to taste our whips and nipple clamps, or perhaps your personal branding iron."

"You know, Tom, I think that you are probably right. I mean, I truly believe that our ladies really would volunteer for that sort of thing, if we asked them to do it. But the question is, would *you* actually ask them to do such a thing?"

"Well, no, I couldn't. Look, I wasn't being serious. The truth is, I feel very protective towards these girls. I don't think that I could hurt one of them if my life depended on it. But I at least I came up with something original. Now it's your turn to think up something for us to do today."

"Yeah. Well, we could always go flying again. We're still a long way from earning our pilots' licenses."

"True, but somehow, I don't feel like flying today. How about if we get some horses and ride down to the factory area? We could nose around there for a while, and maybe find something interesting."

"I think that's a dull, stupid idea, Tom, but it's the best one I've heard today, so let's act on it."

We walked out of Ian's Taj Mahal, to find two dozen of our ladies mounted and waiting for us, along with the two oversized horses we would ride, Diablo and Trigger. All the girls were in jodhpurs, riding boots, and nothing from the waist up except for some oversized sombreros.

As we mounted up, I said, "Ian, have you noticed that our staffs have been wearing less and less lately? I haven't asked them to do that. Is it your doing?"

"Not guilty. Ming Po, why are all of you wearing just jodhpurs?"

"It is vera painful to ride horse with no long pants on, Ian," she said in her best try at a Chinese accent.

"You know what I mean. Why are all of you women topless?"

"It is what we wished to not wear."

"Okay, then *why* did you wish to not wear shirts, or tops, or whatever you call what you're not wearing?"

"It is not me, of course, for I have receive far more than I deserve, but many other have notice that the less clothes a woman wear, the more likely she is to be noticed by two of you men."

"There you go, Tom. It's all just part of our infinite local sex appeal." Ian turned back to Ming Po, and said, "If you don't feel the need for attracting me any further, why are your breasts as bare as everyone else's?"

"Because when everyone does something, then it is the fashion. A woman must be in fashion, yes?"

Ian looked confused, trying to absorb that one.

I could see that he didn't want to say anything, so I said, "It's passing strange, ladies, but I for one will happily suspend my disbelief in the apparent universe, in return for the ample services rendered."

There was no point in having Ian be the only one who was confused.

It was an hour's ride to the industrial area. The distance was only about six miles as the crow flies, but except for maybe the subways, nothing went straight on our island. There weren't any real roads at all. But the ride was enjoyable, and the scenery was good, which was why we rode the horses in the first place.

By scenery, I mostly mean that the ladies on the whole island were wearing a lot less than they had been three weeks ago. Back in the States, that wouldn't have been a good thing, since most people (of both sexes) didn't have bodies that you really wanted to see stripped down. Down here, where everybody looked like they were between eighteen and thirty-five, and physical fitness freaks besides, well, it wasn't bad.

But *why* were they doing what they were doing? Was it just this business of it being the new fashion? Or were they *all* offering themselves to us? That was a scary thought. There were more than thirty thousand women on the island.

It is possible to have entirely too much of a good thing.

I suppose that touring factories might strike most people as a strange way to spend a day, but you have to understand that engineers *like* to do things like that, and we don't think that it's at all strange. It's kind of fun, actually, like visiting museums, but of the present, instead of the past. As a group, we technical types have an abiding fascination with finding out exactly how the world is made.

Because of trade secrets and insurance problems, this sort of sightseeing is difficult to do out in the real world without knowing someone on the inside who can get you an invitation. But on the island, well, we owned the place.

The factories were all big, blocky grey buildings, mostly without windows, and without any signs except for the large street numbers. Except that there weren't any street signs here, or streets either. On the other hand, in the industrial area, everything that wasn't a factory building was paved over. Maybe you could call those spaces streets, except that there still weren't any street signs. I was a long time finding out what they did about the mail.

For our tour, Ian picked a building at random, and we

just walked in, followed by most of our scantily clad entourage. As had happened before, the workers paid little heed to our ladies, but all of them turned and gawked at Ian and me. The plant manager bustled over, smiling and holding out his hand for me to shake.

It was an ordinary factory, making aluminum window frames. They were very well-built window frames, obviously meant to last a long time, but there was nothing very interesting about the operation, except that there didn't seem to be any need for all the windows that they were diligently making.

"I thought that all the buildings on the Island already had windows," Ian said.

"Well, well, I'm sure that they all do, sir," the manager stammered.

"I haven't seen any new construction going on. What are they going to do with all the windows you folks are making here?"

"I'm sure I don't know, sir. I don't get involved with sales, you see. I just make sure that the orders are filled."

"Then show me the orders."

"As you wish, sir, but they won't tell you much."

They didn't. The purchase orders were all on the same standard form, not on forms with the letterhead of the ordering company, as would be the usual case anywhere else I'd ever heard of.

They specified which standard catalog items were to be built and shipped by what time, and they mentioned the catalog prices but made no mention of any discounts expected, a thing unheard of in the real world.

And they specified precisely which numbered shipping containers should be filled, which seemed impossible. How would anybody, except maybe for the shipping company, know which container would be available for shipment at the time the order was filled? Oh, it could be done, I suppose, if you had that particular container especially set aside and waiting, but that would have been terribly inefficient, and why would anyone bother to do such a thing?

A little checking showed that each order exactly filled one container, which was weird, when you thought about it. How would the purchaser know exactly how they would be packed, what the exact external sizes of all the boxes were, so he could know how they would fit into a standard container?

Finally, there was no mention of who was doing the buying, when they had placed the order, nor when their check could be expected to arrive.

"A strange way to do business," I said to Ian as we left. "What kind of a building job is it that always takes exactly one full container of windows to complete the building being constructed? I mean, there would usually be a few windows more or less than what was needed."

"I know what you're trying to say, Tom, but it's just about the same story we got a few days ago at that electric motor shop."

We hit three more shops before noon: an elevator company, a plant that processed frozen fish, and a clothing factory. It was pretty much the same story at each of them: standardized orders for filling particular standardized containers of particular standardized products.

The crowd of girls with us mostly just kept quiet and followed us around, trying not to yawn. Why they came along, I don't know. We never asked to be followed around by a crowd.

Ian said it was a lot like the way the Roman Patricians figured that their status was defined by how many clients each of them had in his train.

"How about we hit a Syrian restaurant for lunch?" I said.

"I don't think I've ever tried Syrian food."

"It's a marvelous cuisine built around odd spices, flat bread, and dead animals. Their best dish is mostly raw lamb's meat. Don't worry. We'll make sure that they cook your kibbie, and that they don't throw in very much in the way of spices."

Ian agreed, and, of course, there was an Eastern Mediterranean restaurant just outside of the industrial area. They had a big table reserved and all set for our party of twenty-six. The place was much like the one that I had frequented back in Ann Arbor, except that here, the black-haired waitresses all wore abbreviated belly dancers' outfits, and

were as bare-breasted as most of their current female customers.

I ordered the lemon-and-rice soup, the fattoush salad, and
my kibbeh nayeh raw and spicy. And sherbert for desert.
All of my girls followed suit, which seemed perfectly sensible to me. After all, it was the best food in the house.

Since I'd warned him, Ian asked for his kibbeh cooked
and bland, but I was surprised when all twelve of his ladies
ordered the same thing that he did.

Dedication on that level amazed me, since the spiced
ground raw lamb's meat and cracked grain—floating in olive
oil and served with quartered raw onions on flat pita bread—
is one of the foods of the Gods! Cooked, it loses a lot. But
here they all were, missing out on one of life's better pleasures, just to suck up to their boss.

I tell you, it does a boss's heart good.

Ian and I chowed down with gusto, the way we'd been
doing since we'd first seen that doctor. These oversized,
muscular bodies burned a lot of fuel, and somehow they
did something with everything extra we packed in, because
my weight hadn't changed an ounce, despite the way I'd
been overeating for almost a month. After a lifetime of
starving myself, and gaining weight anyway, well, eating all
I wanted to was *almost* as wonderful as all the gorgeous
ladies and free sex.

Barb signed for the meal, and we left. Thinking about
it, I realized I hadn't touched any money since the day before
we got here.

That afternoon, we toured a shop that made wrought-iron
railings, and another one that made glassware. Metalworking was old hat for Ian and me, but neither of us had ever
had much to do with glass factories. The technology of making things out of sand heated into a gooey liquid was pretty
interesting, and we spent a few hours there. They sold many
of their consumer products to local shops, but mostly it was
the old story of filling orders that each filled a standard
container.

I was getting ready to knock off, and maybe find a good
bar, but Ian insisted on touring one more factory.

The building he selected was larger than any of the other

factories we'd visited, but when we went in, there was no one around. Curious, we wandered around what was mostly a big, general-purpose machine shop, equipped with some of the newest, biggest, and finest machinery available. Despite the high ceiling, the place obviously had a second floor. We were heading for the stairway in the corner when Ian stopped me, grabbing my left arm.

"Tom, that small stuff by the wall! That's *my* shop! I recognize my equipment!"

We went over there, and yeah, it was our property, neatly separated from the rest of the plant by a waist-high fence. I mean, there were temporal swords instead of cutting bits on all of the tools, and the saws were all just clamps that held the stock in place while letting the swords do their thing. Ian was going over each tool, making sure that nothing was missing or broken.

"I'll bet that my old electronics shop is upstairs," I said. "I'm going up there to find it."

Ian nodded, but was too busy to answer.

Half of the second floor was an engineering design shop, with dozens of drawing boards complete with parallel bars instead of the old T-squares, and even one of the new drafting machines that I'd heard about. There were a dozen glassed-in offices along the walls, with one posh and much larger office in the far corner. All of the furniture in it was oversized, and done in Danish Modern teak.

You entered the big office by first going through a nice secretary's office. The other door led to a hallway with a big restroom complete with an oversized shower, and a private elevator, so the big boss could sneak in (or out) without letting the peasants know about it.

I knew that the door at the end of the hallway had to lead to my office. It was as big as Ian's, only my furniture was American walnut, and heavily carved with a strange mixture of electronics symbols and naked ladies. I liked it.

My office had two more heavily carved doors, one that went to a secretary's room, and the other, at last, to my old electronics lab. The equipment was old and shabby, with dozens of cigar burns on the upper edges, but for the first time in weeks, I felt really at home.

As I walked in, I just automatically turned on my soldering iron and my battered but dependable Textronic 545 oscilloscope, the way every good tech does. I put my feet up on the solder-splattered workbench and debated with myself about brewing up a pot of Maxwell House coffee. I was home. I don't know how long I sat there before I got up and continued my tour.

Beyond my personal area, I found a big, well-equipped electronics shop, which took up about a third of the whole second floor. There was room there for maybe thirty guys to work with plenty of workbench space and more than decent elbow room.

Except that it was empty of people, and felt almost dead. It shouldn't be that way, I thought. It should be full of people, enjoying themselves while doing good, useful work.

I retraced my steps, and found Ian admiring his new office with his feet up on his new desk.

"You look contented, my young friend. I take it that you are pleased with the arrangements made for you."

"Indeed I am. I presume that your facilities are equally efficacious. They're down that hallway, I suppose?"

"Your presumption is indeed fortunate," I said, sitting down on the Danish Modern chair in front of his desk. It was a lot less uncomfortable than it looked.

"My own lab is in proper condition, and the larger lab for my nonexistent assistants is more than adequately appointed."

He waited a while before answering.

"Of course. Around this strange little island, how could it possibly be otherwise?"

I waited a bit as well. Ian was thinking of something, and on such occasions, it was best to give him plenty of time. I slowly realized that we were alone in his office. The girls had dropped back some time ago, although in fact I wasn't quite sure when they'd done that. In only three weeks, I had actually become blasé about beautiful women. Remarkable!

After a few more minutes of silence, I said, "My formerly runty friend, I perceive that you are about to eventually give vent to some momentous thought, or bold decision, or otherwise profound statement."

Several minutes later, he said, "Tom, let's go back to work."

"I had been thinking much the same thing. The only thing that deters me is that I don't know how to break the news to Hasenpfeffer."

"Yeah. It's going to be rough, telling him that we've decided to do things his way after all."

"I've really gotten used to his daily morning shouting solos. There is a certain harmony in the way his discordant rantings balance our beautiful surroundings, the way his ugly facial contortions offset the smiles of our lovely maidens," I said.

"True, all too true. Maybe we could just not tell him of our decision to somewhat modify our lifestyle. Look, the girls have always done exactly what we've asked of them. Do you think that they'd tell a few lies for us as well?"

"You know, I believe that they would, loving creatures that they are. I mean, they'd only have to say that we were out skin diving today, and cannot be disturbed, or flying the heavens with our newly invented gossamer wings, or raping, in friendly fashion, the eager peasant girls."

"Or developing our expertise at floral arrangements, basketry, and the proper placement of nipple clamps. Yes. You know, this could be fun, Tom."

"Considering his arrogance, profound rudeness and insufferable presumption, he certainly has it coming. Of course it will be fun."

"Then let's act on it. The girls have to be waiting out in engineering. Let's go explain our little joke to them."

"Seconded, and carried by unanimous vote. We're also going to have to tell them to call in a suitable workforce for us."

"Yeah. We'll have to work out our manning requirements. Well, let's get on it!"

CHAPTER TWENTY-FIVE
Ve Vas Only Filling Orders

The girls had all laughed and giggled at the thought of lying to Hasenpfeffer, so much so that I figured that he'd hear about it in a few hours. Just as well. The important thing was that he should know that his nagging morning lectures had had the opposite effect of what he had desired. They had slowed down our return to work.

My original thoughts had been that I would take on one or two techs or engineers, teach them what we had learned about time travel, and get them to work. That is to say, if I *had* to become a manager, I wanted to sort of ease myself into it, kind of the way you ease yourself into a cold lake, hoping that once you're over the shock, it won't really be so bad.

The first thing that Ian wanted to do was to convert all of his spanking-new machinery over from conventional cutting bits to temporal swords, which would require that my people build several hundred industrial swords for the purpose. This would mean that I had to provide several thousand electronic man-hours to satisfy him. I'd need a few more techs than I'd planned.

My stomach started grumbling, so I sent four girls out for a supply of cheese-and-anchovy pizzas and a few cases of beer, enough for everybody. Ian immediately counter-manded my order, such that his half of the crowd got cheese, ham, and green pepper pizzas. He's a nice guy, but he's got no taste.

The girls were back so fast that they must have passed themselves on the steps going both up and down, a fre-quent occurrence on this strange little island. Not that they'd ever let the two of us see how they did it.

Barb helped herself to a can of Budweiser and entered the discussion by saying that while Ian and I were tour-ing our new offices, she had found the accounting office of our new company. There she had found purchase orders from our small Army, our smaller Navy, and our tiny Air Force. An army colonel, who said that he had met me in that reception line, wanted swords, like the ones Ian and I wore on our belts, for all of his men, and could we please develop something larger along the same line to replace the small arms his men carried? Was anything possible for the artillery? This was followed by some simple sketches of a rapidly spinning artillery shell with six swords built into it.

"What he really wants is a circuit like the one we found in the first place in the Upper Peninsula. We could put one in an artillery shell, with some sort of adjustment on it to control the size of the hole. You could do that, couldn't you, Tom?"

"Yeah, but I don't know about building a circuit that could stand the shock of being shot out of a cannon," I said.

"It can be done," Ian assured me. "They make proxim-ity fuses for antiaircraft shells, don't they? Aren't they a sort of tiny radar rig?"

"I suppose that's true, if you wanted to stretch a few definitions. Prox switches are electronic, so the technology must exist somewhere. It might take me weeks to look it up, though."

"No, it won't," Barb said. "That's the sort of thing that you have secretaries and librarians for. You'll have the information you need in the morning, unless you need it sooner. But let me continue with these military purchase orders."

The Navy had similar requests for side arms, and requests

for quotes on the research and development required to design a heavy, turret-mounted weapon, for which they had incidentally left space in their existing deck turrets (sketch included).

And the Air Force had a similar bunch of requests, only with aerospace specifications, instead of the naval requirements for salt-spray tests.

Then there were orders from three local industrial supply houses, saying that they had heard of our swords, and couldn't something similar be used for cutting very hard materials? Assuming that this was so, they wanted to buy them, and they didn't care about the price.

Ian said, "So what it comes down to is, we've got a fistful of production orders on stuff we already know how to make. If we're going to fill them, we're going to have to put on a lot of people in a hurry, and back off on R and D for a while."

Somehow, we never wondered if we *should* fill those orders.

I said, "Nah. I can't see getting involved with the headaches of mass production. There are lots of shops with good managers on this island. They can make anything you want, so long as you don't expect them to get too creative. All we have to do is to design the products, build some prototypes, and test them. Then we can hand it all over to someone else."

"We'd lose a lot of the profits, that way, Tom."

"What profits? Don't you realize that all these things we're going to develop and make are going to be used inside of our own organization? That everything on this whole Island is *already* ours? How could we possibly make a profit off that? We'd be as likely to make a profit by taking in each other's laundry!"

"Huh. You've got a point there, only we will profit, in the increased equity of our holdings. But okay, we'll get an accountant to handle whatever accounting they need to do around here, and after that, we just won't worry about the money."

"Agreed. I haven't seen any money around here anyway. Everybody just seems to sign for stuff, however that works. So where are we?" I asked.

"Well, first, we have to take those items that have already been built and tested—the temporal swords, the machine-tool adaptations of them, and the bomb—and document them so that other people can build them."

"But before we can do that, we'll need people who know as much as we do about this whole thing. I hate to say it, Ian, but I think that you and I will have to become school-teachers for a few weeks."

"What a depressing thought."

"True. And we have to make sure that we have some real schoolteachers in that first class, or we'll have to keep on teaching the damn thing ourselves. Are you taking notes, Barb?"

That last was for Ian's benefit, since I knew that Barb either had an eidetic memory or a built-in tape recorder. She not only didn't sleep, she never forgot anything, either. Sexy, too. I definitely had to marry that girl, one of these days.

Barb said yes, and that if we going to teach a class, something that we did not enjoy doing, it would make sense to teach as large a class as possible. A large auditorium was available, and did we want to have the first class in the morning?

Ian said, "No. We'll need at least a day to get our class notes together. We'll start on Thursday morning, at eight. Ming Po, set it up. Two four-hour sessions a day. In the meantime, I found Hasenpfeffer's old sword in one of the drawers in my toolbox downstairs. Shirley, get it over to some engineering outfit or other, and have them make formal drawings of all the parts, since we built them from rough sketches. Warn them not to turn the thing on until after they've been to our lectures. Can you think of anything else that needs doing before we get going on the class notes, Tom?"

"Nothing except to say 'What you mean "we," White Man?' You're the one with all that wonderful formal education. You do the notes, and I'll kibitz."

"Deal. But you have to give half of the talks, and we're both going to have to be up on the stage together. For moral support, you know, and making sure that we get it right."

"Stage, huh? We're going to have *that* big an audience?"

Barb said, "The hall I had in mind seats three thousand, Tom. If we use anything smaller, the V.I.P.s will crowd out all of the engineers and technicians."

"V.I.P.s!" Ian shouted, "We don't need no stinking V.I.P.s! We're doing this to educate our workforce, not to entertain the brass!"

"Anyway, if the brass comes, Hasenpfeffer will come too, and that'll blow away our joke on him," I said. "No. No V.I.P.s. If they come, I won't."

"Tom, you must remember that most of the people on this island have been waiting for this lecture series for most of their lives. You can't expect them to pass up seeing it in person. No manager is going to send his subordinates, when he himself has to sit home."

My mind had stuck on that "waiting all their lives" line, and hadn't gotten much farther.

"Then how are we going to insure that Hasenpfeffer doesn't show up?" Ian said.

"I don't think that we can, sir. But what we could do is see to it that he doesn't come for two more weeks, subjectively, while your joke is being played on him. Then he can double back for the lecture series," Barb said.

"I don't think that I could have thought of that," Ian said. "How are you going to keep him from knowing about our talks, if everybody on the whole damn island is so eager to go to them? He's sure to hear about it."

"It will not be difficult, sir. We will simply let everyone on 'the whole damn island' in on the joke being played."

"You know, Ian, I think they could do that. It couldn't happen in our world, of course, but we're not in Michigan any more. Look at the way these people have stonewalled us on a dozen different topics."

"Yeah. And I'll bet that most of that stonewalling was at Hasenpfeffer's instigation. Nailing him back is only fair. Our little joke is getting better all the time."

I said, "Barb, let's go back to that line about how everybody here has been waiting all their lives to hear our lecture series. What's so new about what we're going to say? I mean, you people use time machines as often as the average American uses a telephone. It can't be any big deal to you."

"Tom, we use temporal products in *exactly* the same way as the average person uses a telephone. We know how to use them, but we don't know how they work. None of us do!"

"Well, some of you must. I mean, you have repairmen, don't you?"

"Of course. But the repairmen don't do anything but replace defective sealed boxes with functioning sealed boxes that are shipped to us from the future. Those boxes are tamper-proof, and naturally, we're all dying to find out what's inside of them."

I spent a long while mulling that one over.

CHAPTER TWENTY-SIX
Baboons and the Ladies

We spent a day and two nights getting our class notes together.

When Hasenpfeffer came by at eight in the morning, one of the girls told him that we were out hunting for a narwhal in our scuba rigs. We needed it so we could make ourselves some drinking cups out of the tusk; that would protect us against the ever-present danger of being poisoned.

By noon, we had decided that the best way to explain the whole thing was to do it as a narrative, explaining our actions and thoughts in chronological order. We still didn't know enough about the theory to present it in a more logical fashion.

I dug out those same notes to write this book, years later, but like I said, it's best to tell the whole thing in the order in which it all happened.

It's a curious thing, but it simply never occurred to us at the time that we should worry about security. After two and a half years of keeping absolutely mum to outsiders about our project, here we were, not just telling someone about it, but about to give a definitive lecture series to three thousand people! And it never occurred to us to wonder about this, any more than we gave any thought as to whether we should equip a tiny island nation with a new set of very powerful weapons.

There was something about the Smoothies that just naturally made you want to trust them. I *liked* the Killers, but I *trusted* the Smoothies.

They had placed some orders for the weapons, and it seemed only natural at the time to fill those orders without question.

The lecture series went off without a hitch, even though it was the first experience either of us had with public speaking. There was a huge crowd of carefully groomed people there to watch us, and it was strange to think that a few hours before, every one of them had been sitting naked in a bathtub, in ablutions to prepare for the momentous event of hearing Ian and me talk.

I vaguely recognized a few people in the crowd, and Hasenpfeffer was there in the first row, cheering us on. But mostly it was a sea of eager, but anonymous, faces. As best as I could tell, all of them were Smoothies, with not a Killer in the bunch.

I expected to be nervous, at first anyway, but I never was, and neither was Ian.

Somewhere along the line, we'd both picked up a lot of confidence that neither of us had had when we'd first gotten to Morrow.

"I saw a thing on television, once, about baboons," Ian said over a boomba of beer, the evening after our first lecture. "The baboon leaders are actually chosen by the females of the pack, or tribe, or whatever you call it with baboons."

"Let's see. Wolves come in packs, whales come in pods, quails have coveys, geese have gaggles, and owls belong to parliaments. Nobody ever told me about baboons," I said.

"No shit? Parliaments? Are you sure?"

"Would I lie?"

"Constantly. Sometimes, I think that you only tell the truth to set me up for your next lie. But I remember now. Baboons belong to troops. The females of the troop select the next leader by giving him all the sex he wants. When this happens, he grows bigger, sleeker, and more powerful. The females groom him a lot, too, and kowtow to him, and before long, he's strutting and swaggering like a medieval Japanese warlord. All this adds up to making him boss. The other males knuckle under or get beaten up."

"Are you saying that that's what's been happening to us? That all these women decided to make us the leaders, so we became the leaders?"

"I wouldn't swear as to who made the decision, but it's a fair bet that the women are playing a prominent part in carrying it out. Or at least, it's a good working theory, Tom. I observe that we're both remarkably well groomed, and have been since we first arrived here. Back in Michigan, I never saw you even clean your fingernails, let alone trim, buff, and polish them to the state of perfection that they presently enjoy."

"You still won't see me do it. Every morning, a half dozen naked women spend an hour or more on me, scrubbing me down with all of us in a huge tub, then doing my fingernails and my toenails, trimming my hair and my beard and the hair in my ears. They even brush my teeth with a rig like a dentist uses. I get rubbed down and polished up like you wouldn't believe, except that your crowd of groveling ladies obviously does the same thing to you."

"True. I resisted it at first. It seemed like an invasion of my person, and sinfully decadent, besides, to have someone else do such private things to my body. But I guess that I'm a decadent bastard at heart, because I don't resist it any more. The fact is that I enjoy the hell out of it."

"Yeah, so do I. So much so that I was too embarrassed to talk about it, before this. All this cleanliness, it just doesn't seem . . . manly, somehow."

"By the standards of a lower-class working man, it isn't, and that's the subculture that both of us were brought up in. A working slob can't help having dirty fingernails, but I've gotten a good look at a General Motors vice president, or two, and let me tell you, those guys are well groomed. Not as well groomed as we are, though," Ian said.

"I'll bet that they have their women, too. I mean, besides a wife, often a second 'trophy' wife at that, they all have a secretary or two, a female chauffeur, a few housemaids, and as often as not a few girlfriends. Nothing like what we have, but you see the pattern. The cluster of women around each of them helps make him a leader of men."

"You're cutting with a sword, Tom. Then there's our clothes. Back in Michigan, you had exactly three pairs of pants that fit you, and you never wore one pair, but saved it in case you ever got a hot date. Furthermore, you were almost as poorly equipped when it came to shirts, socks, and underwear."

"No fair! Do you realize that a man my size had to pay three or four times as much for clothes as you little critters did? And every time you gain a few pounds, you have to go out and buy a whole new set! I tell you that a fat boy ends up spending five times as much for clothes as you Munchkins do, and then we still look shabby despite the expense!"

"Hey, lighten up, Tom! I'm not passing out blame. I'm explaining a situation. There's no denying that you are dressing well now. Even though we've never worn anything but casual clothes around here, I'll bet it cost at least three thousand dollars, cash money American, to dress each one of us today."

"Yeah. It was weeks before I found out that the only shirts I have that aren't made out of silk are made of Egyptian cotton, and every one of them is hand stitched," I said. "I've got three sports jackets in my closet made of vicuna."

"Shades of the Great Inca. Not only did he keep more women than the three of us put together, he was the only person in his entire empire permitted to wear that precious cloth, vicuna, and he never wore the same garment twice. The Queen of England can't keep a harem, but she follows the custom of never being seen twice in the same dress to this day. What's more, I'll bet that our ladies will never let either of us wear a single article of clothing for more than one day, even though buttons are hand carved out of jade where they aren't made of precious jewels, or cast in twenty-two-carat gold. What's more, we'll be doing it for the rest of our lives, and radiating the purest mana in the process."

"Then what's going to happen to all of those clothes?

Nobody could wear them secondhand. Who could fit into clothes big enough to fit us?" I asked.

"Who wears Queen Elizabeth's old clothes? I don't know, either. My advice is don't worry about it."

"It seems so damned wasteful."

"Oh, it is. But it's all part of the program of making the two of us into great world leaders. In fact, it's probably one of the cheapest parts."

"Make that the three of us, since Hasenpfeffer's doubtless getting the same treatment."

"Probably. But at least *he* knows what the hell is going on!" Ian said.

CHAPTER TWENTY-SEVEN
The Loss of a Friend

We soon found that speaking in public for four hours a day, each, was a lot, so we cut the lectures down to a ten to noon matinee and a two to four afternoon show.

It was yet another revelation. Up until then, I'd thought that the twenty-hour workweeks that most teachers did was sheer government worker-style featherbedding, but four hours a day whacked us out, even though we didn't have to correct any papers or tests.

All the while, Hasenpfeffer was coming by every morning, and being handed each day a more improbable tale of our whereabouts than he got the day before. Sometimes it took Ian and me hours each evening to come up with a new story.

We survived the course, and at the end of the last class, we were each presented with bound galley proofs of a book that somebody had put together from our lectures. This meant that we each had to read the whole thing over one more time, making corrections as needed, and making sure that what this guy had thought he heard was what we had meant to say.

Hasenpfeffer came around to the small party we threw after the last class at my place, celebrating the end of school.

It was good to see him again, but somehow, he wasn't the same.

"Dammit! He was *polite* to me! To both of us! What the hell is the matter with him, being *polite* to his best friends?" Ian said, after Jim had "made an appearance" and departed.

"Maybe we've been a little rough on him."

"How so? I mean, we took a vacation when he didn't want to, and when he got to yelling and screaming about it, we ignored him. That seems normal enough. It's not like we made *him* take a vacation, when he didn't want to take one. Then, we played a trivial joke on him, where for a few weeks, while we were giving those lectures, which was what he wanted us to do in the first place, we made him think that we were still goofing off. Is that anything to get *polite* about?"

"But Ian, to play that joke, we had to organize the entire population of Morrow into a conspiracy to tell lies to him."

"We didn't organize anything. We just gave your house-keeper permission to go ahead and do as she suggested. These islanders are the most organizing people in the known universe, I swear it."

"Well, we did make up all those stories our girls told him, but the big thing is that he'd just spent a month or so, working his buns off, being diplomatic to everybody, while we'd gone around being fornicating playboys. And then, for his reward for being such a good boy, everybody in the whole country ganged up on him to play a joke. Think about it. Every single person on the island sided with us. Everybody he saw for two weeks knew what he didn't, and was laughing at him for it."

"So? Is that so much different from what's been happening to the two of us? Everybody in Morrow knows what's going on but you and me, Tom, but do we go around being *polite* to old friends? Of course not!"

"Yeah, but we've still got each other. Hasenpfeffer is out there all alone."

"All alone with nobody but his hundred and fifty naked ladies and a few thousand sundry others."

"Yeah, but those people aren't *friends*. It makes me feel rotten. We gotta do something about it."

❂   ❂   ❂

It had taken us eleven days of lecturing to explain everything we knew, or thought we knew, about time travel. After
that, we took a long weekend off, and vowed to start work,
bright and surly, on Monday morning. Which implied having
some manpower there to help us out.

Talking it over on Friday morning, Ian and I decided that
we didn't know anything about hiring people. Neither one
of us had ever had any significant number of people working
for us. Barb and Ming Po, on the other hand, were both
experienced managers, so we gave them the job of hiring
the men who would work at our factory.

Oh, Ian and I had sketched up the job description for each
slot to be filled, but after that we let the girls handle
everything, including salaries.

Having thus performed my managerial duties by delegating
them all away, I spent the rest of the day curled up with
a book and a bottle, in that little room Ian had found on
our first morning in Morrow. Sometimes, a man just has
to get away from the rest of the world for a while.

Early on Saturday morning, I walked over to Hasenpfeffer's
glass-and-chrome monstrosity, to talk to him and see about
mending some fences. A man has very few true friends in
this world, and you can't just let them slip away.

It was actually the first time that I had ever been inside
of Hasenpfeffer's house, after living next to it for over a
month. Most of the time, the three of us had met over at
my place, I suppose because the Gothic styling there was
more conducive to comfortable living than Ian's rather
austere Taj Mahal, or Hasenpfeffer's sterile, modernistic glass-
and-metal thing.

Aside from the splashy but ugly architecture, which had
all sorts of elevated platforms and walkways cutting at
different levels through huge volumes of space, the first
difference I noticed was the women.

At my place, the girls were naked or nearly so, and openly
friendly, cheerful, and energetic. Thinking about it, this was
doubtless a response to my lecherous but essentially egali-
tarian personality.

Ian's women wore a bit more clothing than mine did, but

they all were still pretending to be Chinese slave girls, with a lot of bowing, kneeling, and groveling. The Oriental kow-towing had happened at first due to one of my suggestions, when I was trying to get Ian over a hump, but the fact that Jim hadn't changed it probably said something about the man. But then again, maybe all it said was that he had simply never noticed it. For all his education, intelligence, and perception, that boy could be godawful dense, sometimes.

The ladies of Hasenpfeffer's harem were all fully and properly dressed, generally in shades of grey, black, and white. Many of them wore well-fitted ladies' business suits. They all acted as if they were at a major corporate head-quarters, with stiff, artificial smiles and quick, efficient motions.

In his glassed-in breakfast room, atop a clear, round glass tower which faced the city and not the sea, Hasenpfeffer, too, was in a three-piece business suit. It was carefully tailored of grey wool with a thin, dark blue pinstriping. He wore a silk Rep tie, a diamond tie tack, and had a gold chain running from a twenty-carat diamond watch fob to a priceless antique gold watch.

All this to meet an old friend on a Saturday morning.

He met me in a friendly enough manner, but with a touch of formality, too.

We had breakfast, served by a quiet woman with her hair in a bun, wearing a black-and-white English maid's outfit. She had long sleeves, her top was buttoned up to her throat, and the hem of her black skirt almost brushed the floor.

Jim's old casual manner and slovenly ways were entirely gone. He was as well groomed as Ian and I had become, but it was more than that. He was now a corporate executive, a consummate politician, a manipulator of people. Even his table manners were now disgustingly impeccable.

Between the power suit, Hasenpfeffer's formal politeness, and his new table manners, I felt as intimidated as all hell, despite the fact that I was still twice his size.

Nonetheless, I pushed onward.

I started out by apologizing for the joke we'd pulled on him, but before I had even finished, he brushed it off as not worth bothering with.

"Think nothing of it, Tom. It was nothing but a youthful prank, and a harmlessly amusing one at that."

"Youthful prank? Jim, we are the same age. You are just as youthful as I am."

"Of course we are. Did I tell you what an outstanding job you and Ian did with that lecture series? It was remarkably well done. Why, even I got the feeling that I understood this time travel business myself, by the time the two of you were finished. Everyone has been talking about it, of course, even those who could only catch it on television."

"I never realized that we were being televised. I never saw any cameras. Where were they?"

"I haven't the foggiest notion. The people here have their ways, of course. I'm told that the two of you will be starting back to work on Monday."

"Yes."

"That is excellent. You will be accomplishing great things there in your new facility, never doubt it for a moment."

I tried repeatedly to get him talking about the strange things Ian and I had discovered about the island, about the two distinct types of people who lived here, and the strange cultural quirks that each type had, but I might as well have been talking to a college advisor, for all the personal interest he took in it. He acted as if I was a small child, telling him about all the things that had happened today in the third grade.

"Yes, the two of you are far too intelligent and observant for anything to remain a mystery for long. It's one of the many things that I have always admired about you both."

"Jim, this is Tom. Do you remember? Your friend Tom?"

"Of course I remember. We've always been the best of friends, and we always will be!"

"Yeah."

I left, feeling saddened and sickened. One of my two best friends was gone. Grown up, maybe, while I was just abandoned like Puff the Magic Dragon. The fact was that, in a few weeks, Jim Hasenpfeffer had somehow grown *old*.

Ian was waiting for me when I got back.

"So how is he, Tom?"

"Uh, I'd rather not say, just now. Why don't you visit

him tomorrow, before church. After that, we can compare notes."

But on Sunday afternoon, Ian was looking as sad as I felt.

Hasenpfeffer, at least the old Hasenpfeffer that we knew, respected, and, yes, loved . . . was gone.

CHAPTER TWENTY-EIGHT
Womaning the Factory

Ian and I showed up promptly at eight on Monday morning, ready to meet our new workmen and get them all to work.

We'd taken the subway there, and rather than ride our private elevator up to our offices, we went up the public elevators to the main plant floor. Barb had said that our new people would be there at seven, to start getting things squared away, so we expected to find dozens of men working diligently. The doors opened and we got our first shock of the day.

We didn't have any manpower in our facility.

We had woman power. Working around the huge lathes, mills, and overhead cranes, there was not a single male human being. All of the machinists, skilled tradesmen, and repairmen were beautiful young women.

Now, back in Michigan, I'd heard all of the women's complaints about inequalities in the workplace, and for the most part, I sympathized with them. I mean, if somebody was working next to me, doing exactly the same job that I was doing, but was bringing home twice what I was being paid, I wouldn't be happy. And if I was making half what that person was, just because of a little biological accident, I'd be downright pissed! If I was being passed up for promotions, if the good work I'd done was not being credited, and I was simply not being taken seriously for the same non-reason, I'd be ready to revolt! If I was the last to be hired, and the first to be laid off, and given all the shit jobs in between, I'd be about ready to head up into the hills with a rifle and a bandolier of ammo to rectify the situation!

But I was never on the receiving end of that sort of discrimination, so my feelings were all sort of on an intellectual level.

On that spring morning in 1971, I couldn't help having a gut feeling that there was something inherently *wrong* when you see a small, pretty woman in coveralls loading a three-ton casting into the jaws of a lathe with an eight-foot throw. Yes, she was using an overhead crane to do it with, just as any man would have had to do, but there still seemed to be a wrongness about it all.

I could see that Ian was even more upset about the whole thing than I was, so I steered him back into the elevator, even though half the women in the shop had seen us come out. We went down to the subway level, crossed over to our private elevator, and then went up to the hallway between our offices.

I made a right and went to my office, and Ian followed me. I sat behind my desk and pressed the button marked "secretary."

An attractive woman came in immediately, smiled and said, "Yes, sir?"

Which was just fine, except that she was dressed in the fashion which most of the women at my mansion had adopted. That is to say, in nothing but a pair of skimpy shoes. I mean, yes, she was pretty, she was well built, and nakedness looked very nice on her, but was this lack of clothing conducive to a proper working environment?

Ignoring the clothing issue for the moment, I said, "Please have my majordomo, Barbara, and Ian's Ming Po come here immediately."

"Yes, sir."

As she left, Ian said, "From the looks of things, we don't have a workforce, here. We've got another fucking harem!"

Before I could answer, and explain that fucking was what harems were for, our housekeepers came in. This sort of instantaneous appearance had happened so often that I had come to expect it.

"Okay, Barb. *Why* did the two of you decide to 'man' this installation entirely with women?"

"But Tom, we made no such decision!"

"Well, somebody sure as hell did!" Ian said, "There isn't one single male human being out there. Are you claiming that not one single qualified man applied for a job here?"

"No sir, many qualified men applied for work here."

"Then why in hell didn't any of them get hired?"

"Because in all cases, women outbid them for the jobs available, sir."

I said, "Hold it. What do you mean, 'bid for the jobs'? Just how do you go about filling a working position around here?"

"When a position becomes open, the prospective employer posts a notice at the Employment Office, describing the job, the maximum salary that might be paid, and the qualifications necessary to fill it. The Employment Office screens job applicants, and decides who is qualified for what. Job applicants read these postings, offer to fill those that they are qualified for, and bid a minimum salary that they would be willing to work for. In our case, all of the women who applied were willing to work for less than the equally qualified men were."

"That seems like a reasonable enough system, but why were the women willing to work so much cheaper than the men?"

"A person expects many forms of remuneration from their job. Besides money, one wants a chance for personal growth and advancement, a pleasant working environment, interesting, challenging work, and . . . other things."

"*Other things?*" I asked.

"Tom, she's saying that the women were willing to work cheap because by working here, they'll get a chance to meet us," Ian said. "Those who didn't get jobs at our palaces figured that this was their next best shot."

"The mind boggles. Barb, how much are the girls out there

working for? For that matter, what do the women at the palaces make? How much are you, yourself, paid?"

"Minimum wage, Tom. We're all earning the least that the regulations permit."

"Uh huh. And how does this minimum wage compare with the usual salary paid to an experienced skilled tradesman or a good engineer?"

"Usually, such people would make about six times minimum wage."

"And all of these women are willing to work for starvation wages, just to get a chance to meet Ian and me?"

"Yes, Tom. Although no one is starving, of course. All wages include food, housing, and medical insurance."

Ian said, "Barb, I want you and Ming Po to go out and wait for a while. Tom and I need to talk."

When they were gone, Ian continued, "Tom, there are a lot of things that I don't like about all this. One of them is that I don't like wearing solid gold buttons on my silk shirt while I'm paying people scab wages."

"Agreed. As of now, everybody who works for us gets paid as much as they would earn if we weren't here."

"No way. We've got to make it retroactive to the date of hiring. And all of Hasenpfeffer's women have to be included in the deal."

"Seconded and so moved. Next, what do we do about the hundred or so women out there? If we replace them with men, what do we do with them? Do we fire them because they're women?"

"Tom, how could we do that and still be honorable men? No, we have to keep those women who have already been hired, and try to treat them just like men."

"But they don't *want* to be treated like men. They offered to work for nearly nothing because they expected us to treat them like women! Are you going to decline the services of the next attractive woman who works her way into your bed? Could any normal man turn down that many decent, gorgeous women? I mean, there are these biological imperatives that a man doesn't have all that much to say about!"

"And there are some religious reasons for doing the same

thing. God's very first commandment was for us to be fruitful, to divide and multiply. But what I meant was that in the work situation, we should try to be as fair as possible, and keep our private, sexual lives separate from our working lives."

"Good luck. I'll tell you what I'm minded to do. Aside from Barb, I've followed Hasenpfeffer's original suggestion, and put all the girls at my place on a schedule. They each have their occasional night in bed with me, and if it happens that they get laid before then, they forfeit their next turn, until all the others have caught up."

"Yeah. I've done about the same, Tom."

"So, I'm going to tell Barb to put all the women who work for me on the same schedule. Those who want to, that is. If the girls at the palace don't like it, well, they can blame the whole thing on Barb."

"Okay. Then I'll do the same. But it's not going to be easy, treating the girl you slept with last night like she's just another worker."

"It's a rough life, Ian, but England expects every man to do his duty."

"I've got a better idea. How about if the girls who work here for you belong to my harem, and your new harem girls all work for me? After that, we try not to mess around with each other's girls, and pillow talk about work isn't allowed."

"A good thought! We'll act on it."

We called in Barb and Ming Po, and explained the new program to them. I was surprised that they weren't happier about the way we'd just octupled their salaries, retroactively to last month, but they weren't. It was like they actually didn't care, one way or the other.

"One other thing," I said. "Dress codes. Anybody working down below on the plant floor is expected to wear proper safety equipment, including safety glasses, steel-tipped shoes, hard hats, and sturdy garments that completely cover them. People who might occasionally need to go down there shall wear safety glasses and hard hats, at least, when they do. And people who work in an office environment must wear shoes and other clothing that completely covers at least their torsos. Anyone dressing too sexy, in our opinion, will be sent home to change. This last is for our benefit, not yours. All play and no work doesn't get the job done."

"Yes, Tom."

"Good. Now, let's go meet the managers you've hired for us."

As we walked past my new secretary, I noticed that she was now properly dressed in a skirt, blouse, and sensible shoes.

I decided right off that I would stay on a last-name basis with the women who worked for me, in an attempt at keeping our relationships as businesslike as possible.

I told them that they could call me "sir."

I later noticed Ian doing the same thing, I suppose for the same reason. Something had to be done, since every woman in the shop was as beautiful as any of the women at the palaces. By ordinary American standards, they were all knockouts, each as beautiful as any leading lady that Alfred Hitchcock ever put on the screen.

I soon met the five key people I had working for me. There was Kowalski, my secretary. She was one of those extremely organized people who always knows where everything and everybody is. She had two other secretaries subordinate to her.

Preston was primarily a mathematician, although she got her Ph.D. in physics. I figured that we'd be working together a lot. My math has always been a bit poor, and up until then, I'd had to ask Ian's help when I needed to get into anything beyond calculus. Preston didn't have a solid place in our table of organization, and her name just appeared near the top boxed in with dotted lines that didn't connect to anyone else, not even me. She had no subordinates, but she was sort of on call to anybody who needed theoretical or mathematical help.

As the weeks went by, she got to spending much of her time at the coffee bar located between engineering and the technicians' assembly area. When I asked her about that, she said that some people were hesitant about "bothering" her in her office, and she worked better on an informal basis, anyway. Later, she admitted that the biggest reason for her new location was the two hundred pounds of Jamaica Blue

Mountain coffee I had donated to the bar from my palace's stores.

DuBoise was a solid electrical engineer, and she was competent and disciplined, if not overly imaginative. She did everything exactly "by the book," and kept copious notes on everything she did. Everyone was encouraged to keep a journal of the work they did, but DuBoise filled them up at the rate of three a month. She headed a team consisting of eight other engineers, two computer programmers, and nine draftsmen.

O'Mally was an engineer, too, but of a more practical bent than DuBoise. Like me, she was of the "make it work, and fill out the paperwork later, if you have time" school of thought. She headed up a group of eighteen assorted technicians.

Brown was in charge of purchasing and liaison work with both suppliers and customers. We didn't have a sales or marketing group, since for the foreseeable future, all of our products would be used internally within our own greater company, KMH Industries, which consisted of the entire City of Morrow, and much else, besides. Not that we planned to let any of our temporal devices get off the island.

We didn't have an advertising group, either, since everybody on the island already knew about us.

The accounting people reported to Brown, as well, as did the janitors, for a total of twenty-one subordinates. It seemed like an odd bag, but those functions had been grouped under her, and her under me, primarily to make my group the same size as Ian's group.

Which meant that when Barb had set it up, she was thinking more about a balanced harem than of an efficient workforce.

Someday, I'm going to get ahead of that little girl.

Still and all, it was a day well spent. The six of us had gotten ourselves shaken down, then, in a four-hour meeting with Ian and his people, we had figured out what we had to do, and had a schedule that said when we were going to do what.

⚙   ⚙   ⚙

Late that night, after four new ladies (two mechanical engineers, a draftsman, and a machinist with a Ph.D.—a woman also strange in other ways) had come and gone, I was alone in bed with Barb.

"Barb, you're awake, aren't you?" I said quietly.

"Of course, Tom."

"I should have asked you sooner, but is it inconvenient for you to lie beside me every night while I sleep? I mean, what with you not sleeping and all. Doesn't it get boring?"

"Not really. My mind doesn't need to sleep, but my body still needs to rest, and if I wasn't by your side, I'd be lying down somewhere else, alone. I like being by you, and it gives me time to think."

"What do you think about?"

"Nothing important, usually. I go over the events of the day, and sort of mull them over. I plan the things that I'll be doing tomorrow. That sort of thing."

"Hmm. Well, if I ever do something that you are not happy with, be sure and tell me about it, won't you? I want you to be happy. You've become a very important person to me."

"Thank you, Tom."

"There's another thing that I've been meaning to ask you about. It's been more than a month since that first night we spent together. At the time, you said that there was a sixty-percent chance that that you had conceived a child."

"Yes?"

"Well, have you? I mean, a month has gone by and all. Did you miss a period? Are you pregnant?"

"I am not pregnant now, Tom."

"Oh. Okay. To be honest, I don't know if I'm disappointed or relieved. I mean, you'd be a wonderful mother and all, but at the same time, having a child is such a huge responsibility, and I'm not sure whether or not I'm ready for it. I doubt if any man is, until after it happens to him."

"Not being a man, I couldn't advise you on that one, Tom."

"True. And what's more, I find it *good* that you are not a man. Good night, Barb."

"Good night, Tom."

I fell asleep kicking myself, because once more I had lost my nerve. I had not asked this perfect little woman to marry me.

CHAPTER TWENTY-NINE
Different Kinds of Power

Tuesday being a day when Ian's people cooked our breakfast, I met him there in his Taj Mahal.

"Tom, I've been playing with an idea for a logo for our new company. M and K Temporal Engineering."

Ian was already working on his usual stack of Famo Buckwheat pancakes with Vermont maple syrup. I'd gotten into the habit of asking to be surprised with something completely different each morning, and on that particular morning I was served some poached herring, English style, the waitress said. It seemed like a strange thing to eat for breakfast, but it didn't taste all that bad.

"Catchy name, and I guess it's your turn to get your name first."

"My thought exactly. Look at these."

I looked over the sketches he had done up, and the truth was, they were better than the usual stuff you see plastered over the world's billboards.

"They look good to me. Better, in fact, than anything I could come up with. Only, I've got this one nagging question."

My breakfast waitress was wearing a loose top of some very flexible material that covered her to American television standards when she was vertical, but fell away and exposed her torso completely when she bent over to serve me. Thus, she was able to satisfy both Ian's desire for decorum and my own desire for lechery at the same time. I thought it an interesting engineering solution to what was essentially a social problem.

Ian said, "Yeah?"

"Do we really have a company?"

"Well, of course we've got a bloody company! Just where did you think you spent all day yesterday, you silly twit?"

"I'm not sure, but I just might have been at the Temporal Engineering Research and Development Group, a loyal subsidiary of KMH Industries. A separate name and logo sort of implies that we're an independent company, doesn't it? But when all of the money, personnel, and other useful things are coming, I suppose, from KMH, just how independent can we be?"

"Your comments are rude, Tom, your demeanor is insufferable, and your timing is abominable. I was sitting here, bothering no one, and having a lot of fun, designing these logos. I was halfway there to designing us a corporate blazer for everyone to wear at company functions, where we could all sing the company song together. Then you came along with your unwanted existence and fucked it all up, for no other reason than that you stupidly picked this precise moment to have a rare flash of common sense. Furthermore, you insisted on performing your vandalism before I'd even had a chance to finish breakfast. You know, I think that if we ever discover who your parents were, they will turn out to be brothers."

With that, he crumpled his sketches up and threw them over his shoulder. An obsequious blond maid, kneeling behind him in proper Oriental fashion, picked up the papers and put them out of view, probably to hand them down to her grandkids, thinking, *"Actual drawings by the hand of the great Ian McTavish himself! Yes, I knew him back then. . . ."*

"Well, look Ian, if you have these inner needs to get creative in that direction, why don't you do something about a new KMH logo? We could probably use a company song or two, even if you can't carry a tune in a backpack or hold a note with a pair of Vise-Grips, and even if I've never once seen you wearing a blazer, company or otherwise. Together, we own two-thirds of KMH, don't we? We thus constitute a solid majority on the board of directors, so we can do anything we want with it. We can even make it sing, if we want to!"

"Apparent power and actual power are often two different things, my poorly educated young friend. As to the Board of Directors of KMH Corporation, or whatever it's called, are you really positive that it has one? Have you ever seen it? And is this weird little Magic Fairyland of an island really owned by KMH?"

"I have been under those distinct impressions."

"Yes, but are you resolute in your convictions?"

"It beats me. Tell you what. This morning, instead of going to work, let's march over to Hasenpfeffer's Monstrosity and demand our rightful places on the Corporate Board of Directors!"

"I suppose that we could do such a thing, but what would it prove? The locals hereabouts have the wealth and organization to sit the two of us at some huge, impressive table, surround us with dozens of equally impressive suits filled with distinguished-looking people inside them, and then bore the shit out of us with accounting figures until we give up and go back to work at our own little company. And for all we know, everything we see could be just another Potemkin Village."

"A *what* Village?"

"Okay. Time for another history lesson. Catherine the Great of Russia wanted to lead an enlightened nation into the Western World. She wanted all of her peasants to live well, and to be happy and healthy. She even gave orders to that effect. Her nobles wouldn't go along with it, figuring it would be too expensive, and what was the point of being a nobleman if you couldn't make a few peasants miserable now and then? They said that it would take all of the fun out of being boss, but Catherine was adamant. She actually did the unprecedented thing of going out into the country and seeing for herself that her orders were being carried out. To forestall any unpleasantries, one of her ministers, Potemkin, arranged that everywhere she went, she was met by healthy, happy peasants, living in nice, clean peasant villages with healthy cows and happier chickens. The problem was that Catherine went in for long road trips, and Potemkin couldn't afford to build that many idyllic villages, let alone hire enough actors to play all the peasants. So, as an economy measure, he only built a few villages, and had them moved, buildings, happy peasants, fat cows, contented chickens and all, such that as the Empress of All the Russias progressed through her country, she always had nice villages to look at. Of course, they were always the *same* villages, with the *same* peasants and the *same* cows, but who looks all that closely at a cow, a chicken, or a peasant, anyway."

"Good God! And this really happened?"

"Oh, yes. And similar things go on all over the world to this day. So just because they call you the Emperor, the Chairman of the Board, or whatever, don't go believing that you are really in power."

"Well, if we're not, then who is?"

"A good question. If you study any one of the thousands of books on conspiracy theories that have been filling the world's bookshelves for the last three hundred years at least, you can convince yourself that some secret group of sinister individuals actually rules the world."

"But you don't believe this?"

"Oh, I do believe it, but only on Thursdays and Saturdays. The rest of the time, I think that the world is so complicated, confused, and corrupted that there isn't anybody smart enough to comprehend the whole of it, let alone manage the place. I don't think that *anybody* is actually in charge. Sometimes, I think, perhaps, the world is like a huge but poorly constructed ship, designed by a madman, and crewed by billions of people who refuse to talk to each other. It is a ship with a hundred propellers all pointing in different directions, and with a thousand rudders each with a thousand helmsmen, and every one of them is trying to get her safely into a different port."

"Ian, sometimes you paint some *very* strange pictures inside my head. Come on, let's go to work."

❁   ❁   ❁

With plenty of competent help around, things progressed quickly at work.

The temporal product that was farthest along, the temporal sword, was properly documented in a few days. That is to say, we had good engineering drawings of every part, complete assembly instructions written up and printed, and a user's manual had been sent to the typesetters.

One of Kowalski's people, Downing, turned out to be a first-class technical writer. Incredibly, she was able to write instructions that even I could read and understand. We promoted Downing up to her own office, and had Kowalski find herself a new receptionist.

Our vendors started delivering civilian versions of the sword within the month, and our military got its first temporal side arms a few weeks after that.

The "Temporal Bomb" was next off the line. This was little more than a toughened-up version of the device we had originally found in that woods in Northern Michigan, years before. It had been adjusted so that the sliced-up bits returned to our normal three dimensions within a few microseconds, rather than the hours that original circuit had taken, so that the noise and implosion effects didn't have time to take place. There was just a loud *click*, and everything within the designated sphere crumbled into very small pieces. Since the bits and pieces didn't have time to fall down into each other, and air didn't have time to get in, the bits reemerged in a fairly good vacuum, and there wasn't much radiation at all.

Designed to fit in the nose cone of one of the small, two-inch mortars our infantry carried, it had a calibration ring on it that let the operator adjust the radius of destruction from three feet to three hundred feet. Thus, the same weapon could be used to take out anything from a machine-gun nest to a football stadium, at the operator's discretion. Destruction within the radius was absolute, with everything within the sphere just suddenly collapsing into thin shards. Destruction outside that volume was nonexistent.

Our little army was very impressed with it.

We also made the Army a hand grenade version of the bomb, with a smaller radius of destruction for operator safety.

The Navy promptly requested their own version of the hand grenade for use as a depth charge. The main difference between the two was that the navy version left a hard vacuum behind for several seconds. In the atmosphere, a near miss by a temporal bomb caused little or no serious damage, but under water, at a depth of a few hundred feet, the implosion of seawater into a large sphere of hard vacuum was remarkably deadly.

Shortly thereafter, the Air Force got its version of the bomb, designed to fit on the nose of a small, two-inch Mighty Mouse rocket. It was made to aerospace specifications, of course, rather than to army specs. That is to say, it wasn't dust proof, mud proof, or rust proof, but it could function at two hundred thousand feet. Since pilots are customarily farther away from the damage they do than foot soldiers are, the radius of destruction was adjustable out to five hundred feet.

When fitted with some stabilizing fins, the same nose cone could be used as a gravity bomb. Once somebody else had designed, built, and installed suitable bomb racks, they gave one of our fighter jets the firepower of a World War II-style thousand-plane raid.

And, of course, the Navy got its own version, to its own specifications, for its rockets, guns, and depth charges.

Near the end of the Temporal Bomb Project, Ian and I heard one of my engineers referring to the thing as a "Time Bomb." I chuckled at the pun, but Ian's reaction was a bit different.

"Tom, have you ever heard a Smoothie tell a joke before?"

"Well, no, thinking about it."

"Right. That's because in order to be funny, a joke has to be new. But these people already know everything that is going to happen to them. They don't tell jokes, ordinarily. Making up a new joke, even a silly pun, is an act of creation, something that these people are not capable of. Yet here we just heard one of them use a pun. Did one of them think it up herself?"

"I don't know, but I can find out. Who knows? Maybe there's hope for these people yet."

I put one of the junior assistant secretaries on it. I asked her to trace the joke back, going from person to person, asking each of them when and where they had first heard the pun, and who they had heard it from.

The result was disappointing. It turned out that the originator of the pun was none other than my friend, Leftenant Fitzsimmons, and he wasn't a Smoothie at all.

Farther down the pipeline were bigger, longer-ranged versions of the temporal sword, with ranges of up to fifty miles. They replaced our infantry rifle, various army machine guns, aircraft machine guns, and so on. All told, there were twenty-three distinct versions of these high-powered swords. Or perhaps I should say *relatively* high-powered, since the biggest of them only consumed nine and a half watts.

The military gadget that I was proudest of was the "Escape Harness." This thing looked like a pair of epaulets with arm loops under them, and straps across the back and chest. The chest strap had an arming button, a kill button, and a control knob on it.

The tops of the epaulets functioned like the beam of a temporal sword, except that instead of focusing the temporal distortion into a fine thread, the entire tops of the shoulder boards became active. Air rushed into the things at almost supersonic speeds, to be sent a short while into the future. The undersides of the epaulets were still at normal atmospheric pressure, of course, but the tops felt only a hard vacuum. Since the total active area was about forty square inches, the escape harness had an effective lift of up to six hundred pounds at sea level.

This was plenty of power to pull a pilot right up out of his aircraft at four Gs, eliminating the need for the ejection seat as well as for the parachute.

The real beauty of the gadget was that here was something that you could wear on a regular basis, that weighed less than a pound, but that would let you fly! It was easy enough to steer. You just moved your legs one way or the other. The knob on your chest controlled the amount of active area, and thus the lift.

It was noisy as all hell, but the pilot's crash helmet protected his ears well enough.

I thought of these things as being strictly for emergency use, since the amount of air they sucked out of the present was pretty huge. They seemed wasteful to me, but Preston proved that there was no danger of dropping the world's air pressure by any measurable amount, even if everyone in the world used one all the time. The air being sent elsewhen wasn't being wasted, after all. It all came back in a short while.

The night after the first successful test, I was having a drink at the Bucket of Blood with Captain Stepanski, an Air Force pilot. I showed him one of the prototype escape harnesses my people had made up, to get his opinion of it, and, well, to show off.

He was impressed, and after a few more beers, we went outside so he could try it out, ear plugs and some helmets having been scrounged out of the sporting equipment in the basement.

Naturally, a crowd followed us, so I had to explain all over again, loudly this time, what it was and how it operated.

Captain Stepanski was a natural pilot, with a plane or without one. In moments, he had it all figured out, and he was doing aerial acrobatics in minutes. Once he came down, he said, "Beautiful, sir, but it needs a bit of work. At one point there, the suction of these plates on my shoulders nearly snapped my neck! I think you will have to equip these things with something like the fishbowl helmets they put on space suits, to protect the pilot."

And that's the way the escape harness looked when it went into production.

Leftenant Fitzsimmons of the Navy stepped up, and thinking that he wanted to try his hand at flying, Stepanski gave him the harness.

Instead of putting it on, the leftenant proceeded to fasten the harness to a log, a big section of tree trunk that was set upright in the concrete, and normally used as a target for knife, sword, and javelin throwing.

"What are you doing?" I asked him.

"Just trying out an idea I had. I won't be but a minute, sir."

Soon, the harness was howling away, trying without success to pull the log over sideways. Fitzsimmons walked back ten paces, borrowed a snub-nosed .44 Magnum pistol from one of his men, and proceeded to put all six slugs into the harness!

I was at first shocked, that someone would dare to try to destroy my latest brainchild, but I quickly saw that it was unharmed. The leftenant went over and shut off the screaming harness, so we could talk again.

"What? You missed all six times?" I said.

"No, sir, I could hardly miss at that distance. All six rounds went into the active area of your new device. Where they went after that is something that you'll have to tell me about. You have more than an escape device or a flying machine here, sir. You have also invented the world's first perfect armor!"

After Ian watched the first test of the escape harness, he went back to his desk to sketch up an "Emergency Power Generator." This had an area at the back that was essentially the same as the top of an epaulet, creating a hard vacuum. Before getting there, inflowing air was ducted over an air turbine, which was in turn connected to a standard electrical generator.

It worked the first time we tried it out. As we watched it run, I gave Ian a copy of Prescott's writeup on air consumption, and told Ian that he had to take the word "Emergency" out of the name of the thing. There was no need to burn coal, oil, or any other fossil fuel at all, ever again.

CHAPTER THIRTY
The Second Law

"You know, Tom, I think that I was happier back when the Second Law of Thermodynamics still worked."

For whatever reason, our best conversations always seemed to take place at the breakfast table. It was my table this time, and my serving wenches.

"Nah. You were just brainwashed like almost everybody else in the technical world, except for me, of course, and Einstein and Bronowski."

Over the months, my ladies had refined their appearance to coincide with what they had apparently decided was what attracted me the most. This involved very long hair, usually straight, but curly if it was naturally so. They wore high-heeled shoes, and were otherwise naked, devoid even of body hair. They had light suntans, without strap marks. Facial makeup was minimal to nonexistent, but more and more lately I was beginning to notice a slight glistening of body oil.

"I'd heard that Einstein had doubts about the Second Law. Who's Bronowski?" Ian asked.

"A mathematician. He did a show called 'The Ascent of Man.' You should watch more television."

"I shudder at the thought."

"Elitist."

It's odd to think that my tastes had been so carefully studied, by so many and for so long, with this as the result. I would have thought that I would have preferred more variety, but there it was. And the high-heeled shoes! For many years, I had ridiculed women for wearing them despite the pain they caused and the damage they did to the feet.

Now, they were apparently being worn by hundreds of women because I found them to be attractive!

On reflection, I begin to think that what attracts me is not the shoes *per se*, but the way a woman walks when she's wearing them.

"You never believed in the Second Law?"

"Of course not. Among other things, it implies that the universe as a whole is constantly getting more random. But if you'll look around you, you'll see that everything around us is *not* getting more random. It is obviously getting more ordered."

"Bullshit!" Ian said, which of course meant "give me some concrete examples of that."

"You will observe that I am currently eating breakfast. My body, in the meantime, is turning this breakfast into me. I am obviously a more ordered system than this breakfast is. Q.E.D. Thus it is demonstrated."

The waitresses and other ladies who constantly surrounded us were used to our continual arguments by now. I sometimes wonder if they kept recordings of them, so as to write up an academic paper or two, once their present charade was over.

"Your body is turning a small portion of your breakfast into you, which person, incidentally, never struck me as being particularly orderly. Most of your breakfast will be converted into carbon dioxide, water vapor, and one of your major constituents, shit. These are blatantly disorderly, not to say downright messy on occasion, being end products, as it were. On the average, your strange eating habits have decreased the order of the universe, not increased it."

"I deny all of the above. One glance at the evolution of life on the Earth should convince you that the universe strives upward, not downward," I said.

"If things are becoming more orderly in one place, they must be becoming less orderly in another. Earth is only one tiny bit of the universe."

"You are suggesting that on Mars, perhaps, there are animals that are evolving into beings that are slower, stupider, and in general less well adapted? Earth is the only part of the universe that we humans know much about, so I suggest that we confine our arguments to its surface. Or, if we *must* go into outer space, I point out that current cosmological theory has the universe starting out containing little else but hydrogen, the simplest of the elements. After a few eons of star formation, stellar burning of various sorts, and the occasional supernova, the other elements were gradually built up. Notice again, please, that we went from a disorderly cloud of hydrogen to very complicated constructions like stars, planets, the hundred-odd higher elements, and me. I stands my ground."

"In the short run, you might be right, but eventually the universe will consist of nothing but lukewarm iron, the element lowest on the energy curve."

"In the short run? I'm talking about fifteen to twenty billion years, here! And as to the famous heat death of the universe which you allude to, just how do you adjust, rectify, and justify this Second Law of yours with the Law of the Conservation of Mass and Energy? If matter is convertible into energy, why can't I take some of that lukewarm iron of yours and turn it into energy to warm up the rest of it?"

"I confess that I have occasionally been troubled over that one."

"As well you should be. In truth, your rational self was rebelling against the brainwashing it had received in that overvalued university that you are so proud of having attended. They did a similar job on you young earnest types with their Laws of Momentum. They gave you a formula that said that the mass of a bullet times the speed of that bullet must equal the mass of the cannon that fired it times the speed of the cannon moving backwards. Thus, for hundreds of years, every properly educated young engineer knew, *absolutely knew*, that you couldn't possibly shoot a gun without that gun having a kick. It wasn't until World

War Two (when someone was given the problem of making the plume of smoke from a tank's gun a little less obvious to the enemy), that the gas brake was invented. This was nothing but a bent piece of metal with a hole in it that fit over the muzzle and let the bullet go on its way, while sending some of the propelling gasses out sideways. It sent a smaller plume of smoke into the sky, but the tankers soon noticed that their guns kicked less than they had before. Notice that the improvement was made by accident, or at least for the wrong reasons, because every engineer in the world had been blinded by a formula."

"MV is still equal to MV," Ian said. "Gun designers were just a little bit slow in noticing that you not only shot the bullet out the end of the gun, you shot the propelling gasses out as well. If you send those gasses out sideways, or better yet backwards, you can significantly reduce the total kick of the weapon, and even eliminate it in some cases. So what?"

"So what? So a whole lot! Had that advance been available around the turn of the century, in the days of the All Big Gun navies, it would have made possible a ship the size of a destroyer that could have taken out a battleship! It could have shifted the basis of world power! But it wasn't done because the engineers of the world had been blinded by their own neat little formulas."

"And what does that have to do with the Second Law of Thermodynamics?"

"A lot," I said. "People were as brainwashed by the Laws of Momentum as they currently are by the Second Law, when all along, there were ways around them both."

"Oh, I suppose you're right, of course. After all, in a few months, we'll be powering the whole damn island with a system of generators that the Second Law says can't work. I just feel less comfortable without a new law to replace it with," Ian said.

"You're just asking for a new set of horse blinders. 'Beyond this point you must not see, much less think about.' "

"Knock it off. A man needs guidelines."

"Well then, have one of mine. If it works, it's not only good engineering, it's also good science as well."

"I guess I'll have to take that as a working hypothesis."

"Hey. It's all that John Roebling, Isambard Kingdom Brunel, Major Armstrong, and all the rest of the great old engineers had to go on, and they did good work. Finish your breakfast, and we'll go do some of it ourselves."

I was sketching up plans for an entirely new type of military aircraft, based on what we had learned from the escape harness.

It would be a small craft, consisting mainly of a chair inside of a hermetically sealed geodesic ball for the pilot, a big temporal sword, and a bomb rack. This was entirely surrounded by plates that acted like the shoulder boards on the harness. They provided the lift necessary to keep the thing in the air, and they provided all the forward acceleration, braking, and maneuvering required. Also, they could be selectively switched on by a proximity sensor such that if anything solid came quickly at the craft, a bullet, for example, it would be atomized and sent safely into the future. When this happened, a plate opposite was also switched on, to keep the plane from accelerating in the direction of the bullet.

Streamlining? We didn't need no stinking streamlining! Who needs streamlining when you can make all the air in front of you disappear? At that point, you are moving into a hard vacuum, no matter what your altitude is!

This puppy would be small, inexpensive, fast, maneuverable, and indestructible.

"Tom, it looks great to me, and in time I think we should build one of them. But we have been working on military equipment for months now, and we haven't ever asked ourselves *why* we are doing what we are doing. What do we need with all these super weapons, anyway? Nobody is bothering us."

"Well, we had all those purchase orders . . ."

"Orders? Those weren't *orders*! Those were written requests sent to us by our subordinates!"

"Huh . . . Okay, I suppose you could think of them that way. But you were the one who was so adamant about filling the damn things."

"So I was. I just hadn't thought it all out, back then. We wanted to get our own company going, and here suddenly were all these military orders. Back home, military orders are government orders, and patriotism, the law, and common sense say 'fill them.' I hadn't figured out yet that when you own the whole country, all that changes."

"I suppose it does. But I still don't see where we've done anything wrong. Having a more effective military never hurt any country, even if we do own it, ourselves. The military contracts have given all of our people here some valuable experience with temporal equipment, and all of it has been relatively simple stuff, and free of the kind of brain-busting headaches our earlier work entailed. The fact is that it has been fun, and you enjoyed it as much as I did."

"True. There's something about making weapons that sort of grabs a man's attention. It's probably something in us left over from the Paleolithic Age, when man first learned that a pointed stick and a sharp rock are handy things to have around."

"Right, only it's not something just 'left over.' It's something we still need today. The fact is that the need for protection has been around long enough for it to be hard wired into our systems, just as all of the rest of our basic needs are. Food, air, water, shelter, procreation, and protection. Without them, we can't continue to exist. So, you feel pain when they are lacking and pleasure when they are satisfied. Evolution, or God, if you prefer, set it up so that we do what we have to do, without much recourse to our brains, which are still expensive, unproven, and newfangled gadgets, anyway."

"Save it for a breakfast-table discussion, Tom. Only, why do you call the brain expensive?"

"The brain makes extremely high energy demands on the body. The average person, sitting quietly, has an energy requirement of around a hundred watts. About thirty-five of those watts are consumed by two pounds of brain tissue. The other hundred and fifty odd pounds burns only sixty-five watts. It's no big thing in our overfed civilized world, but we humans evolved out in the wilds, where the big problem is usually getting enough to eat. Back then, it was a very significant expense."

"Huh. Is human energy output really that much higher than that of all the other animals?"

"Without your clothes, you're naked, aren't you? We are just about the only land mammal that has had to dispense with the thermal insulation and the physical protection that a coat of fur gives you. There has to be a reason for that."

"It's a thought. But back to what I was saying, Tom, I think that we've been spending too much of our effort on military weapons, and none at all on making the time machine work. I mean, isn't that what we were originally planning to do? Build a time machine?"

"Yeah, but right now we've got thirty projects going, in every stage of development. There'd be hell to pay if we stopped them all dead."

"I'm not saying that we should do that. I'm just saying that we should stop, or at least slow down, initiating new military projects, and start spending more real effort on our main job."

"I'll agree with that in principle, but I still want to see this little fighter plane of mine fly," I said.

"Fine, so put a small crew on it, if you want, even though you can't properly call it a 'plane,' since it doesn't use one to fly with."

"Picky, picky, picky."

So we went back to what we were doing in Michigan, before we were so pleasantly interrupted.

First, we had to map out the lateral displacement drifts in the local area. These turned out to have almost nothing in common with those we saw around Ann Arbor, except that the drift was still lateral, and the test object reappeared with the same gravitational potential as when it left. And the drift still tracked with the sidereal day.

But where it went and in which direction was now totally different. In one sense the project was set back a long ways.

On the other hand, we now had the incredible mass-production facilities of the entire island behind us, so we could send out a lot more canisters, collecting a lot more data points, and without having to worry about salvaging anything.

Also, the canisters we now used were far more sophisticated, and better engineered. Before, we were just kluging up something workable, using existing components to get the job done in a hurry. Now, we had teams of technical people who were, I have to admit, better engineers than we were.

Beyond all doubt, the women we had working for us were extremely competent, superbly trained, and very hard working.

What they weren't was creative.

It was hard to understand. You'd give a team of them a project, and they'd come back with something that was exactly what you had in mind in the first place. It was almost like magic, seeing your own thoughts rationally developed into something that was truly beautiful, in the esoterically technical sense of the word. And it was flattering as well. Because of this, it took a while before Ian and I realized that they weren't putting anything of *themselves* into their projects.

There weren't any of those little jumps of insight that a good engineer can't help but put into his work, often to the frustration of his managers. After we realized what was happening, Ian and I each got to checking the work of the other's teams, trying to find small creative things that would improve the final products.

Being inventive young men, we found a lot of places where we could make small improvements. These suggestions were always sent back to the team that did the original engineering, for incorporation into the design, or for rejection, if they could prove that we had screwed up, which we occasionally did.

It was the reactions of our engineers to what was really managerial meddling that confounded us. We expected them to feel anger and frustration, since we were messing with the children of their brains, and people are usually just as protective of those as they are of the children of their bodies.

Instead, they acted as if they were awestruck at our brilliance! At first, we both took that as mere sucking up to the boss, especially since our smiling subordinates were all women who badly wanted to get into our beds, and there to make full use of our willing bodies. Remember that these chicks were willing to eat *cooked* kibbie, if that's what their boss was eating. But as the months went by, we became convinced that their feelings of admiration were actually genuine.

These intelligent, competent people were absolutely incapable of doing anything creative, and were truly amazed to see anyone else doing anything new!

Once our original incredulity wore off, our feelings became a bit more mixed. Mostly, they became sadness and anger.

"Dammit!" Ian said one day as we were discussing the situation. "This sick little culture has got to be all Hasen-pfeffer's doing, and that bastard has one *hell* of a lot to answer for!"

CHAPTER THIRTY-ONE
I'm Getting Married!

After living on the island of San Sebastian for six months, it was time to have a talk with Barbara. I mean, I talked with her every day, since I slept with her every night, but she was as slippery as Hasenpfeffer when it came to side-stepping things she didn't want to discuss. The only thing for it was to hit it straight on.

"Barb, we have been making love almost every night for six months, and you are still not pregnant. You once told me that you wanted to have children by me, so what's the problem? Is it me? Should I have a doctor check out my sperm count, or something?"

"No, Tom. Stop worrying and go to sleep. You are perfectly healthy. Your last doctor's visit proved that."

"Your flat tummy suggests otherwise. Do *you* have some sort of problem?"

"No. I, too, am healthy. Roll over and I'll rub your back."

"Not right now. I want to know why there isn't anybody on this island who's pregnant. I don't know about Hasenpfeffer, but Ian and I have been doing yeoman service around here for half a year, nailing well over five hundred women regularly, and I have yet to see one bulging belly on the whole damn island! Explain to me how this is possible."

211

"James Hasenpfeffer has been as sexually active as you and Ian have."

"That's nice, but it wasn't my question."

"We get pregnant, and we have children, but you can't expect us to have them *here*!"

"So what's wrong with here? This island is a beautiful place. It's idyllic, by any normal standard!"

"By your standards, maybe, Tom. Not by ours."

"Then tell me one single thing that's wrong with it."

"It's as I just said, Tom, our standards differ."

"That's a bullshit answer and you know it."

"Tom, can't you see that it's *dangerous* here?"

"Dangerous? The only thing that I've seen around here that's dangerous are the sharks at the north end of the island, and your people never swim there."

"Tom, this whole twentieth-century world that you've lived in all your life is dangerous! There are dozens of countries out there with atomic bombs! There are hundreds of people dying every minute of horrible diseases! There are psychotics and gangsters and whole governments that kill people without any more reason than just for the fun of it! Why, the future history of this time isn't even known! Anything could happen! We are willing to be here, for a while, because it is necessary, but you can hardly expect us to subject our precious children to all of this danger!"

"So you're telling me that your people are so cowardly that you can't face each new day without being afraid of it?"

"I face each day here with some fear, yes. But I do what must be done, and if you want to call that cowardly, then do so. You and your people face the future by pretending that all the bad things that could happen won't happen *to you*. You lie to yourselves, and then you live within your lies, until you are no longer aware of the harm that can come to you and those that you care for. Our standards differ, Tom. By mine, it is *your* people who are the cowards!"

"Huh . . . Well, there is a lot of truth in what you just said. But let's go back to my original question. Have I ever gotten you pregnant?"

"Tom, enough has been said tonight. Go to sleep."

"I'm not sleepy, you can't sleep, and I want some answers. Do I have a child?"

"You have hundreds of children, Tom. I'll get you the exact number in the morning."

Well, that's as heavy a kick in the head as a normal man ever gets, but I still wasn't satisfied.

"Nice of you to tell me about it. Did you think that I didn't care? I mean, most of those had to be by women that I didn't love, but I certainly cared for them. You, however, are a very special case. I love you, and I want a straight answer. Have we made any children together? Answer me."

"Yes, Tom, we have. We have created three lovely sons together. When last I saw them, they were six years old. And since you were about to ask it, no, I have never had another child by any other man."

If I knew anything at all about this woman, I knew that she had doubtless been with each of the kids for every minute of their time since they were born. And if she had last seen her kids when they were six, that meant that she knew that I had not see them during that time. As I understood the laws of causality, this all meant that my children's early childhood was forever lost to me.

It is not nice to rob a man of his children's childhood. Nonetheless, I resolved to keep my cool.

"I didn't know that I was going to ask about your previous love life, but thank you, anyway. So, the boys are all six, now? You'd better explain that."

"Very well. Among my people, it is customary for a woman to live with each of her babies alone for the child's first year. After that, she usually brings all of her children together, and raises them as an equal age group from their first to their fifteenth year, when they all go out on their own."

"Then from what you've said, you are what? Nine years older now than when I first met you?"

"It's just over ten years, Tom."

"You don't look any older."

"My people don't age as quickly as your people do."

"Then how old are you now?"

"Please, Tom, leave a girl with *some* secrets."

"All right. I guess it doesn't really matter. You said that your people let your kids go pretty early. Fifteen seems a bit young, but I guess in your sort of world, nobody can possibly get hurt. But mostly, I'm more than a little angry about this business of my children being six years old, and I've never even seen them yet. They're my kids, too, you know, and I should have some say-so as to how they're brought up!"

"In your culture, perhaps. Not in mine. Even in yours, a woman must be married to a man before he has any rights over her or her offspring."

"Which gets us to something that I have been wanting to do since the first morning I spent on this weird little island. Barb, I want to marry you. You are the most beautiful woman I've ever met, the smartest, and the most desirable. I love you. Will you marry me? Please, say yes."

"But there are so many things that we have to discuss first. . . ."

"Then we'll discuss them, but later. For right now, answer me. Yes or no."

"Well then, yes, Tom. I will marry you."

A double victory! First I got my nerve up to ask her, and then she said *yes*!

The next morning, I bounced into the breakfast room in the Taj Mahal.

"Ian, I want you to be the best man."

"My impression was that I always had been, though I didn't want to rub it in. Still, it's rather nice to hear you admit it."

"No, stupid! I want you to be *my* best man. I'm getting married!"

"Married? To what? A woman? Just who is this poor deluded girl?"

"Barbara, of course."

"The poor thing. And I'd had such hopes for her." Ian shook his head and went back to eating his inevitable stack of pancakes.

My brilliant parry and tart riposte were forestalled by a

waitress bringing in my breakfast. She said it was Eggs-Something-or-Another-in-French, and it mostly involved a lot of heavy cream and garlic. It smelled good but looked sort of wimpy.

Before I could remember what I was going to say, Ian interrupted.

"Tom, would you please tell me why any sane man, or even one sadly like yourself, would want to get married? I mean, consider your position. You are sound of body and perhaps even of mind. You are infinitely wealthy, for all practical purposes, and you are currently surrounded by hordes of attractive women who have somehow been deceived into thinking that you are sexually desirable. You should be happy as you are, especially since you are presently in a position to make hundreds of those sadly deluded women happy as well. Yet instead of simply enjoying yourself, you are proposing to abandon all of your advantages in order to make just one woman miserable. Please attempt to explain your ridiculous line of reasoning."

"There's nothing to explain. I love the girl, and I want her to stay with me, even when this whole stupid charade ends. And it *will* end, you know, someday."

"I know that nothing is forever, this side of heaven, and okay, I can see some sense in wanting to nail down a good one before she gets away. What I can't see you doing is giving up the vast harem of increasingly naked ladies that you currently enjoy."

"Well, I hadn't planned to give it up. Why should I? I mean, Barb doesn't mind my sexual generosity. In fact, she schedules it, and seems to think to think that I am just doing my manly duty. Furthermore, all of the other girls are pretty enthusiastic about the arrangement, as you well know."

"So you are planning on committing adultery even while you are planning your marriage?"

"How can there be a crime if all the parties involved are willing, consenting adults?"

"Oh, there can, there can. Ask any politician or police chief. Victimless crimes are where all the graft is, which is of course why we had so many of them, back home. Whenever you hear somebody screaming about how we have to stamp out prostitution, or pornography, or drugs, or gambling, or anything of the sort, you can be certain that the people behind him, or more likely her, are sure to make a lot of money out of it. Real crimes, like murder, or assault and battery, or theft, simply don't lend themselves to the paying of political contributions and other graft. But I wasn't talking about crime. I was talking about sin, which is a different matter entirely."

"I don't see how I can be sinning, either, especially since I don't believe in your strange religion in the first place."

"Your position on religion is common knowledge. By the way, what is Barbara's religion?"

"I don't think she has one. Religion doesn't seem to fit into the Smoothies' way of thinking."

"I've noticed that. Tom, I strongly advise that you sit down with Barbara and talk out exactly what you expect from one another in this marriage. I shudder to say it, but you might even want to get a lawyer involved, and write up a pre-nuptial agreement, because what you are calling a marriage doesn't have much in common with what most other people would call a marriage."

"All right. I'll do both of those things."

"You really are serious about this marriage business, aren't you?" Ian asked, "I mean, this isn't just another one of your illiterate jokes, is it?"

"Ian, I am dead serious. I asked Barb to marry me, and she said yes. It's that simple."

"Nothing is *ever* that simple. Now, about this best man thing. As I recall, the bride's parents are responsible for the reception, so I don't have to worry about that. Who are Barb's parents, by the way?"

"I haven't the foggiest idea. People around here don't seem to have parents. At least, nobody ever seems to mention them."

"I've noticed that, as well. Maybe they just don't mention them to *us*, since you and I are both orphans. Maybe they simply don't want to hurt our feelings. Anyway, I hope that you realize that when you marry a woman, you are not only marrying her, you are marrying into her family as well."

"Assuming that she has parents and a family."

"Well, of course she must have parents, at least. It's a biological requirement. Whether they're on this island, or even in this century, is another question, of course. That's the third thing you'll have to do, look up Barb's parents. To be properly engaged to her, you will need her father's formal permission. The list is growing, so you'd better start writing all this down."

One of Ian's girls immediately put a pad and pencil in front of me. I was used to that sort of thing. Without comment, I wrote down: 1) Talk to Barb about what getting married means. 2) Talk to a lawyer. 3) Find out who her father is. 4) Get his permission to marry his daughter.

"Don't look so upset," Ian continued. "Barb knows everything that has ever happened to her, and except for her time here in the twentieth century, she knows everything that ever will happen to her. She will certainly know where her parents are to be found. Now, as your best man, I believe that traditionally, I am in charge of the groom's party, and thus responsible for the service, itself. Being an atheist or worse, I suppose that you'll be wanting a simple, Justice of the Peace sort of wedding?"

"Justice of the Peace! Ian, I may be an atheist, damn you, but I'll have you know that I'm a *Catholic* atheist. I want Barbara to have a full Roman Catholic service, complete with an ordained priest, four altar boys, an organist on the big pipe organ, and a full choir besides. And I want it held in that big, empty cathedral we found in the city. Now, at least, we know why it was built."

"You expect me to find a genuine Roman Catholic priest who is willing to marry a professed atheist to a woman who has no real idea of what religion is in the first place? You're asking a lot of a man who hasn't even finished his breakfast!"

"I am doing no such thing. Please, by all means, finish your customary breakfast first. There's not that big of a hurry."

"But Tom, well, I don't know all that much about the Catholics, but I can tell you this— They take their religion *very* seriously. Getting a genuine priest to do what you want him to do is not going to be like getting a Baptist minister who is currently working out of a storefront in the ghetto."

"My oversized friend, you have the resources of the whole island, not to mention the rest of KMH Corporation, behind you. Just delegate the job to somebody. It sounds like a natural for the Mayor of Morrow. You know, the one who did everything 'personally.' I think his name is Jennings, or something like that."

"The things one does in the name of friendship. Okay, Tom, I'll see that the job gets done. Now finish that French garlic stuff that I'm smelling too much of, so we can get to work."

"Good. Did I tell you how happy I am that you are no longer bashing your head on doorframes as often as you used to?"

"No, but thank you. I too am pleased by this development."

CHAPTER THIRTY-TWO
You Still Have to Start at the Beginning

Our earliest devices simply sent things forward into the future, to merge into whatever hapened to be in that time and place. This had the effect of causing dangerous explosions and radiation from the strange isotopes caused when two atomic nuclei happened to emerge close enough to fuse. Eventually, getting a strong handle on Dimension Five, we found that we could simply leave things we didn't want out there, wherever "out there" was. As far as we were concerned, things simply disappeared, when we wanted them to.

We debated using this for trash disposal, but decided that in the very long run, we were better off recycling. Consider that everything in our trash was something that we once needed, and that we would probably need to use those elements again. Otherwise, future generations might someday start running out of planet, or scarce materials, at least.

We also decided that the Dimension Five route was the way to go when it came to our own tunneling. It was safer, cleaner, and the world had plenty of rock, anyway.

The engineering on the "Temporal Test Canisters" was pretty slick. Instead of our old basement, we were now operating from the bottom of a shaft bored twelve hundred feet into the coral, limestone, and granite under our island. This was to eliminate any danger of hurting anyone when the canisters reemerged into our continuum.

Tunneling and excavation had become simple jobs, since our people were now equipped with our new line of temporal digging tools.

The simplest of these was a variation on the escape harness. A sturdy, temporally active area like the ones on top of the shoulder boards was fitted out with a swivel, on the end of a hefty, two-yard-long stick, which contained the circuitry and a battery pack. To use it, you set a dial to the thickness of rock that you wanted to eliminate, usually around a quarter of an inch. You put the active area, the pad, on the rock you wanted to go away, and you pulled the trigger. It went pop, and a layer of the rock under the pad vanished.

The first models had a continuous-discontinuous mode switch, where the operator could elect to continue scooping away rock as fast as he could swing the hefty gadget, but this proved to be dangerous. It was too easy to let it get away from you, and we had two serious accidents before we made it a discontinuous mode only device.

With the pad swiveled all the way out, the thing looked vaguely like a shovel, and that's what the men got to calling our invention.

And yes, most of the construction workers were men. After the "manning" fiasco of our engineering outfit, Ian and I made sure that sexual bias in hiring—in either direction—didn't happen again.

We also made bigger machines, where an operator sat in a sealed cabin, and simply drove in the direction he wanted to go. When cutting through good, solid rock, this could be just as fast as he felt like driving, but in most cases it was prudent to take the time and money to line the tunnel with a sturdy steel tube.

The only disadvantage to our excavation techniques was that besides the rock and dirt that was vanishing, a lot of air was sent to somewhen else as well. When cutting down from the surface, this wasn't a problem at all. If anything, it greatly improved the ventilation. But when you had to start from a canister buried you didn't know how deep, you either had to bring a lot of bottled air with you, or your workers had to be equipped with space suits! But I'm getting way ahead of myself.

As before, we were sending back a sturdy steel canister first, to insure that the test canister emerged in a hard vacuum. Now, however, we could afford to make all of our canisters out of stainless steel, to cut down on the corrosion problems we'd seen before.

The first canister, over a yard long and a foot wide on the inside, was sent on a programmed course, sideways into the fifth dimension, then back in the fourth for a programmed duration. This was followed by a return trip in the fifth in the opposite direction, at the end of which it returned to our continuum, but earlier in time.

Within nanoseconds of arrival, before its circuitry could degrade, or the whole thing had time to explode, it sent itself, with its new contents (the dirt and stone it emerged in) out into the fifth dimension, in a dispersal mode which broke it up into atoms. We hoped that these atoms wouldn't cause any future problems.

We'd never run into anything while traveling backward in the fourth dimension, but we didn't see any sense in leaving any rocks out there that we might ram into later on some other test or trip. The truth was that we didn't know exactly what happened to those canisters of rock that we were blithely throwing around the other dimensions.

There was a great deal that we didn't know about a lot of things.

A few nanoseconds after the first canister departed, leaving a chamber filled with a hard vacuum in the past, a second canister arrived that was slightly smaller than the first. This had to get there before the walls of the chamber, if they happened to be made of something soft, started to collapse.

Inside the second canister was a small machine that we called a "surfacer." It had a top made just like the active surface of an escape harness. The sides of the machine had four caterpillar treads set at right angles to one another, and the rest of it was taken up by a radio transmitter, a power supply, control circuitry, and a timer.

The little machine sat there, under the ground, for as long as we had sent it back in time. If we sent it five hundred years back, its timer had it wait there for five hundred years, doing nothing.

Once its timer said "GO!" the temporally active area was turned on, its treads started moving, and it ate its way through the top of its canister, and then through the rock above it, crawling slowly upward on its treads until it eventually reached either the air, or, as was more likely, the bottom of the sea. If it reached air, it would send up an antenna and broadcast its ID number. If it found water, it dropped its treads and their drive as an anchor, while the rest of it floated to the surface, connected by a few thousand feet of fishing line, and again it radioed its presence.

Then someone, usually from the Navy, went out and found it with the aid of radio direction finders, carefully noted its position using the Loran system we had installed, and brought it back for possible repair and reuse.

As the project continued, we found a major long-term drift to the east, far out into the Atlantic Ocean. This meant that we had to operate from deeper and deeper shafts, to make sure that one of our canisters didn't emerge deep in the ocean water. If that happened, there was no telling where ocean currents would take the thing, and if we ever did get it back, its positional data would be totally useless.

The design of the canisters and the surfacers they contained had to be changed as time went on. Making machinery that could sit idle for thousands of years, and then function properly on command, was no trivial task!

Eventually, we were building the surfacers mostly out of stainless steel, with gold bushings on all moving parts, and then filling the canisters with a fluorinated oil to keep moving parts from welding themselves together over the ages. Whole categories of electronic parts had to be eliminated. There isn't a battery or an electrolytic capacitor that will last more than a few decades, and these things had to be designed around. Power supplies were a particular problem.

A version of Ian's emergency generator eventually pow-ered the things. It made a partial vacuum that the encap-sulating oil boiled into. The resultant gas went through a piston-type motor which in turn powered an electric gen-erator.

Even so, a small atomic battery was needed to get the Rube-Goldberg affair started. These batteries had been developed in the late fifties. They consisted of a thin rod of a radioactive isotope that emitted alpha particles. These particles struck a surrounding layer of a phosphor that gave off visible light. This light, in turn, energized a layer of solar cells, which converted the light into a small trickle of elec-tricity, enough to run a clock and keep a large, mylar capacitor charged. It was a matter of one overly compli-cated Rube-Goldberg device starting another.

We also had to modify the six ships of our small navy, so they had the range to go out on the high seas and recover our transmitters. Their huge Rolls-Royce gas turbines were removed and replaced with things that worked on the same principle as Ian's emergency generator, but which turned impellers rather than electric generators. They now had essentially infinite range, especially after we added a small galley, a shower, and some submarine-style bunk space, where the engines and fuel used to be.

Even so, toward the end, only one surfacer in three was being returned to us.

We sent out some sixty-seven thousand of the things before we were sure that we had the local drifts mapped for the last fifty thousand years. We would have gone back even farther, except that we weren't up to designing machinery and electronic equipment that could last much longer. In the end, we decided that we'd have to someday build a beachhead back there, and then use it as a base for fur-ther temporal explorations into the past.

Mayor Jenkins managed to find a genuine Catholic priest who was willing to commit the unspeakably sinful task of marrying two people who were not of his faith. He turned out to be an impoverished fellow of mostly Indian ances-try who hailed from one of the poorest sections of Paraguay.

Even so, he didn't come cheap. In return for his services, KMH bought and installed a complete water and sewage system for the extended village that was his parish. He also got a small, but well-equipped hospital, two food processing plants (to get local products ready for market), and a small fleet of trucks (to get those processed products to those markets). Finally, he gouged us for the materials necessary for the building of a church, a rectory, and a minimal house for every family in the parish.

The priest figured that if he was going to sell his only soul to the rich and boorish, he might as well charge all that the traffic would bear!

It was months before he arrived, since he demanded his pay, or rather his loot, up front. Then, once he got here, he insisted on taking six weeks for the posting of the banns, time which he planned to use to educate us in the one true religion. Fortunately, he spoke no English, we spoke no Spanish, and the translators that I was paying for somehow found more pressing things to do, so his plan didn't quite work out.

He then demanded that I cease sleeping with Barbara until the wedding.

I politely suggested that in return, it would only be proper that we should burn his building materials, put sugar in the gas tanks of all of his pretty, new trucks, and dynamite his nice, new water and sewage system. Eventually, he saw the light.

It's a hell of a thing. A sold-out sky pilot who won't stay bought!

Meanwhile, work on the Time Train went on.

With the local temporal drifts mapped out, we went into Phase Two of the project. This involved canisters big enough to transport equipment, supplies, and people. After some debate, we settled on a canister sixteen feet in diameter and sixty feet long, big enough to take a standard shipping container and the truck it drove in on, or to comfortably seat fifty people, along with all of their luggage.

Long hours were spent in meetings, hammering out our plans. After months of debate, what we came up was this:

The first part of the drill was to be much like that used on the smaller, exploratory canisters, except that now we knew where we were going, as well as when. The first canister would weave its way through five dimensions, arrive at the predetermined site for a few nanoseconds, and then go away, taking nine thousand cubic feet of rock away with it. The second would arrive by the same route, a few nanoseconds behind, and materialize in the vacuum left by the departing first canister.

And yes, we probably could leave the first canister in position, and discard only its contents, saving the cost of the second canister entirely, but this procedure would leave the walls of the canister impregnated with rock, which weakened the metal in an unpredictable way, and made it radioactive. In addition, the temporal circuitry itself wasn't all that dependable after it had emerged once in solid rock.

Time, money, and human effort weren't among our problems. We had plenty of resources, so there wasn't any incentive to chintz on the job.

The second canister sat there until the the third canister was scheduled to arrive. Just before that point, it sent its contents (mostly air, along with anything else that might have leaked in) out into the fifth-dimensional void so that the third canister could emerge into a truly hard vacuum.

Once the third canister made it safely back to the twentieth century, that particular leg of the Time Train was declared ready to be put into service.

Then, a work crew could be sent back, armed with temporal digging tools, to tunnel their way up to the surface.

The temporal drifts were such that we were able to put our first big canister back some two hundred and thirty-five years, and still be under the island. Before that, and they would emerge in the rock under the sea, and that didn't seem like something that I'd personally want to dig my way up from.

Intuitively, one would think that the sensible thing to do would be to go in small steps, sending the first canister back one year, say, and the next back for two. I mean, that's the way things are normally built. If you are building a railroad, you start from where you are, and build in the direction that you are going to. Then you continue the proscess until you finally get to where you want to be.

But it doesn't work that way when you are building a railroad line into the past. Consider that tunnels, by their very nature, tend to last a long time. Starting out below ground, we had to first tunnel our way out.

Suppose that we made our first canister emerge in 1900, planning to have other canisters emerge earlier than that. In 1900, we couldn't know what we would find out there in 1890, so we couldn't possibly know what we would need to build in 1890 once we got there. And since we didn't know exactly what we would need in the past, we couldn't be sure that we wouldn't wreck some of it as we dug ourselves out. If we made sure in 1890 that there would be plenty of empty space for the 1900 people to dig themselves out, we would be seriously reducing our building options.

Then, of course, when we went back to 1880, our problems would be even more difficult, and by 1750 . . . well, you see the problem. Even when you have a time machine, you have to start at the beginning.

CHAPTER THIRTY-THREE
Barbara's Family

One evening, I was sitting on a couch in the American Room of Camelot with Barb snuggled up comfortably at my side, as naked as all of my other servants around the place. Fumbling through my pockets, I dug out the list of things I had to do prior to marriage.

"Ian says that to do things properly, I need your father's permission to marry you."

"Tom, we are both adult human beings. Neither of us needs parental approval to do anything."

"I agree. However, I think that it might be a good idea for me to meet your relatives in any case, and if that satisfies Ian, well, so much the better."

"Very well, if that is your wish."

"Is there some reason why I shouldn't? Is there some problem between you and your folks? I mean, you've never mentioned them, or anything."

"My siblings and I maintain a normal relationship with our parents and our other ancestors, and meet them at all the usual quarterly meetings."

"Quarterly meetings? Now you've got me confused again, Barb."

"Among my people, it is customary to spend a day with

227

one's biological ancestors every three months, at the solstices and equinoxes. This permits parents to observe the developments of their offspring and their further descendants."

"Sort of a culture-wide family reunion, huh? Not a bad idea, I suppose. I'm surprised that I've never been invited to one."

"Well, you don't have any ancestors here, Tom. But I expect that the real reason for the lack of invitations is that these meetings are terribly boring, even for those who are seeing their relatives again. An outsider would simply feel lost."

"Well, if everybody is bored stiff at them, why do you hold them at all?"

"Because not *everybody* is bored. The older people enjoy the meetings immensely. Parents are naturally far more interested in their children than the children are in them. This is even more noticeable between grandparents and grandchildren. And when they are eight or ten generations removed, well, I'll let you imagine the results for yourself."

"Eight or ten generations! Good God, Barbara, I knew that your people lived longer than mine, but that's ridiculous! Even at twenty years per generation, you are talking about people who are more than two hundred years old!"

"I think that the average length of a generation among us might be closer to fifty years, Tom, although people over two hundred years old subjective are extremely rare. And since you are about to ask it, no, I am nothing close to fifty years old. You got me started on raising children quite early, as it turned out."

"Please don't tell me what I'm going to ask you next. I'm never sure if it's just an expression of yours, or if you really have read my next statement out of one of your history books."

"It's simply that your facial expressions are very telling, Tom, so your thoughts are easy to guess. I never *really* know what you're thinking. The history of this century has never been written. Quite possibly, it never will be."

"One strange statement at a time, young lady. Back to

these ancestors of yours who are ten of your fifty-year generations old without pushing two hundred."

"Isn't it obvious? After they reach retirement age, people in my culture have a great deal of freedom. They can do just about anything they want, go anywhere, or any when. Many of them become extremely interested in their descendants, and attend two, or three, or sometimes even seven successive quarterly meetings a week, subjectively. There are some who have made meeting their descendants the major hobby in their lives, and attend all of the meetings for thousands of years."

"So the world for them becomes like a series of conventions, with the same old pros there every time, and an ephemeral bunch of young neos bubbling through and going their way."

"Yes, I suppose that it could seem that way to some of them."

"Huh. Back home, I knew a couple of old guys who treated science fiction conventions that way. So, do I have to wait for the next solstice to meet your folks?"

"Of course not, Tom. They'd be delighted to meet you at any time. My siblings would like to meet you as well. Shall I invite them here? I know that they'd all like to see this place."

"It sounds fine to me, and let's do it as soon as you feel it's appropriate. I'd just as soon get this thing over with as soon as possible."

"As you wish. Would this coming Saturday at six be acceptable to you?"

One of the glories of having time travel available was that you never had to check with anyone else before you scheduled any sort of gathering, party, or other event. If your guests had something else going on at the same time, they could always go to both things if they wanted to. On the other hand, if they didn't show up, they had no possible excuses except that they simply didn't want to go.

Most people had a long list of social events in the past that they had promised to attend, and simply hadn't gotten around to showing up at yet. It wasn't considered wise or even polite to mention those events to them. After all, if a hostess chided you for not coming to her party, she was proving that you never would go to it, thus relieving you of having to worry about it in your subjective future.

Not that it made any difference to me back then, since they still weren't letting Ian and me use the time machines that we hadn't completely invented yet. It wasn't so much that they forbade us to use them; it was more that they had hidden the things, and try as we might, we hadn't been able to find them. Yet.

When Saturday afternoon came around, I found that a silk tie and a vicuna sports jacket had been laid out for me. Barb had apparently decided on the evening's dress code, and I wasn't about to argue with her about it.

I noticed a more startling change on my way downstairs. All of the usually nude serving wenches that filled the place were now properly dressed. This took me aback for a moment, but then I realized that having a naked harem girl answer the door for my fiancée's parents would not be the socially corect thing to do.

Ian had invited himself over, with Ming Po on his arm, I suppose mostly to lend me his moral support.

I was in good hands, but I was still nervous as all hell.

Meeting Barb's parents was less of an ordeal than I feared it would be, once I got over their appearance. They both looked to be incredibly young, about my own age. That troubled me a bit. Your girl's folks are supposed to look *old*.

Furthermore, Barb's mother is every bit as beautiful as Barb is.

Barb introduced everyone, using first names only, as was customary among these people. Except in work situations, you almost never heard anyone's last name.

Her parents were both charming and intelligent people, as were Barb's two sisters, her brother, and her three siblings-in-law. Over drinks and then dinner, I found that they all had productive jobs on the island, in everything from accounting to agriculture. Indeed, Barb's brother Justin ran the island's only dairy farm, a major installation with over a hundred workers and five hundred cows that turned out milk, butter, yogurt, and twenty-two varieties of cheese.

It turned out that Barb was very close to her siblings, more so than the usual American woman would be with hers. It made sense, though, considering the way they were all the same age when they were raised together. It was almost as though they were fraternal twins.

As the pleasant evening ended, I formally asked Barb's father's permission to marry his daughter and he just as formally granted it.

When I thanked him, he said, "According to the standard formulas that Barbara made me read, I was supposed to inquire about your finances, to be sure that you could support her properly, but since you are known to be one of the wealthiest men in history, I thought it best to forget about that requirement."

Finally, the day came when we sent a full-sized canister back to 1737, and had it return safely.

"Are you all ready for our little jaunt?" I asked Ian at breakfast.

"I've been looking forward to this moment since we started fiddling with time. I wouldn't miss this trip for the whole world and a certificate that the taxes had already been paid on it!"

Ming Po, who was present, looked distressed, and Barbara said, "You mean that both of you are planning to test that thing out personally? Together?"

"Of course. It should be safe enough, and if it isn't, that's all the more reason for us to go ourselves, at first. What kind of men would we be to send someone else out on a job that we wouldn't go on ourselves?"

"This is no time to be heroic!" Barb said, while Ming Po nodded vigorously. "There is not only the danger of a technical malfunction in what is still an experimental device, there is also the fact that you know nothing about the local terrain back then. Why, there could be a sinkhole right below where your canister materializes. There could be hostile natives living there in that period, which was also noted for pirates, and various wars between England, France, and Spain. You might dig your way up right into the middle of a battle!"

"Or maybe, we might have to rescue a Spanish virgin princess from the English pirates, and we will come down with a case of the Spanish pox each, as a result of accepting the lady's gratitude," Ian said. "Who knows? It might be worth it. But when you consider the probabilities . . ."

The normally obsequious Ming Po threw a serving of Cherries Jubilee at Ian, splattering the delicious stuff across his black silk shirt. Completely unfazed, he took no particular notice of her uncharacteristic actions except to remove his stained shirt right there at the table, while he continued talking. Without looking, he gave it a toss behind him where a maid was ready to catch it and take it out of the room to wherever they went with such things.

Again without looking, he reached out to the side and another maid put a clean shirt in his hand, which he then donned while two more women cleaned off a few small splatters from his hands and face, and yet another one tidied up the table in front of him. He never stopped talking the whole while.

The way these people always seemed to know what was going to happen, even the most trivial or unusual events, never ceased to amaze me, any more than did our complete acceptance of their well-coordinated actions.

" . . . so logically, there can be no possible danger to either of us," Ian concluded.

"Nonsense," Barb said. "The two of you are the only indispensable people on this entire island. It is totally absurd to risk either one of you, much less both of you for absolutely no good reason at all!"

Ian looked aside to me and said, "Have you noticed how feisty they get once they think that you're going to marry them?"

"I have. But, given your last statement, taken together with the cherry sauce that recently decorated your shirt, am I to assume that you have followed my lead and proposed matrimony to Ming Po?"

"You are not, for I have made no such decision. It's just

that she thinks that I might do some such thing, and is already acting as though it is a done deal."

"I see. Well, keep me posted as to the state of your current thinking on the subject."

"I shall do so."

"Good. Now then, to answer your last assertion, Barbara, Ian and I are not beholden to this island and the people on it. Rather, we own the place, and the people here are all our employees, including the particularly lovely one that I intend to marry in a few weeks. After that time, you might have some substantial claim on me, but until then you do not! For the time being, Ian and I feel absolutely free to risk our own silly necks in any fashion that we see fit. Am I understood?"

Our ladies' response was sullen but affirmative.

"Good. Now then, one thing does occur to me. We just might run into some people back there, and I think that it would be advisable if our party was dressed in clothes appropriate to the period. Also, we should have a squad of ground troops along with us, just in case. They should be appropriately dressed, and equipped with weapons that at least look period. Have it all ready for us in six minutes, when we get to the shop."

Again, Barb nodded a sullen assent.

As we got up to leave, Ian said, in a girlish, falsetto voice, "Oh, Tom! You look so manly when you get assertive!"

This statement earned him a heavy fist on the shoulder.

CHAPTER THIRTY-FOUR
The First Expedition

When I got to my office, there was a costume waiting on my desk for me. It consisted of a wide-sleeved white cotton shirt, white canvas pants, and a pair of sturdy leather slip-on boots. A broad-brimmed felt hat with a white ostrich plume, and a real steel rapier, complete with a sheath and a wide, over-the-shoulder leather sword belt completed the outfit. It was sturdy, work-a-day stuff, and looked well worn. The only decoration was on the baldric, where it disguised a red emergency button. Just what good that would do me back in 1735 was a moot point, but there was no point in removing it, either.

I stripped off my usual finery and put on the coarse-feeling clothes. Months of wearing silk, vicuna, and the like had spoiled me for more plebeian fabrics. Nonetheless, I felt jaunty, mostly because I liked the plume in the hat, and the long, thin sword. I was clipping my temporal sword to the belt on the pants, next to my calculator and my Swiss Army knife, when Ian walked in. He was similarly attired, except that his outfit had brown leather accessories instead of black.

I said, "Shouldn't we have a pistol or two, and daggers in our boots?"

"I suppose we could, Tom, but do you really know how to operate a flintlock?"

"No, but there can't be all that much to learn. I'm sure that somebody at the Bucket of Blood could show us."

"The canister is scheduled to leave within the hour, and I can't see delaying the trip by a sidereal day just so you can have both a sword and a pistol by your side, just like the Froggy who Went Acourtin'."

"I suppose you're right. But next time we should plan these things out better."

"Making the damn time machine work was mental exercise enough for me," Ian said.

The elevator in the hallway now went all the way down to the upper time-canister chamber, three hundred feet down. When we got there, a fair-sized welcoming committee was waiting for us, headed by Hasenpfeffer, and including Barb, Ming Po, all of our senior technical staff, and a few dozen other, officious-looking people.

None of them looked happy.

Jim Hasenpfeffer stepped pompously forward with his hands on the lapels of his grey wool suit. He said, "Gentlemen, surely you realize that this action on your part is inadvisable."

"Hello, Jim," Ian said. "We haven't seen you in months. It's good to see you out slumming with us working folks. You should do it more often. It would work wonders on your stodgy personality. Do you have any idea of what a pompous ass you've become?"

"This is hardly a suitable occasion for name calling. You youngsters are about to do something stupidly dangerous, and it was felt that I was the only person who had sufficient authority to dissuade you from your childish foolishness."

"'It was felt?' By who? Last time I heard, Tom and I owned two thirds of this outfit, so we're the only ones around here with any clout!"

I cut in with, "'Youngsters'? 'Childish'? When we arrived here, Jim, we were all the same age, and the fact that you have decided to act like an old fart doesn't give you any enhanced authority in our eyes. If you want us to have any respect for you, you should start by coming around now and then and having breakfast, or better yet a beer with us. As things are, well, you are just a silly, old fool who used to be a friend of mine. I mourn the loss of that friend, but you aren't him any more."

"Please, gentlemen, you are embarrassing me in front of my associates. This should be a memorable occasion, the first test of our first temporal canister with human occupants. Please, boys, just step aside and let those who are properly trained for the task enter the device."

"Wrong," I said. "First off, there's nobody who's 'properly trained' because nobody has ever done this before. Secondly, Ian and I know more about it than anyone else, so we're going on the first trip. We have a digging crew scheduled to go with us, and a squad of infantry to handle any emergencies. The rest of you are not supposed to be here. I want you to leave. Please. Do it now."

The managers and officials in the crowd looked uneasily at Jim and me, and then at one another, uncomfortable with receiving contradictory orders from the various parts of their upper-management team. They didn't like what was going on, but they didn't leave, either. Not even my own damn subordinates.

Well, they'd hear from me later. First things first.

James Hasenpfeffer was not about to be ordered out. He marched ostentatiously over to the front of the canister's heavy, vacuum-proof door and stood obstinately in front of the thing with his arms crossed. I glanced over to Bob McMahon, an infantry lieutenant I knew from drinking with him at the Bucket of Blood. He was wearing a period outfit, so I assumed that he was in charge of the infantry squad I'd ordered up. I was about to ask him to clear the area of nonessential personnel, but then I changed my mind.

Asking Bob to decide which of his bosses he was going to obey wouldn't be fair to him. It would be better management technique to handle the problem myself.

With that thought in mind, I walked over to Hasenpfeffer, grabbed him by his carefully tailored wool lapels, and lifted him up in the air at arm's length. I've always been a lot stronger than most people, and the modifications made on me by that annoying Killer doctor hadn't weakened me one bit.

Jim was so shocked that someone would actually use physical force on him that he didn't even struggle. I carried him like a limp doll over to the opposite wall and set him down. Meanwhile, Ian had cranked open the canister doors and was gesturing the construction workers inside. Embarrassed at being present at a disagreement among their upper management, they obeyed him with alacrity.

Hasenpfeffer got over his initial shock and became furious. You could see his complexion go from dead white to beet red, starting at the top of his slightly balding head and progressing downward. He started to move toward the opened canister when I heard a hissing, crackling sound.

A thin line appeared on the pavement in front of Hasenpfeffer's polished, wingtip brogues. He came to an abrupt stop, and his face went from red back to white again.

Ian had his temporal sword in his hand.

"Jim, we just had a meeting of the Board of Directors, and you were outvoted on this one. Tom and I want to take a ride in our new time machine, and we're going to do it. Now, go back to your office and administer something. Leave the technical stuff to the technical people."

I could tell that Hasenpfeffer wanted to rant and rave a bit, but seeing that we were willing to use both force and violence, he thought better of it. He stalked away, muttering under his breath like a very old man.

I said, "Lieutenant, get your men in the canister. The train is leaving the station."

As we sealed the door on the stationary vacuum canister and then the door on the traveling can, the orange, glowing Nixie tube numbers on the countdown timer said that we had four and a half minutes to go.

The controls used on these big canisters were almost exactly the same as those used on the small test canisters we'd used in the early part of the program. After all, we knew they worked, and we were producing them on an assembly line, so they were fairly cheap. They were automatic, and worked whether people were around or not. The only difference was that on the big canisters, there was a keyboard available, and if you knew what you were doing, you could reprogram the thing. Normally, though, it was to be just a matter of going aboard and letting it take you where you were supposed to go.

I sat down next to Ian, carefully sliding my steel sword down between the seats, and said, "Maybe we were a bit rough on our old friend. Maybe we shouldn't have humiliated him in public the way we did."

"Well, he was the one who made it public in the first damn place! If he wanted to talk it over with us, he could have come over to our places, or to our offices, or even invited us over to his. We could have discussed it privately, but no, he had to round up all of our managers at the shop, and our girlfriends, and act the thing out in front of them."

"I didn't like Barb and Ming Po being there either. I mean, yes, they're both managers subordinate to us, but they both are a lot more than that, too. Jim used to be so slick when it came to handling people, but he sure botched this one. He didn't really leave us much choice but to do what we did. It's like he was having some sort of mental aberration, or delusions of power."

"I don't think he's gone crazy. I mean, all three of us are getting used to being big shots, and generally getting things done our own way, but you and I have had the advantage of being engineers. Mother nature has a way of maintaining the humility of a man who works with her. Jim has had nothing to work with but people. It's like you said, he's not the same man any more. He's gotten so used to having his every word be the law that he's forgotten that he has partners in this business. *We* are the ones who made this whole thing possible. Jim just helped out with the business side of things," Ian said.

"I don't think that he looks at it that way. I think that he really has gotten old, administering this island and everything else. I think that he has put many, many years of his life into this project, doubling back and forth through time in machines that we haven't even thought of yet."

"So? Did we ask him to do that? Did we ever authorize him to go off on his own, and create this sick little society of time travelers who can't think up a new joke, or invent a widget, or even whistle a tune unless somebody else plays it for them first? Was our opinion asked before the fruits of our labors were used to create an entire culture that I, for one, consider to be downright immoral?"

"Well, no, to all of your questions. But you've also got to ask, could we have done all of this without him? And you've got to answer no to that one, too."

"True, but neither of us would have *wanted* to do all of this. We would have been quite content to run a profitable little business just outside of Ann Arbor, and maybe not so little a one at that. We probably wouldn't have had all the palaces, and certainly not all the women, but we would have built a good life for ourselves, Tom."

"I can't argue with you. But things are what they are right now, and we've got to play it from here."

"Right. And what we'll do now is make our first trip into history."

Ian's timing was dead on, because just then the Nixie tubes read six zeros, and we left home.

Our first surprise was the lack of gravity. It was just like being in a space ship, I suppose, with things floating up and out of our pockets, and us floating out of our chairs. It had never occurred to us that we'd need seat belts.

"Why didn't we expect this?" I said. "It would have been easy enough to build an instrument that could check for gravity, and put it into a test canister."

"Because we never thought of it," Ian said from six feet "above" my head. "Still, it makes perfect sense. We are not on Earth any more, so we aren't affected by Earth's gravitational field."

I would have been more upset, except that I saw the eight soldiers we had with us, sitting in their chairs with their hands firmly gripping the armrests, grinning at the two new kids. They and the construction workers were used to this sort of thing. I made a mental note to have someone put safety belts on all the seats, next time.

"Well, if it makes so damn much sense to you, why didn't you predict this null gravity thing?" I asked, floating upside down to everything else.

"I said it made sense, not that I knew it was going to

happen. It would also have made sense if the gravity slowly went away as we got farther and farther away from Earth in the fifth dimension."

"Only that didn't happen, so the fifth dimension must be impervious to gravity waves, whatever they are."

"That, or we are moving a lot farther into the other dimensions than we thought. I mean, if we were billions of miles away from home, there wouldn't be much of Earth's gravitation field to feel."

"Well, I've already thought of a use for the effect," I said.

"Yeah?"

"Sure. Get a weight and put it on top of a spring. The weight pushes the spring down. Take the contraption out into the fifth dimension, and the spring pushes the weight away. Attach the weight to a crank, and turn the time circuit on and off quickly. You get free power, and I bet it would be a lot cheaper to build than that emergency power machine of yours. No turbines, for one thing, and it doesn't need a bodacious supply of air."

"Tom, that sounds just stupid enough to work. You know, we could have powered the surfacers with something like that. We'll put a technical team on it when we get back."

"Okay. You know, maybe you shouldn't have pulled your sword on Hasenpfeffer."

"It got his attention, and we were running out of time. If we'd let him delay us past the departure time, it would have given him another day to think up things to delay us further."

"I can see your point, but while we've done impolite things to each other before, we've never used real weapons up till now."

"All right, all right. I'll send him a formal note of apology as soon as we get back."

"Thank you. I just don't want this whole thing to escalate."

Another set of Nixie tubes said we had forty-one minutes until we arrived. We'd known that it took time to travel in time almost since the beginning. We still didn't know why that was so, and it still bugged me.

Free fall was starting to get fun, now that I was no longer startled by it. I would have suggested some sort of free fall game, except that if the troops and workers got out of their chairs and got involved, the place would have gotten crowded in a hurry.

Besides fifteen people, we had power, food, and water aboard for a year. We had bottled oxygen, calcium oxide, and activated charcoal to last us a week. We had digging equipment to get us to the surface, tools and materials to set up a small station in 1735, and a small observatory to let us ascertain our exact geographical position. What we didn't have was much room for a game of null-G touch football.

We were all in our seats when the Nixie tubes counted down to zero again.

Nothing happened. Gravity did not return. We weren't on Earth in 1735, or anything like it.

I heard a nervous voice behind me say, *"Boss, I think we're in big trouble."*

CHAPTER THIRTY-FIVE
Big Trouble

Ian said, "Tom, you checked this program yourself, didn't you?"

"No. I wrote it myself. Prescott checked it. I'll go take a look at it."

I opened the control cabinet under the Nixie tubes, and turned on the cathode ray tube display. While it warmed up, I fumbled around and found the program, a long column of nine-digit numbers, all of them ones and zeros, written in my own handwriting. Ours was a stripped-down system written in straight, efficient machine language, without benefit of Fortran.

What I didn't find was my flowcharts, our volumes of charts and tables of lateral drift, and everything else I needed to write a five-dimensional program from scratch. They weren't here because it had never occurred to me that I might need them anywhere else except at my desk in my office.

In hindsight, I know that this sounds incredibly stupid, but please remember that we had written more than sixty thousand of these programs before, and all of them had been for test canisters without any humans aboard. Including the volumes of tables in a small, unmanned test canister would not only be stupid, it would have been flat impossible.

After a while, you settle into habits, solid routines of how things are done. Ian and I had been so eager to make this trip that we hadn't bothered to think everything out again from the beginning.

As it was, we were lucky that we had even the program itself with us. It was here only because the typist and her checker hadn't bothered to take it back with them.

Working the controls with one hand while I held myself in place with the other was annoying. I put my sword inside the cabinet, took off my shoulder belt, and used it to fasten myself to the stool in front of the cabinet.

I tediously checked the screen against my written program and found the problem in about ten minutes. Two zeros in one line had somehow become ones.

"Had only one error occurred, it would have been caught in a parity check. What we're seeing here is pretty improbable."

"You think somebody did it on purpose?" Ian said.

"I don't know, but we can worry about that one later. The point now is that we've missed our target, both in time and in space. From here, I don't think that I can steer us back to there. Not without all the stuff I have back in my office."

"Can you get us back home again?"

"That's what I'm going to try, even though I don't have any of our charts or tables with us. I think the easiest thing to do will be to simply retrace our steps. I'll pick a time in our subjective future, and have it reverse our directions from that point."

"Why do it in our future? Why not do it now?"

"Because it's going to take me some time to change the program in the first place, stupid, and I don't want to rush myself. I may not get a second try. *We* may not get a second try."

It took me a half an hour to modify the program to run us backward, and load it into the buffer. I had to use some educated guesses as to estimating our drift, and that troubled me. If I was off by twenty feet sideways, we would emerge in solid rock, which would not only instantly kill all of us, but would likely take out the entire factory as well. Being off by only two inches would wreck the canister, and it just might kill us anyway, although in a less spectacular fashion.

Ian spent another forty-five minutes checking over my work before he would approve of what I'd done.

I'd allowed two hours for the job, so we had another forty-five minutes to chew our nails before we could load the modified programs into the machine proper.

The squad of infantry, all being of Killer stock, spent the first half hour of the emergency quietly talking to each other. You could see that they were worried, but on the whole, they were taking it pretty well.

After that, someone got out a deck of cards and a poker game was soon in progress, played in zero gravity. They hadn't brought any money with them, but they had an empty Kleenex box Scotch taped to the middle of a makeshift table, and IOUs written on scraps of paper were being stuffed into it as the game progressed. The winner of each hand got to empty the box. Since their period outfits didn't run to pockets, cards and IOUs of various denominations had to be stuffed under one's belt. It slowed down the game, but killing time was the object of the exercise in the first place.

Had there been anything that needed doing, I could see that these troops were ready to do it.

The construction workers were all Smoothies, and they were in much worse shape. One burly sandhog had simply fainted the moment that it was obvious that we were in trouble. Most of the rest just sat it out in a blue funk, with sweat beading up on their zero-G faces like monstrous zits. About an hour and a half in, one of them freaked out, screaming and clawing his way towards the canister door, for what reason none of us could imagine. There wasn't anything outside the door, not even air. Maybe not even space.

At least we didn't think there was anything out there. The temporal screen that surrounded the canister reflected back everything in the electromagnetic spectrum, including light and radio waves. Some of the test canisters had been programmed to turn off their screen so we could get an instrumented look around, but none of those had ever returned.

Bracing himself between two seats, Lieutenant McMahon

simply threw the screaming worker back to the other end
of the canister, and when the man immediately tried for the
door again, Bob just kicked the fellow in the jaw, knocking him out cold.

"Nice job," Ian said, as he helped haul the unconscious
worker back to his seat.

Finally, the timer I'd set up to dump the buffer into the
machine proper timed out, and we were, in theory at least,
heading home. Not that we felt any change in our direction.

From there, it was another three hours of sitting around
to see if my fix had really fixed anything, and if, indeed,
we would survive this trip.

Ian had two of the workers break out some food and we
had a quiet, nervous lunch.

The canister didn't have a john, but the only sergeant
we had along, a fellow named Kuhn, emptied a keg of
ancient-looking, hand-cut nails into a plastic sack, and we
made do with the keg. You had to be quick with the lid,
or you had a mess floating around, but we made do.

After a bit, I joined the poker game, and was soon
followed by Ian. We all fit around the small table because
half of the troops were upside down, and holding themselves to the ceiling by means of the cargo straps up there.
None of the Smoothies asked to play, because Smoothies
never gambled. With their lifestyle, there wasn't any point
to it.

The game broke up a few minutes before we were due
to arrive home. It was just as well, since by then I was
fourteen thousand dollars down, and Ian had lost more than
twice that. When you know that there's a fair chance that
you won't live to settle up your debts, there's not much
incentive to scrimp on your betting. Sergeant Kuhn was the
day's big winner, being over twenty thousand ahead. I don't
think he cheated, but that man is one mean poker player!

Everyone got back to their seats. Most of the people had
improvised some sort of seat belts by then, and the rest
of them just held on.

The timer hit six zeros again, and this time something
definite happened. The canister wall to my right was

suddenly three inches closer to me, the "POP" nearly burst my eardrums, and gravity had returned.

"It seems that we have arrived!" I shouted, and got a cheer out of the troops. The Smoothies just sat there and looked relieved.

Ian and Lieutenant McMahon got to the door at about the same time, but when they tried to turn the crank, it wouldn't budge. We were home, or at least we were someplace with earth gravity, but we were still trapped in the canister!

The lieutenant started beating on the door with the butt of what looked like a "Brown Bess" musket, and a few minutes later, someone else started beating on it from the outside. Another cheer went up.

Our good lieutenant knew Morse code, and a few moments later, someone was found on the outside who could understand him and reply.

It seems that besides being welded to the side of the stationary canister, we had also come back a few inches too close to the door, such that the two doors were now welded together. We were instructed to wait until cutting torches could be brought down to our area.

"This is not good," I said. "I can smell ozone. We are taking a dose of ionizing radiation right now."

"Right. To hell with obsolete technology, anyway." Ian said. "Bob, tell whoever is out there to back off! We're cutting our own way out."

Bob quickly beat out a message that I later heard read, *"run away!"*, because Ian was already positioning himself in front of the door with his temporal sword in his hand.

Ian gave whoever was out there a count of five to be gone, and then, with a quick rotation of his wrist, cut a six-foot circle in the big door. As it began to fall, another fast wiggle of his hand cut the circle into six pieces, which came to the floor with a loud clatter.

"Everybody out!" I shouted, and was almost trampled by the little, ordinary-sized people scrambling past me. I was the last one out, proudly wearing my white plumed hat and my fine steel sword.

Naturally, there were medics and ambulances waiting to

take us all away. I felt just fine, but after my earlier experiences with radiation damage caused by temporal reimmersion, I thought it best not to argue with them.

Arguing with a medic doesn't do you much good anyway. Their egos are such that if you disagree with whatever strange thing they're doing to your only body, they'll automatically assume that you're in shock, or otherwise out of your head, and sedate you so that you can't disagree with them any more.

Our exalted status did get Ian and me to the front of the line at the hospital, and we were out of there in an hour. It turned out that the dosage we'd gotten wasn't at all serious. Of course, had we waited around in the canister for a few hours, things would have been much different.

I soon discovered that we had returned to our own time only a half hour after we'd left. Had we gotten back much sooner, we'd have run into Hasenpfeffer and his crowd again before they'd had a chance to leave. This was good, because I wasn't ready to talk to him just yet.

"Lieutenant McMahon, you did well today. Now, I want you to look up Leftenant Fitzsimmons of the Navy and Captain Stepanski of the Air Force. I want the three of you at my office in a half hour. I have another job for you to do."

"Yes, sir." He saluted and left.

"What's that about?" Ian said.

"We need some detective work done, and one thing this strange little island doesn't seem to have is a police force."

"True enough. But soldiers aren't cops."

"They're the closest thing that we have available. If those three can't do the job, I think that they'll know who can. What's more, I have the feeling that they'll be on our side, no matter what, and that's something I'm not sure I can say about all the Smoothies," I said.

"Unfortunately, after this morning I agree with you. I didn't like the way all of our managers were down there backing up Hasenpfeffer. Not to mention Ming Po and Barbara."

"Yeah. Something stinketh mightily around here, and I intend to dig it up before we bury it again."

CHAPTER THIRTY-SIX
Sabotage?

Still in my eighteenth-centuary getup, with my steel sword at my side and my plumed hat hanging on a convenient peg behind my desk, I filled the officers in on the problems we experienced on our first attempted time trip, with Ian sitting in.

"... so what we need to know is what went wrong, and how do we fix it, if it was some sort of technical problem, or who did it and why, if we're looking at sabotage. You can call in any help you think you may need, and spend as much time and money as you want, just as long as you all show up here again in an hour with some answers. Are you three up to the task?"

Leftenant Fitzsimmons had turned out to be the senior man in the group, so he answered, in his almost accurate upper-class English accent, "Yes, sir. You will be seeing us back here shortly, I expect."

They snapped to and saluted. It felt strange to be returning a salute to a bunch of officers, but I saluted them back, rather than make them hold that silly posture. Then they did an about-face and left. I guessed that they must figure that I was their Comander-in-Chief.

Maybe I was.

"They'll be doubling back, of course," Ian said. "Why was *Lieutenant* Fitzsimmons acting as if he was superior to *Captain* Stepanski?"

"Because by their rules, he is. Not having had the benefit of a proper military education, you never learned that a navy lieutenant is equal in rank to an army captain, for some strange historical reason. After that, Fitzsimmons had more time in grade. Also, a navy captain is equal to an army colonel, but why should I tell you this when you're the one with the exalted history major?"

"Oh. Someday, I'll look it up. For now, I think our next step should be interviewing our subordinates."

"Right," I said, pushing a button on my desk. "Kowalski, come in here."

She walked in immediately, and stood before my desk, looking worried. I didn't feel like setting her at ease.

"Kowalski, a while ago, you were down in the time canister area, standing behind Hasenpfeffer and apparently supporting his demands that our trip be aborted. Why did you do that?"

"But, I didn't! I mean, I was there because Dr. Hasenpfeffer had invited me, but I never took anyone's side on anything! I never said a word!"

"You didn't have to. You stood there behind him, literally backing him up. Also, you heard me order you and the rest of the crowd out, and you didn't obey me. Why was that?"

"But, you wanted one thing, and Dr. Hasenpfeffer wanted another, and I didn't know what to do, so I didn't do anything!"

"For future reference, this outfit is owned by three equal partners. If we ever have the bad taste to disagree in public again, remember that any two of us can outvote the third."

"Yes, sir."

"Now, did you know of any reason why we should not have taken that trip?"

"Well, when you got back, you were all sent to the hospital! Isn't that reason enough?"

"Yes, but did you know about that before we left?"

"No, sir. But Dr. Hasenpfeffer did say that your trip was 'ill advised,' and that was hint enough for me."

"Huh. Well, go, for now. Send in the rest of my senior staff, one at a time, and don't tell them what all this is about."

"Yes, sir."

The rest of my people came in one at a time, and they all said about the same thing as Kowalski. They were there because Hasenpfeffer had invited them, and they didn't do anything because they didn't know what to do.

We went to Ian's office and he repeated the procedure with his people.

We got the same results.

"Maybe we're reading more into this thing than we should," I said.

"Maybe. Let's see what those military types of yours have come up with. We've kept them waiting for over an hour."

"Oops! I forgot about them."

We went back to my office and had Kowalski send in the three officers.

"I'm sorry to keep you gentlemen waiting for so long, but we got involved in something else, and I lost track of time."

"No problem, sir," Fitzsimmons said in his best phony British accent. "With any appointment, it's common to make a TARR—that's a Time Actually Required Request—to a bloke's secretary. It saves all sorts of time that would otherwise be wasted sitting around and waiting. Your Miss Kowalski informed us of when you'd really want us here, so we got here just in time."

"A TARR, huh? I see that you are as efficient as ever. Well then, what can you tell us about the 'accident' we had earlier today? What are we up against? Technical failure or sabotage?"

"Technical failure, beyond all doubt. Last night, all electronic systems in the canister were completely torn down and everything was carefully checked. The controls of the canister were in perfect working order. Early this morning, a technician typed the program in accurately, checked it herself, and then had a coworker check it all again. I then personally verified that the program installed was the one you wrote. No one went into the canister from then until your group entered an hour later."

"How can you be so sure of all of this?"

"Besides our personal checks, we used various classified surveillance devices to verify everything."

"What sort of 'classified' devices?"

"I'm not at liberty to disclose that, sir."

"I don't like that answer."

"I'm sorry, but it's the best answer you are going to get, sir. Please consider that these devices will someday be invented by the two of you gentlemen. If you learned about them before you had invented them, you would be messing with the laws of causality, a most unsafe procedure."

"So just what would happen to me if I did break these laws of yours?"

"I haven't the foggiest idea, sir. To the best of my knowledge, there has never been a well-documented case of anyone ever daring to break those laws."

"Then how can you possibly say that breaking them is dangerous? The best you can honestly say is that it is unknown."

"Sir, you haven't taken the time to consider the facts carefully. We have two entire cultures where millions of people have been using time machines for many thousands of years. Thus, there have been untold trillions of opportunities to violate causality. Consider that some of those people were probably dishonest, and that many more of them were doubtless curious. Yet there is not one single verifiable case of violated causality on record. Do you know why?"

"No, I don't."

"Neither do I. The best guess is that nature has some mechanism that corrects these violations. How it does this is unknown. My own thought is the data can also be stated thusly—'There is no one still in existence who has ever violated causality.' Given that, the short of it, sir, is that I prefer existence to its alternative, and therefore I have no intention of ever messing with the laws of causality."

"Interesting, but let's get back to the problem at hand,"

Ian said. "You said that we had technical problems. What do you recommend that we do?"

"Your equipment was designed with simplicity and efficiency in mind, which was appropriate for use in disposable canisters when only discrete electronic components were available. Now, with large, non-expendable canisters, we recommend that you redesign your circuitry for greater safety. For example, you are using only a simple, horizontal parity check. We suggest that at the least you add an additional, vertical parity check. A good investment might be in a military-style, triple-redundant circuit, where two out of three circuits must agree for anything to happen. With the new integrated circuits, this shouldn't cost much in terms of bulk or power requirements. There are many other security techniques to be found in the textbooks."

"Very good, gentlemen. Thank you for a job well done," I said as they left.

While Ian and I mulled their report over, I called Kowalski in and asked her to tell me exactly how she used TARRs.

"Well, sir, when those three officers first left your office a few hours ago, one of them, the Air Force captain, told me that they had an appointment to see you in an hour, so I wrote it down in your appointment book. Then the Navy lieutenant asked me for a TARR, and I wrote down the time he had asked for it. Then my mailbox dropped a letter from its *out* slot addressed to him. I gave him the envelope without opening it, of course. Then, a few minutes ago, after you'd actually called them in, I wrote down the time you called for them, and sealed the note in an envelope. I addressed the envelope with my own address but the lieutenant's name, and the time when he asked for the TARR. Then I put the envelope in the box's *in* slot."

"So this mailbox of yours has a time machine in it?" Ian asked.

"No sir. At least I don't think it does. My understanding is that it just has a timer to drop out each letter at the proper time. I go to the post office about once a week, drop off my old box and pick up the new one at the same time, with the right letters all set to come out at the right time. Only they're both the same box, of course. I mean, it's my personal property, you know."

"So the post office does the time traveling. How do they know when a letter should be delivered?"

"From the address, of course! Oh, I remember that in America, a letter is just addressed for the place you want it delivered to. Here, we have to state both the place and the time it should get there."

"I see. And these letters are not only from yourself, but from others as well?"

"Of course. You can use a letter to talk to anyone when a phone isn't handy. Or to talk to people in other time periods. I mean, my sister is back in 43,519 B.C., and we write each other all the time."

And here I had been thinking that these people had no more curves to throw at me!

"What would happen if you broke open the box and got all your mail at once?" Ian asked.

"Oh, that would be very dangerous, sir. The box and all the letters would burn up!"

"I see. Booby-trapped to conserve causality."

I thanked Kowalski, and asked her to write up something nice and appropriate to put in the personnel files of each of the three officers and then bring it back for my personal signature. That sort of thing was very important to American officers, and I imagine that all military outfits are pretty much the same.

"So. It was just an electronic glitch, and all of this detective work amounts to little more than a wasted exercise in paranoia on our parts," Ian said.

"Paranoia, probably, but I wouldn't call it all a wasted effort. I intend to redesign the temporal circuits as the leftenant recommended, no matter what it costs, or how much it delays our next try at time travel. It makes you wonder how many of those test canisters that didn't return failed because of this same glitch."

"Another point is that even paranoids can have people who are trying to kill them," Ian said. "The only question still in my mind is why did Hasenpfeffer raise such a stink about our going on that trip, and why did he choose such a strange way to stage his protest?"

"Why indeed? I suppose that we could go and ask him."

"We could, but I'm not sure that I will like his answer. Tom, my gut-level feeling is that we should just let this one lie."

"Moved and seconded."

CHAPTER THIRTY-SEVEN
Wedding Preparations

As the day of my wedding approached, things got increasingly hectic around Camelot, and around the Taj Mahal as well, since with Ian as best man, and Ming Po as Barb's bridesmaid, all of Ian's ladies were soon roped into helping out my girls.

Barring attendance at a few rehearsals, I managed to stay out of the loop as far as most of it was concerned, but I couldn't help noticing a few of the stranger things go by.

A special issue of a book on Catholic American wedding customs was printed and distributed to everyone concerned, including yours truly. It's strange, the things people do simply to state publicly that they intend to shack up together. Rings are exchanged; bouquets are thrown about; brides are denuded of their garter belts, which are then thrown to the bachelors in the crowd; and atrocious things are done to the groom at bachelor's parties.

I wanted no such things to happen to me. This wedding was a serious thing to me, and I didn't want it spoiled by any nonsense. I talked about it long and hard with Ian, and he eventually promised that a surprise bachelor party wouldn't happen. Then I took steps to insure that no one else would try any stunts by posting public notice, promising to fire anyone involved with any crude jokes on my person.

I wanted Barb to go through the whole, days-long ritual, mostly to impress upon her the seriousness of the whole thing. Once we were married, I wanted us to stay that way.

The book said, among a huge number of other bits of trivia, that Barb's father was to pick up the bill for the wedding reception. Since some three thousand people were eventually scheduled to attend, it seemed a bit much to ask the guy to pay for all of it, and over breakfast, I asked Ian to see to it that I caught the bill instead of him.

"Not a good idea, Tom. It would embarrass him. Wedding ceremonies are much like the potlatch festivals that the Northwest American Indians used to throw. They are a display of wealth and power that vastly increases the prestige of the guy throwing it."

"I've heard about those things. Isn't that where the guy hosting it gives away absolutely everything he owns, and if he can't find somebody to take the last of it, he'll burn whatever was left over, just to make sure that he's totally destitute?"

"Usually, it doesn't go quite that far. Anyway, in the long run, he comes out way ahead, because everyone who accepts a gift is morally, or at least socially, obligated to give his host a gift of far greater value, once it's *his* turn to throw a potlatch."

"Weird custom, sort of like a voluntary income tax, except that with the Indians, you eventually get something back for what you have to shell out. So the Smoothies have a custom like the potlatch, too?" I asked.

"Damned if I know. Nobody ever gave me a handbook of Smoothie customs. But you know, I'd be willing to bet that from now on, they adopt your Catholic-American customs as the standard way to get married."

"Bullshit," I said politely. "There is no way that so many couples could possibly get a real Catholic priest to marry them."

"Okay, you've got me on that one. But the huge ceremony, the massive display of wealth, and the social commitment that these public displays enforce, could well become permanent things hereabouts. For one thing, marriage customs quickly become permanent anywhere. Look at the way that the giving of a diamond ring to announce an engagement quickly became universal. Most Americans would say that the custom was ancient, whereas it really has only been around for less than a century."

"The reason for that one is obvious. Besides the millions that the DeBeers diamond cartel spends on advertising, a woman naturally wants to know that the guy has made a serious commitment to her before she makes the commitment that he wants from her. I'm surprised that the custom wasn't invented sooner."

"Without any sort of dependable birth control device, and what with the social stigma placed on giving birth to a bastard, most properly brought up women back then weren't likely to give in to their man's desires before marriage, in any event," Ian said.

"What about the medieval lord's *droit du seigneur*, where he got to take all of his peasant girls?"

"Traditionally, he only had the right to take them on the night before their wedding, so her husband to be was there to take care of the kid, in case the lord's sperm got lucky. You know, there is a similar custom in Southeast Asia, where the Buddhist monks take on the hard duty of relieving the local maidens of their maidenheads."

"Purely for religious reasons, of course."

"Of course. The causing of pain and the spilling of blood are sinful acts according to Buddhist tenets. Due to the strength of his soul, a monk is best suited to do the onerous task. They even get paid for doing it."

"A typically religious justification for the defloration of the youth, while raking in the money," I said.

"Some religions, perhaps. Not mine, of course."

"You figure that the Smoothies are going to pick up on that one, too?"

"No. But they have a culture without much real depth, and such cultures are quick to adopt new customs. Like any other new culture, they slosh around a lot, like water carried in a shallow tray."

"How do you get off calling them a 'new' culture? We

keep hearing that they've been around for thousands of years!"

"They have and they haven't," Ian said. "Don't forget that almost everyone here left wherever they came from when they were teenagers, and spent at least their next ten years scattered throughout the United States. That amounts to a very definite cultural break. Now that they are together again, they want a feeling of cultural solidarity, but they don't have the customs, the symbols of cultural solidity, to work with. Being absolutely uncreative, they have to get those customs from us, the only creative people around."

"Huh. I don't mind being responsible for creating the technical basis for their sick little culture. I mean, they're not an evil people, or anything like that. But I don't know if I feel right about being the cause of their social customs as well. I don't feel that I'm competent to handle a job like that."

"You're not. Neither am I. But then again, I don't think that we'll do more than modify a few surface things, like wedding customs. The real basis for their culture, and the reason for their uncreativity, is the way they use time travel. For that, we certainly are responsible, perhaps to the damnation of our souls."

"I can't buy that," I said. "We just made a machine. We never forced anyone to use it, to make it the basis of their whole culture."

"Once the machine was there, it was going to be used. I've heard it argued that Henry Ford, along with the other early auto makers, was responsible for the change in morals that occurred in the first half of the twentieth century. Maybe all Henry wanted was to give people a cheap, convenient means of transportation, and to make a fortune doing it, but he also gave the average young man an enclosed, self-mobile box to take his girl out with. No longer was he forced to spend his Sunday afternoons sitting with her in her father's well-chaperoned parlor. He now had a way to take her somewhere else, as well as a convenient place to have sex with the girl."

"He could have done the same thing with a horse-drawn carriage," I said.

"Only if he was rich. Even if the horse and carriage had been free, it still took a lot of time and effort to take care of a horse, more than the typical working man could afford. A Model T Ford could be bought new for ten weeks' pay, and you didn't have to feed it, curry it, shoe it, and do everything else that a horse needs to stay healthy."

"So you're blaming the automotive engineers for the breakdown of morals during the 1920s? Well, good for the engineers! And to hell with drinking tea and eating crumpets with a bunch of maiden aunts, anyway!"

"It's a judgement call, and if that's yours, go wallow in it," Ian said. "Some of us have a different opinion. None of which changes our responsibility for the Smoothy lack of creativity."

"There's got to be a better way. There has got to be a way that we can use time travel and still be creative."

"When you figure it out, tell me about it. For now, let's get to work. You have to find where that glitch is in our time circuit, fix it, and then design a triple-redundant version of it, with backups and extra parity checks. I have to take a look at the damage we did down below, and do something about it."

Our best guess turned out to be that a single energetic bit of radiation managed to upset two adjacent registers, which caused the entire circuit to malfunction. A single bad register would have caused a parity error, and the canister would have returned home immediately.

Our circuit could malfunction under these circumstances because those two particular bits changed a legal command into an illegal one. Of the sixty-four codes allocated to control functions, only sixty-two were actually in use. I had used a simple diode decoding matrix to do the job, with each function incorporating a transistor circuit for amplification, which also performed the pull-down function. I had not included an amplifier for those two codes that had no use. This meant that those two codes didn't have a pull-down resistor, and various "sneak paths" existed when either of them was called up.

We had tested the circuit extensively, but we had never

tested for things that "couldn't possibly happen," like codes that weren't in use. So what *could* possibly happen was that several functions were activated simultaniously, and your humble heroes were left drifting in the sixth dimension for a while there.

In Standard Engineering Terminology, this situation is called "Fucking Up." I suppose that I could mumble and grumble about how my uncreative staff, acting like I was God, had a lot to do with the way my error wasn't caught, but the truth is that it was my mistake.

I'm glad that I made that first trip, and took my chances dying on it. If somebody else had died because of my fuck-up, well, I couldn't have lived with it.

Two cheapshit quarter-watt, carbon pull-down resistors cured half the basic problem. Hardening our registers with their own, separate, triple-redundancy circuits (plus a bit of lead shielding) did most of the rest. The triple redundancy with backups for the whole circuit came later. Fortunately, I had help with that.

Actually, the triple circuit didn't take us all that long to build and test. There were books and papers available on how to make any electrical circuit more reliable, provided that you didn't mind spending money, space, and power to get it. Nothing creative was required on our parts. I had a lot of good engineers who could do a very competent job under those conditions.

Within two weeks, we tested the new circuit out on a small test canister, and it worked. We ran two hundred more tests, going as far back as fifty thousand years, and had a success rate that was almost twice as good as we'd ever had before, all of which was pretty damned embarrassing. It meant that we had lost thousands of canisters on our earlier tests, not because of problems with making machinery last fifty thousand years, or because of geological accidents, but because of a simple electronic glitch!

Ian ragged me about it for years, and while the Smoothies were all far too polite to ever mention it, the people in his mechanical design team acted smug, aloof, and superior to my electronic people from that day on.

We then ran ten tests on full-sized canisters, shuttling back and forth from 1735 to our newly rebuilt terminal in 1972. We were now ready to make our trip into the past, except that I had this wedding to attend.

My own.

Even though Ian promised that there wouldn't be any bachelor party stunts, I was increasingly watchful as the day of the wedding approached. I *knew* that he was going to pull something. But nothing happened.

With the ceremony less than an hour away, my bath girls got me into the formal, full-dress with tails outfit that somebody had decided was absolutely necessary. Just as well, since I never could have figured out how to get into it on my own, what with the shirt studs, the bow tie, the gaiters and all. It even came with a spring-loaded top hat, an opera cape, and a walking stick. I'd hoped that there was a sword hidden in the walking stick, but no such luck. Or if there was one in there, I couldn't figure out how to get the damned thing out.

My usual accessories, my calculator and my temporal sword, didn't seem appropriate with the formal outfit, and what with all the new stuff, I failed to notice the lack of a red button on the belt buckle.

Ian showed up with six other friends of mine, Killer drinking buddies from the Bucket of Blood, who had volunteered to act as ushers. They were all in the same uniform that I was, and they said that they were going to escort me to the church.

"Sort of an honor guard, as it were," Leftenant Fitzsimmons said, as we got into the subway car.

But when the car door opened, I could see that we weren't in the basement of the church. We were in the time canister test chamber below our shop!

"What? You pressed the wrong button by mistake, Ian?"

"No . . . Tom, listen to me. First, you must understand that I am your best friend. That all of us here are friends of yours. And as your friends, we can't let you go out and make the biggest mistake of your life! Deep down inside, we know that you realize that Barbara is simply not the right girl for you, and that by marrying her, you would not only be making yourself miserable for the rest of your life, you would be ruining her life as well."

"I realize no such God damned thing!" I said, standing up and trying to make it to to the car's control panel.

I never got there. All seven of those guys piled on me, and while they did no damage to anything but my pride, they held me down in the aisle.

"We were afraid that you would take it this way," Ian said. "We sincerely regret being forced to put you in bondage, but sadly, you leave us no choice."

My arms were forced behind my back, and a set of handcuffs was snapped on my wrists. I was furious! Not only were they doing their damndest to upset a ceremony that I had been looking forward to for months, but they were actually overpowering me, physically! Such a thing had never happened to me before. I had always been the strongest person I knew, and I hadn't realized how much of my ego was involved with that fact.

But the seven of them were more than I could handle. I was helpless against the fighting skills of the six Killers, and Ian's towering strength. I never even got a single good lick on any one of them.

Once the handcuffs were on, most of them worked their way down to my feet, and put a set of leg irons on me. I was squirming and shouting loudly for help. At first it didn't seem to bother them, but my increasingly vulgar cursing ended when they held my nose closed and stuffed a ball gag into my mouth.

"Now don't get yourself into too much of a dither," Ian said calmly as they carried me at shoulder height over to a time canister. "We're only sending you back ten years, to when the island was unpopulated. That ought to give even you enough time to get over your present, doubtless temporary, insanity."

CHAPTER THIRTY-EIGHT
Kidnapped!

With Ian giving directions, my six other "friends" carried me from the subway car to the back of a big canister, half loaded with boxes and crates that were strapped down to the deck. They laid me down, face up, on a big, inflated air mattress.

"You've got all the supplies you need here to keep yourself healthy and happy until you catch up with the present again. Food, camping gear, clothing. Even your favorite cigars, and plenty of beer."

Leftenant Fitzsimmons took an oversized can of Australian beer from one of the cases, opened it, and set it on the deck near my head with a friendly wink. Not that I could drink any of it, bound and gagged as I was. Captain Stepanski returned my top hat, opera cape, and walking stick, which had been scattered in the struggle. He dusted them off, folded the cape, and set it all neatly on the floor near the beer can.

"We've jimmied the time circuit so that this machine can only travel backward. Without test equipment or even a soldering iron, there's no chance that even you could fix it," Ian said, tossing the keys for the cuffs to the floor near me. "I doubt if it will take you more than a few hours to get yourself free. Again, sorry, but this really is for your own good, you know."

And with that, Ian hit one button on the canister's keyboard and they all filed out of the canister. I heard them close both vacuum-tight doors, and in a few minutes I was suddenly in zero-G, traveling back in time.

There was enough spring in the air mattress to push me high into the air. Floating upward and rotating slowly, I could see that the beer can was also afloat, and that a growing blob of frothy beer was extruding itself from the opening. I soon bounced gently with my back to the ceiling, and lost my rotation in the process. It wasn't a big immediate problem, but I knew that when we arrived and gravity returned, if I wasn't back down I had a nasty fall coming!

Coming slowly back towards the deck, I saw that the glob of beer had grown much larger than the can it had come out of. It was bigger than my head, and it was coming directly at my face!

I had ugly visions of the blob fastening itself around my face, suffocating me. Beer foam is a mixture of carbon dioxide gas and a liquid made up mainly of water. Not the sort of thing you can breathe. A hell of a thing! Tom Kolczyskrenski, drowning in a single can of Foster's Lager Beer!

I couldn't change the vector of the beer, and I couldn't move my head more than a few inches. All that I could think of to do was to blow at it, and what with the ball gag, I was limited to blowing through my nose. This was not an efficient procedure, and the deadly glob of beer came closer and closer.

Gyroscopic action! If I could spin myself around and catch it on the back of the head, I just might survive. While I normally don't use hair oils, this time my bath girls had said that the slicked-down look was right for the outfit I would be wearing, and had greased me up. The hair oil, being non-polar and thus hydrophobic, ought to repel the hydrophilic beer! I tried moving my head around, to my left shoulder, then my chest, my right shoulder, back, and repeated the procedure as rapidly as possible.

There was some gyroscopic reaction, but not nearly

enough, and the beer blob was still growing, turning from yellow to foamy white, and still coming at me.

I did some rapid mental calculations for a journey of ten years, and came up with a subjective trip length of four minutes, assuming that the program was using our usual temporal velocity, and assuming that Ian hadn't been lying about sending me back for ten years. If both of these assumptions were true, I could hold my breath if the blob covered my face, and probably stay conscious until gravity returned to splatter the beer on the deck. But that was two too many assumptions, when my only life was on the line!

By swiveling my legs rapidly around my hips, I was able to turn myself ninety degrees or so, and from there I could bend over to let the dangerous beer slowly cruise past my head.

Victory! Now I only had to worry about breaking my neck, falling from what could be fourteen feet up when the gravity came back. I had to time it so that I was at or near the deck when that happened.

The problem was that, because of the handcuffs, I couldn't see my watch, and when I had been high enough above the boxes and crates to see the Nixie tubes on the control panel, I was facing in the wrong direction.

I drifted back towards the air mattress, and tried to flex my body so that I wouldn't bounce as hard next time. I was only partially successful. The next time I got to the ceiling, I could see the orange numbers, telling me that I had nine seconds to get down before I fell four yards to the floor. Squirming, I bumped the ceiling as hard as I could, and got to within three feet of the floor before gravity returned.

I missed the air mattress, and the fall knocked the wind out of me, but at least I hadn't broken my neck. Moments later, a gallon and a half of beer foam hit the deck, splattering my face and chest. Damn Ian, anyway!

I could see the keys to my handcuffs, and had started to wiggle my way towards them, when I heard someone opening the big steel door on the canister. Some rapidly chattering feminine voices echoed in the canister, and my first thought was that Barbara and some of her friends were coming to my rescue!

"Great! It's a cargo canister!"

"Yeah, but it's ancient. Can you handle the programing on one this old?"

"Are you kidding? I could reprogram Methuselah, if he had a keyboard!" They spoke to each other very quickly, in something like an Australian accent, with no time wasted between when one left off and another began.

"Then get on it, girl, before somebody comes by!"

I heard the doors being closed while the first voice said, "I'm working, I'm working!"

These weren't friends of mine. These people were some sort of temporal hijackers! Still, I tried to get their attention by mumbling past the damn ball gag and bumping my feet on the deck, on the theory that once I was free, I could deal with them somehow or another. The trouble was, they were making too much noise to notice me.

Whoever she was, she must have known her stuff, because in a few minutes we were in zero-G again, and presumably going farther into the past.

I drifted up to the ceiling once more, and got a look at my new set of abductors. There were three of them, a blonde who was taking off her backpack, a brunette sitting strapped to the chair at the keyboard, and a real redhead, with freckles and everything. All three had their long hair pulled back into ponytails. They were dressed for roughing it, in flannel shirts, blue jeans, and hiking boots.

I could tell at a glance that they weren't Smoothies. The girls of Morrow were almost all slender with a lot of hidden muscle, having the sort of bodies you see on ballerinas, lithe figure skaters, or rhythmic gymnasts.

These women were of a different sort, with large, firm breasts, wasp-tiny waists, and flaring hips, a bit like a slender version of the Victorian ideal, or perhaps like exaggerated Playmate-of-the-Month types. Not the sort that I'm usually attracted to, they were none the less very fine looking women.

I was still near the ceiling when they noticed me.

"Hey! We've got company!" the blonde shouted.

"He's all tied up! Shouldn't we free him?" the brunette said, undoing her safety belt.

"What makes you so sure about that? Maybe he's some kind of criminal!" the redhead said.

"Muff muff!" I said through the ball gag.

"But he dresses so nicely!" the brunette objected.

"I'll bet he undresses nicely, too!" the blonde said.

"And quickly, if I have anything to do with it!" the redhead said.

"Muff?"

"You know, I've always wanted a slave boy!" the blonde said.

"Muff!?!"

"You've always wanted anything that involves sex!" the brunette said.

"So what's wrong with that?" the blonde said.

"Nothing, except that I get him first," the redhead said, as she took her shirt off.

"No way! You got to pick the restaurant we ate lunch at!" The blonde was furiously unlacing her boots.

These women were experts at maneuvering in zero-G, and had apparently been together long enough to be well coordinated in their actions. As a group, they swarmed over me, disrobing themselves and me with equal efficiency. In seconds, they were all naked, and over my strenuous objections, I was floating with gobs of clothes at my bound wrists and ankles, but was otherwise naked save for a ball gag.

I've heard it said that it is physiologically impossible to force a male *Homo Sapiens* to have sex, but I can testify that such a statement is a patent lie. Even if you are not a volunteer, and have no intention of participating in their pleasures, when enough beautiful, naked women spend enough time stroking your body (about thirty seconds, in this case), the gallant reflex occurs.

From then on, they have you at their mercy.

Oh, for a little while, there, I thought the fact that we were in zero-G would save me from further molestation, but as I said earlier, these women were experts at maneuvering without gravity. Furthermore, despite her earlier

kindly thoughts, it was the brunette who impaled herself on me first.

The short of it was that I was soon forced into submis-
sion and raped six times.

Yes, raped!

I wasn't in charge, I wasn't a volunteer, and I didn't like
it.

That having been said, I don't think that the women
involved deserved twenty years in jail apiece for their crimes,
which is what would have happened to three men back in
the States, if they had done to a woman what these three
did to me.

But God dammit! A good spanking was definitely in
order!

Towards the end of my ordeal, they used my socks as a
blindfold to add to the ball gag, cuffs, and leg irons.

"Whoops!" one of them yelled. "It's time to hit the deck!"

I was woman-handled to the ground just before the gravity
returned.

I heard one of them opening the steel door. "Come on,
you two! We gotta get out of here!"

"What about our boy toy here?"

"What about him? We gotta quit this place before we're
caught! Leave him where we found him!"

"No! I like him. I want to take him along."

"Yeah, me too!"

"Then grab him and let's run! We can't stay here!"

It took all three of them to set me up on my feet, but
I didn't feel much like cooperating. I went down on my
knees, and tried reasoning with them.

"Muff. Muff!" I explained.

"Look fellow, you can come with us or you can stay here,
but either way, I'm going and I've got the keys to your cuffs
in my pocket."

"Muff." I capitulated, and they set me upright again.

I was hustled naked out of the capsule, barefoot with my
pants at my ankles. From the sound, I'd guess we went down
a long corridor, and then into a much larger room. We came
to some steps, where I tripped and fell forward. Before I
landed, I was picked up by two pairs of strong arms and

hauled up onto some sort of platform. Somebody turned me ninety degrees to the right.

"Gentlemen! May I present our guest of honor!" Ian's voice boomed out.

The blindfold was ripped off, and I found myself on a stage in front of an audience of at least a thousand men!

"Yes, Tom, this is Your Bachelor Party!"

CHAPTER THIRTY-NINE
A Bachelor Party from Hell

Things got worse.

I was hauled to the side of the stage, still bound, gagged, and naked. Meanwhile, my three former captors and molesters, who had somehow managed to get dressed in evening gowns, were acting like the models on a TV game show. With much swirling, smiling and hand waving, they opened the big curtain behind me, exposing a movie screen, and bowed out stage left.

I was forced to stand there while every man I had ever met on the island watched a movie of everything that had happened to me from the moment Ian and his henchmen walked me down to the subway.

The shouts and catcalls were loud, the display was vulgar and obscene, and I was royally pissed. People thought that assaulting me seven to one was funny. They thought that leaving me bound and gagged in a damaged time canister was a great joke, and that my vigorous avoidance of being drowned in beer foam was marvelous comedy.

The girls got special applause for every nefarious crime they committed on my body, and came to the front of the stage individually or in a group, each time, to take a bow.

And when the bloody-be-damned thing was finally over,

the crowd demanded to see it all over again. But for this performance at least, Leftenant Fitzsimmons came around and undid my cuffs and shackles. I was able to get most of my clothes back on, although I was still barefoot.

"All in clean fun, what?"

"No. Not clean fun at all, Ensign." I left him looking stunned and went out hunting Ian. I found him in the middle of a laughing crowd.

"Damn you, Ian! You promised me that nothing like this was going to happen!"

"Not quite, Tom. I promised that I wouldn't throw a *surprise* party. But you know me well enough to know that I couldn't possibly let a once-in-a-lifetime opportunity like this go by without doing something about it. You *knew* I'd pull something, now didn't you? And if you knew that it was coming, it couldn't possibly have been a surprise, could it? So I couldn't and didn't throw a *surprise* party, and therefore I never broke my promise!"

Faced with that line of reasoning, there was only one sensible thing I could think of to do.

I hit him.

My fist caught his jaw just off center, and I heard his jaw bones make a satisfying snapping sound. He went over backward and was out cold on his back.

Then I felt much better.

There was a gasp from the crowd. A single, white-suited man flicked into and out of existence a few feet from me. A half dozen white-coated men with a stretcher blinked in, put Ian on the stretcher, and then the lot of them disapeared without a sound.

Apparently, somebody had pressed his red button. Under other circumstances, I would have been fascinated, but just then I didn't give a damn.

People backed away from me as I went over to the bar that ran down the left side of the room. The bartender handed me a quart-sized boomba of full of dark beer, and I drained it on one breath.

"You know," I said to the man next to me, a plant manager whose name I didn't remember, "maybe tonight *is* a good night to throw a party."

The guy gave me a nod and an overly eager smile, but after seeing me deck the last person I'd talked to, you could tell that he didn't want to get involved.

Halfway through the next beer, Captain Stepanski came over with the rest of the wedding ushers. "Sir, you weren't serious about busting Fitzsimmons down to ensign, were you?"

"No, I wasn't. I meant to make him a midshipman, Cadet Stepanski."

Seargeant Kuhn was about to say something, but I cut him off with, "And that goes for the rest of you as well, Airman Basic Kuhn, or whatever that comes out to in army rank. Did you assholes actually think that you could get away with kidnapping, sexually molesting, and then publicly humiliating your Commander-in-Chief? After I had stated publicly, and in writing, that this sort of thing would not be tolerated? Because if you did, you are not only ignorant, but you are stupid as well, and both of those conditions are capital offenses in this universe!"

They were all appalled. Somehow Ian had convinced them that I'd be a good sport about it all, once I got over being angry. Well, maybe I would be, but I wasn't anywhere near over being mad. Maybe later. Much later. Or maybe not.

"Yes sir," Fitzsimmons said. "What are your orders for now, sir?"

"For now, well, you might as well enjoy yourselves, since your next assignments are going to be pure Hell, the absolute worst things I can think up. However, you might get some small joy in telling everybody else who participated in this fiasco, or even showed up at this party, that *their* careers have been wrecked as well, for laughing at the boss when he was tied up and naked, among other things. For myself, there are three women that I promised would get one hell of a spanking for the abuse they did me."

"You're angry at them as well, are you sir? Perhaps I can be of some assistance in locating them, in partial amends for my transgressions, as it were."

"Assist all you want to, but it won't do you any good. You know where they are, Fitz?"

"Well, I bloody well should! They are my wives, after all.

I thought that you'd enjoy some decent, full-bodied women, after all the thin-flanked fare, hereabouts."

"Your wives?! You sent your wives out to rape and fornicate with a stranger?"

"Well, I hardly 'sent them out,' sir. Actually, it was their idea, once they heard that the job was open. As to that fornicating business, you must understand that these are my wives, not my slave girls. We're not barbarians! Our contracts call for me to be the biological father of their children, to share in their upbringing, and to support the family during that period. After that, we all get to discreetly play around a bit, when the mood strikes."

"And you figure that raping your boss counts as 'discreet'?"

"In this case, discreet means that the children shouldn't be affected."

"Getting yourself fired just might affect the way you support them."

"I rather doubt that, sir. At worst, it might mean that I'll have to work for longer periods between home leaves. It might take me eighty years subjective to raise the lot, instead of forty. Maybe not a bad thing at all."

"Your people are weirder than the Smoothies."

"We have a saying, sir. 'Weird depends on where you came from.' By my lights, the really weird bunch are the Incas. If you keep me around, I'll tell you some tales about them."

"Fitz, you have more gall than any twelve people I've ever met."

"Well, sir, it's just that after a certain number of ass chewings, there's not much left but scar tissue, which is low on nerve endings. Did you want me to send the girls over in a group, or one at a time?"

"One at a time." I figured that it might be difficult getting the bunch of them over my knee without hurting one of them.

Where I grew up, you don't hit a woman, not ever. But hitting someone means striking them with the intention of doing physical damage to their person, and spanking is another matter entirely. It involves deliberately causing someone pain and humiliation, but not actual damage. In spanking, you strike with the palm of your hand, and only on the bare buttocks of the person being punished. The human butt contains the biggest, strongest bones in the body, which are covered with the biggest normal muscles in the body, which are covered by an inevitable layer of fat, and lastly by some sturdy skin with lots of sensitive nerve endings.

I expect that Ian might say that God built the human fanny with a definite purpose in mind.

"Right sir. There's a small room with a chair in it that might serve your purpose. It's through that door. I'll send Judy around first. She's the redhead. She rather enjoys a bit of spanking."

Suddenly, I had bad feelings about all this.

CHAPTER FORTY
The Wedding

I spent a day and a night sobering up. Then Prescott, my mathematician, showed up with a blindfold and said that if I wanted to get to my wedding on time, I had to put it on.

After a very short trip, she took off my blindfold and I was in one of my rarely used guest rooms, where my bath girls had a duplicate of my last wedding outfit all laid out and ready. Or, maybe, they'd just had the old one cleaned up. In an hour, Ian and my ushers arived looking not a bit abashed, and we rode on horseback to the cathedral, waving to the cheering crowds.

The sky was clear blue, and spotted with white clouds. The cathedral was beautiful, and decked with white flowers. My Barbara was the most beautiful of all, swathed in acres of white lace, and just stepping out of her father's white carriage as my party arrived.

Inside, after an abbreviated mass, Barb's father presented her to me before the thousands of people present, and she was by ancient custom officially mine now, once the Spanish-speaking priest mumbled out a few memorized lines in English.

On the way to the reception hall, in an open white carriage

drawn by four white horses, Barbara said, "On the way to church, I heard about your bachelor party."

"Ian gets carried away, sometimes."

"So do you. Are you really planning on demoting every man on the island?" Barb was smiling and waving to the crowds.

"I've been thinking about it, and you know, it's just not logically possible. Every man who is in any kind of managerial position in the entire organization was at that party. If I demote every one of them, all that happens is that the whole company goes down a few pegs, but their relative positions go unchanged. So what's the point?"

"Not quite, Tom. Half the managers on the island are women. Demoting the men would put them in charge. Smile. Wave to the people."

I smiled and waved.

"And you think that this would be an improvement?"

"It might be fun, but seriously, no, it would cause many more problems than it would cure."

"Right. I think I'll just let them all worry about it for a few days, to get back at them for what they did to me, and then rescind the order."

"Good. Next question. Did you really spank all three of Leftenant Fitzsimmons's wives?"

"No. That wouldn't have done any good, either. The first one showed up already naked, with a bag full of handcuffs, whips, and chains. I didn't know what half of that stuff was for, even. She had all these suggestions about how I was supposed to tie her up, dangle her upside down from the ceiling, and go at her with this cat-o'-nine-tails whip she'd brought. There were these *fish hook things* at the end of each goddamn strand, and she was really looking forward to getting swatted with it! Short of killing her, there wasn't anything that I could do to that woman that she wouldn't have considered entertainment!"

"So what did you do?"

"I told her to get out of Morrow, and promised that if she ever returned, I'd have her executed. Painlessly."

"It was probably the cruelest thing you could have done to her. What about the other two?"

"The second one showed up with a bag of her own, but

I threw her out before she had a chance to open it. I left before the third one got there."

"Poor baby. Left alone with all the difficult decisions of command." She giggled at me, then went back to waving at the crowds.

The reception was a long, boring affair, with ridiculously expensive foods and wines being consumed by the ton, and Barbara's father smiling throughout while his gluttonous friends and alcoholic aquaintances impoverished him. Yet he seemed to be genuinely enjoying himself, so maybe there was something to Ian's potlatch theory.

With my ushers prompting me, I went through a dozen silly ceremonies. I threw Barb's garter to the bachelors in the crowd, danced the first dance with her, and then the second with her attractive mother. Barb's bouquet went the way of all wedding bouquets, a six-foot-tall wedding cake was cut into thousands of pieces and handed out, for eating and for souvenirs, and everybody kissed everybody of the opposite sex.

I'd thought that the reception should be held at Camelot, since so many people had expressed curiosity about the place, but Barb wouldn't have it. It seems that we were only equipped to entertain a thousand people, and that wasn't nearly enough. A suitable hall was rented. I have no idea what they did with the place when the boss wasn't getting married.

In the course of the evening, Barb told me about her plans for Camelot, which—thankfully—did not include redecorating, since she'd been in charge of decorating the castle in the first place. She figured that if she threw one party a week for sixty-five weeks, with a carefully controlled guest list, everybody on the island could have their curiosity satisfied. I figured that if that was all the mischief that she planned to get into, I was getting off light. Just so long as I was not required to attend every one of them, if they turned out to be boring.

It was after midnight when we finally got home, and because of the tradition of the wedding night, the other girls left us in bed alone. Or maybe Barb had just scheduled it that way.

After we'd made love a few times, I said, "So how does it feel to be Mrs. Kolczyskrenski?"

"Oh. I hadn't really thought about changing my name. Do you want me to?"

"Since everybody on this island is on a first-name basis, I don't suppose it much matters. If we ever move back to the States, though, I'll expect your papers to say 'Barbara Kolczyskrenski.' But for now, well, what's the local custom?"

"You keep the name you were born with. A girl is given her mother's last name, and a boy, his father's."

"You mean his biological father's? So then our three boys are already named Kolczyskrenski? I was worried that I might have to adopt them, or something."

"Yes, yes, and adoption isn't necessary. Your other three hundred and eighteen sons also share that name. Your two hundred and ninety-six daughters have their mothers' names."

"Six hundred and twelve kids?"

"Conceived as of yesterday morning, Tom. Most of them are still in their mothers' wombs."

"I'd better get a will made up! Otherwise, the lawyers are going to have a field day when I kick off."

"I can't imagine why. We don't have that many lawyers, and inheritance doesn't play much part in our lives here."

"Your people don't inherit anything when your parents die?"

"Not in the normal course of things. So many of our older people spend their time traveling up the time stream, that not all that many of them have actually died. When they do, it's often by arrangement, and any property is given out as gifts by the person dying."

"They arrange their own deaths? You mean suicide?"

"Hardly ever that. But there are limits to what the doctors can do, and when those are reached, and the body is failing, a person usually simply gets tired of living, and welcomes death. One's best friends generally attend the gathering."

"I'll bet that they sometimes go to each other's Death Party. 'I'll go to yours if you'll come to mine.' "

"Yes, of course."

"You know, this is one hell of a topic of conversation for a wedding night! What I was trying to get around to was that since I am now officially our children's father, I want to see the little buggers! I want them brought here, to the palace, by ten o'clock tomorrow morning, so I can start getting to know them."

"Tom, I don't like that idea. We've talked about it before. This is a dangerous world up here! Too dangerous to raise children in!"

"I am going to meet and have a hand in raising my own children! The causality laws won't let me go back to whenever it is that you keep them, so they will have to come here to me!"

"You'd risk their lives just to satisfy your ego?"

"I'm not risking anybody's life, my ego has nothing to do with this, and my children are not going to be raised to be three more of your dull, cowardly, uncreative drones! They are going to have every possible chance of becoming bright, curious, and inventive people. The kind of people their ancestors were, out there in the real world."

"Tom, you can't make me do this."

"Maybe I can't, but if you don't bring them here, I'll have a military platoon go back and get them for me."

"You'd never do that!"

"Oh, yes I would, lady. Don't make me prove it!"

"Tom, I believe you would."

"That's what I've been telling you!"

"Tom . . . Could I have a few weeks, to, to get used to the idea?"

"Well . . . Okay, if you need it. But one limitation. You may not go back to see them until the day they leave for here and now. I don't want to discover that they're all fifteen years old when they arrive."

The honeymoon was not the delightful affair I'd hoped it would be. I'd made arrangements for us to tour Niagara Falls, plus the four other biggest and/or tallest waterfalls in the world, with fake ID and so on, but Barb couldn't see them as being anything but examples of the horrible, powerful destructiveness of the world I lived in. I finally gave in, and called the tour off after five days.

"You got back early," Ian said as I was sitting down at my desk. "You want to talk about it?"

"No, I just want to get back to work."

"When you're ready, then. Your managers tell me that everything is pretty much on schedule, but you'll want to get the details from them. Our first time trip is ready to go, again. I've had it on hold, pending your return."

"Thanks. How about if I spend the day around here, and we leave for the eighteenth century in the morning?"

"Suits. There's one other thing that I want to talk about, Tom. They tell me that after you coldcocked me at the party, somebody hit a red button, and you saw the whole procedure."

"You figure that you didn't have it coming?"

"No, it's not that. What's a broken bone or two, between friends? It's not like I felt any pain. I went out like a light, and woke up feeling fine in the hospital. I even went back to the party, once you were too drunk to notice. No. What bothers me is that we're now up against a violation of causality, and from everything I've heard about it, that's about the most dangerous thing a man can possibly do."

"Naah. Don't worry about it."

"You've got a new slant on causality?"

"Nope, but I've got a fix for the problem at hand."

"Enlighten me, my master."

"Now, you're showing the proper attitude! The solution is simple. I saw the Red Button Drill, and how they took you to the hospital. You didn't, since you were out cold, enjoying your just deserts on the floor. Therefore, I won't tell you what I saw, and you will have to invent the whole thing all by yourself, without any input from me."

"Yeah, I guess that would work. I'll do some thinking about it this afternoon."

CHAPTER FORTY-ONE
The Second Expedition

This time, there wasn't anybody waiting for us near the opened time chamber except for a few guards, the construction crew and the military squad who were scheduled to go along. Everybody who was going was all decked out, as we were, in eighteenth-century finery.

We were getting ready to shut the steel doors when Barbara, Ming Po, and a half dozen other women arived in the wide-bottomed feminine equivalents of our outfits, and tried to join us inside.

"Whoops! Hold on, there!" I said. "You people can't come with us!"

"And why not? We are man and wife, joined until death do us part, in your theory of things. Where you go, I go."

"But you can't! It might be dangerous!"

"If it is, then it's all the more reason for me to be along, to protect you. But it's not. You've said so repeatedly."

"But . . ."

"Two minutes, Tom. Give in or give up for today," Ian said.

"But . . ."

"You should have thought of that before you insisted on marrying the girl."

"But . . ."

Barb and her friends brushed by me, and I had no choice but to step in after them.

The interior of the canister had been redesigned with the storage area nearest the door, where the dirty work of digging up to the surface could go on without messing up the living quarters in the back. The pile of supplies and machinery was bigger than it had been last time. There was so much stuff that I had to duck my head and go sideways through the storage area.

The passenger area resembled the first-class section of a modern airliner, with wide, tilt-back seats, a small kitchen, and *two* rest rooms. There were eight more seats than there had been before, and feminine-looking suitcases were strapped to three walls and the ceiling. Damn. I'd been had, again.

I managed to sit in a chair next to Barb without getting my long sword tangled up in the armrest. "Extra supplies, two johns, and eight extra seats. You had the canister redesigned for this expedition."

"Not really, darling. I merely wrote a note to the design team that was working on this canister, and made a few suggestions."

"It would seem that a suggestion from the boss's wife has a lot in common with an order."

"So it would seem."

"I trust that you arranged for extra compressed air for breathing, as well?"

"They said that it wouldn't be necessary. They're using tanks of liquid air, now, since they discovered that the field that surrounds the canister is a perfect reflector of heat. Ian used the same sort of field to surround the liquid air tanks. It's safer, and holds a lot more air in the same space."

So she'd done more than just write a note. She'd had a hand in the design! But, there was nothing I could do but take the Chinaman's advice, and let the adventure we'd been looking forward to for years get turned into a family outing. Shit.

"So you and Ming Po just had to come along. Okay. But what are the other six women for?" I asked.

"Somebody has to take care of the two of you and keep you neat and clean, or you'd fall back on your old slovenly habits. Also, from a management standpoint, your men might get frustrated if they had to stay celibate when their bosses didn't."

"Yeah, sure. Anything for the troops' morale."

It was shaping up to be a dull trip, and as it turned out, I wasn't disapointed. For a while, anyway.

We arrived precisely on schedule, and the construction crew dug us up to the surface in about five hours.

When Ian opened the second, huge, air-tight door, we found ourselves facing a solid granite wall. The first machine to go out was the tunneler, a sturdy tracked vehicle that cut a hole eight feet wide and eight feet tall. The square front of the thing was one big "shovel" that made dirt and rock go away. Behind it was a gasket that cut down on the air we would otherwise send elsewhen with the rock, followed by a sturdy, air-tight cage that protected the operator in the event of a cave-in.

In normal operation, the shovels took a quarter-inch bite, and the *click-click-click* of the thing made it too loud to talk in the enclosed space, but our crew was equipped with earphones, throat mikes, and CB radios.

The tunneler went forward fifty feet with the operator stopping every two feet to check his leveling gauges, to open a hatch in the front to make sure that he was still going through solid rock, and to peek through a rear-facing periscope to make sure he was going straight. Then he backed out, and a crew bolted on two "wings," "shovels" that pivoted outward to make the hole he cut thirty-two feet wide. Again, he went forward and then backed out. A third pivoting wing was then bolted to the top of the tunneler. Finally, the operator drove forward two hundred feet, leaving behind an arched tunnel with polished walls that was thirty-two feet wide and twenty-four feet high at the center. This was our staging area, where we could get the rest of our stuff unpacked and assembled.

The pivoting wings were removed and a smaller semicircular shovel was bolted to the top, to give the stairway up an arched ceiling. A step-cutting gadget was set up to be towed behind the tunneler. It left a narrow ramp on each side for a special cart to roll on.

Most of the construction crew spent their time setting up the electric generator, and installing lights and handrails, using our temporal version of a half-inch drill, while our guards spent their time unloading the canister.

In an emergency, the tunneling machine could go faster than a man could run. Hell, in an emergency the damn thing could fly right out of the ground and keep on going, using the same flight mechanism as the escape harness and the fighter plane that was still under construction. Since there were no springs or shocks in the suspension system, and forward visibility was nonexistent, this procedure was not encouraged.

The tank tracks were used to get the tunneler into position, but in operation they did not drive it forward. Air pressure behind the machine did that. The tracks and their electric drive motors dynamically braked the forward motion, to keep the machine from slamming into the tunnel face. On long runs, you actually had to stop on occasion to discharge the batteries.

Since we were in no big hurry, we followed the safe procedure of going forward for two feet, stopping to see if the roof wanted to collapse, checking the instruments, opening the front window to make sure that we were still in solid rock, and then going ahead two more feet, stopping, and et cetera. Actually, when we got to the dirt a few feet from the surface, the roof did collapse, but that was no big thing. The top and sides of the tunneler also had "shovel" surfaces that the operator could switch on. The dirt was cleaned away in moments.

Ian handled what little supervising was necesary, so I went back to the passenger section, tilted my seat back and downed a dozen or so cold beers.

The girls who pulled waitressing duty felt obligated to strip out of their eighteenth-century finery to do the job in their traditional attire. It got a bit chilly towards the end, what with all the liquid air boiling off to replace what our "shovels" were sending elsewhen, but it never got cold enough for my waitresses to ask to put some clothes on.

Finally, word came that they were through to the surface, and your intrepid adventurer picked up his beer and wandered out. The new tunnel slanted upward at a thirty-degree angle through solid rock for a few hundred yards or so. It was nicely equipped with electric lights, handrails, and steps that a building inspector would have approved of. So much for adventure.

The last twenty feet of the tunnel passed through loose rock, sand and dirt, and so was lined with prefabricated, interlocking steel arches that I had been pretty proud of when I thought them up.

I stepped up into the sunshine of an eighteenth-century morning, feeling very anticlimactic. It was the same old island, only now it seemed completely empty except for the abundant plant life.

Ian was waiting for me a few feet away. Our guards had set up a perimeter defense against nothing in particular, and the construction crew had gone down to rig up the freight cart cables and start bringing up equipment and supplies. In a small valley with a nice view of the ocean, the girls were already laying out a campsite.

As luck would have it, the tunnel mouth came out at the top of a low hill, which looked to be the highest point on the island.

I said to Ian, "Pretty good shooting. A few yards either way, and you would have had to stop tunneling sooner."

"And shorten the scenic walk up here? For shame! Anyhow, this way we eliminate the drainage problems. Are you ready to join us working slobs?"

"There was something useful for me to do?"

"There's a town to design and build. If I'm going to get the definitive history of mankind written, we ought to start here and now."

We had long ago decided that if you put a secret installation in the middle of the wilderness, somebody is sure to notice all the people coming and going. But if you put it in the middle of a town, or better still a city, where strangers are wandering in and out all the time, your chances of going unnoticed are much better.

Since we could not be sure of the exact layout of the land

back in this century, we had deferred the design of the town and its defenses until we actually got here. Our plan was to make this island the base for our exploration of the Western Hemisphere. In time, we figured to have three thousand people living here, with about ninety percent of them being locals who didn't have any idea of what was really going on.

The obvious first step was to map the island and select a site for the town. A group of three Smoothie surveyors was getting itself together, to be accompanied by three Killer guards. I decided to tag along, for lack of anything better to do.

The surveyors planned to walk around the island, surveying as they went, staying near the beach so we wouldn't have to clear much vegetation out of their way. Tomorrow, they would walk across the island a few times, to get an idea of the interior.

Despite the fact that I'd been living a sedentary life for the past few years, my new body took to a day's brisk walk without difficulty. It's remarkable what a little biological reengineering can do for you.

It was mid-afternoon when we came on the cannibals' campsite. What had happened here was pretty obvious. The roasted and chewed bones of three people were scattered on the sand, skulls and everything. One of the broken-open skulls was pretty small. It must have been a child.

The Smoothie surveyors just freaked out, shaking, breaking into cold sweats, or vomiting on the ground. I was more than a little queasy, myself.

Sergeant Kuhn was in charge of the Killer squad. "This happened last night, sir, judging from the bones and the campfire," he said.

"You've seen something like this before?" I asked.

"Yeah. This was probably the work of Caribe Indians. They made a point of hunting the Arawaks on these islands. Or, it could have been the Arawaks. They were cannibals, too. Whoever it was, they could still be around here. We'd better call the base and warn them to be on their guard."

"Good idea. Do it."

Our little hundred-milliwatt CB radios carried a long way in this century, with its clean, empty airways.

The other two guards had followed a trail into the brush. One of them gave a shout, and I went in to see what they wanted.

They'd found a fourth victim, a naked woman. She was unconsious, but still alive, barely, and dangling upside down from a tree.

"Well, cut her down!" I said.

"Are you sure we should get involved, sir?" a private said.

"What? Of course I'm sure! What are you worried about?"

"Causality, sir."

"Causality be damned! We can't just let a woman die without trying to help her!"

"Yes, sir."

His "Brown Bess" had a temporal sword built in it, and with it he quickly cut the rope a foot above her feet while his partner caught her and laid her on the ground. She was filthy, and wouldn't have been pretty if she'd been cleaned up, but she was human, cannibal or not, and she needed help. I took out my leather canteen and got a bit of water into her. She revived enough to drink the canteen dry, and then she fell asleep again.

"You want us to rig up a stretcher for her, sir?"

"It might come to that, but let's give her a while to see if she comes around. I'll stay with her. You two go farther up this trail and see what you can find."

"We'll be back in half an hour, sir."

There was a fallen tree a few yards away. I sat down on it and lit up a cigar, waiting.

I was halfway through my stogie when this Indian with a big steel lumberman's axe broke out of the brush not twenty feet from me. He ran right past me while I was too startled to move, and planted his axe in the woman's head. Then he noticed me, pulled out his axe, and started to run towards me. He was yelling something that I couldn't understand, with his bloody weapon held high above his head.

By that time, I had my temporal sword out. It never even occured to me to draw the steel one. When he was six feet from me, I slashed him across the middle, cutting him in half, but he kept on coming.

Both halves hit me hard enough to knock me down.

I heaved the pieces off me and got up, shaking. I looked down at what I'd done to the man.

"Why?" I said, knowing that he couldn't understand me. "Why did you kill her? Why did you try to kill me?"

He looked back at me. He blinked, and then he died.

CHAPTER FORTY-TWO
Building a Small City

I was covered with blood and shit. My hands were shaking so bad that it was a few minutes before I could get the radio working to call back the troops.

All six of the people on the surveying team got to me at about the same time. The Smoothies got sick all over again, while Sergeant Kuhn led me away from the carnage.

"First time you ever killed anybody, sir?"

"Yeah. Richards told me we shouldn't get involved, but I figured I had to help the woman. Now she's dead and the other Indian's dead, too. I feel sick."

"Look, sir. A man's got to do what a man's got to do. As to causality, well, we're still here, aren't we? Before long, all of the Indians on these islands will be dead and gone, be it from European diseases, slavers, or their fellow cannibals. And don't feel ashamed of being shook up at your first kill. Most of us go through the same thing. You want me to send one of the men back to camp with you?"

"No. No, I'll be all right. We've got a job to do."

"That's the spirit, sir. Richards! Take that axe back with us. Leave everything else as it is. We're moving out!"

"What do you want with the axe?" I asked.

"Nothing. But it's a very valuable tool in this time and

289

place. That Indian's friends would think it very weird if we left it."

That evening, I changed outfits as soon as we got back. Barb took one look at my dirty clothes and threw them into the campfire. Even the boots. I had to rescue the sword, sheath, and baldric from the fire, since I didn't have any spares with me.

There were three Canada geese roasting over that fire. Lieutenant McMahon had bagged them that afternoon in a small nearby stream.

"I didn't know that Canada geese lived in these islands," I said.

"Neither did I," Ian said. "It's the sort of information we came here to find out. You want to talk about what happened this afternoon?"

"Not just yet."

The women and the Smoothies turned in early, talking about tomorrow being a long day. Two Killers stood guard duty, but the rest gathered around the fire, passing around cold beer, whiskey and ice cubes. After a few beers, I found that I needed the whiskey. Before long, Sergeant Kuhn was talking about the first man he'd ever killed.

"I was on point, going down a forest trail in what is now southern England, with the whole Ninth Roman Legion strung out behind me. Suddenly, this tall guy wearing nothing but blue paint and a scowl jumps out from behind a tree, swinging a big, two-handed sword. I took it on my shield, just like in training, and got him in the gut with my gladius. That was the way the Romans fought. Big shield, short sword. He went down, but I had to stab him three more times before he quit moving. It was strange, everything seemed to be moving so slowly, but somehow I was still faster than the other guy, which is why I'm still here, I guess. They gave me a triple ration of wine that night, and I needed it."

Three of the other guards told stories of their own, before I was ready to talk about what had happened to me.

Much later, with a lot of empty bottles lying around, the lieutenant explained, "We call it debriefing, sir. When you're in a fight, and it's kill or get killed, you have to do things that are contrary to everything they taught you about morality and decency, ever since you were old enough to walk. After something like that, a man has to talk it out, among friends if possible. You have to settle it all out in your mind. And maybe it's a little like confession. But not doing it makes a man crazy, and old before his time."

It turned out that there wasn't a better site for a town than the place we'd come up at. The island didn't have a natural harbor, and since we wanted this to be a base for further exploration, we would have to build one ourselves. Our tunnel entrance had to be hidden and protected, and the eighteenth century being a rather violent time, we planned to build a fort covering it. The fact that it had come up at the island's high point didn't hurt a bit.

One of the construction crew, Jolsen, was an architect who had spent years studying the construction techniques of this century. Not that we planned to use those techniques, but, for obvious reasons, it was important that when we got finished with construction, it had to look period.

Jolsen looked rather sheepish when he unrolled his plans for the town. It took me a while to find out why.

They showed a town that could hold three thousand people by the cramped standards of the eighteenth century. It was built around an irregularly shaped deep-water harbor that was big enough to hold two of the largest ships of this century and a dozen smaller ones. There were eight big stone piers and a largish dry dock. The main road of the town followed the shore. Most of this was to be cut from solid rock.

The town's defenses looked like something the Spanish would have done in this century, with two small forts guarding the harbor entrance, a thirty-foot wall with fourteen towers and three gates surrounding the town, and a powerful castle on the hill. Where these defenses couldn't be cut from bedrock, they were to be built of cut stones weighing two tons each, the limit of what our lift truck could handle.

It was when we got down to details like the water and sewage systems that we found out what our architect was so sheepish about. You see, he wanted to put in water and sewage systems, and that just wasn't done much in the eighteenth century.

"Yes, sir. You're right, sir. But without these systems, life in this town would be smelly and uncomfortable by modern standards, not to mention disease ridden. What I want us to build is well within the limits of eighteenth-century technology. The sewage system consists of a single tunnel that runs under the main buildings of the town. The bottom of the tunnel is at the level of low tide in this area. At one end of the sewage tunnel, a gate connects with the harbor. This is manually opened at high tide twice a day, flooding the tunnel. At the other end is a second gate that connects with the sea. This is opened at low tide, flushing the sewage out to sea."

"Yeah, that much is fine," Ian said. "But somebody is bound to get curious about the flush toilets."

"I hadn't planned to use flush toilets, sir. Just a seat with a hole in it. A tight-fitting lid should keep the smell down."

"If we can teach the men to put down the toilet seats," Barbara said.

"I suppose I could hinge the lids so that you had to hold them up, ma'am. That way they would close automatically."

"Why couldn't they do that in our century?" Barbara said, but I shushed her.

"What about the water system?" I asked.

"There's a nice steady breeze here most of the time, sir. A well and a windmill in the next valley should provide for our needs, with a simple aqueduct system to deliver it to the town. Much of it can be built within the outer city wall. Each major building will have a cistern that is also filled by rainwater. A second windmill on the castle can pump the water for its requirements."

"It might be better for the castle to have its own well. And if we ever have to stand a siege, we'll want to have the windmill inside the town. We can run a tunnel from some underground aquifer to the windmill. But all told, I suppose it beats having two hundred slaves to do the hauling. Is this okay with the rest of you? Then let's do it," I said.

"And we'd better get it done fast, since this island isn't as uninhabited as I'd like it to be," Ian said. "We need defenses in case we're seriously attacked, and we don't want any of the locals to see how we're going to build them. This is going to have to be an all-out effort until at least the exteriors of things are up."

The next step was clearing the land that the harbor, the town, and the castle would be built on, or more often carved into. It would have been easy enough to just run the tunneler over it all, but most of the area was heavily wooded, and we would be needing the lumber.

Felling the trees was no problem, not when every one of us carried a temporal sword. The problem was hauling the usable logs out of the way, when we had only one small lift truck and the tunneler. We also had a small traveling crane, though, and the tunneler soon cut some straight temporary roads that let the crane drag in logs for the lift truck to stack.

We cleared the top of the hill first, because building the castle would be the biggest job, and we had to get going on it soonest.

Barbara liked operating the tunneler, and proved to be very competent in operating it. This was good, since unlike the rest of us, she didn't have to sleep, and we needed more than twelve hours of work a day out of that machine. Ming Po commandeered the lift truck, and one of the other girls, Kelly, took over the traveling crane. The other five women were on kitchen and housekeeping duty, leaving us mere men to do the grunt work. Two of the Killers were always on guard duty, but the rest were put to work.

Within a day, the hilltop was logged over, and by working through the night, Barb and "her" tunneler had us down to a big flat piece of limestone bedrock by morning. The hill and the tunnel mouth had become thirty-five feet lower, and my nifty interlocking steel hoops were gone.

The town and the harbor covered over six hundred acres, and logging it took us over a week. The tunneler easily kept up with the rest of us. For this sort of work, digging with an open sky above you, the tunneler was equipped with a periscope that let the operator see over the front shovel. With its side wings on, and driving an easy seven miles an hour, that thing was capable of sending twenty-five hundred cubic feet of rock into oblivion every second. By the time we had the tree trunks hauled away, Barb had the harbor cut down to fifty feet deep, complete with stone piers, a launching ramp, and a dry dock. A thirty-two-foot-wide road surrounded it, a road of equal width ran on both sides of the town wall, and some of the connecting roads were in as well. A big town square was cut, with a big block of limestone left in the center to be eventually cut into a fountain. She had been able to leave enough good rock in position so that half the outer wall, complete with towers and gates, was already built, and the larger buildings closest to the castle, where a hill used to be, could be made by simply hollowing them out, rather that having to build them up out of cut stone. The architect calculated that there was enough good limestone left inside the buildings, and in the unfinished roads, to complete the town.

We quarried the stone for the castle out of the granite walls of the staging area down near the canister we'd arrived in. It would have to be hauled up the tunnel to the top of the hill, but there was already a freight elevator of sorts to do the job. Well, it was a cart that ran on stone rails cut on either side of the steps going up. An electric winch moved it up and down.

With a temporal sword, cutting stone was no problem. You just switched it on and whacked away. Cutting it accurately, however, required that you carefully place a simple aluminum frame with an adjustable rail that you set up to where you wanted the cut to be. There was a sword that cut a quarter-inch-wide hole mounted on a little wheeled trolly that rolled along the rail. You needed that thickness to slide metal bars between the blocks before you cut them loose from the wall. Without the bars, you couldn't get a lift truck fork under a block to lift it.

The lift truck operator took the blocks to the stair elevator and sent them up in groups of four. At the top of the steps, a worker checked the blocks and if necessary did some trimming on them. He also put two holes in each one, so the crane would have something to grab onto, and attached them to the end of the traveling crane's cable.

Our crane was small, and had to drive along on top of the eight-foot-thick wall it was building. A fifth worker eased the blocks in place and mortared them down.

Our usual block was two feet wide by two feet high by four feet long, and weighed about two tons. Once we got into it, a team of five of us averaged one block— cut, hauled, and mortared into place—every minute and a half. The Smoothies were amazingly coordinated, and worked together like a well-designed machine. Every one of them seemed to know exactly what everyone around them was doing, what needed to be done next, and what their part in that ought to be. They did construction work the way auto workers built cars—with calm, cool effiency, even though each of their jobs was new and different, and the car workers had been doing the same things over and over again for years. The Killers were competent and hardworking, but at the end of the day, they each got only half as much done as a Smoothie. And despite our advantages of size and strength, Ian and I weren't quite as good as a pair of Killers when it came to getting things done.

We started quarrying a rock face that was eight feet tall, as high as the little electric lift truck could lift. Being taller than the rest, Ian and I spelled each other doing the cutting. Even so, we were a week getting the outer walls of the castle built, and that was working a twelve-hour day. Putting in the interior partitions, floors, and ceilings, with all the supporting arches required, was going to take months, but that could be done after company came, working behind the shield of the outer walls. We made a point of leaving plenty of extra stone over and around doors, windows, fireplaces, and banisters, so that decorations could be carved in later. Doing all that fine work might take years, but that could be done at some future date when people felt bored and artistic.

Actually, after years of skull sweat, doing manual labor was kind of fun. These new bodies of ours gloried in hard work. I suspect that the construction workers had had similar treatments, since they didn't seem to have any trouble keeping up with us big guys. Or maybe Smoothies were just built that way.

CHAPTER FORTY-THREE
Barbara's Tunneling Machine

Barbara and her tunneler pretty much worked straight through, barring quick stops for meals and occasional bouts of lovemaking with me. She was a few days getting all the sewers and secret passages in, including a second set of both that extended outside the town's walls. This was her idea, for future expansion, she said.

She also went way overboard when it came to getting our water supply in. She cut twenty-two miles of tunnels, twelve feet high and eight wide, eighty feet below sea level in the remarkably solid limestone under the island, and then rigged a dozen half-inch drills in a fan-shaped array on her tunneler to punch millions of holes in the roof all the way to the surface. This drained groundwater into two huge underground vaults that the windmills could draw water from.

It also punched holes in thousands of trees that would otherwise have been good timber. When I complained about this, Barb said that there wasn't any way to be sure exactly how far up the surface was, and it was better to be safe than sorry. The damage was done, and it wouldn't be repeated, so I let the matter drop.

The architect calculated that once the system filled with water, if the island suffered from a total drought for twenty years, we would still have plenty of water for all of our needs.

Personally, I think Barbara just liked digging tunnels.

Another crew was working with the logs we'd collected during the ground clearance. There wouldn't be time to season the wood properly before we turned it into furniture, doors and window shutters, but any seasoning was better than none, so we got on it soonest.

Our "saw mill" looked like a long, aluminum sawhorse that you set up above the log you were planning to turn into boards. Up to sixteen temporal swords fit on a wheeled trolley that ran along the bottom of the long beam of the sawhorse. Pulling the trolley the length of the horse sliced the log into nice, smooth lumber.

The hard part was stacking the wood in neat, rectangular piles so it would dry out properly.

Despite the long hours we all put in, it wasn't all work, not by a long shot. Every Smoothie can play at least one musical instrument, and most of them brought one along. Being ungodly cooperative, group singing came naturally to them. Furthermore, Barb was a world-class ballerina, and her friends weren't far behind her.

The sea was full of fish, and there was plenty of game on the island, from wild pigs, birds, feral goats and cattle, to sea turtles. Ian claimed that many of them had been put on these islands by Christians to feed shipwrecked sailors, and to give the cannibals something to eat besides each other.

The trick with the cannibals hadn't worked. Apparently, once you develop a taste for human flesh, nothing else quite makes it.

The Killers liked to hunt and fish, so we didn't have to live on the canned food we'd brought along. A bakery, a brewery, and a still were among the first things they got going and, weather permitting, we usually ate around a campfire.

With the Killers providing the food and drink, and the Smoothies the entertainment, a very good time was had by all.

❂   ❂   ❂

When there was nothing else for Barbara to do but cut the canal that would connect our harbor to the sea, she warned us, and we all knocked off work to watch. She had already cleared the canal down to a few inches above the high-tide level.

The tunneler was sealed against both a hard vacuum and high pressure, and was as sturdy as a submarine, so taking it into the water wasn't what bothered me. I was having visions of the sea water driving her backward into the harbor, and smashing her against a pier or something.

Most people just don't realize the force of moving water. Thousands of people are killed in floods every year all around the world, but very few of them actually drown. Most often, they are ripped to naked pieces by the force of the water smashing them into things.

But Barbara insisted on doing it herself, and out-arguing her was a lot like out-stubborning a cat. You can do it, but it usually isn't worth the effort.

She got the tunneler into position on a notch that she had cut earlier for the purpose. She swung her wings out to their full thirty-two-foot width, and took off at about thirty miles an hour. She ran out of stone to drive on about the time she hit the beach, but that didn't slow her down. She just pressed on regardless, eating up prodigious amounts of rocks, sand, and then water. She didn't even stop when she was completely submerged, but continued on with the water flowing over and around the big wings.

With hindsight, I can see the wisdom of her actions. She had to get out and away from the backwash she was kicking up. At the time she scared the shit out of me!

Watching her, I almost missed the start of the hydraulic show she'd kicked up. Water gushed up her recently cut canal at what must have been sixty miles an hour. It made a spectacular waterfall as it splashed down into a harbor that you could hide a five-story building in.

In a few minutes, Barb and her tunneler drove up onto the beach. She shut down the shovels, folded her wings, and hurried back to see the waterfall she'd made. She needn't have rushed. The harbor was more than six hours filling

up. Only then, when the rapid flow had ceased, was it safe
to go back and cut the channel wider and deeper.

We spent another two months getting the town pretty
much finished. The buildings were all up, with walls and
roofs, and had doors and window shutters, but were lacking glass windows, and were mostly without furnishings.
They were connected to the sewer tunnels, but not to the
secret passageways that would let our agents and historians communicate with the modern libraries and workrooms
in the basement of the castle. The secret entranceways would
be installed later on an "as needed" basis.

The castle had four floors, stairways, inner walls, partitions, and nicely arched ceilings, but was still pretty bare
inside. The drawbridge was in, spanning the moat, but we
didn't have the chains and mechanisms needed to draw it
up. The moat was still dry, except for some rainwater. The
wells were in, but we didn't have the pumps or the windmills to bring up large quantities of water.

Barb had talked the architect into letting her put a seawater moat all around the town, and this meant that we
had to put in drawbridges at each of the town's three gates.
They didn't work yet, either. Ian came up with a system
of two floating check valves that, with the action of the
tides, kept the water in the moat circulating in a clockwise
fashion, keeping it fresh.

Next, somebody made the mistake of telling her how a
fish weir worked, and the area near the town soon sported
two big ones. We soon had more fish than we could eat.
The ones we couldn't eat were eaten by the bigger ones,
and nature took its course.

Then, she decided that she didn't like the way the
town was situated in a notch cut into the surrounding
hills, so, without informing the rest of us, and working
at night, she eliminated the hills. She didn't even let us
save the lumber. Except where it abutted the cliff, with
the castle above, the town was now surrounded by a
smooth, stone plain. I suppose that this was good, from
the standpoint of defense, but esthetically, well, it looked
like the parking lot of a big shopping mall. How she was

planning to get some soil and plants growing there was beyond me.

She just *liked* playing with that tunneler.

To keep her out of further mischief, I had the architect draw up plans for a road system that she could cut through the whole island, and that had kept her busy for months. We rigged a temporal sword to the front of the tunneler, and cobbled up a bulldozer blade for the front of it so she could cut the trees and push the logs off the roadway, rather than sending them to wherever such things went when we sent them elsewhere.

I made her promise to stay inside of her beloved machine whenever she was outside the town walls, so the natives couldn't hurt her. They never tried to. If they were still out there, we didn't see any of them.

To look authentic, the castle and the forts guarding the entrance to the harbor needed dozens of ornate, eighteenth-century cannons, which we didn't have yet.

Only the Red Gate Inn was really complete, sitting on the town square, with the big fountain in front of it. The fountain was empty, but we didn't have any horses that needed to drink from it anyway. At least Ian claimed that that was what public fountains were really for, originally.

You'd think that I would be the one who wanted a good bar in operation, but no, it was Ian who pushed the inn into completion first, even ahead of the church across the big square.

He explained himself one night in the common room of the inn.

"I'll get the church finished, don't worry about it. But right now, I'm the only one here who would use it, and I can pray just fine in my room."

That surprised me. I'd never actually seen Ian praying. Then again, I'd never seen him shitting either. I guess that they were both very private occupations with him.

"The inn is another matter. Our people, the historians, are going to have to spend much of their time traveling around. They are going to want to see everything that goes on, but not draw too much attention to themselves. Now I ask you, where is the one place where a stranger is not much noticed? Obviously, at a hotel or inn. And where are other travelers most likely to gather and swap their stories? At a bar in an inn, of course. Therefore, the centers that the Historical Corps will build and use will have to be inns. Eventually, we'll need to build thousands of these, in every age and culture the world has known. And to make sure that our agents can find those inns, we are going to mark them all with a bright red front door, and all of them are going to named 'The Red Gate Inn,' or some variation of that in the local language."

"It sounds like a program," I said. "Do you suppose that the Red Gate Inn, back in the twentieth century, is one of your Historical Corps centers?"

"I expect that it might be. We'll probably decide that the history of the island is just as important as the history of everyplace else."

"You keep saying 'we,' but you know, Ian, it's really *your* program. I mean, I'd be happy to help out and all, but you are the one who is so fascinated with history. I'm interested in what happened in the past, but it's nothing that I want to spend my whole life working on."

"Huh. Then what *do* you want to spend your life doing?"

"I really can't tell you. I've never had anything like a life plan. So far, I've been like most people, just doing what comes to me, and trying to roll with the punches. We've still got years and years of work ahead of us, developing this time travel thing, and after that, well, who knows?"

"Agreed. But what do you yourself want to do. What really turns you on?"

"You know, before we built this town, I wouldn't have believed it, but I find that I enjoy the hell out of building things. You know, we could have turned this job over to a bigger, better equipped crew months ago, but nobody has suggested that we do so. I think that everybody here has been having as much fun as I have."

"It's been a real vacation, and no mistake," Ian said. "But if what you want to do is to build things, well, there's the whole culture and city that the Smoothies come from. Somebody's got to build that."

"Let Hasenpfeffer do it. I still think that that whole sick

culture is all his fault, anyway. I mean, I may not be a Christian, but I'm not totally immoral, either! Do you think that I want to be responsible for creating a civilization full of people who are as absolutely uncreative as those Smoothies are?"

"They can't be that bad. You married one of them, didn't you?"

"Yes, and it's not turning out as well as I'd hoped it would."

"Like, what's the trouble?"

"Mostly, it's the way she won't let me see our kids. They're already six years old, somewhen back there, and I haven't met my own children."

"Huh. But then, we each must have hundreds of children, what with all the fornicating we've been doing, and I haven't seen any of mine, either."

"I know I'm not being rational, but somehow, it's just not the same thing. Barbara is my wife, and not just another bedmate."

"Well, if it's really bothering you, when we get back, we'll both do something about it."

"It *is* bothering me, and I thank you. It is very good to have a real friend, Ian."

"And I love you, too. So just what is it that you want to build?"

"I think that I want to build a culture, all right, but I want it to be a place where intelligent, creative people can enjoy themselves being intelligent and creative."

"And how would that be possible if they have time travel? It's the fact that they know their own futures that makes the Smoothies what they are, and what they aren't."

"I've been thinking about that, and I've got some ideas, but they're too hazy just now to be worth talking about."

"Well, you keep thinking about it, and when you're ready to talk, I'll be ready to listen. For me, well, I haven't been staying here for the joy of getting my hands dirty. The real reason that I've been hanging around is that I've been hoping that some ship will come sailing into our new harbor, and we can make contact with the locals. The civilized locals, I mean, although I'm almost ready to go out and look for those cannibals of yours, I'm getting that frustrated."

"A ship will happen by eventually, and when they do, they're all yours. Do you have any idea how you're going to explain how this town just sort of popped up one night like a mushroom?"

"I plan to wing it on that one. I mean, if we find out that nobody much has been here for fifty years, there's nothing to explain. If the guy was by here three months ago, we'll have to convince him that he was someplace else, I suppose. I'm smart. I'll figure something out."

CHAPTER FORTY-FOUR
Visitors

Two weeks later, I was in what was now the carpentry shop in what would later be the town hall, making table legs. Three thousand people end up requiring over a thousand tables, and that means four thousand table legs. It was a matter of taking a four by four from one stack, putting it in a homemade lathe, spinning it up and making one swipe with a temporal sword sliding along a bumpy template, then taking it out and handing it to Ian, who was cutting some slots in the big end for the tabletop supports to go into.

Farther on, two more guys were assembling the tables, using wooden pegs but modern glue, and painting them with twentieth-century polyurethane varnish. Cutting with temporal tools, everything was so smooth and accurate that we didn't have to bother with sandpaper. We wanted everything to look authentic, but it wasn't like anybody was going to send this stuff out for chemical analasys.

This was not intellectually stimulating work, but we'd done all the fun things first. Like making four thousand chairs. Maybe in the eighteenth century, they wouldn't have made them all identical, on a production line, but our carpenter assured us that using green wood the way we were, everything would soon warp all to hell, and then it would all look as individualistic as you could possibly want.

I felt a definite relief when one of the sentries ran in and shouted that a ship had been sighted. Ian ran out to get a look at it, while I told everybody else to hide everything anachronistic, and then clean the place and themselves up, in that order.

I found Ian on the fighting top of one of the harbor forts, holding his body rigid and staring out to sea.

Besides being able to see clearly under water, our new eyes had another trick, but we didn't know about it until Lieutenant McMahon had showed us how to use it, a few weeks before. We had telescopic vision, just like an eagle. It didn't come naturally, like the underwater thing. You had to hold yourself very still, and concentrate on it, but when you got the hang of it, it was better than a pair of twenty-power binoculars.

"He's a Frenchman," Ian said. "At least, that's an eighteenth-century French flag on his mizzenmast."

"No. The flag on top has some kind of a cross on it. That's got to be one of the Scandinavian countries, doesn't it?"

"That's probably the house flag of the merchant company it belongs to. On these old sailing ships, it isn't the highest flag that counts, but the one nearest the poop deck."

Our flag poles all flew a blue flag with a gold emblem of Ian's own invention on it. The girls had made them up rather than getting involved with building furniture.

"He's taking in his sails."

"And getting ready to drop anchor," Ian said.

"Why doesn't he just sail in?"

"He probably doesn't know that he can. There didn't use to be a deep-water harbor here. Also, he doesn't know if we're friendly or not, so he's staying out of gun range."

Sergeant Kuhn and a squad of Killers were setting up some of our temporal weapons out of sight, behind the battlements: a mortar and two heavy, tripod-mounted temporal swords with telescopic sights. Across the canal, on the other fort, Lieuteant McMahon was getting similar things done.

"He's not out of range of *our* guns."

"He doesn't know that either."

Our visitors took half an hour to get their sails in, drop anchor, and put a small rowboat over the side. During that time, our ladies showed up, wearing their finest outfits. They each sported more lace than Barb had worn when getting married, plus a few dozen yards of embroidered silk and velvet with lots of brightly colored ribbons thrown in just for the fun of it. They were carrying fresh finery for Ian and me.

Under Barbara's supervision, three women took me below, stripped me, washed me down, shaved me, and trimmed my fingernails. They got me into a pair of white silk stockings, silk shorts, and a white silk shirt with lacy ruffles at my wrists and neck. I squirmed into tight knee-length sky-blue velvet pants that were covered with gold embroidery, as was the thigh-length matching jacket with a flaring skirt. Together, they weighed at least seven pounds extra because of all the real gold embroidered into them.

The girls wanted me to wear makeup, but I absolutely nixed that one. They did make me wear a white powdered wig, for God's sake, and the ornate hat they gave me was huge, with at least six white ostrich feathers on one side. The lavishly decorated sword was small, poorly balanced and useless. The skimpy shoes looked like a pair of lady's flats, except for the heavy gold buckles. A ridiculous outfit.

I clipped my temporal sword to the belt and glared at the girl who told me it didn't match.

I hadn't even known that we had such clothes with us. If I'd had any say in the matter, I would have dumped the clothes and brought along a second lift truck, but I hadn't so we didn't.

All this heavily embroidered velvet was entirely too warm for the climate, but fashion was fashion, and I was stuck with it. The only good thing about it all was that when Ian came out in a mostly pink and gold outfit, looking even stupider than I did, I got to sneer at him.

"Your mother dresses you funny," I said.

"So does yours. But in European society in this century clothes don't make the man. They *are* the man."

Sergeant Kuhn came over with a polished helmet topped by something like an ancient Greek crest, only it was curly instead of being made out of straight horsehair. He wore a polished steel breastplate, and the rest of him was covered in tight-fitting, spotless white wool, with a lot of red trim. He wore a more practical sword than mine, and carried a short, sturdy, and very ornate spear.

"These clothes may state your status to the world, but they're damned uncomfortable, sir. If we get into a fight, this outfit is going to be trash in thirty seconds," he said.

The ship's boat was being rowed in to us from about a mile out. There was plenty of time.

"Well, you can always throw the spear at them," I said.

"Oh, no sir. This isn't a throwing spear. Well, you *can* throw it, but normally you use it sort of like the way you use a bayonet on a rifle. If you'd ever served with the Ninth Legion, you would have spent half your time working out with one. It's a fine weapon, if a bit fancy. I'd take it over a sword, any day."

"Do say," I said, noticing that he, too, wore a temporal sword on his belt.

Lieutenant McMahon was back on the fighting deck of the opposite harbor fort, wearing a white-and-red outfit with gold epaulettes, a red helmet crest taller than the sergeant's, and almost as much gold braid as I was. His squad, like ours, wore white-and-red outfits with fewer doodads than the officers were allowed, but carrying "Brown Bess" muskets. I waved, but neither one of us felt the need to get out the CB radios.

As the boat rowed closer, I could see that the two men in the rear were wearing outfits as ornate as ours, but in much darker colors. Seamen usually wore darker clothes than landsmen, probably the result of the poor sanitary facilities on board one of those old ships.

In the front of the rowboat, a man was throwing a weight on a string to check the depth of the water. They had found the channel Barb had cut, and seemed amazed that it was a steady fifty feet deep.

Barb had cut some slips for small craft near the harbor forts, and after some discussion, we decided to greet our guests there. Leaving the troops to man the weapons on the forts, Ian, our eight ladies, and I went down to the slips.

As the boat pulled up, Ian shouted, "Welcome!"

A guy in the rear answered something polite-sounding in French, which I expected, considering the French flag on their ship. What I didn't expect was the way Barbara stepped forward and answered them in their own language. My wife was a never-ending string of surprises.

Ian soon took over the conversation, as we had agreed, with Barb doing the translating. Her version of French must have not been quite the same as theirs, since a lot of side conversations took place, clearing up minor points, but they were communicating. Talking through a translator is a long, slow process, but the gist of the conversation went something like this:

"Welcome to San Sebastian," Ian said, and formally introduced the ten of us.

"I thank you, sir. We are astounded to see you here," and just as formally introduced himself as Rene DuLac, Count of Lorraine, and the representative of the merchant company who owned the ship. His silent but smiling companion was the ship's captain. He didn't bother introducing the guys who had rowed them in here. You could see that the Frenchman, who was shorter than Barbara, was trying hard not to stare at Ian's astounding size. He was also trying, with less luck, to not stare at Barbara and her lovely friends.

"Indeed? And why are you so astounded?"

"Why, because I sailed by this island not two years ago, and it seemed then to be uninhabited."

"We bought this island three years ago, but we did not get here until a year later. We must have just missed you."

"But these well-built fortifications look to have been many years in the construction. How did you get them completed so quickly?"

"It's an interesting story, my noble guest, and you have not seen a tenth of it yet. But there is time enough for that tale later, over dinner, and a glass of wine, perhaps. For now, there must be some reason why you have stopped at this place. Tell us, please, what can we do for you?"

"Your courtesy and understanding are remarkable, my lord.

In truth, we have been becalmed at sea for over a month, and our supplies, especially of water, are almost exhausted."

"We have two good wells, my friend, and you and your crew are welcome to all the water that you want. Our supplies of food are not limitless, but we can spare you some beans, peas and rice. Also, the forests here abound with game, and we can easily shoot and smoke you enough meat to last you for the rest of your journey."

"That is most generous of you, my noble lord."

"Then it is settled. You and your captain shall accompany us to a suitable inn, since our castle is as yet but sparsely furnished. We will lend you a pilot to bring your ship into our harbor, and we will see to it that all of your immediate needs are attended to."

Barb wanted to guide their ship in, since she had made the channel herself, and knew it better than anybody else. Ian squelched that idea, saying that in this culture, women weren't trusted with doing anything technical. It turned out that our architect also spoke French, and so he accompanied the boat back to the ship. He didn't know anything about piloting ships, but he knew where the channel was.

CHAPTER FORTY-FIVE
Telling Lies

That evening, over dinner, while the ship's crew of twenty-six men, having drunk their fill of clean, cold water, and eaten a good meal, were drawing up buckets of water from our well and filling their ship's barrels, the count said, "You men and your ladies are obviously of high and noble birth, but you have not mentioned your titles to me."

After translating that, Barb whispered that his accent was from the lower classes of Brest, and that she doubted if *he* was a nobleman at all. I said that I had once read of a small lizard who claimed to be a dinosaur, on his mother's side, and that if it made the Frenchman feel better, why not let him claim it? She smiled and nodded agreement.

"The answer is simple enough, my noble guest," Ian said. "You see, when we left home, we renounced all of our titles, privileges, obligations and allegiances, in return for a cash payment from our brother, so in that respect, we have no titles, and indeed may not claim that we ever had any. On the other hand, we are now in sole possession of this island, and owe allegiance to no nation or king. I suppose that one might say that we are minor kings ourselves, but I would feel very awkward claiming such a title. It is more convenient to simply claim nothing at all, and to live with what is in fact a comfortable situation."

"You are at least the lord of a remarkably well-built city. But you were going to tell us how you got it all built so quickly."

Once Barbara translated that, Ian said, "It was a lucky matter of coming across a company of four hundred Italian stonemasons who had just lost a contract with the Spanish government, and who were desperately in need of work. At the same time we found that a convoy of slave ships had discovered that the market for their wares was very poor when they got to Cuba. We hired the Italians at a very reasonable price, and rented two thousand slaves for almost nothing for two years, although we had to feed them, of course. You see, as seasoned slaves, those who survived (most of them, really) will now be worth more than twice as much as they had been when they were fresh out of Africa.

"We had assumed that it would take at least ten years to get our new home suitable for occupancy, but as it turned out, we were very lucky. The slaves, their owners, and the masons all left less than a month ago."

"I see. They certainly did fine work. I don't think that I've ever seen better stonework anywhere in my entire life. I don't think that you could get a thin knife between any two blocks in your entire city. Yet it is strange to see it so empty, so devoid of people and animals."

"Our horses all died of some sort of disease, and we have not been able to replace them. Two ships full of colonists and supplies were supposed to have gotten here two months ago, but they have not yet arrived, and in truth we are becoming worried about them."

"Just what sort of supplies were you needing, my noble friend?"

"As I have said, we may not claim nobility. But we need many things. We are at present in possession of only small arms, and we need dozens of cannons for the forts and the castle. When the slaver's ships were here, they were well enough armed to protect us, but now, well, I worry. We also need glass for the windows of all these buildings, and machinery for the windmills we want for pumping water, and the mechanisms for the drawbridges at the town gates and the castle. And animals, of course, especially horses. And colonists, thousands of them, mostly craftsmen, tradesmen, and farmers."

"As to the colonists, the animals, and the machinery, I fear that I can be of no assistance at present. However, it happens that much of my cargo consists of armaments, bronze cannons of the finest French workmanship that I had intended to sell to the Governor of Cuba, plus ammunition for them, and a large supply of the finest French black powder. You have been so generous with us that I would be ashamed to charge you much more than what it cost us to purchase them, plus a modest fee for shipping. Also, we have a supply of excellent window glass on board, but I think not as much as you will want for this entire city. We might, perhaps, have enough for your inn, your town hall, and your castle, though."

"We will have to spend tomorrow morning inspecting your cargo, my friend. I trust that Spanish gold would be acceptable to you?"

"Most assuredly, my lord. So you are Spanish, then?"

"As I have said, I may not speak of such things. But for now, would you care for some more of this wine?"

The French ship also contained a fair store of luxury items, like fine China dinnerware, cut glass ware, and rich cloth for clothing, curtains and furniture. In the end, we bought almost their entire cargo, except for some wine that the count praised highly, but which was really bad stuff. French wine has always been vastly overrated.

We emptied out their ship to such an extent that we had to sell them twenty tons of granite bricks that we said were left over from the building, for ballast, so their ship wouldn't fall over.

But mostly, we now had forty-three bronze cannons of various sizes. They were gorgeously ornate and absolutely authentic. We now had enough weapons not only for the forts and the castle, but for the city gates as well.

Our guests left with a long list of things we needed, and they promised to return in the spring.

"So, Ian," I said, as we watched the ship clear the harbor. "Can we go home now?"

"Yes, Tom, now we can go home."

Most of the construction crew stayed behind to finish up the job, and to get some farmland cleared. Since most Smoothies were good artists, when they could copy somebody else's work, and since we had books on eighteenth-century decorative art with us, they were looking forward to decorating our new buildings with their temporal swords.

I gave them my blessings. I also told them that it might come in handy to have a sailing ship of our own, and that they might want to get started building one, once the gates on the dry dock were constructed. Our Smoothie carpenter drooled at the idea. Building an eighteenth-century ship suitable for the needs of a wealthy merchant-adventurer was something that he had fantasized about for most of his life. He said that it would take him a few years, and he made me promise to come back and sail it when he had it completed. I said I'd do that, provided that he made the ceilings high enough so that I wouldn't bump my head.

Lieutenant McMahon and his men elected to stay on for a while to protect them, they said. Mostly, I think, they wanted to get the cannons mounted so that they could have some fun shooting them.

Four of the ladies who had formed attachments with men from one group or the other stayed on to do the cooking, but the rest returned home with Ian and me.

Our carpenter said that it seemed wasteful to send the canister back empty. He had our storage area filled with wood that he said was very rare in our era, and he asked us to have it sent to his furniture factory in the twentieth century.

Our time canister was such that in order to safely return, since we had spent four months in the past, we had to return four months after we left.

My mathematician, Preston, was the only person waiting to greet us.

"Boss, if the shop has to go four months without the two of you being there, we are going to run out of stuff to do.

Things will go a lot better at work if we have the two of you there in charge. If you don't mind, I'll blindfold both of you, and take you back in time, the same way I got you to your wedding."

It didn't make sense to let things at the shop stall out for lack of direction, so Ian and I went along with it. After ten minutes of stumbling around in the dark, we found ourselves back home in my palace.

I said, "Someday, we are going to have to figure out how we are going to *did* that."

"Yeah. It's really annoying to have to work on something that you don't completely understand. But we'll do it someday. We'll have to. It's preordained."

"Right. Well. First things first. Ian, you promised to help me to get my children up here. Barbara, I have been very patient with you in this matter, but enough is enough. You now have two-thirds of the Board of Directors of this place ordering you to produce our three children. Are you going to bring them to me here and now, or am I going to send a military detachment back to wherever and whenever they are to get them?"

"Damn you, Tom! Can't you get it through your thick skull that it's dangerous up here?"

"Okay. If you're worried about the kids' safety, I'll have a squad of very polite and discreet soldiers on duty twenty-four hours a day, guarding them. If you want, I'll have Lieutenant McMahon do the job. Now, are you going to get them, or do I send out the troops?"

"I'll do it myself, damn you. It's better doing it that way than to have a squad of Killers handling my children."

"Come on! You've just spent four months in close company with a bunch of those Killers. They're not such bad guys."

"They are still Killers! My people don't kill the way you and those hired guns of yours do!"

"Me? If you are referring to that cannibal I killed, well, just what was I supposed to do? He had just murdered a woman, and he was charging at me with a bloody axe in his hands! I waited till the last possible moment before I cut him down! I didn't have any choice!"

"You could have run away! You could probably have outdistanced him without any difficulty."

"*Probably* is not a very encouraging word when somebody is trying to chop you up with an axe! Running might have worked, but what was I supposed to do if it didn't? What if that cannibal was faster than he looked?"

"Maybe you could have led him back to the others. Then one of the Killers could have done the dirty work."

"So now it's evil to defend myself, but okay to get somebody else to do my killing for me? You have a lousy concept of ethics, lady! Anyway, what if I had tripped, or the Indian had caught up with me, with my back turned and my weapons still at my belt? What then, huh?"

"Then you could have *died*! That's what one of my people would have done, rather than be guilty of killing somebody else. *We don't kill!*"

"Is that so? Then why haven't I noticed that all of you are vegetarians? Why were you enjoying the roast meat around the campfire with the rest of us?"

"That's not the same thing! Those were animals, not people!"

"That cannibal didn't see much difference between the two! Killing is killing."

"He wasn't civilized, and neither are you! Anyway, those animals we ate were already dead when the Killers brought them in."

"So now you're back to having somebody else doing your killing for you! To hell with this! Shut up and go get my boys!"

"You don't have any respect for life at all!" she said as she stamped out.

On the island, everything always happened when you wanted it to happen, without all the inevitable time lags that occur in the real world. Therefore, I was taken aback when six hours went by before Barb returned with my three sons. Maybe she was punishing me, or maybe she wanted to give me a chance to cool down. Whatever she had in mind, it didn't work.

But when she finally got there, she was trying to be

pleasant. Trying, but not exactly making it, and what little I know about kids says that they are a lot like dogs when it comes to picking up on the mood of those around them. We all tried to make the best of an awkward situation.

They were good-looking boys, blond and big for their age, but they didn't seem to have the energy, the spunk, the just plain bad manners that you expect from healthy youngsters.

They were named Tom, Ian, and Jim, after me and my friends. I thought that was a nice gesture on Barb's part, but that she really should have asked my opinion about it before she named them. When you name little people after big people who are still alive, they end up being called things like "Junior," or "Butchie," or "Little Tommy," which doesn't do the kid's ego much good.

Still, it was done, and the best thing to do about it was to live with the situation, and use middle names when necessary.

I told them that they were welcome to our island.

They didn't say much. They acted as though they were afraid of me, or of the world around them.

I said that my partners and I owned the whole place, and if there was anything that they wanted, all they had to do was ask.

They didn't ask for anything.

I told them that we had horses here, and that we could go horseback riding in the morning, if they wanted to.

Apparently, they didn't want to.

I talked about scuba diving and flying airplanes, but I didn't get much of any response. Camping and fishing didn't get me anywhere, either.

The whole thing was depressing. I mean, I know that I don't know anything about kids, but I was a kid once myself, and back then I would have lied in the Confessional to get the kind of offers that I was giving these boys. It was like there wasn't any "boyishness" in any of them at all.

I don't know.

Maybe I was coming on too strong. Maybe I really was a barbarian, and they were the civilized ones. Or maybe they had been given too God damned many lessons in how to be a Smoothie.

Individualism, that's what they needed. The three of them had been living together in one room for too long. I had each of them assigned a big suite of rooms, in three different corners of the palace. I gave each of them a half dozen women as their personal servants, in addition to the four Killers who were assigned to guard each of my boys around the clock. I made sure that all of their teachers would be Killers, too. The program might turn them into spoiled-rotten brats, but they sure as hell wouldn't be Smoothies for long.

When I got to my office in the morning, I found that I had been gone for only two days. There hadn't been time for any management problems to crop up, so I could spend my time playing engineer. After four months as a construction worker, it felt good.

The architect had given me sketches of all the special machinery we would need in the eighteenth century, as well as lists of other supplies that would be needed to complete the job properly. It looked as though we would have to send about twenty cargo canisters to haul it all back there. Besides furnishings for the castle, there were the ordinary household supplies needed by three thousand people. Plates, cooking pots, silverware, towels and an almost endless stream of other things. I gave it all to my secretary, and told her to get it done.

Ian was busy working out the manning requirements for his Historical Corps, so I got busy on a few pieces of machinery that we hadn't considered before.

Feeding the people of our little town would require about thirty thousand acres of farmland, if what I understood about the productivity of eighteenth-century farming techniques was correct. Clearing the land of trees could be done with temporal swords, if we could do it privately, or the hard way, with axes, if the locals were around. But chopping down the trees was the easy part. Something had to be done with the tree stumps and roots, and after that, the soil would inevitably be full of rocks and stones that would take millions of man-hours to remove.

I sketched up something I called a shredder, a simple two-wheeled vehical twelve feet wide that could be pulled with a farm tractor, a horse, or even by hand, if the ground was level. It contained six hundred temporal swords, a third of them pointing straight down, and the rest at a forty-five degree angle to one side or the other. As you pulled this over a field, everything under it for a yard down was sliced to bits a half inch across at most. Going over it a second time, at right angles to the first pass, should mean that you would be able to get a plough through it immediately. The rocks and bits of wood would have a lot of sharp edges, and it might be years before you could work in the fields barefoot, but the chips would round out eventually.

I calculated that one shredder should prepare about forty acres for planting in an eight-hour day. I ordered ten of the shredders to be made up, along with an equal number of light farm tractors to be powered by something like Ian's emergency generators. Then I doubled the number of tractors, since they could be used for dragging logs as well.

CHAPTER FORTY-SIX
The Appearance of the Teacher

The next morning, there were a lot of changes at my breakfast table. Barbara, Ming Po, Ian and I, our usual "Gang of Four," were there, but now my three boys had joined us as well, and that somehow made a dent in the usual freewheeling conversation. We just didn't feel comfortable enough with each other to get into a decent argument.

The maids were fully clothed now, as were all the other women around Camelot and quite possibly the whole island. I guess that the ladies had decided that running around naked didn't generate the right atmosphere to raise young boys in. I had to agree with them, in a way, but a part of me missed the old ways.

The breakfast conversation had degenerated into a monologue by Barbara about the necessity of leading a virtuous life, of being careful and considerate of others, and never harming anyone, and so on. She went on and on about how *she* had never hurt anyone in her entire life. It was nothing that you could really object to, but it was getting damned boring, nonetheless. Thus, I welcomed the interruption when a maid came and announced that we had a visitor with an urgent message.

We got very few visitors at Camelot, and time travel being what it is, we *never* got unexpected guests.

Bemused, I said, "Well, send him in."

He was a young man of proper size. That is to say, he was about six foot ten, about halfway between Ian and myself. He was well built and had those straight features that most women seem to find attractive. Clean shaven, and with short blond hair, he wore the same sort of hyper-expensive silk and vicuna outfit that Ian and I usually sported.

"I see that we have the same doctor," Ian said.

"No, we don't," the stranger said. "But I can understand why you would think that, since my exterior form was patterned after you and your partner's."

I said, "You were 'patterned' after us. Great green gobs of greasy gopher shit. This might turn out to be an interesting day after all. Barb, call the office and tell them that Ian and I will be late for work. I expect that this conversation might be a long one." Barb nodded but of course she didn't have to leave and do it right now. "So, stranger, do you have a name?"

"From studying your people, I assumed that you would expect one. Would 'Teacher' be adequate? Or perhaps 'Ambasador'?"

"Those are more like titles than proper names," Ian said. "Unless you want to be 'Mr. Teacher,' of course."

"I would be happy with any designation that you would care to use."

"I'd be happier to know what your real name is," I said.

"In reality, I don't have a name. My people don't use separate names for individuals, although we occasionally use job classifications. Any name I use will be strictly for your convenience."

"Tom, assuming that this isn't an elaborate practical joke, it looks like we've just come across our third cultural group. First the Smoothies, then the Killers, and now this bunch."

"I'd like it to be a joke. It would mean that Hasenpfeffer is becoming human again. But I don't think that it is," I said. "Okay, Teacher, so what are your people called?"

"It might be best if you called us 'The Travelers,' since

it is in that connection that I was made to contact you with a message."

"Before we get to this message of yours, you say that you were 'made'? Do you mean that you are some sort of machine, a robot?" Ian asked.

"Not in the sense of what you think of as a robot. I am a biological construct, not a thing of metal. If your biologists were to examine me, they would find hydrocarbons, proteins, and DNA that is not too different from what they are accustomed to seeing. They might find some differences in my gross anatomy that would suprise them, but then again they might not. The Travelers would not have been able to come to you themselves, being physically incapable of surviving on this planet, and being mentally incapable of having a meaningful conversation with you. You, of course, have the same incapacities with respect to them. An intermediary was therefore necessary. I am it, or *he*, if you prefer."

"And just what are these physical incapabilities you are referring to?" I said.

"There are many. At the most basic level, your body chemistry is based primarily on carbon, oxygen, nitrogen, and hydrogen compounds surrounded by water. The Travelers use those elements, plus a lot of silicon and fluorine compounds all surrounded by ammonia. You are quite poisonous to each other."

"And mentally?"

"You are individuals who exist in a diffuse cultural matrix and communicate in a serial fashion using modulated sound waves. The Travelers have a hive mind, and while they are physically individuals, they are mentally a single entity. They communicate in a broad-band, parallel fashion using modulations in an energy field that you have not yet discovered. In addition, your people live in three dimensions while traveling through a fourth, which you call time. The Travelers live in five dimensions, while traveling in two others. In addition, your people have a rather stodgy disposition, while the Travelers have an extensive sense of humor that I don't think that you could ever comprehend."

"Ian, that sounds like such a crock of shit that it is almost certain to be true."

"Yeah. So you can somehow communicate with these seven-dimensional Aliens who built you?"

"That might be a fair statement. Or, it might be more accurate to say that I am a seven-dimensional Alien, as well as being a four-dimensional creature who strongly resembles you humans. In order to do my job properly, I had to be made with a dual nature. You might say that I am an interface."

"I always wondered what it would be like when the Aliens finally landed. I never expected them to walk in for breakfast," I said. "In any event, please sit down. Would you like some breakfast? You do eat, don't you?"

"Oh, yes. This part of me was made to be perfectly human, as nearly as possible."

"Good. Make yourself at home."

The maids quickly brought in another chair and a large tray of assorted breakfast foods.

"I hope to. After all, this part of me will be spending the rest of my life here."

"No way of going back to the seven-dimensional world, I take it?" Ian said.

"Not with this body, and of course my other half can't exist in this world. I exist, must exist, in both. It's rather difficult to explain. These pancakes are absolutely delicious. I've never eaten anything before, you know."

"Well then, you have a lot to learn, as well as teach, I suppose. There was some talk about a message that you had for us?"

"Oh, yes. Your activities here, your clumsy muddling with some of the aspects of the multidimensional universe have caused a certain degree of distress to the Travelers. I am instructed to inform you that you must cease and desist in these activities immediately, or the Travelers will destroy your entire Solar System. These sausage things are good, too."

There was about thirty seconds of silence, and then I said, very quietly, after getting a nod from Ian, "Barb, put out the word to everybody on the island. Do it right now. Tell them that absolutely nothing of a temporal nature may be used in any way until further notice. Every device that does anything concerning other dimensions is to be collected up and locked away, or locked off, or something done to it to make sure that nobody makes a mistake."

Barb left quickly.

Barb returned, saying that she had made the order retroactive to the moment that the Teacher had walked in the front door.

I was about to start shouting that that in itself was a use of time travel on her part, in direct contradiction to my orders, when the Teacher said, "Yes, that was quite wise of you. The Travelers really would have done it, of course. Having a hive mind, the lives of mere individuals don't mean much to them."

"If they had destroyed the Solar System, you would have been killed, too, wouldn't you?" I said. "Why doesn't this trouble you?"

"Because I would only be destroyed as an individual, and as I just said, we aren't very concerned about the life or death of a single individual."

"Okay," Ian said. "I'm trying to absorb this. You say that these 'Travelers' can't live here, and if they can make somebody like you, they obviously have a technology that is vastly superior to our own. Given that, there can't be much that we have that they could want. So why are they threatening us?"

"You are quite right. You have nothing that they want, or could possibly use. All they want of you is to be left alone. They have threatened you because you have done them a great deal of damage. Among other things, you have caused the death of several million of their component parts. Their people, as it were."

"We have killed millions of them?" I said.

"Quite so. You have been taking millions of tons of stone and other materials and dumping it into what you have been calling the 'Fifth Dimension.' The Travelers use that dimension, very regularily, for traveling in. The speeds involved are of course astronomic, so that even quite small particles can cause catastrophic damage to their vehicles and 'people.'"

Barbara entered the conversation for the first time. "Just what millions of tons of stone are you talking about?"

"Why, that installation you recently built a few hundred of your years ago on this very island," the Teacher said. "You not only dirtied our shipping lanes to an unprecedented extent, but you sent out several times the amount of rubbish than was necessary to complete your project. You wantonly destroyed several hundred of our, well, I suppose you could call them 'Passenger Liners,' and did it for no apparent reason at all."

"I did that," Barbara said, a look of absolute horror on her face.

"True. We examined the incident quite carefully before I was sent here."

"I murdered millions of people?"

"I suppose that you could say that. They were certainly terminated without their permission, and by your standards, I suppose that you could call them people."

"I was having fun, playing with a piece of machinery. I didn't know that I was hurting anybody."

"We know that, and of course you meant no harm. By our standards, you did no great wrong. To us, it was as if you had deleted a few million cells in our body. A minor injury at most. We don't hate you for it, but you must understand that this practice must stop."

"By our standards, ignorance is no excuse in the eyes of the law," Barbara said, starting to cry.

I said, "Hey, Barb, lighten up! He has said that all you did was mess up a few million cells in their body. That's like falling and scraping your knee. No big thing, pretty girl! It's not like you killed a human, or something."

"But of course, she did that, also. When she was perforating the roof of the overly extensive water-collection system she was putting in, she inadvertently also perforated eleven canibals who were sitting hungrily around a campfire. But they were from a culture that was soon to be extinct, so the incident shouldn't trouble her," the Teacher said.

Barbara's eyeballs rolled up and she crumpled silently onto the floor. As I bent down to pick her up, I said, "Oh, but it does trouble her. It troubles her greatly."

"We are not concerned with either your emotional reactions or your primitive legal standards. Since you have agreed to stop your offensive practices, my other task is to teach you how to do things properly. Simple modifications to your equipment will enable you to dispose of your trash in such manner that you won't cause anyone else any damage. I left a suitcase in your entranceway that contains a complete set of textbooks, written in your language, that will allow you to continue with your lives without disturbing ours."

"You are going to teach us everything there is to know about traveling in the other dimensions? Give us the theoretical background that we presently lack?"

"Of course. It is really preferable to killing you all, and it doesn't actually cost us anything. I mean, I had to be made to deliver the message, and since I'm here, I might as well live somewhat longer and spend my time being a teacher. Also, it is quite possible that as I learn more about you, the knowledge might be useful to the Travelers. In fact it is more than possible. Already, I have learned much that is valuable. The whole phenomenon of taste is new to us. Your pancakes, sausages, and this 'coffee' are absolutely delightful!"

"You are going to have a marvelous time when you discover sex," I said, making Barb as comfortable as I could. I didn't realize then that the damage to her psyche was permanent.

Ian said, "Okay. You've got a deal. You teach us everything we need to know, and we'll do the same. We've got a good, complete university sitting empty on this island, and we've always wondered what it was for. Now we know. It's all yours, Teacher. Take it, staff it and run it any way you want to. Have a ball!"

CHAPTER FORTY-SEVEN
The Departure of the Smoothies

The Teacher started out by writing down a few simple equations on a piece of paper, and Ian and I stared at them for a few minutes.

"That's it," Ian said. "That's what we've been busting our balls on for years, trying to figure out."

"Yeah. I sure wish it was more complicated, so I wouldn't feel so dumb."

"All the world's great ideas are simple, and always have been, all the way through history."

"I'll take your word for it," I said. "Anyway, these equations prove that the Teacher's for real. I don't see that we have any choice but to do everything that he says."

"Yeah. And here I was hoping that I would go down in history as one of science's greatest thinkers."

"Me too. But we have to either give up on that dream, or have our Solar System destroyed because we are guilty of Interstellar Littering. On the other hand, well, we're still filthy rich. That's got to count for something."

"It always has, Tom. It always has."

The first major effect of having the Teacher around was that, since it was obvious that Ian and I hadn't invented all this time travel stuff in the first place, it would not violate causality if we got to see some of it, and learn how it worked.

It turned out that there were four time travel terminals on the island, which were connected to the subway system. All you had to know was which destination button to push, and there you were.

Actually, I don't remember ever pressing any of those two-hundred-odd buttons on the wall of each subway car. I was always with a crowd of girls, and one of them always pushed the buttons. In my years on the island, I had never dialed a telephone, rung a doorbell, or written a letter. It was easy to see (now) how they had so easily kept so many things from us. I began to realize that having too many servants makes you a rather limited person.

Anyway, you stepped across the hallway from the subway door and into a small room. A panel on the wall let you dial in the time that you wanted to arrive at, and you pushed a button. The door closed and in a little while it opened. Then you were then. There was no free-fall, since the room was able to maneuver within Earth's gravitational field, now, but the transit time was still there, which was why people used the more spacious and comfortable canisters for traveling long temporal distances.

I was told that if I was going to start using the Local Temporal Transport System, one thing that I had to be careful of was to keep a close watch over my own circadian rhythms. It was all too easy to get them out of step with one another, and there was a danger of getting yourself stuck in a permanent jet lag.

It was frustrating to see how simple it all was, and embarassing to realize that we hadn't been smart enough to figure it out by ourselves.

The next thing we did was to take the Teacher around, and show him every bit of temporal engineering that we had on the island. He passed judgement on each device, saying whether it was okay to use, needed modification, or if it had to be destroyed immediately.

It was our tunneling and digging equipment that caused

most of the problems. Mechanically, the devices were okay, but the electronic controls had to be destroyed, and entirely new ones built and installed. The same went for some of the weapons we'd been so proud of. Not the bombs, since they returned all the matter involved back to our own dimensions, as did the emergency power generators and the escape harnesses. But all the variations of the temporal swords were no longer allowed, not without a complete redesign. The earliest models, which caused some residual radiation, were deemed acceptable by the Teacher, but they had all been replaced years ago by what we thought were cleaner models, which dumped the trash into the fifth dimension, rather than into our own future. It was with great regret that I unclipped my temporal sword from my belt, and handed it to the Teacher.

The Teacher took over the university that we had given him, hired some administrators at our expense to schedule classes and keep student records, and put on some more housekeepers, janitors and gardeners to keep the place very neat and clean. Then he proceeded to teach every class himself, doubling back in time as much as necessary to get the job done. You could go through the school and see what appeared to be hundreds of him, teaching hundreds of small classes of typically ten students. He soon took over an entire student dormitory for himself, and lived in all of the rooms, aparently simultaneously.

And it wasn't only multi-spatial engineering that he was lecturing about. The Travelers were way ahead of us in almost everything scientific, cultural, mathematical or philosophical. The Teacher was prepared to teach anything to anybody at any time. New textbooks somehow materialized on a regular basis and were sent to our print shops for duplication. Of course, you had to be a Smoothie, a Killer, or a member of the Historical Corps to get on the island, so enrollment at the university was somewhat restricted. Maybe we'll change the rules, later. Maybe much later.

The Teacher always dressed very well. He discovered that with a little re-tailoring, Ian's worn-once outfits fit him very well, and that he liked them. My old clothes, being a bit small for him, continued to fill up the closets in my palace.

The ladies of the island were as attracted to the Teacher as they were to the three of us, but I think for different reasons. He liked them as well, and he found sex to be as marvelous a thing as I had promised him it would be. Sex, but not reproduction. For whatever reason, he proved to be sterile, with human women, anyway.

Ian and I got private tutoring, of course, but we didn't do all that well at it. We'd been the bosses for too long to slip easily back into the role of being mere schoolboys, but we did pick up a few pointers.

One thing that I was delighted to learn was that the Second Law of Thermodynamics was a purely local phenomenon that only applied to some aspects of a three-dimensional universe. I'd known it all along. With a bit of digging, I found plans for a simple device that turned water into ice cubes, and produced electricity as a by-product.

I also finally learned why it took time to travel in time. The way the Travelers looked at it, what we were doing when we traveled in time was taking a defined portion of our space-time continuum, and bending it into the other dimensions. Within that defined portion (think of it as sort of a pipe), space and time remain completely normal. They have to, since if they ever became discontinuous, even for an instant, anyone inside would cease to live, or even to exist.

Now, this wasn't the way I had been looking at what we were doing. It seemed to me that I was working with fields and forces, not bending continuums. I don't know. Maybe I never did really understand time travel. I've heard that DeForrest never really understood what was going on in a vacuum tube. He only invented the thing. Other people, like Major Armstrong, figured out *why* it worked.

So our island was finding a new role in life. It was now becoming a university town. This was good, since its other functions were starting to shut down.

At the shop, all of our subordinates had enrolled at the university as soon as it was opened, and doubled forward and back as necessary, usually completing several years of graduate work in what appeared to us to be a single night.

Within a few days, all of the people in our little company were retrained, barring two of the janitors (a musicologist and a history major, who weren't interested in technical things), and within a few weeks, all of our old machinery and weapons were operational in the new, safe mode.

Sometimes, when there was some bit of trash that we were sure that the world would never need again, we would simply dump it into the sun. More often, it was sent to a recycling center where the stuff was broken down into its constituent atoms, sorted, and stored. Well, things like pure oxygen, argon and nitrogen were usually just released into the environment. Then, if you needed a few tons of pure silicon, titanium or gold, well, you knew where to go.

Now that our engineers had textbooks to go by, they didn't need to be creative at all. They had all the answers that a culture a thousand times older than our own had come up with. If you had a problem, all you had to do was look it up. The girls turned out some marvelous things, but for Ian and me, well, they didn't need us anymore.

We were still in charge and all, but there weren't many opportunities to earn the undying admiration of our loyal workers because of our astounding creativity.

Work got very boring, for me at least. Ian was so wrapped up with getting his Historical Corps going that he usually didn't have time to eat, let alone talk to old friends.

In many of the manufacturing plants around, work was getting nonexistent. One day I noticed that the window-frame plant, which we had toured in one of our first weeks on the island, was closing down. All of the stock bins were empty, the last of the finished windows were being hauled away, and the machinery was being packed into shipping containers.

Ian and I found the plant manager.

"What goes on here?" I asked.

"Why, we're closing down, sir."

"I can see that. But why?"

"Lack of work, I suppose. We've filled all of our orders and used up all of our raw materials, so it is time to close it all up."

"They stopped ordering windows? Strange. But then, I never could figure out where all of those windows were going in the first place."

"Going, sir? Why, look around you! Every window on this entire island was manufactured right here in this plant, and so was every window at Atlantic Ridge City. All of the necessary repair and replacement windows have been manufactured and stored, so they won't be needing this facility ever again. The machinery is all being sold to a company in Mexico, they tell me. It will be working for many years yet, but I won't. I'll be retiring as soon as we finish getting the building cleaned out."

"I hope you enjoy the rest," Ian said. "But what was that you were saying about a city on the Atlantic Ridge?"

"They never told you about that, sir? How odd. Well, anyway, during the Ice Age before last, the level of the oceans got so low that a few hundred square miles of the Atlantic Ridge became exposed to the air. It's a perfect place for all of us Smoothies to live, for thousands of years. The climate is lovely, there's no local ecology to disrupt, so we can bring in modern plants and farm animals without endangering existing species, and when it eventually sinks back into the sea, there won't be any possibility of problems with causality. My plant made all the windows we'll ever need for the city and all the surrounding countryside."

"I guess they never told us because we never asked. What are they going to do with your old factory building?" I asked.

"I'm sure I don't know, sir. Maybe the university will find some use for it. It's not my concern. I'm leaving tomorrow afternoon."

"You're going to Atlantic Ridge City?"

"Yes. The wife and I have bought a nice apartment there, with a good view of the ocean. It's a two-week trip, going back that far, but we've booked a private canister, and we're looking forward to the trip. The wife is calling it our second honeymoon."

"Well, enjoy yourself. I wish you both the best of everything."

"Thank you, sir. I'll give the wife your regards."

As the weeks went on, more and more factories and shops

were closing down, their purposes for existing having been completed. In time, I began to notice that the crowds were thinning down, that the concert halls were no longer full, and that the plays often had fewer actors and were being given shorter runs.

Ian asked me if I didn't want to go back and see this Atlantic Ridge City that everybody was abandoning our island for, but I didn't want to do it, not now, anyway. When we got to talking about it, he said that he felt about the same way as I did. Later. We'd do it later.

Then one night I found a new woman in my bed.

Barbara's depression had grown until she had stopped sleeping with me. The doctors couldn't seem to do anything for her. I figured that maybe if I let her have her space, and gave her enough time, she would eventually recover. It wasn't like I needed the sex, what with all the other girls around.

Anyway, having lived with them for years, I had of course gotten to know my household staff pretty well, as well as the ladies who worked at the shop under Ian.

Natually, I asked the new girl what she was doing there.

She said that she worked at Camelot now, in gardening, replacing a woman who had decided to get married to a man who was going to the Atlantic Ridge.

I said that that was nice, and we had a fine night together.

Then, the next day, I found another new girl waiting in the bedroom. I soon discovered that over half of my household was scheduled to leave soon, and that in a few months, they would start having difficulty finding replacements. I decided, what the heck? The place didn't really need a hundred and fifty women to keep it up. Thirty or forty of them could handle things (and me) well enough.

Ian was having similar experiences. It seemed that since we were no longer necessary for the continuation of the culture, our previously infinite sex appeal was starting to wear a little thin.

Barbara's depression didn't wear thin. Instead, it got worse. Much worse. In a few weeks, she became impossible for anyone to talk to, and the Head Chef, a woman named Julia, started taking over most of her duties.

Barbara stopped spending her days with me, as well.

I was making some progress with my boys, but it was slow going. Scuba diving and flying ultralights still frightened them, but we often went horseback riding now.

But I couldn't get them to race each other on horseback. The closest they got to it was galloping three abreast across the fields, like an old-time cavalry charge. That gave me an idea. I had uniforms made up for the four of us, the infinitely flashy outfits worn by the ancient Polish Winged Hussars, complete with golden helmets, leopard-skin sashes, scale mail breastplates, sabres, and long lances. Plus, of course, the great feathered white wings going from their backs to high above their heads. Then I found a Killer corporal who had actually served in the Winged Hussars in the early fifteenth century. He showed up in full regalia—just Absolute Panache—to give them some pointers. The boys actually got fairly good with those long, hollow lances, skewering brass rings at a full gallop, but when it came to using a sabre, well, they just couldn't bring themselves to swing one at somebody.

Often, the four of us went sailing. I tried to talk the boys into each taking one of the three yachts, using their servants as a crew, and racing each other, but they didn't want to. They prefered to work together, as a team. Turning them into individuals was going to take time.

One night, at the Bucket of Blood, I got to talking to Leftenant Fitzsimmons.

"Look, Fitz, you are a multiply married man, with lots of kids. You have more experience with children than I'll ever have. I've told you the kind of problems I've been having with my boys. What am I doing wrong?"

"Wrong, sir? Why, nothing that I can see. Look. A boy needs a mother who loves him no matter what, and a father who spends enough time with him to show him what being a man is all about. See that he gets those two things, and enough to eat, and he'll grow up all right. But I get the feeling that that's not exactly what you want. You want those boys to grow up like twentieth-century Midwestern Americans, and there's only one way to do that. You'll have to take them to twentieth-century America, say, about 1945, a healthy, peaceful time, really, although it didn't seem that way to the people who lived there. Raise them in the American Midwest, and they'll grow up to be just like you. I mean, if you raise them in Inca Land, they'll grow up being good little Incas, if you get my meaning."

"But how can I do that? My job is here."

"You can do what I do, sir, if your wife will go along with it. Spend your working life wherever the job takes you, and spend your vacations with your boys and their mother. Do it right and they won't even be aware of the fact that you spend most of your time elsewhere."

"But don't you see, my wife is my biggest problem! She is a Smoothie who considers herself to be a murderer, and I'm beginning to realize that Smoothies have a bigger guilt complex than anything a Pagan or a Jew or a Catholic ever suffered from."

"Sir, it sounds to me like the two of you are in need of professional help. You need a psychologist from your own American culture, and there's only one of them on the whole island. He's a friend of yours."

CHAPTER FORTY-EIGHT
A Talk With Hasenpfeffer

I mulled it over for weeks, and in the end I knew that Fitzsimmons was right. I had to talk with Hassenpfeffer. Still, I procrastinated until one day Barbara was gone. She simply could not be found anywhere on the island.

Frantic, I called together the three Killer officers who had helped me back when we thought that somebody might be sabotaging our first time canister.

"Find her," I told them. "Find Barbara."

"Right, sir," Leftenant Fitzsimmons said. "We'll be back directly, I expect."

They all returned to my living room in five minutes.

"Yes?"

"She's left, sir. She went back to 1965, when the local time transports were first put in. She went directly to the harbor and talked her way onto a freighter that had just delivered a load of building materials here. She sailed off with them, sir, headed for New Orleans."

"Well, stop her! Get her back here!"

"Yes, sir, if that's what you really wish. But have you thought it all the way through? Do you really want us to have a military squad waiting for her when that ship docks in New Orleans? What if she doesn't want to go back?

Should we force her to come with us? What should our response be with regards to the local people and authorities? To them, this might look like a kidnapping, and then the use of force would seem appropriate to them. When that happens, do we fight back?"

"Oh, how the hell should I know? Why can't you stop her before she gets on that ship?"

"Causality again, sir. You see, the three of us have watched her get on the ship and sail off. Not directly, but through the means of certain surveillance devices available to us. Anyway, her sailing off is now an established fact, and there's no way in the world to change that."

"Shit. Just what kind of surveillance devices are you talking about?"

"Right. Well, there isn't any reason to keep anything from you anymore, is there? We use these 'bugs' that actually look like insects. They can crawl, fly, and have enough intelligence to follow their target at a discreet distance. They have enough sensors to observe everything that happens and enough memory to record about six hours of it. Then they fly home, and let you see what they saw."

"Are these some kind of living thing, or a sort of tiny robot?"

"As I understand it, they are somewhere in between, sir."

"Then how can what a machine knows stop you from doing anything?"

"Well, we know it too, sir, now that we've looked at what it saw. But their very act of recording it makes the event immutable. If we were investigating a murder, for example, and there was a dead body on the floor, we could bug the place, and find out exactly what happened there. We could prove conclusively who did the killing, and have a one hundred percent expectation of bringing him to justice. But we couldn't do a thing for the victim of the crime, except avenge him, of course."

"Well, damn causality!"

"I've often felt that way myself, sir. But for now, may I point out that the events we are talking about happened many years in the past? That you have plenty of time to think everything through, before you take any action? Time enough, say, to discuss the matter with your oldest friends and business partners?"

I sat there a while, thinking. "Yeah. I suppose you're right. Okay. Thank you, gentlemen, for another job well done."

Ian was getting more and more involved with his Historical Corps, to the point that it was difficult to get him to talk about anything else.

Anyway, I had a people problem, and only one person I knew of had the expertise to help me. I asked my secretary to make me an appointment to see Hasenpfeffer.

He said that he'd be right over.

In ten minutes, he was in my living room. He was much older than when I'd seen him last, and he had shrunk, somehow. His hair, what there was left of it, was grey turning to white. His skin was a bright, untanned pink, and there were crow's-feet around his clear blue eyes. More importantly, he seemed to have mellowed out with age, with a steady, sincere smile on his lips and in his eyes.

"Come in," I said. "Have a seat. Can I get you anything?"

"Thank you, and perhaps we'll have some refreshment later. For now, there is much to discuss, and this talk is long overdue."

"You know that Barbara is gone?"

"Oh, yes. Is that where you want us to start?"

"Well, no. Maybe we'd best start at the beginning. Jim, just what in the hell has been going on around here?"

"I was sure that you had figured that out by this time. No? Let me explain it from my point of view, and then it will all make sense to you. The obvious first point was that once we had formed the partnership, we were faced with a basically technical problem, that of developing a time machine. We had two people, you and Ian, who were very competent, technically, but who were woefully incompetent in their interpersonal relationships. Great leaders you were not. You couldn't even talk a girl into having sex with you. Then we had one person, me, who was competent in managing people but equally incompetent at anything technical. Therefore it made perfect sense for me to handle all the business, financial, and management tasks, and for the two of you to do the technical things. Are you with me so far?"

"Yes, of course, that much is obvious. But this island, these cities, all these women? Wasn't that going way overboard?"

"I don't think so. You see, it eventually became obvious that your technical endeavors were going to be sucessful far beyond our earlier dreams. This brought on the need for elaborate security provisions, since wealth of the magnitude that we were soon generating could not possibly be hidden. At the same time, you and Ian would soon have to become competent managers in your own rights, since we were growing outside of the backyard inventor's millieu. You had to be able to run at least a major engineering company, and lead the people in it. Ian was quite right about the similarity between humans and baboons. If you wish to be a great leader of men, you must first have a considerable following of women. I'm sure that if you asked him, he could give you hundreds of historical examples."

"So you were deliberately manipulating us from the very beginning?" I said.

"True. Sometimes it was an overt manipulation, as when, just before your first time trip, I forced you and Ian to stand up to me publicly, and assert yourselves as equal partners in this venture. More often, I could be more indirect, or even subtle. But I was also manipulating myself, for a few months there, until I figured out precisely what I would have to do, and what it was that, in a sense, I had already done. Convincing the women that the three of us were sexually desirable was a relatively simple matter of adjusting the parameters of their culture, to make us be perceived as the most desirable possible fathers for their children, and making it socially permissable for them to aggressively pursue us. After which, well, Mother Nature simply took her course."

"Horseshit. You were always a lady's man, from the first day that I met you."

"Again true. Or, to put it another way, I was fortunate in being somehow a culturally approved ideal mate for women in the second half of twentieth-century America. You and Ian were not. As the saying went, some get it, and some don't. I arranged matters such that all three of us were in that exalted category in the Smoothie culture. Surely you can't be angry with me for that."

"Maybe not. But you just happened to have a whole bloody culture around that you could manipulate in any way you wished?"

"In a manner of speaking, yes. Like many other thinkers, psychologists, and philosophers throughout history, from Plato on down, I had often dreamed of creating a perfect culture, a place of peace and harmony where people could live long, rich lives completely free from the deprivations, the horrors and the anxieties that the rest of humanity has always been heir to. Unlike the rest of them, I had the wherewithall, thanks to you and Ian, to actually create it, and the time to guide it to fruition."

"And you are proud of this thing that you have done?"

"Oh, yes. Infinitely so."

"I think it's a fucked-up mess. You have created a huge mass of mental cripples who can't think for themselves! They can all play musical instruments, but not one of them can compose a simple tune! They can each paint a beautiful picture, but not one of them can create anything original! They can do sound engineering work, but not one of them can actually invent anything! They can't make up a fucking joke, for God's sake!"

"I don't completely agree with you, but even if what you claim is true, well, so what? In the world we both grew up in, not one person in ten thousand was truly creative. All the rest worked their butts off trying to survive as best they could, eking out some sort of a living in an absolutely insecure world. My people feel secure precisely because they know what their futures will be. There is no crime because everyone knows that every criminal will be caught and punished for his transgressions. There is no material want because we know exactly what will be needed and when, and have various sensible means of providing it. My people live long, contented lives. If that one person in ten thousand who wants to be creative gets eased out of my society and into one where he will be appreciated, well, is that so great a price to pay?"

"What 'society where he will be appreciated'?"

"Why, the one that you will build, of course. You know, for quite a while, there, after you married Barbara, I had hopes that you would change your mind about the Smoothies, as you call them. I had hopes that you would one day become my successor, as the leader of this society. I see now that you will never want to do such a thing. A pity. Ian, of course, has found a lifetime avocation in running his Historical Corps. I suppose that I will end up having to choose one of my own sons, and train him to succeed me. Interesting."

"Okay," I said. "To be fair, I have been thinking about some sort of thing like a culture for creative people, but that's not what I want to talk about. Barbara is gone, and I want her back!"

"My old friend, Barbara is gone, and you will never get her back."

"What the fuck are you talking about? She's just having some emotional problems. She'll straighten out and come home, eventually."

"No, she won't. Barbara is gone forever. You must somehow reconcile yourself to that. Look, by her standards, she committed two great crimes, one almost has to say two great sins. Her carelessness killed some cannibals living on the island, and then her rambunctiousness with a piece of equipment that you and Ian had designed caused the deaths of a few million Aliens from the Travelers' culture. By our standards, neither of these acts could possibly be considered murder. Even the Aliens don't hold her personally responsible. But by her standards, she sinned the greatest possible sins. She felt that she had to atone for those sins, and that she could only do that by giving her life for the betterment of her society. And that's exactly what she did. It was a lot like a Greek tragedy, really. The beautiful, innocent young mother going willingly to her death because of circumstances totally beyond her control."

"Then we will damn well stop her! And don't give me any of that causality shit!"

"I must give you that causality shit, Tom, because you yourself have already seen her dead body. Remember that day in Northern Michigan when this whole thing started? Those thin slices of human being that you scooped up with that contraption you'd made out of your sleeping bag? That was Barbara, Tom. She had learned enough about how time travel worked from sitting in on the tutorial sessions that the Teacher gave you and Ian. She took a supply of money with her from your accounts here—You didn't even know that you had such accounts, did you?—and went north to set up the demonstration that resulted ultimately in the creation of her entire society, her entire world. When the story gets known, I am sure that she will become the equivalent of the Patron Saint of her world."

"Holy shit, Jim. I don't know what to say," I said, no longer able to hold back the tears.

"Then don't say anything. There are drugs and therapy that might help, but sometimes the old remedies are the best ones," Jim said, pulling out a fifth of the Jim Beam I used to favor in the old days. "Come, old friend. Drink with me."

Much later, and three fifths of sour mash later, I said, "My boys, Jim. What am I going to do with my boys?"

"You must find them a new mother, Tom. Or perhaps, mothers. If you really want them to grow up as individuals, I would recomend that you separate them as soon as possible. Are you ready to get married again?"

"Married? Me? No, I don't think that I'll ever do that again. The first time was too painful."

"Then you must either send them back to Barbara's family, where I'm sure her parents would be happy to raise them, as good little Smoothies, or you should follow Leftenant Fitzsimmon's recomendations and take them to the early second half of the twentieth century, in the American Midwest. That is to say, put them up for adoption, with good families."

"Smoothies? My boys? Never! Adoption? I wouldn't have any idea how to go about doing such a thing."

"I could take care of that for you, if that's what you really want."

"Let me think on that for a few days."

"That is very good thinking."

"Another thing, Jim. You've been telling me about all these things that you shouldn't be able to know. Things like what

Ian said to me when we were all alone. What gives? You've been spying on us the whole time?"

"Of course! If you are going to manage a culture, and tweak it to perfection, you have to give up on things like a concern for privacy. Oh, we never intrude on anyone's life. They probably know that we are watching them the way a Christian believes that God is always looking over him, but it rarely affects them personally, unless they are desperately in need of help, or are in the act of committing some crime, so no one ever minds it."

"I mind it."

"Do you really? Would you like us to stop it?"

"Damn straight!"

"It might be dangerous for you. We help a lot of people in trouble, you know. When that shark bit Ian's foot off, it wasn't the flare that got the Air Force there in seconds, you know. It was one of our bugs."

"I'll take my chances."

"Come back to me when you're sober, tell me the same thing, and and I'll act on it."

"I'll do that."

"Very well. In the meantime, think about that fine, creative world that you are going to build. The world of the Killers."

THE END